"*W*HAT HAPPENS

"Will you take you
Scotland?" If he did, th
able after all.

"Not directly. I wish to purchase a herd of English cattle for Glen Alpin. After I do that, I will return home."

"Forever?" she asked hopefully.

"I certainly have no desire to stay here," he said, flicking a disdainful glance around the beautiful room.

Her brows knit thoughtfully. "Under those circumstances," she said slowly, "I might consider your proposal."

"Do that," he replied. He came around the game table to stand next to her, forcing her to tip her head way back in order to look at his face.

You can't intimidate me, she thought, glaring up at him defiantly.

Their gazes locked, and the air between them felt as charged as it did just before lightning struck. An intensely blue flame flared in his eyes, then he scowled and stepped away from her.

Alexandra's heart was pounding. *He feels it too . . .*

❦

ACCLAIM FOR JOAN WOLF'S *GOLDEN GIRL*

"Delightfully romantic."
            —*Southern Pines Pilot* (NC)

more . . .

"Wolf delivers this sparkling historical with a purity of storytelling that's 24-karat treasure."
—*BookPage*

"A tender romance that warms the heart like sunshine on a spring day. . . . Wolf's writing is as smooth and polished as ever. . . . A delight."
—**Bookbug on the Web**

"A truly delicious story that keeps you right in the flow [and] the heart racing. . . . A wonderful . . . charming, poignant story with strong characters and vivid prose."
—*Rendezvous*

"Wolf once again works Regency magic . . . a cast of convincing and likable characters . . . with suspense and a believable romance."
—*Booklist*

"Wonderful prose. . . . The particular beauty of a Joan Wolf book has always been the rich emotional and cognitive lives of her characters, often reflecting larger social and political issues, set against a historical background brought to life with an abundance of carefully conveyed, accurate detail."
—*Romance Reader*

"Suspenseful plotting and solid characterizations will keep readers riveted."
—*Publishers Weekly*

Someday
Soon

BY JOAN WOLF

The Deception
The Guardian
The Arrangement
The Gamble
The Pretenders
Golden Girl

Published by Warner Books

ATTENTION: SCHOOLS AND CORPORATIONS
WARNER books are available at quantity
discounts with bulk purchase for educational,
business, or sales promotional use. For
information, please write to: SPECIAL SALES
DEPARTMENT, WARNER BOOKS, 1271 AVENUE
OF THE AMERICAS, NEW YORK, N.Y. 10020

JOAN WOLF

Someday Soon

WARNER BOOKS

A Time Warner Company

If you purchase this book without a cover you should be aware that this book may have been stolen property and reported as "unsold and destroyed" to the publisher. In such case neither the author nor the publisher has received any payment for this "stripped book."

WARNER BOOKS EDITION

Copyright © 2000 by Joan Wolf
All rights reserved. No part of this book may be reproduced in any form or by any electronic or mechanical means, including information storage and retrieval systems, without permission in writing from the publisher, except by a reviewer who may quote brief passages in a review.

Cover design by Rachel McClain
Cover illustration by Franco Accornero
Hand lettering by David Gatti

Warner Books, Inc.
1271 Avenue of the Americas
New York, NY 10020

Visit our Web site at
www.twbookmark.com

 A Time Warner Company

Printed in the United States of America

First Paperback Printing: June 2000

10 9 8 7 6 5 4 3 2 1

For Claire Zion, with appreciation
for all that she has done for my books.

Prologue

May 1813

Lady Alexandra Wilton regarded her father with apprehension. Her answer was going to make him furious, but unfortunately it was the only answer she was capable of making. Bracing herself to withstand the storm, she said, "I am very flattered by Lord Barrington's offer, Papa, but I cannot marry him."

The Earl of Hartford's once-handsome but now-dissipated face began to turn the color of a tomato.

"What?" he roared. "God damn it, Alex, Barrington is the biggest catch of the year! He has a fortune in the funds as well as a very decent title. True, a viscount may not be the equal of an earl, but the Barrington name is even older than ours."

"I know, Papa," Alexandra answered unhappily.

The earl and his daughter were sitting in the library at Gayles, the earl's country house in Derbyshire. The bright spring sun poured in through heraldic glass windows, illuminating the rich leather covers of the myriad shelved books. The earl regarded his daughter, who was seated on the opposite side of his mahogany desk, with distinct disfavor.

"Barrington is a very decent fellow," he said.

Alexandra sighed. "He is very nice, Papa, I will agree with you. It is most unfortunate that I cannot love him."

The earl clasped his hands in front of him on the desk. "You cannot love Barrington," he said ominously. "Nor could you love the Earl of Ashcroft, to whom you actually became engaged last year. After you jilted him, I despaired of you ever getting another offer. Now here you have the Catch of the Season asking for your hand, and you are going to turn him down?"

The earl's voice had become progressively louder as he listed the details of Alexandra's transgressions.

"If I become engaged to him, I would only jilt him, too, Papa, and you would not like that at all," she replied in a reasonable tone.

The earl pounded his clasped hands on the desk. "This obsession of yours with love is ridiculous. Has it never occurred to you, my girl, that love might come *after* marriage?"

A tiny frown indented the smooth perfection of her forehead. "But what if it doesn't, Papa? Then I would be forced to spend the rest of my life shackled to a man I didn't love."

"Believe me, Alex, there are worse things in life," her father informed her.

Alexandra shuddered. "What could be worse than that?"

"Ending up your life as a bloody spinster, that's what!" the earl roared. "And that is precisely what is going to happen to you, my girl, if you continue on in this fashion. You may be as beautiful as Helen of Troy, but no man is going to offer for you if you get the reputation as a flirt as well as a jilt."

"I am sorry to upset you, Papa . . ." Alexandra began, but the earl swept on.

"You do upset me! You are the only child I have left, the only chance I have of seeing my blood carried on into another generation. Don't you think I already have enough to bear? Because of your brother's suicide, I must see my title and property go to my cousin's son, not my own."

Alexandra was very white. "I wish to marry, Papa," she said. "I want a husband and children. It is just very important to me that I marry a man I love."

The earl made a visible effort to control himself. "My dear, I can assure you that most young girls do not love their husbands when they wed. They marry because their husbands are compatible in temperament and in worldly position. Love grows after the knot is tied. Viscount Barrington seems to me a perfectly lovable young man. I am sure you will grow to hold him in affection."

"I already hold him in affection," Alexandra said. "I just do not love him."

"What the bloody hell do you know about love?" the earl roared, turning a dangerous shade of red once again. "You are twenty-one years old and a virgin! Believe me when I tell you that your husband will teach you to love him."

Alexandra lifted her chin. "I know enough about love to know that it can't be taught, Papa. It is either there or it is not."

"Please don't tell me that you're waiting for Romeo to come and climb up your balcony, Alexandra," the earl said with heavy sarcasm.

"But suppose he did come, Papa, and I was already married?" Alexandra said with perfect logic. "*That* would be truly terrible."

The earl looked exasperated. "Alex, you have had too many Seasons not to know the way of the world. Should your Romeo eventually come along, there would be nothing to stop you from having him. As long as you were discreet."

Alexandra shook her head. "That may be the way of the world, Papa, but it is not *my* way," she said.

"I will never know how I came to have such a simpleton for a daughter," the earl said disgustedly.

I am this way because I don't want a marriage like your marriage to Mama, Alexandra thought. But she said nothing.

"Listen to me, my girl. I want you to take Barrington," the earl said. "He loves you, and I guarantee that in time you will learn to love him in return."

"Lord Barrington is a very fine man," Alexandra said. "He is generous and kind, and I think he does love me. If I were going to fall in love with him, I would have done so already."

The earl regarded his daughter with frustration. His comparison of her to Helen of Troy had not been exaggerated, but her face was more than just classically beautiful. There was a suggestion of great sweetness about the curves of her cheekbones and mouth that produced an effect that was intensely stirring.

He thought that one would never know to look at her that she was stubborn as a mule.

The earl had presented his daughter to society three years before, and since then she had collected more marriage offers than her father could remember. The previous year she had finally accepted one of them, only to decide a month before the wedding that she had made a mistake. Now here she was, turning down the finest young man available on the Marriage Mart today.

The future was suddenly very clear to the earl. If he didn't do something to force her hand, Alexandra was never going to marry at all.

Chapter One

October 1813

The sudden death of the Earl of Hartford shocked both his family and society in general. While he had not been a robust man—too many years of dissipation had made inroads on his health—there had been no suggestion that he was nearing the end of his life. Consquently it had been a stunning surprise when he died in the arms of one of the girls at Madame Dufour's, an upper-class establishment discreetly tucked into a side street off of St. James's Square.

To give Madame Dufour her due, she tried to keep the venue of the earl's death quiet. Her motivation might not have been completely selfless (it could not help business if customers began to think that the activities she specialized in were dangerous to their health), but she certainly acted in the best interest of all concerned. She sent one of her footmen to fetch the earl's heir, Mr. Geoffrey Wilton, who came in a carriage to collect his cousin's body. The earl was taken home to Hartford House in Grosvenor Square and put into his own bed, where his unfortunate demise was "discovered" by his valet in the morning.

The ruse might have succeeded if Lords Middleton and Calder hadn't happened to be passing by the side door of Madame Dufour's at the very moment that the earl's body was being carried out. Geoffrey Wilton, who was supervising the removal of his cousin's remains by two of Madame Dufour's minions, hastily assured the two curious lords that the earl was only "a little under the weather" from having had too much to drink. However, the following morning, when Middleton and Calder heard about the earl's death, they immediately raced to their respective clubs and recounted the story of their strange nocturnal meeting with the Earl of Hartford's body. Soon the whole of London was speculating about the earl's end.

"I am so sorry, Alex," Geoffrey said earnestly to his cousin as they stood together in the library at Gayles the day after the earl's funeral. "It was just rotten luck to have run into Middleton and Calder like that. I told them that your father was ill, but . . ."

"It's all right, Geoff," Alexandra said expressionlessly. "Everyone knows what Papa was. It's not as if the manner of his death ruined his reputation."

She walked to the window, which was open to the warm October day, and looked out, silently staring at the east court of Gayles as if she had never seen it before in her life.

The new earl looked worriedly at his cousin's slim, black-clad figure. Her beautiful pale gold hair was brushed into a severe chignon and there was a rigidity about her posture that he had never seen before.

Geoffrey did not make the mistake of thinking that Alexandra was grieving for her father. He had not been an attentive parent, preferring the company of his cronies to that of his children. She had grieved when her brother died, but the earl's death was less a personal loss than it was a loss of the way of life as she had always known it.

As for Geoffrey himself, the death of his cousin was an unmitigated blessing. It had made him the Earl of Hartford and the owner of Gayles, one of the finest country homes in the nation. A London town house in Grosvenor Square also came with the title, as well as a famous stud near Newmarket. Because of the earl's death, Geoffrey found himself transformed from an ordinary young commoner of small means into a Peer of the Realm, with extensive property and great wealth. Although he was trying valiantly to disguise the fact, Geoffrey was ecstatic.

Alexandra's life was also changed, although not in such a pleasant manner. Geoffrey walked over to his cousin, laid a protective hand upon her slender shoulder and assured her in a gentle voice, "Everything will be all right, Alex. You'll see."

She turned around, effectively moving her shoulder away from his hand, and mustered a strained smile. Before either of them could speak again, the earl's solicitor came quietly into the room.

James Taylor was a small, neat-boned young man of six-and-twenty who had recently taken over a partnership in the firm of Taylor and Sloane from his retired father. He had asked to meet with Alexandra and Geoffrey in order to go over the late earl's will.

"My lord, Lady Alexandra," he said now in a quiet, deferential voice. "If you would kindly take seats I will be happy to acquaint you with the provisions of His Lordship's will."

"Certainly," Geoffrey replied pleasantly. He waited for Alexandra to cross the room and seat herself on the green-velvet settee that was placed catty-corner to the fireplace, then sat beside her. Mr. Taylor faced them in the large wing chair that was opposite to the settee. He smoothed the sheets of paper resting on his lap and regarded his late client's cousin and daughter soberly.

High walls full of leather-bound books looked down on the two men and the girl. The room was rather dark, as the sun was hidden under clouds and the lamps had not yet been lit.

Mr. Taylor began. "For the most part, His Lordship's dispositions are much as you will have expected. The title and the estate are entailed, of course, and by law must go to Lord Hartford's closest living male relative, which, since the death of Lord Hartford's only son, is his late cousin's son, Mr. Geoffrey Wilton."

There the lawyer looked at Geoffrey.

For a brief moment Geoffrey's mind conjured up a picture of Marcus Wilton, the young man whose tragic suicide three years before was the reason all of this largesse was coming to Geoffrey.

The solicitor was going on. "I will acquaint you with the various individual bequests shortly, but I think I must first tell you of the change His Lordship made in his will last May." The young solicitor's blue eyes went from Alexandra's face to Geoffrey's, then returned again to Alexandra. "I advised him very strongly not to do this, Lady Alexandra," he said soberly. "But His Lordship would not be swayed."

Geoffrey frowned and glanced at Alexandra. Her dark gray eyes held an expression of apprehension.

Mr. Taylor selected a single document from among the pages in his folder. "This is the change Lord Hartford insisted upon making. It has to do with the money left to Lady Alexandra." He lifted the paper to the level of his eyes and, in a dry monotone, he read:

"To my daughter, Lady Alexandra Wilton, I bequeath all of my unentailed funds and properties . . ."

A gasp from Alexandra caused the solicitor to look up. He held up his hand to stop her from speaking and said a little grimly, "I have not finished reading the bequest, my lady."

Geoffrey swallowed hard. Surely his uncle could not have wished to bankrupt his heir?

The young solicitor continued:

". . . on the condition that Lady Alexandra agrees to marry the seventh Earl of Wilton within eight months of my death. Should she refuse to do this, then I bequeath all said funds and properties to the Jockey Club to be used as it sees fit."

Geoffrey stared at the lawyer, his mind in a daze. Could he possibly have heard correctly?

"Are you saying that Alexandra must marry me in order to receive her inheritance?" he inquired in a shaken voice.

"That is what the earl wished, my lord," Mr. Taylor replied. "And you must marry her if you wish to have enough money to keep Gayles and live according to your station."

Geoffrey shot a quick glance at his cousin's profile. She was looking stunned.

"Is this legal, Taylor?" he demanded.

"I am very much afraid that it is, my lord," James Taylor replied unhappily. "I did my best to talk His Lordship out of making this demand, but . . . well, as you must know, His Lordship was not an easy man to convince once his mind was made up."

The two young men looked at each other in perfect comprehension. Then, at the exact same moment, they turned to Alexandra.

"The Jockey Club?" she said. Her tone was incredulous.

"Are you saying that if Geoff and I don't marry, all of Papa's unentailed money and property will go to the *Jockey Club*?"

"I am afraid that is what will happen, Lady Alexandra."

A little color crept into Alexandra's pale cheeks. "When did you say my father inserted this into his will, Mr. Taylor?"

"In May, Lady Alexandra."

"I knew it!" Alexandra's gray eyes darkened. "He did this right after I refused to marry Lord Barrington."

The solicitor concurred. "He was very upset with you, I'm afraid. My hope was that either you or your cousin would marry and thus force the earl to change this . . . extraordinary . . . stipulation. But he died before any changes could be made."

Alexandra stood up. "If this isn't just like Papa," she said furiously. "If he weren't already dead, I swear I would kill him myself." And she walked out of the room.

The young men she left behind regarded each other somberly.

"The two of you will have to marry, my lord," the solicitor said bluntly. "If you don't, neither of you will have sufficient money to live upon."

Geoffrey ran his fingers through his butter yellow hair and looked at the door through which his cousin had so precipitously exited. "I have been in love with Alexandra since I was twelve years old," he said soberly. "The problem will not lie with me, Taylor."

"If Lady Alexandra refuses to marry you, she will be left with virtually nothing, my lord," Taylor said. "The income she has from her mother is not nearly enough for her to live the life she is accustomed to."

Geoffrey gave a crooked smile. "Somehow I can't picture Alexandra in a cottage."

The young solicitor agreed wholeheartedly. "You must explain matters to her. She has no choice, my lord. You and she must marry."

Alexandra flew up the monumental seven-foot-wide stone staircase that connected the three main floors of Gayles. Still in full flight, she sped across the length of a spectacular Elizabethan gallery, for once not pausing to look through the great windows that opened the room up to the sky and the gardens. All she wanted was to reach the safety of her bedroom, which opened off the south end of the gallery.

She had begged for this room when she was a little girl and loved it passionately. It was where she always retreated when she was upset, and today she was very upset indeed. And angry as well.

She slammed the bedroom door and stood for a moment, fists clenched, teeth clenched, eyes flashing.

How dare Papa do this to me? This isn't the Middle Ages. He can't make me marry someone I don't want to.

She went to the wide window seat that gave a view of the new west entrance that had been built by her grandfather and flung herself down.

I can't marry Geoff. It wouldn't be right. He's almost as much my brother as Marcus was.

Her heart was pounding with the intensity of her emotion. Her father knew how she felt about Geoffrey. How could he have bound her to a union that felt to her like sin.

I don't have to marry anyone, she thought angrily. *I have some money from Mama. I can live on that.*

She thought about this for a while, her eyes on the delightful Elizabethan pavilions topped with obelisks that bordered the entrance court. Her reflections were not precisely encouraging. Alexandra had received her inheritance from her mother upon the countess's death a few years ago; she used it to buy some of her dresses.

Her next thought was that she was not the only one affected by her father's ultimatum. What would happen to Geoffrey if she refused to marry him?

Without the earl's other sources of income, he would have only the rents from the farms to live on. It had always been a source of pride to Alexandra that the rent money from the estate went right back into maintaining the property. If her father's will held, that money would have to be diverted into Geoffrey's pocket for living expenses.

That solicitor should never have allowed Papa to put such an outrageous demand in his will, she thought. *It can't be legal. It simply can't be.*

She kicked off her soft leather slippers, swung her long legs up to the window seat, and rested her chin on her black-silk-clad knees.

Geoff and I should challenge the will, she decided. *We'll get another lawyer. This one is too young to know anything. We'll get someone older and more experienced. This kind of a condition can't possibly be legal. Geoff and I aren't slaves, for heaven's sake!*

The more she thought about it, the more optimistic Alexandra became. The law would overturn this will in favor of the original one, which had to be more sensible about the disposition of money, and then she and Geoff could go their separate ways.

The stone terrace glimmered in the September sun, and the Elizabethan pavilions looked even more fantastic than usual. Alexandra felt a sharp pain in the region of her heart.

If she and Geoff were successful in overthrowing that ridiculous clause in her father's will, she would have to leave Gayles. She knew how Geoffrey felt about her, and it wouldn't be fair to him for her to remain if she wouldn't marry him.

Alexandra loved Gayles. She sometimes thought that the only time she was truly happy was when she was there. She loved the beautiful old house, where her forebears had lived since it was built by her ancestor during the reign of Elizabeth. She knew and loved every rock and tree in the extensive and varied park, where she had spent so many happy hours riding her beloved horses. She knew everybody who lived in the neighborhood, from the local farmers, to the village merchants, to the upper-class families with whom her family socialized.

One of the reasons she had known that she didn't love any of the men who wished to marry her was that she had not been willing to give up Gayles for any of them. To leave Gayles would be to uproot the deepest part of herself. It would feel like an amputation.

Someday, she had always thought, someday a man would come along whom she would be willing to follow to the ends of the earth. It was one of her most profoundly held convictions, that only her Great Love could take her away from the secure childhood safety of Gayles.

But she was twenty-one years old, almost on the shelf, and still no Great Love had come her way.

Perhaps I should marry Geoff after all, she thought forlornly. *At least I would be able to live at Gayles for the rest of my life. There's really nothing wrong with cousins marrying . . .*

She bit her lip and forced back the tears that were rising to her eyes. The law might allow her to marry Geoffrey, but all her sense of rightness rose up in rebellion at the thought.

One didn't marry one's brother, and that was how she felt about Geoffrey.

"*Damn*," she said with violence, picked up an embroidered pillow from the window seat, and threw it at one of the posts of her bed.

Then the tears began to fall. "Oh God, Marcus," she sobbed, thinking of her brother. "Oh God. Why did you have to die?"

Geoffrey consulted the most well known and respected experts in England as to the legality of his late cousin's will. They all told him the same thing: The earl had the right to dispose of his personal property in any way he chose. Geoffrey was entitled to everything that was entailed, which included Gayles, the London town house, and several smaller properties in other counties. The Newmarket stud and the fortune Lord Hartford had made in investments were not entailed and as such could be disposed of in any way Lord Hartford wished.

If Geoffrey and Alexandra wanted the money, they would have to marry. Otherwise, it would go to the Jockey Club.

This was devastating news to Alexandra. She had put so much hope in the thought that the will would be declared invalid. Geoffrey, on the other hand, was intensely happy, a happiness he struggled to keep from showing to Alexandra as they discussed the situation in which they found themselves.

The two young people were alone in the Great Chamber after the attorney bearing the final judgment had left. It was late October, and the room was chilly. Alexandra, who was wearing her riding habit, walked over to the magnificent Portland stone fireplace that a footman had just lit and stood staring into the flames, her back to the room.

Geoffrey took two steps toward her, then stopped.

"Would our marrying really be so terrible a thing, Alex?" he asked her, his voice very gentle.

She turned to face him. "We grew up together, Geoff. I . . . I . . . just don't think of you that way."

"I know, but perhaps you could learn to," he said. "I love you, Alex. You know that. Nothing in the world would make me happier than to have you for my wife."

"It just doesn't seem right." She was twisting her hands together in distress.

"You need some time to get used to the idea," he said. "I love you, Alex. You know that. I have always loved you. Can't you try to love me back?"

"I do love you, Geoff," she said wretchedly, turning around to face him. "I don't want to leave you without the means to live according to your station, and, to be honest, I don't want to live like a pauper either. But . . . my feelings for you are those of a sister, not a wife."

She looked at him, her gray eyes dark with worry.

He took the last few steps that brought him to her side and took her hand. She bit her lip and allowed him to hold it. "But we aren't sister and brother, Alex," he said steadily. "There is absolutely nothing wrong with the two of us marrying. The Church allows it. The state allows it. It is quite obvious that your father saw nothing wrong with it. The problem exists only in your own head."

"But it's *there*, Geoff," she said.

"It's there now, perhaps, but once we are affianced, and you begin to regard me as your husband, it will go away." He sounded very definite.

"Do you think so?" she asked worriedly.

"I know so," he replied. He cupped his fingers around her chin and held her face as he leaned forward to kiss her mouth. It was a terrific struggle for him not to betray the hunger he felt at the touch of her lips, but he managed to keep the kiss light.

"Once we are married, you'll be fine," he said huskily as he withdrew his mouth from hers. "You'll see."

Alexandra touched her lips with her finger and looked into the blue eyes that were almost on a level with her own.

"I hope so," she said, but she didn't sound convinced.

Chapter Two

March 1814

I have just received the most extraordinary letter," James Taylor said, coming into his partner's office.

Giles Sloane, the Sloane in the firm of Taylor and Sloane, looked up from his desk. He was an older man who had started the firm in partnership with James's father. "What letter?"

"It pertains to the Hartford estate."

Mr. Sloane rolled his eyes. "Will we never see the end of that coil? The earl had to be mad to make such a condition, but it was legal, and his heirs are bound by it. I thought we had clarified that matter sufficiently, James."

"This letter has to do with the succession," the younger man said. "I wish you would look at it."

Giles Sloane took the paper his partner was holding out, settled his eyeglasses more firmly on his nose, and began to read.

Silence fell.

Then, "Good God," Sloane said. He was still reading the

letter. He finished it and looked up. "Good God," he said again. "Can this be true?"

"I don't know," Taylor said unhappily. "If it is, I don't know how I am to break the news to Lady Alexandra."

"It will be even more difficult to break it to the poor chap who thinks he is the seventh Earl of Hartford," Sloane said drily.

The expression on James Taylor's young face was deeply troubled. "What do you think I should do, sir?"

Sloane reread the letter once again.

"The late earl did have a younger brother," he said slowly. "I remember that he died under somewhat mysterious circumstances." He frowned. "And I do believe it was in Scotland. He was buried up there. No one here has spoken of him for years."

Taylor said, "Well, if what this letter claims is true, if he did indeed marry and have a son, then that son is the seventh earl, not Geoffrey Wilton."

"He lives in a place called Glen Alpin," Sloane said, frowning at the letter in his hand. "Where the devil is Glen Alpin anyway?"

"Somewhere in the Western Highlands," Taylor returned. He held up a piece of paper. "Our correspondent has kindly sent directions."

"The Western Highlands," Sloane repeated, in much the same tone he would have used had he said, "Outer Mongolia." He looked back down at the letter. "What of this person, this Archibald Douglas, who has written to you? Are you sure he is reputable?"

"As you see, he claims he is a professor who taught Niall MacDonald, as this new heir is apparently called, at the University of Edinburgh. He appears to be a reputable source, sir. If you notice, he has offered us other names as references."

Sloane blew out of his nose. "If what he writes is true, then why did this Niall MacDonald not contact us himself?"

"According to Douglas, Niall MacDonald does not know he is Hartford's heir. Up until three years ago, remember, Hartford's son was the heir. Apparently Niall does not know of Marcus Wilton's death."

"Hmmm." Sloane's expression was distinctly skeptical. "Then why did this Mr. Archibald Douglas not write to MacDonald himself and leave it to the new heir to make his presence known?"

Taylor, who had been standing all this while in front of his partner's desk, now sat down in one of the office chairs. "I don't know why. He doesn't say."

Sloane regarded his young colleague over the top of his glasses.

"What do you think we should do, sir?" Taylor said.

Sloane sighed. "Unfortunately, we don't have any choice in the matter, my boy. This letter has too much substance to be dismissed out of hand. Lady Alexandra and her cousin must be told of this new claim, then someone will have to go to Scotland to verify if there was indeed a legal marriage between Edward Wilton and this Niall MacDonald's mother. If such a marriage did in fact take place, then the new earl must be informed of his good fortune."

Taylor's slight form shifted uncomfortably in his chair. "Sir . . . what about the marriage stipulation in the earl's will? Surely the earl's intention was that Lady Alexandra marry Geoffrey Wilton. He would never have expected her to marry a stranger."

"Perhaps not," Sloan said gloomily. "But what he wrote was that Lady Alexandra must marry 'the seventh earl.' And if this Niall MacDonald is in fact the seventh earl, she will have to marry him if she wants her money."

Taylor leaned forward. "What if he is already married?"

Sloane tapped his nose thoughtfully. At last he opined, "If he is already married, we may have cause to set aside that infamous clause. We'll cross that bridge when we come to it, however. Your duty now is to inform Lady Alexandra and her cousin of this new development. Then you will have to travel to Scotland and ascertain if this Niall Macdonald is in fact the legitimate son of Edward Wilton."

"This is terrible," Taylor muttered. "Simply terrible. Poor Lady Alexandra."

"It is a damnable situation, I agree, but our duty is to follow the law," Sloane said briskly. "If I were you, my boy, I would pay a visit to Gayles this afternoon. Then you had better make plans to travel north. There are but two months before the time stipulated by the late earl will be up, you know."

James Taylor's young face looked miserable, but he nodded and went to call for his trap in order to drive out to Gayles.

Alexandra had just entered the house when she was stopped by her butler, who informed her that Mr. Taylor had called and requested to see both her and His Lordship.

"I have put him in the library, Lady Alexandra, and I believe His Lordship has already joined him," Stokes said.

"Thank you, Stokes," Alexandra replied with her usual courtesy. She had come in through the west entrance of Gayles and proceeded to walk down the corridor and mount the stone steps to the second floor.

She was wearing her oldest riding habit, and her hair had blown into a tangle around her shoulders, but she didn't bother stopping to change or tidy up. Alexandra rarely thought about her appearance—a privilege afforded to those rare few who knew that no matter what, they always looked beautiful.

What can that bloody man want now? was her thought as she walked past the magnificent second-floor drawing room which, in the time of Elizabeth, had functioned as Gayles's Great Chamber.

Alexandra would never forgive James Taylor for allowing her father to insert that abominable clause in his will.

She stopped for a moment outside the library door, reluctant to go in. In her experience, solicitors rarely brought good news. After a moment, she drew a deep breath, straightened her shoulders, and pushed open the door. Inside two men were standing in front of one of the great windows and, as they turned toward her, an all-too-familiar fog of depression settled around Alexandra.

Will it be like this for the rest of my life? she thought drearily. *Will nothing ever have color for me again?*

"Stokes said you wished to see me, Mr. Taylor," she said to the young solicitor.

"Yes, Lady Alexandra." The attorney looked distinctly distressed. "I am afraid that I am not the bearer of good news."

"Somehow I didn't expect that you would be," she replied resignedly.

Geoffrey said, "Come and sit down, Alex." He came to put a protective hand on her arm and lead her toward the green settee in front of the fireplace.

All of Alexandra's ease in the presence of this cousin whom she loved as a brother had disappeared in the light of their engagement. Geoffrey had been heroically restrained in his behavior toward her, but she saw how he looked at her, and she knew how he felt. Her own feelings were a mixture of guilt that she could not care for him as he cared for her and deep unease at the idea of his touching her like a lover. She had hoped that Geoffrey was right and that her feelings toward him would change, but they hadn't.

Mr. Taylor said, "This morning I received a very disturbing letter from Scotland." Then he went on to tell his clients what he had learned from the Edinburgh professor.

Alexandra stared at Taylor as he explained that he would be traveling to Scotland to verify this claim and that, if it were indeed true, he would bring the new earl south to take up his inheritance.

"Do you mean that, if this man, this son of my uncle, does actually exist, then he and not Geoffrey will be the next earl?" she said in astonishment.

"That is exactly so, Lady Alexandra," Taylor replied.

Alexandra's immediate reaction was one of gratitude.

I don't have to marry Geoffrey, she thought with intense relief. *I don't have to marry Geoffrey*.

She looked at her betrothed and saw that he was deathly pale. A twinge of familiar guilt went through her at her own reaction. This was devastating news for poor Geoffrey.

"I am so sorry . . . er . . . my lord," Taylor said, evidently deciding to accord Geoffrey the title until it was conclusively proved that he did not deserve it. "I would not have had this happen for the world, but we had no inkling that another claimant existed."

Geoffrey shocked her by asking, "Does this mean that Alex must marry this new earl?"

"Of course not," Alexandra replied immediately. "Papa never meant that!"

The solicitor was silent.

Alexandra glared at him. "Surely that is not so, Mr. Taylor. My father did not desire me to marry someone I do not know!"

"Unfortunately, Lady Alexandra, the late earl did not specifically name Mr. Geoffrey Wilton as the man you were to marry," Taylor replied apologetically. "The wording in the will reads: 'the seventh earl.' If this new claimant is in fact the seventh earl, then your father's stipulation will still hold."

Alex stared at him, utterly appalled. "You can't be serious?"

"I am afraid that I am, Lady Alexandra," the solicitor said unhappily. "It is most unfortunate, I agree, but the terms of the will are clear."

"Geoffrey," Alex demanded, turning to her cousin, "can't you do something about this?"

Geoffrey's eyes were blank with shock. He didn't answer.

The solicitor's sympathetic eyes went from Geoffrey's white face to Alexandra's. "If a valid marriage can be proved to have taken place between your uncle and this Maire MacDonald, and if a son was indeed born to them after that marriage, then there is nothing to be done, Lady Alexandra. Their son is the late earl's closest male relative, and, under the entailment, the title and property must go to him."

"Including me?" Alexandra said in horror.

Next to her, Geoffrey moved. "What if this fellow is already married, Taylor?"

"If he is already married, then I think we will have a case for setting aside the marriage clause," the solicitor replied.

Alexandra began to breathe again.

"How old is this person?" she demanded.

"I believe he is twenty-five, Lady Alexandra."

She waved her hand dismissively. "They probably get

married at a young age in the Highlands. What else is there to do in such a wilderness?"

James Taylor did not reply.

"When can we expect to learn the truth of this claim?" Geoffrey asked in a tense voice.

"I am planning to leave for Scotland immediately, my lord," the solicitor assured him. "I hope to return within the month."

Alex leaned against the green-velvet back of the settee and stared straight ahead. "I can't quite take this in," she said.

"It is indeed a shock," Taylor replied. "Allow me to remind you both, however, that this is by no means a sure thing. First I must confirm that there was indeed a valid marriage between Edward Wilton and this MacDonald girl. The Scots have a number of ah . . . arrangements . . . that they refer to as marriage but which are not recognized as such in English law."

"Is that so?" Geoffrey said hopefully. A little color crept back into his face.

"Yes, my lord. It is very possible that even if there was a union that produced an offspring, the union was not what our law would recognize as a legal marriage."

Alex's eyes went from the face of the solicitor to the face of her cousin. It occurred to her that she didn't know how she wanted this situation to resolve itself.

She didn't want to marry Geoffrey, and the presence of another heir would get her off that particular hook.

On the other hand, she hated the thought of her beloved Gayles in the hands of some Scottish stranger.

She gave no thought at all to the idea that she might be forced to marry this newfound cousin of hers. As far as she

was concerned, that was not a possibility she would dream
of considering.

The easiest way to reach the west of Scotland, even in
March, was by sea. Two days after he had spoken to Alexandra and Geoffrey, James Taylor sailed out of Blackpool on a
boat that took him up the west coast of England and into the
Scottish waters of the Firth of Clyde. At Troon he was able
to hire a local boat to take him through the Sound of Jura,
the Firth of Lorne, and up to the head of Loch Linnhe, where
Fort William, the town the English had built after the first
Jacobite uprising of the last century, was located.

For almost the entire trip the sky had been full of rain and
the waters rough, but James Taylor was young and, to his
good fortune, turned out to have a steady stomach. The farther north he traveled, the more he felt as if he had slipped
away from civilization and entered into an ancient and primitive world. The rain-lashed Scottish shoreline looked bleak
and empty, and the stark mountains that soared above him as
his ship traveled toward Fort William were stark and bare.

In a wild and eerie way, it was beautiful, but Taylor shuddered at the thought of actually passing the whole of one's
life in such desolate surroundings.

Fort William, at least, was a recognizable town, with a decent inn and a horse to hire. Taylor spent a night there, and
the following morning, in cold, blowy sunshine, he left to
travel north along General Wade's military road to Fort Augustus, the other town built by the English to control the
Great Glen, the lifeline of the Highlands. Fort Augustus was
situated at the southernmost tip of Loch Ness, that long arm
of the sea that made up the northern part of the Great Glen,
just as Loch Linnhe made up the southern part. Fort Augus-

tus was a town quite similar to Fort William, except the inn was not as good.

It was late afternoon when Taylor exited from the Royal Stag to seek out a local solicitor. He made his way along the windy street, peering at the shops and looking for the name of Mr. Walter Erskine. Taylor had been able to travel from Fort William to Fort Augustus without an escort, but from now on he would need assistance. According to the extremely sketchy information Archibald Douglas had provided in his letter, Niall MacDonald was to be found at a place called Glen Alpin, which lay in the mountains to the west of Fort Augustus. There did not appear to be any main road that led to Glen Alpin.

Gold lettering on a sign proclaimed that Taylor had found his quarry, and he pushed open the shop door and went in. A rotund man with bushy black hair and glasses looked up from his desk and peered nearsightedly at the door.

"Mr. Erskine?" Taylor asked tentatively.

"Aye, I'm Erskine," the man answered in a broad Lowland accent. "What do ye want?"

"My name is James Taylor, and I am an English solicitor," Taylor said, coming all the way into the room. "I am in search of a young man named Niall MacDonald, and I was hoping you could help me locate him."

Erskin regarded Taylor suspiciously. "And what would an English solicitor be wantin' wi' young Niall?"

"It is a matter of an inheritance," Taylor replied circumspectly.

"What kind o' inheritance?" Erskine demanded rudely.

Taylor hesitated, annoyed by the question, then decided that there could be no harm in telling this man the truth. Unfortunately, he did not seem the sort to offer assistance to a stranger out of the goodness of his heart.

"I represent the estate of George Wilton, the late Earl of Hartford," Taylor said. "It has come to our attention that the father of Niall MacDonald may have been the late earl's younger brother, Edward. If this is indeed true, and if this Niall was born in lawful wedlock, then he is the new earl."

The Scotsman's mouth dropped open. "Ye canna be serious, mon," he said, his accent growing thicker with surprise.

"I am perfectly serious. If you can give me any assistance in this matter, I should be grateful."

Erskine closed his mouth. "I didn'a ken that Niall was anything but a MacDonald."

"I need to meet with Mr. MacDonald to inform him of this situation," Taylor said patiently. "It is essential for us to know whether or not Edward Wilton was his father and, if he was, if he was legally married to Niall's mother."

"Mon, would I like to see old GlenAlpin's face when he hears o' this!" Erskine said with a glint of malicious glee in his eyes.

Taylor felt distinctly uneasy about that glee. "I'm afraid I don't understand you," he said a little frostily.

"GlenAlpin is the MacDonald chief in these parts," Erskine informed him. "He's also young Niall's grandda. He willna like some Sassenach lord tryin t' tak his lad awa frae him."

"I didn't think there were any chiefs left in the Highlands," Taylor said in some surprise.

"There's no a lot of them. GlenAlpin is a century behind his time." A distinctly sardonic expression came across the solicitor's face. "The clan reveres him."

Taylor tried to get down to business. "If I sent a message to Mr. MacDonald, do you think that he would come to visit me here in Fort Augustus?"

The Scots lawyer hooted. "Naw, I dinna think he will

come, Mr. Taylor. If ye want to see Niall MacDonald, ye must gae to him."

"Can you tell me how I might do that, sir?" Taylor asked with dogged courtesy.

"Ye'll need a guide. The way to Loch Alpin leads over the mountains."

"Could you procure a guide for me, sir?" Taylor asked, hanging on to his courteous tone with difficulty. The Scotsman was annoying him intensely.

"Ach, I think I can do that for ye. It will cost ye a pretty penny, though."

"I am prepared to pay for guide service," Taylor said austerely.

"Verra weel. I will hae someone here for ye tomorra morn. If that is no too soon?"

"Tomorrow morning will be fine," Taylor said evenly. "I appreciate your assistance, sir."

The lawyer grinned.

Taylor bowed and left the office before he said something he knew he would regret.

Chapter Three

The following morning, in the office of Walter Erskine, Taylor met his guide: a dark, wiry Glen Alpin clansman named Alan MacDonald. Rather to Taylor's disappointment, Alan was garbed in a saffron shirt and brown-woolen trews. Taylor had been expecting to see a man wearing a kilt ever since he arrived at Fort William, but so far the only plaids he had seen were blanket-type garments that both men and women wore around their shoulders and over their heads.

"Y'er verra fortunate that Alan here was in Fort Augustus," Erskine said. "He's just noo goin' home and has agreed to tak ye wi' him."

"That is wonderful," Taylor said, giving the young clansman a friendly smile.

Dark brown eyes regarded him with suspicion and disapproval. "I have a pony for you," Alan said. "The way will be rough for a Sassenach."

To Taylor's surprise, the clansman's English was considerably better than the English spoken by the Lowland lawyer. A strange but attractive rhythm was the only sign in

Alan's speech that gave away the fact that Gaelic and not English was his native language.

It was raining, as it frequently was in the Highlands, and as they prepared to leave the shelter of the lawyer's office, Alan presented Taylor with a red-plaid blanket. "It will keep you dry," he said, flinging an identical blanket around his own shoulders and striding out into the wet street. Imitating his action with the plaid, Taylor followed.

They made their way through the gloomy streets down to the shore of Loch Ness, where Alan had four ponies picketed. Taylor stood watching the rain-lashed waters of the loch while the clansman untied the pony that bore a saddle and brought it over to him.

"But where is your pony?" Taylor asked, looking at the loaded pack ponies that remained.

From under his plaid, Alan gave him a look of magnificent scorn. "I will walk," he said.

"Oh," said Taylor. "Ah."

The Englishman mounted the small, shaggy pony. He was not a tall man but his feet almost touched the ground. He knew he must make a ridiculous sight, sitting wrapped in a plaid blanket upon a pony that was much too small for him, and was profoundly grateful that no one he knew was there to see him.

Alan picked up the lead of the first pack pony and turned away from Loch Ness toward the mountains that lay to its west.

The trip from Fort Augustus to Glen Alpin was something that Taylor never forgot. The road they took was a rough track that snaked between the mountains and across wild, heather-strewn hills and moors. The going was rough, but the scenery was stupendous. The blues and purples of the snowcapped mountains formed a magnificent backdrop to the glens, which were adorned with beautiful little lochs and streams and small waterfalls.

To Taylor's amazement, all of this magnificent landscape appeared to be utterly devoid of human habitation. The only living creatures Taylor saw, besides the birds that circled overhead, were herds of sheep.

He remembered reading in the English newspapers that many of the Highland landlords were clearing their lands of people in order to raise hardy Cheviot sheep. There had been huge emigrations from Scotland to Canada in the last twenty or so years, as the native Highlanders had been forced to seek their living on foreign soil.

In general, the English papers had seemed to approve of this policy. Sheep were profitable; clansmen were not.

After they had been three hours out of Fort Augustus, the rain finally stopped, and as they passed over the low grassy hills that led from Glen Moriston into Glen Alpin, the sun actually peeked out. It was at this point that Taylor saw his first sign of human life: a cluster of mud-walled houses with thatched roofs nestling by the side of a small loch. There was a group of women sitting in a patch of sun that had broken through the high clouds, and a number of small children played nearby.

"Those are the first people that we have seen since we left Fort Augustus," he commented to his guide.

"That is because we are now on the lands of Mac-Mhic-Donnail," Alan said. His face bore an oddly fierce expression. "The chief of Glen Alpin is still a father to his clan." He shot Taylor a dark look. "Unlike some others I could name."

Taylor forebore to comment. As they crossed the low grassy hills that formed the entrance into Glen Alpin, instead of sheep he saw herds of Highland cattle dotting the landscape. They also passed several more small villages, which Alan called *clachans*, and once again Taylor saw women and children.

"Where are the men?" he asked his guide.

"Hunting," came the bland reply.

The path they were following had become quite steep, and Taylor leaned forward to help his sturdy little pony make the climb. Alan stopped at the top and waited for Taylor to join him.

"There," he said, "is the home of Mac-Mhic-Donnail."

The curve of the valley below was like a great green-and-purple bowl, in the center of which was a jewel of a long, stunningly beautiful loch. To the south and north of the loch, peak after peak of snow-tipped mountains stretched away as far as the eye could see. The hazy light from the afternoon sky reflected off the glistening water in tints of pale gold and lavender. The loch was so long that it disappeared from view as it curved northwest into the hills.

On the north shore of the loch, a great stone castle reared up from a promontory that jutted out into the water. Framed by the mountains behind it, the castle's image was reflected perfectly in the still, golden waters of the loch.

Taylor's breath caught audibly.

"That is Eilean Darrach," Alan said proudly as he looked at the castle. "The home of Mac-Mhic-Donnail."

By now Taylor had figured out that Mac-Mhic-Donnail was the Gaelic name for the Chief of Glen Alpin.

"Is this also the home of the chief's grandson, Niall Mac-Donald?" he asked his guide.

Once more Alan directed a suspicious look at the lawyer. Finally, he answered shortly, "It is." Then, tugging on the leadline of his pony, he began the descent into the glen.

The English lawyer, who had been fascinated by castles

ever since he was a boy, stared at this unexpected home of
the Chief of Glen Alpin as they approached it from the
shoreline track. The main part of the castle, which Taylor
judged was probably the original part, was a five-story granite keep. The other castle structure, which Taylor thought
might be original, was a small circular guard tower. These
two ancient stone buildings were connected by a four-story
wing, which Taylor recognized as a more modern addition.

"Do you know when the castle was built?" he asked his
guide as they approached the narrow promontory upon
which Eilean Darrach was perched.

"A long time ago," was the unhelpful answer.

The ponies turned onto the graveled stone road that
crossed the promontory, forming the only access by land to
the castle. Two golden eagles wheeled in the air around the
circular tower. Above them the sky had turned intensely
blue.

For a brief moment, Taylor regretted that he had no artis-
tic skill. What a painting this would have made!

The promontory widened as they reached the end of the
road, and the gravel turned into grass, which went right up
to the walls of the castle. Alan stopped the ponies, and two
men, who had been carrying water, put down their buckets
and came to join them.

"You can get off now," Alan said to his English charge.

The minute Taylor's feet touched the ground, his knees
buckled, and he staggered. The three clansmen looked at
him impassively until he recovered himself.

As Alan gave instructions in Gaelic to the two men who
had joined them, Taylor looked around. A few simple
touches bore witness to the fact that the castle was a home
and not a monument. On the rocks along the sunny side of
the causeway, laundry had been spread to dry and, sitting

upon a bench at a little distance from the west side of the castle, two women were churning butter.

There was a mammoth oak door set into the stone front of the great keep, but Alan led the way to a smaller door placed in the middle of the wing connecting the keep to the tower. He went in through the door, motioning for Taylor to follow him.

Inside, the Englishman found himself in a dark, oak-paneled hall with a fireplace that had two carved chairs placed on either side of it. Several stags' heads sporting enormous antlers hung upon the walls. There was no fire in the fireplace, and the room was colder than it had been outdoors in the sunshine. Taylor found the atmosphere extremely depressing.

Alan said, "I will see if I can find Mac-Mhic-Donnail," and disappeared through a door in the west wall of the hall, leaving Taylor to huddle in his blanket and contemplate the glassy-eyed stags' heads in silent disgust. He was not an admirer of taxidermy.

It was at least twenty minutes before Alan came back, bringing with him a splendid-looking old man with a great mane of iron gray hair and a beak of a nose. To Taylor's delight, the chief wore a kilt of the same plaid as his and Alan's blankets.

"Mac-Mhic-Donnail," Alan said formally, "this is the Sassenach lawyer, Mr. James Taylor."

Alan's manner made Taylor feel as if he were being presented to a prince or a king. He had to restrain himself from bowing.

The old man looked at him sternly. His iron gray eyebrows were almost as formidable looking as his nose. "And what do you wish with me, sir?" he asked in a deep voice.

"I represent the estate of the Earl of Hartford." Taylor

paused, not sure what to call this imposing old man. Finally he added, "Mac-Mhic-Donnail."

A thundercloud had settled upon the formidable old face at the words *Earl of Hartford.*

"Come with me," the chief said abruptly and, turning, led the way into the next room, closing the door behind them.

This room was sparsely furnished with uncomfortable-looking carved oak chairs and a large oak table. The wooden floor was covered with a tattered-looking rug.

GlenAlpin walked to the table and turned to face his guest. He did not sit, nor did he ask Taylor to seat himself. Instead he said, with unconcealed hostility, "What are you doing here?"

Taylor tried very hard not to feel intimidated. He said steadily, "The sixth Earl of Hartford died last October and it has recently come to our attention that his younger brother, Edward, was married to your daughter and had a son with her. If that is indeed the case, sir, then I have come to tell you that Edward's son is now the seventh Earl of Hartford."

"How did you hear about my daughter and Edward Wilton?" the old man demanded.

"I would prefer not to say," Taylor returned levelly. "However, the source was legitimate enough that my firm felt we were obligated to investigate the claim."

High color flushed into the strong, weather-beaten face of GlenAlpin. Before he could answer, however, the door behind Taylor opened, and a very tall young man came in.

Taylor's eyes widened as he looked into one of the most arresting faces he had ever seen. It was not a classically handsome face, by any means, but it was unforgettable. It was so . . . so . . .

Arrogant.

That was the word, Taylor thought. He listened to the

sound of the two men talking in Gaelic, all the while staring in fascination at the young man's face.

It was the nose, the lawyer decided. It was narrow and high-bridged and . . . well, arrogant. The look was reinforced by slashing dark brows, high cheekbones, and a well-formed, thin-lipped mouth.

This has to be Niall MacDonald, Taylor thought. *That nose is a thinner, more refined version of GlenAlpin's beak.*

Switching to English, GlenAlpin turned to Taylor. "This is my grandson, Niall. I believe it is he whom you seek."

"How do you do, Mr. MacDonald," Taylor said, bravely meeting Niall's unfriendly stare.

"And why has a Sassenach lawyer come all the way to Glen Alpin to find me?" Niall replied. His English pronunciation was perfectly pure, but he spoke with the same lilting intonation that had colored Alan MacDonald's speech.

"I have come all this way in search of the son of Edward Wilton," Taylor said. His eyes flicked up and down the tall figure in front of him, from the wide shoulders under an old wool jacket, to the narrow hips from which hung a rather tattered-looking kilt, to the strong bare legs that the kilt revealed. "Have I found him?" he asked.

Niall shot a quick look at his grandfather.

The old man suddenly looked weary. "You will have to tell him, lad," he said.

Niall looked back to Taylor, and said in more clipped tones, "I am the son of Edward Wilton."

"You go by the name of MacDonald," Taylor pointed out.

"Niall will be Mac-Mhic-Donnail after me," the old chief said with a renewal of his initial fierceness. "It is only fitting that he bear the name of his clan."

Taylor hesitated, glancing toward the double window that looked out upon the loch and the mountains. The castle's rooms might be depressing, but the views were magnificent, he thought. Bringing his eyes back to the chief, he said, "I do not wish to sound impertinent, Mac-Mhic-Donnail, but can you tell me if Edward Wilton was legally married to your daughter?"

The old man looked at his grandson and did not immediately answer. It was Niall who replied indignantly, "Of course he was!"

Once again Taylor spoke to GlenAlpin. "Is there legal proof of that, sir?"

The old man's face seemed to crumble, and he heaved a long, weary sigh. "Yes," he said at last. "There is proof. They were married in the Episcopal church in Fort Augustus. The record will be there."

Niall looked from his grandfather to Taylor and scowled. "Why are you asking these questions?"

The lawyer glanced at GlenAlpin to see if he wanted to be the one to break the news. The old chief made a resigned gesture. "Tell him," he said.

Taylor faced Niall squarely, drawing his small, slender figure up to its full height. "I have come all this way to inform you that your uncle, the Earl of Hartford, is dead, and that, as his closest male relative, you are the next earl."

Niall's eyes widened, and Taylor realized for the first time that they were not brown, as he had thought, but blue.

"What are you talking about?" Niall said tensely. There was a deep sharp line between his brows.

"The Earl of Hartford was your father's elder brother," Taylor explained. "His only son died, and when he himself expired five months ago we all assumed that his closest male relative was his cousin's son. Then your existence was brought to my attention. As the son of the late earl's brother, you are the rightful heir, not Geoffrey Wilton as we thought."

"You have come to tell me that I am a Sassenach earl?" Niall repeated incredulously.

"Yes, my lord. That is what I have come to tell you."

Niall laughed, but there was no humor in the sound. He said something to his grandfather in Gaelic. His voice sounded harsh.

The old man replied in the same language, then he turned back to Taylor. "We are forgetful of our manners, sir. You will be tired from your long journey. Let me have someone show you to a bedroom so you may wash and rest."

It was perfectly evident to the Englishman that grandfather and grandson wished to be private to discuss this astonishing news, and so he went compliantly with the girl Niall summoned, leaving the other two alone.

Niall remained with his grandfather for a half hour discussion, then strode out of the castle. In the front hall he was joined by two huge long-haired deerhounds, who followed him across the causeway and down to the shore of the loch. He strode along the track that followed the shore for about a quarter of a mile. Then he stood still for perhaps five minutes, frowning into the water. At last he picked up a pile of small stones and began to throw them into the quiet waters of the loch. The hounds lay down on the rough grass and watched him.

From behind him someone said in Gaelic, "What did the Sassenach want?"

Niall turned and saw Alan MacDonald standing there. The clansman had arrived on the silent feet of an accomplished hunter.

"He came to tell me that I am an English lord," Niall told

his foster brother. "It seems that my father's elder brother died, and I am the closest male relative."

Alan looked incredulous. "What does he want of you?"

"I am thinking he expects me to go to England and claim my inheritance," Niall replied.

"You cannot leave here," Alan said emphatically. "We have too much need of you. Mac-Mhic-Donnail is growing old."

Niall threw his last stone, bent and picked up another handful. "I know."

He began to throw the new stones, one by one, into the loch. The water, which was stained golden by the late sun, rippled around each stone as it landed and sank.

Alan moved to stand beside Niall and silently watched each stone as it fell. When the last stone had disappeared, and the ripples had died away, Niall said, "I am wondering how much money the new Earl of Hartford will have."

At that, Alan turned to look at his foster brother. The wind from the loch was blowing Niall's long dark hair off his forehead, and his dark blue eyes were somber.

Niall said, "There is a good market for cattle in the Lowlands and England, and we have sufficient grass in Glen Alpin to maintain a large herd, but our Highland cattle do not give enough beef. We have talked about this before, you and I. We need to replace our own cattle with a meatier breed, and in order to do that, we need money."

Alan grunted his agreement.

"If this Sassenach earl had money, it will be mine now," Niall said. "I could use it to buy cattle for the clan."

"That is so," Alan said. "But no cattle are worth you having to live in a foreign land."

"It would be just for a little while," Niall said. "Just until I can get my hands on the money."

Reluctantly, Alan nodded. "The Sassenach always have money," he said bitterly.

"I am thinking that it might be wise not to ask too many questions at first," Niall said with a frown. "If the Sassenach believe that I am going to be their new earl, they will not try to hide the money from me."

"That is so," Alan said approvingly.

In perfect accord, both young men folded their arms and stared out across the loch. One of the cardinal rules by which they lived was: *Never trust a Sassenach.*

It would be wisest for Niall to pretend to go along with the Englishman's wishes. Only so would he be able to put his hand upon money for the clan.

Chapter Four

The third-floor bedroom to which Taylor had been shown was spartanly furnished but immaculately clean. It contained a bed, an armoire, one chair, and one small table. The window was open, and a cold wind ruffled faded blue draperies. There was no fire burning in the fireplace, nor did the serving girl make any attempt to light one.

The room was absolutely frigid.

As soon as the girl left, Taylor went to the window and closed it. He remained there for a moment, caught by the magnificent view of loch and mountains framed by the thread-bare draperies. Then he cast a longing look at the empty fireplace. There was not even wood laid in it to suggest that sometime in the future a fire was going to be lit.

His eyes went from the fireplace, to the great oak armoire, to the bed. It was a large oak four-poster, but the posts were bare of hangings. It did, however, appear to be well furnished with blankets.

Taylor was aching all over from being jolted over rough country by a pony, and exhaustion suddenly hit him with all the power of a blow to the jaw. He would just crawl into that bed and take a little nap, he thought. Eventually someone was bound to come along to fetch him for dinner.

He pulled off his boots, but it was too cold to undress, so he got into the bed in his coat and breeches. The wool blankets he pulled up over him were warm, and within five minutes he had plummeted into a deep sleep.

He was awakened by the same girl who had brought him upstairs. He opened his eyes at the sound of his name and gazed at her groggily, as she announced, "Dinner will be in half an hour, sir. I will come back to show you the way to the dining room."

As soon as she had closed the door behind her, Taylor reluctantly extracted himself from his warm nest and went to the basin of water that she had left for him. He told himself that he would feel much better after he had washed in nice warm water

He put his hands into the basin, then leaped back as if he had been stung.

The water in the basin was freezing.

James Taylor was not a young man who ordinarily cursed, but he cursed then. *Have these Highlanders taken some kind of a vow that forbids them ever to be warm?*

The leather bag that contained his clothes had been deposited in front of the armoire, and Taylor approached it reluctantly. The clothes he was wearing were a mass of wrinkles, and he would have to change. Shivering in the cold air, he performed that task as quickly as he could.

It was thirty-five minutes before the serving girl returned to take him to the dining room. His bedroom was on the third floor of the wing that connected the keep to the tower, and he followed her down one flight of stairs to the wing's second floor. On the landing they turned right and passed into one of the most striking rooms Taylor had ever seen.

It was a double room actually, with an archway separating the part that lay in the newer wing from the part that lay in the original keep. What made the room so stunning, however, was the series of large windows set into the north and south walls. Each of these windows was hung with embroidered cream-colored draperies that reminded Taylor of the Jacobean draperies in the Great Chamber at Gayles.

The late Highland sun slanting into the room through the windows bathed the oriental rugs on the floor, the glass-fronted cabinets that held a collection of china ornaments, and the elegant French furniture in a warm glow. Graceful curved-leg chairs upholstered with tapestry designs showing pastoral scenes were scattered throughout the room, and Taylor's eye was drawn in particular to an exquisite faux-marble writing table, whose drawers and legs were painted with swags and garlands.

Everything in the room, from the furniture to the portraits upon the walls to the rugs and the drapes, was beautiful.

To Taylor's huge relief, a fire was burning in the lovely carved wood fireplace. Since there was no one else in the room as yet, he went directly to the fire and stood as close to it as he could safely get. He closed his eyes.

The heat felt wonderful.

"Meditating, Mr. Taylor?" said a voice with a distinctive Highland lilt.

Taylor opened his eyes and found himself looking into the amused face of Niall MacDonald.

"Just enjoying the warmth," Taylor replied.

The expression of amusement on Niall's face deepened. He had been followed into the room by two large, rust-colored deerhounds, which now proceeded to walk in front of Taylor to curl up in front of the fire.

Taylor watched them warily. He was nervous of dogs, and these were exceedingly large ones. His eyes moved back to Niall, taking in his scarlet kilt and black-velvet jacket. Taylor thought that he should be wearing his hair pulled back into a queue, like the men in the portraits on the walls.

How could he stand to go bare-legged in this cold?

Deciding that he wanted to spend as little time in Glen Alpin as possible, Taylor said bluntly, "My lord, I came here to bring you the news that you are by right the seventh Earl of Hartford. I also came here to ask you to accompany me back to England to take up the responsibilities of your new estate and position."

Niall's amusement was abruptly replaced by a hard look that made him look dauntingly formidable. "What kind of an estate are we talking about, Mr. Taylor?"

"The seat of the Earls of Hartford lies in Derbyshire, my lord," Taylor replied. "The estate is named Gayles, and it encompasses some thirty thousand acres, most of which are let out to tenant farmers. There are also three smaller estates in Kent, in Wiltshire and in Sussex. The late earl also owned a stud farm near Newmarket."

Niall lifted one dark, slashing eyebrow. "It sounds as if the previous earl was rich."

"The earl was very rich indeed, my lord," Taylor said carefully, "although the bulk of his wealth did not come from the land. He inherited a modest income from his father, which, by means of shrewd investment, he turned into a fortune."

The reckless eyebrows drew together in a frown. "What do you mean, his wealth did not come from the land? Are these tenant farms not self-sustaining?"

Taylor was surprised by the question. "Of course they are self-sustaining, my lord. They are even profitable. But the bulk of the earl's income comes from investment."

Niall was silent for a moment, obviously thinking. At that moment, the old chief, also dressed in a scarlet kilt and velvet jacket, came into the room. He nodded briefly to his guest, and said to his grandson, "Let us go into the dining room."

The old chief went first, followed by Niall, the two deerhounds, and Taylor, keeping as far away from the dogs as he possibly could. They passed through the part of the drawing room that lay in the keep and out into a small hall, which contained only a set of spiral stairs that started on this floor and wound upward. The door on the left side of the hall led into a small anteroom, and on the other side of the anteroom was a huge dining room, whose door was guarded by a beautiful tapestry screen.

Taylor looked around as he came into the dining room, which must at one time have been the castle's Great Hall. The original stone walls had been covered in oak paneling and a faded Persian rug covered what might be the original floorboards. In the center of the room was a dark, polished-wood dining table with six thronelike chairs set around it. Two four-branched silver candelabra lit the table, illuminating the delicate china and heavy silverware place settings that were laid in front of three of the chairs.

The fireplace was enormous; half a dozen men could easily stand inside it. To Taylor's relief, a fire was burning, its flames leaping high inside the immense opening.

The three places had been laid sensibly at the end of the table closest to the fire. The chief took his seat at the head of the table, with his grandson on his right and Taylor on his left. The heat given off by the huge fireplace was intense, and Taylor could see why the screen had been placed across the door of the room. If the screen had not been there, the immensity of the fire would have dragged a frigid draft across the room, defeating the purpose of the fire.

A young man carrying a tray came around the screen and into the room. He placed the tray on one of the serving tables that stood by the door and filled soup plates from the large tureen he had carried in. Then he brought the soup plates to the table. Following Highland hospitality rules, he served the guest first. Taylor waited for the chief to pick up his spoon before he did so himself.

The soup tasted like beef and barley, and it was hot. Taylor took another spoonful, relished the feel of the hot liquid going down, and glanced surreptitiously at the man who sat directly across from him.

It did not look as if Niall MacDonald were married, Taylor thought. If he had been, then surely his wife would have joined them at the table.

Of course, his wife might be sick, or away visiting relatives, or disinclined to meet strangers.

He would have to find out. Taking a deep breath and holding his empty soup spoon over his bowl, he said baldly, "You are not married, my lord?"

The chief stared at him as if he were mad.

"Don't look so startled, Grandpapa. He is talking to me," Niall said sardonically. He looked at Taylor. "No, I am not married. Does that matter?"

I should tell him now, Taylor thought. *I should tell him about the clause stipulating that he must marry Lady Alexandra if he wants to get the earl's money.*

He looked into the black-browed face of Niall MacDonald and said, "Of course it doesn't matter. I was just curious."

"I fear that we are a bachelor household, Mr. Taylor," the chief said courteously. "My wife died over twenty years ago, and my daughter died giving birth to my grandson. My only hope of acquiring the softening touch of a woman at Eilean Darrach is for Niall to marry."

Niall continued to eat his soup.

The old man gave his grandson a stern look. "If you go to England, Jean may lose patience and marry someone else."

The young man who had served the soup now came around to remove the empty plates. A mutton roast was placed in front of the chief, who began to carve it. Niall reached over to take two pieces of meat from the serving platter and pass them down to the dogs, who were lying on either side of his chair.

Taylor shuddered to think what Lady Alexandra would say if she ever saw this outrageous lack of manners.

"Jean is welcome to marry whomever she chooses," Niall said. "I have staked no claim on her."

"She would marry you in a minute, as well you know," the chief said grumpily. "I don't know why you are being so slow about it."

Niall shrugged and accepted a plate of mutton from his grandfather. He began to help himself to the vegetables, which had been placed upon the table.

Taylor, who had already filled his plate, cut into his meat. He put the mutton in his mouth and his eyes widened.

It was absolutely delicious.

He said so and watched with interest as his two hosts exchanged an amused look.

"I am glad that you like it," the chief said courteously.

"I rather thought we would be having beef, or perhaps fish," Taylor said, curious about that look. "From what I could see, you raise cattle, not sheep, in Glen Alpin."

"Oh, we have the odd sheep or two," the chief said airily.

Taylor continued to probe. "I saw large numbers of sheep as we crossed the mountains from Fort Augustus. To whom do they belong?"

"They belong to a traitor who forced his own people off their land so that he could raise sheep for profit," the chief said contemptuously. "He has left behind a Lowland factor to look after the animals, while he sports himself in England like a lord."

"We do not mention his name in this house," Niall said. His voice was calm, but when Taylor looked at him the expression in his dark blue eyes was not calm at all.

The thought flashed across Taylor's mind that he would not like to have Niall MacDonald as an enemy.

He watched with concealed disgust as Niall handed down more meat to his dogs.

Taylor turned to the chief. "I do not wish to trespass upon your hospitality for too long a time, Mac-Mhic-Donnail. As I mentioned earlier to His Lordship, my aim in coming here was to ascertain whether your grandson's claim was valid and, if it was, to bring him to England to take up his title and his estates. If, as you have said, proof is available that there was a legal marriage between your daughter and Edward Wilton, then I believe it would be in the best interest of your grandson for him to accompany me back to Gayles."

Bleak-faced, the chief looked at his grandson. "What do you want to do, Niall?"

The new Earl of Hartford stared at his family's solicitor. "What kind of farms are attached to this Gayles? Do any of them raise beef cattle?"

Taylor blinked in surprise. After a minute, he answered, "No, I believe there are some dairy herds, but beef cattle—no."

Niall frowned.

Out of his depth, Taylor ventured to ask, "Are you interested in beef cattle, my lord?"

"Yes," Niall replied. His frown had not lifted.

"You might wish to speak with Mr. Thomas Coke, then," Taylor ventured. "He has done many successful experiments with various breeds to find the best cattle for beef."

Niall's head lifted alertly. "Where does this Coke live?"

"In Norfolk, my lord."

"Is that close to Derbyshire?"

"It is not far, my lord. A day's ride, perhaps."

"This fellow is well-known for his expertise in cattle?"

"Mr. Coke is well known for his expertise in everything that pertains to farming, my lord. His estate of Holkham is famous for its up-to-date agricultural methods."

Niall's eyes moved to the man sitting at the head of the table. "I think I had better go," he said soberly.

"You must do as you think best," GlenAlpin replied. He did not look happy.

Niall said something to him in Gaelic, and the old chief raised an eyebrow and replied in the same language.

Niall smiled.

Taylor stared in amazement. The smile completely transformed Niall's hard and arrogant face.

The smile died, and Niall turned to Taylor. "I will go to England with you for now," he said, "but I make no promises that I will stay."

Taylor, still bedazzled by that smile, blinked and replied, "When do you think we can leave?"

In reply, Niall looked at his grandfather.

"Go the day after tomorrow," the chief said. His face looked bleak. "There is no point in delaying."

Niall nodded.

"We must stop in Fort Augustus so that I can verify the marriage record," Taylor said. "I must be able to swear that I have seen it."

"Fine," Niall said indifferently.

Taylor took a long drink of his wine, which was surprisingly good, and thanked God fervently that he did not have to stay for much longer in this freezing castle.

James Taylor left Glen Alpin on a day of mist and rain. He was accompanied by the new Earl of Hartford, the earl's foster brother, Alan MacDonald, and the earl's two huge deerhounds. Two pack ponies carried the luggage. Taylor, who still ached from the pony he had ridden into Glen Alpin, had chosen to walk alongside the other two men.

They all three wore plaids to keep their clothes dry from the ever-present rain.

Once again, Taylor noticed the change as they passed out of Glen Alpin. There were trees in Glen Alpin, and people. In the adjoining glen there were only bare hillsides and sheep.

He remarked upon this barrenness to Niall, who replied somberly, "At one time all these glens were thickly forested with birch, alder, oak, and rowan. These hills"—he gestured to the stark landscape that surrounded them—"were once grazed by sturdy cattle and tilled by clansmen. Now all there is to be found here are these . . . these . . . hoofed locusts." He stared grimly at a herd of sheep who were grazing on the sparse hillside. "Sheep in these numbers keep the trees from regrowing and turn grassy meadows into bogs. It is happening all over the Highlands. It is one of the worse legacies of Culloden."

Taylor did not need to ask about Culloden. One did not have to be a Scot to know that the battle of Culloden Field, where English forces had defeated a Highland army under Prince Charles Edward Stuart, had been the death knell for the ancient clan way of life.

He asked doubtfully, "Is there so much money in sheep that it is worth turning the people off the land?"

"Apparently some think so," Niall replied coldly. "The traitor to his people who owns this land wishes to buy Glen Alpin so he can raise even more sheep."

Taylor thought of the imposing sweep of loch and meadow and hill and mountain that was Glen Alpin. "Does your grandfather legally own all of the land in Glen Alpin?" he asked curiously.

"According to Sassenach law, the land belongs to Mac-Mhic-Donnail," Niall replied. "He is a true chief, however, and believes that he holds it in trust for the clan. He would never betray his people and sell their land—unlike some others."

The look of utter contempt stamped upon his arresting face actually caused a shiver to run down Taylor's back. He said, "So that is why you have cattle and not sheep in Glen Alpin."

"Oh, we have a few sheep as well," Alan MacDonald said with a sly grin.

"I didn't see any sheep," Taylor said.

The two Scots exchanged an amused look, identical to the look that had passed between Niall and his grandfather when sheep had been mentioned at dinner.

"Sometimes the sheep from neighboring glens stray onto our land," Niall answered blandly.

Taylor stared at him. "And you keep them?"

"If they're on our land, then they're our sheep," Alan said with perfect matter-of-factness.

Taylor looked at the two men walking beside him and realized that the MacDonalds probably drove those sheep into Glen Alpin and then claimed them.

He thought of the delicious mutton he had eaten the last two nights and his law-abiding heart was outraged.

Then he thought of Alexandra.

God in heaven, he thought in panic. *What kind of a man am I bringing to Gayles?*

Chapter Five

April 1814

Please God, let him be married.

So Alexandra prayed every day that James Taylor was away in Scotland.

For her, it would be the best possible solution. If this new-found cousin was truly her father's heir, she would not have to marry Geoffrey. And if the new earl was already married, then her father's previous will would take effect, and she and her new cousin would each receive an ample amount of money from the estate. The only one who would not benefit from such a situation was Geoffrey.

I'll give Geoff some of my money, God, Alexandra promised, in a shameless attempt to bribe the Almighty. *Everyone will benefit if things turn out the way I want them to.*

The days of waiting to hear from Taylor went by at a tortoiselike pace. Alexandra avoided the house as much as possible, trying to evade Geoffrey and his mother, who had been in residence as a chaperone since Geoffrey had moved to Gayles. Seeing them made her feel guilty about her own secret wish.

One thing Alexandra resolutely did *not* think about was what she would do if it turned out that this new cousin of hers was the legitimate earl—and not married. Every time this possibility began to surface in her mind, she resolutely pushed it away.

One simply did not think about the unthinkable.

The first word that came to Gayles concerning Mr. Taylor's Scottish quest was brought by his partner, Giles Sloane, who arrived late on an overcast April afternoon requesting to see Geoffrey and Alexandra. The butler showed him to the library and went to inform Alexandra of his arrival.

To Alexandra, the Gayles library always smelled like leather and dust. She knew that the servants diligently cleaned the shelves, but the massive collection of books simply could not be removed and dusted individually. Some were too old and fragile to be handled without the utmost care.

Alexandra had spent many happy hours of her childhood in the library, but of late the dusty-leather library smell had come to be associated in her mind with some of the most unpleasant moments of her life. She had a distinct feeling of dread in the pit of her stomach as she walked into the splendid book-lined room to join Geoffrey and Mr. Sloane.

The two men were standing in front of the fire, talking together in low voices. Geoffrey's mother, Louisa Wilton, the wife of the late earl's first cousin, sat on the settee, her hands clasped together in her lap. Everyone turned to stare at Alexandra as she came across the floor to join the group by the fire.

"My dear," Louisa Wilton said in a strained voice. "Do you know Mr. Giles Sloane, Mr. Taylor's associate?"

"How do you do, Mr. Sloane," Alexandra said. "I understand that you have some news for us."

"Indeed I do, Lady Alexandra," the plump bespectacled attorney replied. "I received a letter from Mr. Taylor earlier this morning telling me that he was halfway through his return journey to England. He wished me to inform you that he has been successful in his search. He has found Niall Wilton, who has been known as Niall MacDonald since his birth. And he has seen with his own eyes the marriage record in the Church of St. Peter in Fort Augustus that proves Edward Wilton legally married one Maire MacDonald on May 18, 1789."

Geoffrey sagged visibly. His mother made a mewing sound, like a kitten that has been wounded.

Alexandra's heart began to thump.

In a tense voice Geoffrey said, "Are you sure that there is no confusion of names? How can Mr. Taylor be certain that the man who married in Fort Augustus wasn't another Edward Wilton?"

"My colleague writes that he is quite certain of Edward Wilton's identity," Sloane replied. "Apparently Edward was staying in Fort Augustus when he met Miss MacDonald. It was generally known in the town that he was the son of an English earl."

Geoffrey closed his eyes. His round, boyish face suddenly looked years older.

"It's not fair!" his mother cried passionately. "It's not fair that some unknown person can step forward like this and take away what rightfully belongs to Geoffrey!"

"The earldom rightfully belongs to the nearest male heir, Mrs. Wilton," the attorney said gently. "And it seems that the nearest heir is this Niall MacDonald."

Alexandra's heart might be pounding but she kept her

voice steady as she asked the most important question of all. "Is Niall MacDonald married, Mr. Sloane?"

The lawyer looked at her over the top of his glasses. "No, Lady Alexandra," he said quietly. "He is not married."

Alexandra's heart plummeted into her stomach. Surely this wasn't possible.

"Not married?" she said faintly.

"My colleague was quite clear on that fact, Lady Alexandra. In fact, one of the reasons he took the trouble to send me advance notice was so that I could prepare you for this . . . ah . . . unfortunate . . . situation."

Geoffrey swore.

Alexandra looked at him blankly.

"Geoffrey," his mother protested in a weak voice.

"Then this means that the marriage clause in my father's will is still in effect?" Alexandra asked in the same faint tones as before.

"I am afraid so, Lady Alexandra," the solicitor replied. "Believe me, if there was anything we could legally do to get around it, we would. But the condition is, regrettably, both legal and binding. All of the entailed property will go to your cousin, regardless of whether you marry him or not. If you do marry him, then you will receive the stud farm and the income from His Lordship's many profitable investments. If you do not marry him, those things will go to the Jockey Club."

"But my father never meant that I should marry a perfect stranger," Alexandra said. Her voice had gone from faint to shrill.

"We all realize that, my lady," the elderly solicitor said patiently. "This is indeed a most unlucky turn of events."

Geoffrey said in a bitter voice, "That has to be the understatement of the century."

Alexandra gazed blindly at the large portrait of one of her ancestors wearing an Elizabethan ruff which hung over the fireplace. "When is this . . . this person . . . coming to Gayles?" she asked.

"I believe they will be here in two days' time," came the reply.

No one said a word.

Sloane pushed his glasses up onto his nose. "Mr. Taylor has also informed me that he has said nothing as yet to Mr. MacDonald about the marriage clause in the late earl's will."

Alexandra's eyes moved from the portrait to the solicitor. "Why not?" she demanded.

"He didn't say, my lady."

Alexandra said icily, "It seems to me, Mr. Sloane, that Mr. Taylor has mishandled this entire matter. He should never have agreed to write that will for my father in the first place!"

"It was Mr. Taylor's duty, as your father's solicitor, to draw up the will that your father wished, my lady," Sloane pointed out with inexorable logic. "In fact, Mr. Taylor tried quite strenuously to talk your father out of inserting that clause, but the earl insisted."

"Damn Papa," Alexandra said through her teeth, turned abruptly, and went to stare out the window, her back to the others in the room.

He came late in the afternoon of a sunny but cold and windy April day. As Alexandra entered the house through a back door she was met by a footman, who announced in a breathless voice, "The new earl is here, my lady. The carriage has just been spotted at the gatehouse."

Alexandra had been riding and was dressed in a dove

gray, beautifully tailored habit. She set her gloves and hat down upon one of the tables in the back vestibule and crossed the Great Hall to the front of the house. She hesitated for a moment, then slipped into the family dining room, which had large windows that looked out upon the stone terrace that fronted the house.

She stood beside one of the windows and stared at the hired carriage making its way up the graveled drive. The large, old-fashioned coach stopped in front of the stone steps that led up to the terrace, and Alexandra's hands closed into fists as a footman set the steps and her butler opened the door of the carriage to welcome the new earl.

James Taylor was the first to exit the coach, followed immediately by a lean, dark-haired young man who was dressed in a nondescript, slightly baggy brown jacket, wool trousers, and brogues.

Oh my God, Alexandra breathed in horror. *He's dressed like a servant.*

The two men moved a few paces away from the carriage door and then, to Alexandra's astonishment, two monstrous dogs bounded out onto the graveled drive.

Oh my God, Alexandra thought again, staring in stunned horror at the immense animals.

And then another man stepped out of the carriage and into the chill afternoon sunlight.

For as long as she lived, Alexandra would never forget her first sight of Niall MacDonald. He stood in front of the coach, tall and black-haired and proud as an emperor, and lifted his eyes to survey the house in front of him. It was a moment before she registered the fact that he was correctly dressed in a black coat, light tan pantaloons, and Hessian boots.

Alexandra knew by heart the magnificent sight that this

Highland interloper was regarding. The east entrance of Gayles had been built between the existing wings of the original Elizabethan house by Alexandra's grandfather. The two-story addition was crowned with heraldic beasts on pedestals and the fantasy outline was continued in the spiky balustrade and the two delightful Elizabethan pavilions topped with obelisks that bordered the entrance court.

Niall MacDonald's hard, arrogant face never changed as he stared critically at the beautiful house he had inherited, and Alexandra knew immediately that she wasn't going to like him.

At last he looked away from the house and said something to Stokes. The butler bowed his head with dignity and turned to lead the way up the stairs. The threesome from the carriage followed, as did the dogs.

Alexandra moved away from the window to stand behind the family-dining-room door, where she could not be seen from the Great Hall. After a minute she heard the heavy front door open, and Stokes say, "If you will come with me into the drawing room, my lord, I will inform Lady Alexandra that you have arrived."

"Thank you," Niall MacDonald responded.

"I will be happy to have one of the footmen take your dogs into the kitchen, my lord. Or perhaps your ... er ... valet would like to take them."

There was a moment of silence.

Then, "Are you perhaps referring to Mr. MacDonald?" Niall asked.

"I am sorry, my lord, if I . . ." Stokes's voice petered out. It was the first time in her life that Alexandra had ever heard her butler at a loss for words.

"Mr. MacDonald is my foster brother, and he will come

with me. As will the dogs," Niall said. His English was clearly articulated, but its cadence was unusual.

What an obnoxious man, Alexandra thought as she listened to the sound of the men's feet receding into the north wing of the house. After a few moments she went back into the Great Hall, which was illuminated by the late-afternoon sun coming in through the heraldic glass in the west-facing windows. The portrait of the ancestor who had built Gayles hung above the original paneling, and a rare seventeeth-century plaster panel adorned the opposite wall. Two footmen, looking rather pop-eyed, were whispering to each other in front of the elaborate stone screen with rusticated arches that ran across one end of the hall. As soon as they saw her, the footmen hurried away.

A flustered-looking Stokes erupted into the hall and stopped dead when he saw her. "Oh, Lady Alexandra, there you are." The butler approached her in a more sedate manner. "Mr. Taylor has arrived with the new earl and I have put them in the B-blue Drawing Room." Poor Stokes actually stuttered, he was so upset. "They have two very large dogs with them, my lady," he went on in a rush. "The new earl refused to allow me to take the dogs to the kitchen, and so they are in the drawing room also."

"It's all right, Stokes," Alexandra said soothingly. "I will go and meet them. Will you find Mr. Wilton and ask him to join us?"

"Of course, my lady," Stokes replied. "I must warn you, however, that there is another . . . person . . . with Mr. Taylor and His Lordship. The earl called him his foster brother."

Stoke's nose quivered as if he had picked up a bad smell.

"I will deal with His Lordship, Stokes," Alexandra said reassuringly.

The butler pulled himself together. "Yes, my lady. I will

inform Mr. Wilton that you desire him to come to the drawing room."

"Thank you, Stokes," Alexandra said.

A slight frown indented Alexandra's forehead as she watched her agitated butler retreat toward the stairs.

It was obvious that this upstart cousin of hers needed to be put in his place, she thought grimly. She lifted her chin, squared her shoulders, and headed for the drawing room, feeling rather like a soldier going into battle.

Niall surveyed the Blue Drawing Room with a calculating gaze. It was a large room, extending almost the full width of the house, with a bank of huge windows along the long exterior wall. The lower part of the other three walls was paneled with a beautiful dark wood. An immense Flemish tapestry of a knight in armor on a gaily caparisoned horse hung above the wainscoting on one of the walls.

The white-marble fireplace had a carved wooden panel featuring a coat of arms above it. Hanging on the wall next to the fireplace was a gilt-framed portrait of an extremely handsome, fair-haired boy of about eighteen. The drawing-room ceiling was timbered, the immense blue rug was Persian, and the furniture was either gilt or painted. All of the upholstery was blue.

One of the windows had been replaced by a French door, and, as they stood waiting for the lady of the house to arrive, Niall walked over to it and looked out at a stone patio with two stone urns filled with brilliant yellow daffodils. Then he turned back to frown at the totally unnecessary fire that was roaring in the fireplace and making the room uncomfortably warm.

Poor Alan was looking very ill at ease, and Niall caught

his eye and sent him a quick, reassuring grin. His foster brother had insisted upon accompanying him on this foray into what all Gaels considered enemy territory. In truth, Niall had not tried very hard to dissuade him. England was enemy territory in Niall's mind also, and he was grateful for Alan's familiar presence.

Fergus and Flora lay at his feet, as close to his polished boots as they could get without actually sitting on them. He had thought about leaving the dogs at home, but he wasn't sure how long he was going to have to spend in England, and they pined so when he was gone that he had decided it would be best if he simply took them along.

He looked at the portrait of a lady with powdered white hair and thought that she might well have been the countess here during the period of the Jacobite rebellion, when Bonnie Prince Charlie had rallied the clans to reclaim the thrones of England and Scotland for the Stuarts. Niall had been brought up on tales of that rebellion, and he was well acquainted with the many English atrocities that had devastated the Highlands after the defeat of the clans at Culloden. In fact, for all the twenty-five years of his life, Niall had thought of himself as purely MacDonald. The fact that he had an English father was something he almost never thought about. In every way that mattered, his grandfather had been his father.

"My lady," he heard Taylor say, and he removed his eyes from the portrait to focus them on the young woman who had just come into the room.

The Sassenach attorney had told him that the old earl had an unmarried daughter who was still living at Gayles, but Niall had never thought much about her. So it was with utter astonishment that he looked now into steady eyes that were as gray as Loch Alpin under a cloudy sky. Lady Alexandra

Wilton had hair that was pale as winter sunlight. Her face was like an angel's, with perfect bones under fair, absolutely flawless skin.

Dhé, he thought in shocked surprise.

"My lord," he heard the attorney saying, "allow me to make known to you your cousin, Lady Alexandra Wilton."

Niall inclined his dark head. "How do you do," he said.

Lady Alexandra looked at Fergus and Flora. "We do not allow dogs in the drawing room at Gayles," she said coldly.

It was a few seconds before he was able to reconcile that frigid voice to that angel's face. Finally, however, he managed to reply in a voice that was even frostier than hers. "I understood from Mr. Taylor here that Gayles was my house now." He flicked a glance at the attorney. "Is that not so, Mr. Taylor?"

Taylor was looking exceedingly unhappy. He gave Lady Alexandra an apologetic look as he answered, "That is so, my lord."

Niall did not bother to point out the obvious implications of this reply. The dogs would stay.

Lady Alexandra looked furious.

Niall regarded her anger with satisfaction. If this ill-tempered Sassenach thought she was going to continue to call the tune here at Gayles, she was much mistaken. "Allow me to introduce you to my foster brother, Alan MacDonald," Niall said to the seething Lady Alexandra.

"Good day to you," Alan said with quiet dignity.

"How do you do," the lady replied icily.

There was a movement in the doorway, and she stepped aside to allow an immaculately dressed young man with butter-colored hair to come into the room. He bore a noticeable resemblance to the boy in the portrait.

"Geoffrey," Alexandra said in a steely voice, "this is the

new Earl of Hartford." She regarded Niall with flinty eyes. "My lord, may I introduce the man whom you have displaced, your cousin, Mr. Geoffrey Wilton."

Geoffrey was staring at the dogs.

"Stay," Niall told them in Gaelic. Then he walked across the room, with his hand held out. "How do you do," he said to Geoffrey.

The hand the young man put into his was as soft and smooth as satin. Niall looked down at the yellow head that came only to the level of his nose.

Dhé! Surely his father could not have looked like this!

"It is a little difficult for me to say truthfully that you are welcome." Geoffrey was speaking with careful dignity. "As you can imagine, this situation is not easy for either Alex or me." His blue eyes flickered. "Not to put too fine a point on it, we were shocked to our very marrow to learn of your existence."

"I was shocked myself," Niall replied easily to this boyish-looking Sassenach. "It is most unfortunate that you were led to expect an inheritance that was not yours. It must seem very unfair to you."

"To be honest, it does seem rather unfair," Geoffrey returned. "It is not your fault, however, my . . . my lord . . ." Here his voice trailed away.

The look Niall gave him was more sardonic than sympathetic.

You are left with more than you left us with after Culloden, he thought. *At least you are not going to be driven out of your country into a foreign land, as my great-grandfather was.*

"You must be fatigued from your journey," Alexandra said. "I will summon our housekeeper to show you to your rooms." She favored him with a scornful look. "I gather that you did not bring your valet with you."

"Alan will look after me," Niall said.

She frowned. "I thought he was your foster brother."

"He is."

She shot Alan a look that was distinctly unfriendly, then went to ring the bell to summon the housekeeper.

Chapter Six

As soon as the two Scots had been led away by Mrs. Moreton, a grim-faced Geoffrey said to Alexandra, "I must find my mother and tell her that they have arrived."

"Warn her is more like it," she returned darkly.

He attempted a smile, nodded, and left the room.

Alexandra turned to James Taylor, who was standing a little awkwardly in front of the French doors. "So, Mr. Taylor," she said in ominous tones, "might I inquire as to why you have not yet told my cousin of the marriage clause in my father's will?"

Taylor looked at the heart-stoppingly beautiful face in front of him and thought that the answer to that question should be obvious. He said with circumspection, "I thought it would be best to wait until he had met you, my lady, before I told him about that particular clause."

Two straight, silvery eyebrows lifted in inquiry. "And why was that?"

Taylor smiled. He couldn't help himself. "You must know that His Lordship will be much more inclined to look with favor upon that clause once he has seen you, Lady Alexandra."

Alexandra's eyes turned their darkest gray. Spacing her words with deliberate emphasis, she said: "I Will Never Marry That Man."

Taylor's heart went out to her. She had been placed in an impossible situation, but there was nothing he could do about it. In his most gentle voice, he said, "You must marry someone, my lady. Your father made no provisions for you, and your inheritance from your mother is nothing more than pin money."

She was even beautiful when she scowled. "It's too bad Barrington got himself engaged to someone else," she muttered. "Under the circumstances, I might have changed my mind about him."

"Viscount Barrington's engagement notice appeared in the *Post* last month, my lady," Taylor said.

"I know, I know," she returned irritably.

In the same gentle voice as before, he added, "I might also remind you that your father did not provide you with a marriage portion other than the inheritance you will get if you marry His Lordship."

She threw up her hands. "What was Papa *thinking* of, Mr. Taylor? How could he have done such a dreadful thing to me?"

"He was in a temper, my lady," the attorney replied. "I truly think he would have changed his mind if you had expressed the desire to marry someone else."

Alexandra rubbed her forehead as if she had a headache. "Well," she said, "first you must inform His Lordship of the strings that have come attached to his inheritance. Tell him this evening, after dinner. It isn't fair to keep him in ignorance about this matter."

Taylor bowed his head in acquiescence. "I will do that my lady."

At this moment, Gayles's housekeeper came into the drawing room. "Oh Lady Alexandra, I am so glad I found you." The usually unruffled housekeeper was clearly agitated. "Can you tell me what I am to do with this Mr. Alan MacDonald?"

Alexandra regarded the small, birdlike figure of her housekeeper with some impatience. "What is the difficulty, Mrs. Moreton?"

"His Lordship says Mr. MacDonald is his foster brother, Lady Alexandra, but the man is going to sleep in His Lordship's dressing room and act as his valet." The housekeeper was completely flustered by this social conundrum. "Who is he to eat with, my lady? The family or the servants?"

After a brief moment Alexandra turned to Taylor. "You have traveled with Lord Hartford and Mr. MacDonald, Mr. Taylor. Exactly what is the situation between His Lordship and this so-called foster brother he has foisted on us?" She frowned. "The man is certainly not dressed as a gentleman."

"As I understand it, His Lordship's mother died when he was born and he was fostered out to Alan MacDonald's mother," Taylor replied. "Apparently His Lordship was raised equally by his foster family and his grandfather."

Alexandra looked grim. "Does that mean this Alan MacDonald person will expect to eat in the dining room?"

Taylor gave her a reassuring smile. "Alan would never regard himself as the equal of the future Mac-Mhic-Donnail. He would be extremely uncomfortable eating in your dining room, Lady Alexandra."

"Mac-Mick-Donyail?" Alexandra repeated. "What are you talking about?"

"Mac-Mhic-Donnail is the Gaelic title for the Chief of the MacDonalds of Glen Alpin, Lady Alexandra."

"Good God."

"My lady?" said the housekeeper, determined to get an answer to her problem. "Where should Mr. MacDonald eat?"

"Invite him to dine with you and Stokes in your sitting room," Alexandra said.

Mrs. Moreton did not look at all happy with this recommendation, but she curtsied to Alexandra and went on her way.

Taylor thought that Alan would be more comfortable in the kitchen than in the housekeeper's sitting room, but he understood that Alexandra had elevated the Scot's status by assigning him to the level of the upper servants, and so he said nothing.

Alan would just have to fend for himself.

The only person who was more unhappy than Alexandra about the introduction of Niall MacDonald to Gayles was Geoffrey. He, too, had been praying that Niall would be married, and the news that he was not had been a hard blow.

"He is an impossibly arrogant man," Geoffrey said to his mother where he had sought her out in the privacy of her bedroom. "Alex will never marry him."

"What Alexandra does is no longer your concern, Geoffrey," Mrs. Wilton replied steadily. "It is cruelly unfair that your expectations should have been raised in such a manner, but it is all over now. You are not the earl, and you are not going to marry Alexandra. You must accept this and look to your own future."

Color stained Geoffrey's fair skin. "She may still wish to marry me! We have grown very close these last few months,

Mother, and I'm quite sure she will prefer me to MacDonald."

Mrs. Wilton rested her head against the high back of her wing chair. "You and Alexandra cannot marry, my dear," she said wearily. "Neither of you has any money."

Geoffrey was standing in front of the chimneypiece, facing his mother. "I have Highgate," he said.

"Thanks to your father's profligacy, Highgate is mortgaged to the hilt," his mother replied even more wearily than before. "You must marry a woman with money, just as Alexandra must find a husband of means. You must forget her, Geoffrey. I think we should leave Gayles immediately and go home."

"We can't do that," Geoffrey said instantly. "Someone must be here to chaperone Alex. She can't be left alone with that man."

There was a little silence as Mrs. Wilton regarded her son. Then she said, "Very well, then, I will remain here at Gayles, but you should go home."

"No." Geoffrey's round boyish face suddenly looked older. "I won't desert Alex, Mother. I understand what you are saying, but as long as she needs me, I will not desert her."

Mrs. Wilton closed her eyes and did not reply.

Alexandra was greatly relieved when Niall appeared in the drawing room before dinner correctly dressed in a double-breasted black-wool evening coat with tails, an immaculate white waistcoat, shirt, and cravat, and long trousers with a strap under the shoe to prevent wrinkling. The cut and quality of the clothes, though clearly not the work of a Bond Street tailor, were decent.

Her approval quickly vanished, however, when she saw

the two dogs that trailed at his heels. Mrs. Wilton was not quite successful in stifling her high-pitched cry. She was terrified of dogs.

Geoffrey introduced the new earl to his mother and mentioned her fear.

"They won't hurt you, ma'am," Niall said, looking down upon Louisa Wilton's small, fair-haired person with what Alexandra thought was an expression of contempt. "They are very well trained."

"I am sure they are," Mrs. Wilton managed to reply faintly.

Alexandra opened her mouth to say that she hoped the earl wasn't going to inflict his dogs upon them in the dining room, then closed it again without saying anything.

No sense in inviting another snub, she thought grimly.

Stokes appeared in the doorway to announce dinner. Alexandra said stiffly, "If you would escort me, Cousin, then Geoffrey may take in his mother."

"Certainly," Niall replied, and held out his arm with perfect correctness. She cast a quick glance up at him and caught him looking down at her. Their gazes met.

His eyes were not brown, as she had thought, but blue.

Her heart thumped once, loudly, and then began to race. To disguise her sudden confusion, she rested her fingertips on his outstretched black sleeve and began to walk in the direction of the family dining room.

The dogs followed.

"This is the formal dining room," she said nervously, as they passed from the drawing room into the room that was situated next to it. "We only use it when we entertain."

"The table is rather large for just the family," he replied. His voice was deep but very clear.

Alexandra looked blankly at the long mahogany table,

which was flanked by twenty-four brocade-covered chairs. Two crystal chandeliers hung over its gleaming surface. The huge gilt-framed mirror over the fireplace afforded a glimpse of her and Niall as they passed in front of it.

The top of her head came to just below his chin. Alexandra was a tall girl, and she was not used to being dominated by the superior height of a man. It was not a feeling she enjoyed.

She removed her hand from his arm as soon as they entered the family dining room. The table there had all its leaves removed and was set for five persons.

"My lord," Alexandra said and gestured regally to the place at the head of the table. She herself took the seat opposite and Geoffrey and Mrs. Wilton sat between them on one side of the table while Mr. Taylor sat by himself on the other side.

The dogs took up their stations behind Niall's chair.

Soup was served. As Alexandra lifted her spoon to take a sip, she felt Niall's eyes on her. She lowered her spoon and looked across the table in inquiry.

His blue stare held distinct disapproval. "Do you not say a prayer before your meals?"

She stared at the lawless face of her newfound cousin.

"Do you wish to say grace?" she asked, trying to disguise her astonishment.

"Surely it is only courtesy to give thanks to the Lord for our food," he replied.

"Very well." Alexandra folded her hands in her lap. "Will you say the prayer, my lord?"

He bent his dark head. "We thank you, dear Lord, for your bounty of the day," he said simply.

"Amen," chorused Alexandra, Geoffrey, Mrs. Wilton, and Taylor.

Alexandra once again picked up her soup spoon and began to eat.

It was a strained meal. The conversation was sustained mainly by Mrs. Wilton and Mr. Taylor, the one asking questions about Scottish scenery and the other replying in voluminous detail. Geoffrey offered an occasional courteous comment as did Alexandra.

The new earl ate, fed his dogs from his plate, and spoke only when he was asked a direct question.

Alexandra found his manners revolting. Conveniently forgetting the beloved spaniel that had slept in her bed for almost all of her childhood, she stared with condemnation at the huge, well-behaved hounds whose only movement was the slapping of their tails when they were given food.

Nor did she mistake the earl's taciturnity for shyness. The sardonic expression on his face as he listened to the conversation made her fingers itch to slap him.

At last the dessert had been served and eaten, and she could rise, along with Mrs. Wilton, and leave her disagreeable cousin to his port and to Taylor's revelation.

The two ladies retired to the upstairs drawing room, which was still called the Great Chamber. The windows there were set with stained glass tracing the genealogy of the Wilton family. The paneled walls were topped with an ornate plaster frieze, and the whole of the immense room was dominated by a spectacular black-marble chimneypiece. The drawing room still contained the high green-velvet chair that had been the first owner's chair of state, but the rest of the furnishings were more modern and included a piano.

Gayles had been built during the reign of Elizabeth by Alexandra's ancestor, John Wilton, who had been born in a modest manor some three miles away. After rising to a position of power at court, he had returned to his home county to build Gayles, using glass from his own glassworks for the enormous windows, Derbyshire alabaster for the extensive plasterwork, and Derbyshire marble from his own quarries for the fireplaces.

Alexandra looked at the portrait of John Wilton, which hung on the wall to the right of the magnificent fireplace. She loved the thought that her family had lived in this house for over two hundred years. The thought that a stranger who called himself MacDonald would be the new owner dismayed her unutterably.

What would he do with Gayles?

"I am so sorry, my dear, that things have turned out this way," Mrs. Wilton said. "It is as bad for you as it is for Geoffrey."

Alexandra did not wish to talk about her problems, and said with a smile, "Shall I play for you, Cousin Louisa? Perhaps some music will distract us from our difficulties."

Mrs. Wilton smiled in acknowledgment, and Alexandra went to the piano. She was halfway through a Mozart sonata when Stokes came into the room. She stopped playing as soon as she saw him.

"Lady Alexandra," the butler said in his deliberate, sonorous voice, "His Lordship requests your presence in the Blue Drawing Room."

Alexandra's heart began to slam.

He knows, she thought. She bit her lip. What was he going to do?

Somehow she found the composure to reply to her butler, stand up steadily, and smooth the skirt of her elegant low-cut lilac-silk evening dress. Her hands felt clammy as she descended the stairs, and she could feel the pulse beating in her throat. She stopped outside the Blue Drawing Room for a moment to collect herself before opening the door.

He was standing in front of the French doors looking out into the twilight-lit garden when she stepped into the room. He was alone.

"You wished to see me, my lord?" she asked, annoyed to hear the faint quiver in her voice.

He swung around, his face absolutely shuttered. She had no idea what he might be thinking.

"Yes," he said. "It seems that you and I have things to discuss."

She had only come a few paces into the room, and now she regarded him across the wide expanse of rich Persian rug. "I assume that Mr. Taylor has told you of the marriage clause in my father's will."

"He has told me."

"He should have told you immediately, when he informed you of the inheritance," she said. "I can't think why he delayed like this."

He flicked his eyes over her, from the tips of her soft ivory-colored shoes to the top of her elegantly coifed head. "I think I can guess."

Something in his gaze made her want to back away. Instead she raised her chin and came farther into the room. "It is all a horrible mistake. My father wanted me to marry Geoffrey. He would never have written such a clause if he had known of your existence."

He lifted one of those slashing black eyebrows, making him look even more arrogant than usual. "Taylor told me that it is written using the words 'the seventh earl.' No specific person is named."

"And that is Mr. Taylor's fault," she replied bitterly. "He is the one who wrote that damn clause, and it was his mistake not to name names. You would think that he could come up with a way to get us out of this impossible situation he has created, but apparently he is not clever enough to do that."

There was a deep line between his black brows. "You have sought other legal opinions?"

"We sought many legal opinions, my lord. All of them say that the clause is legal."

He muttered something under his breath in a foreign language. Then he stepped away from the French doors.

"Come and sit down," he said abruptly. "We need to talk about this."

"There is nothing to talk about," she replied, not moving from where she stood. "I am certainly not going to marry you."

He ignored her and went to sit in one of the chairs next to the rosewood game table to the right of the French doors. A chess set was arranged upon the black-and-red board painted on the tabletop.

Alexandra glanced toward the warmth of the fireplace, and for the first time realized that the dogs were in the room with them. The two great deerhounds were stretched out close to the fire, apparently asleep.

She looked back at Niall, who had rudely seated himself before she did, and felt a spark of temper ignite within her. Without speaking, she crossed the room and sat down on the opposite side of the chessboard from him.

"It's a shame I wasn't already married," he said. "Apparently that would have negated the clause."

"It certainly is too bad," she returned sharply. "You're old enough to be married, for heaven's sake. Why aren't you?"

"Why aren't *you*?" he retorted. "Taylor tells me you're twenty-one years old."

His comment made her furious. "It's none of your business why I'm not married."

"I am thinking that it certainly is my business," he snapped back. "If you had been married, I wouldn't find myself in this damnable situation."

Alex tapped her fingers on the arm of her chair and thought that there was no point in trying to be tactful with this savage. "Do you need the money?" she asked with brutal bluntness.

"Of course I need the money," he replied irritably. "Why else do you think I came here? I have no desire to be an English lord. I came because I need money for Glen Alpin."

She scooted to the front of her chair and glared at him across the beautifully carved ivory chess pieces. "What? You want to take my money and spend it on your *Scottish* lands?"

"That is right," he replied. There was a lilting cadence to his words that was oddly attractive. "I wish to introduce a new breed of cattle into Glen Alpin, but I do not have the money to purchase a foundation herd. Foolishly, I assumed that a Sassenach earl would be rich enough to allow me to divert some money to my own projects." His brows drew together, making him look very formidable. "And now I find that all of the money is tied up in you."

The way he said the word *you* was not flattering.

"Well I was hoping that the heir to a chiefdom would have enough money that he would not need to marry for it!" she shot back.

A small silence fell as they gazed at each other across the chessboard. Hostility, and something else that Alexandra did not want to think about, crackled in the air between them.

He said in a milder voice, "It seems we were both wrong."

One of the tendrils she had left loose when she swept up

her hair for dinner was tickling her cheek, and she reached up to push it behind her ear. His eyes followed the movement of her fingers.

She said tightly, "It appears that the Jockey Club is going to become very rich."

He steepled his fingers in front of his chest. His hands were slim, but they looked like hands that knew how to work. "You were ready to marry Geoffrey," he said. "Why won't you marry me?"

She stared at him as if he were a madman.

"Well?" he said impatiently.

"I don't know you," she returned.

"You'll get to know me once we're married."

"I don't *like* you," she said furiously.

He looked amused. "I don't know if there's anything I can do about that."

"There isn't," she informed him.

"Look here," he said. "The situation as it was presented to me is thus: I have inherited several houses and properties that I cannot sell, as they are entailed. You have inherited a stud farm, which can be sold, as well as a great deal of money. But you only get those things if you marry me." He cocked an eyebrow. "Is that a correct assessment of our respective circumstances?"

She was staring at his ringless hands. "Yes."

He tapped his forefingers together once. "I am thinking that I have two options. Either I marry you and thus gain access to the money from the stud farm and the investments, or I bleed Gayles dry of all its income and use it to buy livestock for Glen Alpin."

Alexandra jumped to her feet and glared at him. "You wouldn't do that! The farm rents are meant to be used for the benefit of Gayles!"

He rose more slowly. "All of the income from Gayles and the other properties is mine. That is what Mr. Taylor has told me. I am the earl and I own the land and there is no way that I can be replaced. Is that not so?"

Silence.

Finally, "Yes," Alexandra said through her teeth.

Her hateful cousin went on. "You, also, have two options, my lady. You can marry me, collect your inheritance, and live in the fashion to which you have become accustomed. Or you can try to live on your mother's income, which Mr. Taylor informs me is *not* what you are accustomed to."

"There is a third possibility," she flashed. "I could marry someone else!"

His eyes were the darkest blue she had ever seen. "You don't have a marriage portion."

"Not all English gentlemen are as venal as you appear to be," Alexandra said icily.

He ran his fingers through his hair, which was thick and black and wavy. "Perhaps I have not made myself clear. When I speak of a marriage between the two of us I am speaking of a business arrangement."

Her eyes narrowed. "What do you mean?"

His face took on the sardonic expression that she already disliked intensely. "I mean that we would go through a marriage ceremony, collect the inheritance we both need, then go our separate ways." His eyes glinted. "Believe me, my lady, I have no more desire to be a husband to you than you have to be a wife to me."

Illogically, Alexandra felt insulted.

"I certainly don't wish to be a wife to you," she said. "And if we should do this, you must know that I have no intention of sleeping with you. Ever."

"That is perfectly fine with me," he replied.

A taut silence fell in the room as they stared at each other over the chessboard.

"How would we do this?" she said at last.

He shrugged. "First we should probably sit down with Taylor and draw up a contract about the disposition of the money. You are entitled to half of it, I think."

"You are too generous," she said with lethal sweetness.

"I have often been told that," he agreed.

Alexandra clenched her fists.

He went on, "Once we have the money issue settled, we simply stand up in front of a clergyman and get married. I am an Episcopalian, so we have no religious differences to deal with."

"How fortunate."

"I think so."

She bit her lip in indecision.

"What happens after we are married? Will you take your money and return directly to Scotland?"

If he did that, Alexandra thought, this idea mightn't be so unpalatable after all. True, she would never have a real husband, but she would have Gayles.

"Not directly," he said, shattering her brief moment of complacency. "I wish to inspect some English cattle in order to determine which breed will thrive best in Glen Alpin. Then I will need to purchase a foundation herd. After I do that, I will return home."

"Forever?" she asked hopefully.

"I certainly have no desire to stay here," he said, flicking a disdainful glance around the beautiful room.

Her brows knit thoughtfully. "Under those circumstances," she said slowly, "I might consider your proposal."

"Do that," he replied. He came around the game table to

stand next to her, forcing her to tip her head way back in order to look into his face.

You can't intimidate me, she thought, glaring up at him defiantly.

Their gazes locked, and the air between them felt as charged as it did just before lightning struck. An intensely blue flame flared in his eyes, then he scowled and stepped away from her.

Alexandra's heart was pounding. *He feels it, too,* she thought in confusion.

"Where can I take the dogs for their last outing?" he said.

His face looked perfectly composed, but she saw a muscle twitch in his jaw.

"You can go out through the French doors and around the house to the garden," she said.

He nodded, turned, and whistled softly. The two immense shaggy hounds got up, stretched, and came to join him. He pushed open the glass doors and, without another word to her, exited into the garden along with his dogs.

Alone, Alexandra raised her hands to cover her face. She was furious to discover that she was shaking. She breathed deeply and slowly. Then she dropped her hands, straightened her shoulders, and went to find James Taylor.

Chapter Seven

That night, Alexandra lay awake for a long time, thinking about Niall's proposal. From a financial point of view, she supposed that it made sense. But what would it mean to her personally?

If Niall kept his word and took his half of the money and returned to Scotland, she would find herself a virtual widow. This was a position that many women would relish. She would have all the freedom of a wife and none of the obligations. As long as she was discreet, she could take as many lovers as she wished and society would never blink an eye. Plus, she would have complete control of her own money, as well as all the earl's extensive property.

If you had to marry a man you didn't love, then, Alexandra thought, this was the way to do it. The problem was, she didn't want to marry a man she didn't love. The reason she had infuriated her father by turning down the offers of so many eligible suitors was that she didn't want to marry a man she didn't love.

Now this man, this stranger with his hard face and arrogant manner, had proposed that they marry.

He doesn't even like me, Alexandra thought, as she huddled sleepless under her blue-satin quilt. *And I certainly don't like him.*

Finally, she drifted off into a restless sleep filled with weird, chaotic dreams. She awoke to find her maid quietly setting a cup of chocolate down on her bedside table.

"Meg," she said in a foggy voice, "what time is it?"

"It's almost nine o'clock, my lady," the woman replied.

"Good heavens," Alexandra said. She always rose before eight.

She glanced at the window, which was still covered by drapes, and said in true English fashion, "What is the weather?"

"It's lovely out, my lady," the maid replied. "What clothes shall I lay out for you? A riding habit or a morning dress?"

Alexandra swung her long legs out of bed and went to the window. She pulled open the drapes and brilliant sunlight flooded the room. Outside, two men accompanied by a pair of large dogs were passing between the Elizabethan pavilions that bordered the front entrance court. One of the men was very tall and dressed in a brown riding coat while the other was dressed in workman's garb.

It was Niall and Alan MacDonald. The two men were deep in conversation, and the dogs were trailing behind them, having stopped to sniff at a particularly redolent piece of shrubbery. The sky was clear and deeply blue, and the sun glinted off the dogs' rust-colored coats and Niall's uncovered hair.

As Alexandra watched, the two Scots were joined in the front court by a man whom she recognized as Gerald Mason, her father's steward. The three paused to exchange a few words, then Niall and Mason went together into the house while Alan took the dogs around the side of the house.

Alexandra went into her dressing room, where she allowed Meg to help her put on a scoop-necked, high-waisted muslin morning dress sprinkled with small pink flowers. A delicate gold locket was her only jewelry. She went downstairs to the family dining room and demanded of the first footman she saw, "Where is His Lordship?"

"I believe that he is in the office with Mr. Mason, Lady Alexandra," came the courteous reply.

Alexandra pressed her lips together. Somehow the knowledge that Niall was in conference with her father's steward made the actuality of his ownership frighteningly real. Suddenly, her appetite deserted her.

She drank some coffee, then left the dining room and walked in the direction of the back door, where she met Alan MacDonald, who was coming in with the dogs.

"Good morning, Lady Alexandra," the man said politely, calling her by her name and not "my lady." He met her eyes in a most unservant-like manner.

Alexandra was not in a good mood. "Good morning, Mr. MacDonald," she said frostily. She glanced at the dogs. "I hope you are taking them to the kitchen."

Alan looked at her out of inscrutable brown eyes. "Niall told me to bring them to him," he said.

Alexandra's perfect nostrils quivered, and she replied in her haughtiest manner, "I believe His Lordship is in the estate office." She signaled to a footman. "George will show you where it is."

Alan's level gazed continued to regard her for a moment, then he turned away and fell into step with the young footman, who was clad in the green-and-gold livery of the earls of Wilton.

Alexandra's temper rose as she stared after the poorly dressed young man who called an earl by his first name and acted as if he were her equal.

Niall was closeted with Mr. Mason for the entire morning. Alexandra knew this because she herself spent the morning in the small room that jutted out into the East Court directly opposite to the estate office. For the past several years this room had been her own office, the place where she did the household accounts and met with her housekeeper and cook and butler. This morning she sat at her elegant French desk, account books unregarded in front of her, and stared across the stone terrace of the East Court at the windows of the estate office, which had been opened to admit the chill morning air.

It was well after noon when the figures she had been watching through the windows left the estate office. Alexandra hastily closed her account book, in which she had not made a single notation, and went out into the Blue Drawing Room, through the anteroom, and into the hall. She was just in time to catch Niall and the steward, who were coming from the opposite wing. The dogs were at Niall's heels.

"Mr. Mason," she said with creditable surprise, "I did not know that you were here."

"Lady Alexandra." Gayles's steward, with his ruddy face and stocky build, looked more like a farmer than a man of business. He sketched a small bow in her direction. "I have been explaining to His Lordship the extent of the Hartford properties as well as their financial situation."

"I see," Alexandra said.

Niall said to her, "At home we have dinner in the afternoon, but I understand that you dine in the evening. I hope there is some kind of meal in between?"

She answered in a cold voice, "A luncheon will be served at one in the family dining room."

"Good." He turned to the steward. "After this luncheon, you and I can take a drive around the property, Mason."

"Very good, my lord," the steward replied.

Niall favored both Mason and Alexandra with a single nod, turned, and strode off down the hall in the direction of the door. He was followed by his faithful deerhounds.

"He is quite the rudest man I ever met," Alexandra said furiously as soon as he was out of hearing.

"He is extremely intelligent, Lady Alexandra," the steward replied earnestly. "He asked very pertinent questions and appeared to grasp things very quickly."

This was not quite the answer that Alexandra desired to hear. "How nice," she snapped. "I will have Mrs. Moreton show you to a room so you may wash before luncheon."

Before the steward could reply, Alexandra had turned away.

Niall had been astounded by the extent of his inheritance. Gayles itself was the center of over thirty thousand acres of tenant farms, woodlands, cottages, and villages. On paper, all of the properties had appeared to be wildly prosperous to Niall, but Mason had made clear to him that all of the people who worked on the farms and lived in the cottages and villages were in one way or another dependent for their prosperity upon the Earl of Hartford. Then, in addition to Gayles, Niall learned he had inherited a London town house, a hunting box in Leicestershire, and a house in Bath, which was occupied by two elderly unmarried aunts of the late earl, who, Mason told him, existed solely upon the earl's largesse. There was also a small estate in Kent and one in Hampshire.

To Niall, the income from the estates seemed a staggering amount of money. However, the expenses of the earl were enormous as well. The list of retainers who received a pension was extensive.

He had had no idea that he would be responsible for so many lives.

His afternoon tour of Gayles with Mason made him even more conscious of the difference in wealth between the English tenant farmer and his own clansmen. The farms they visited were wealthy beyond the dream of any of his own people. Even the horses in the Gayles stable lived better than did most of the clan back in Glen Alpin.

The horses who inhabited the stables were a shock as well. Niall's eye was accustomed to the shaggy, sturdy Highland ponies they had at home. He had ridden regular-size horses, of course, but these tall, elegant aristocrats, with their long narrow faces and glossy coats, were a revelation. They almost seemed a different species from the animals Niall had known in Scotland.

The way Alexandra Wilton seemed an altogether different species of female from the girls that Niall had known. Like her horses, she was glossy and elegant and beautiful.

These Sassenach surely live off the fat of the land, he thought resentfully, as his long Highlander's stride ate up the ground between the stable and the house after he and Mason had returned from their inspection. Abruptly, he realized that Mason was almost running to keep up with him, and he slowed his steps and surveyed the east front of the house with hard, flinty eyes.

Mason had told him that when Gayles was originally built in 1601, the East Court had been the front of the house. The image that came to Niall's mind as he regarded the great home he now owned was that of a highly stylized medieval fortification. Statues, which Mason had told him represented the Nine Worthies of medieval lore, were placed above the entrance and between the first-floor windows. The rest of the house showed an ingenious use of what Mason called Renaissance motifs. Classical entablatures separated the three stories, and segmental pediments surmounted the projecting bays to either side of the entrance as well as the two wings.

Niall had never seen a house like it. Great houses in the Highlands ran more to stark stone castles, such as his own Eilean Darrach.

Walking side by side, he and Mason mounted the five stone steps to the terrace, then entered the house through the heavily carved door. Alexandra was standing inside, under the large plaster panel which bore the Wilton coat of arms.

Dhé, but she is beautiful.

The thought was almost hostile. Niall had no intention of finding anything to admire about this English cousin. If he had to go through a marriage ceremony with her in order to get his hands on the money he needed, he would. But he wanted nothing to do with her, or with any of her prosperous countrymen.

Alexandra looked up at him out of eyes that were colder than the snow that covered the top of Ben Nevis.

I pity any man who has to rely on her to warm his bed, Niall thought cynically.

"Mr. Taylor has called, my lord," she said. "He wishes to see the both of us."

Niall had been looking forward to some quiet time so he could think about everything he had learned today, and he frowned in annoyance at this news.

Alexandra's chilly expression became even frostier.

Fergus and Flora came galloping down the hall to greet him. Alan's raised voice, calling them, came from the direction of the back door.

The hounds were wet, their rust-colored coats matted

against their lean, elegant bones. They pressed against Niall's legs, dampening his boots and breeches.

Alan said in Gaelic, "I was meaning to take them to the kitchen, but they saw you first."

"Where did they get so wet?" Niall asked in the same language. He made no motion to push the dogs away.

"I took them for a swim in that wee loch with the fake waterfall," Alan replied. "They made the mistake of chasing the swans. *Dhé*, but they are nasty creatures."

"I hope they did not eat the silly birds," Niall returned.

His foster brother shook his head. "In truth, I am thinking that the swans won that particular battle."

Niall pictured the scene in his mind, his huge shaggy deerhounds and the elegant white swans. He grinned.

Alan grinned back. "This is a very fancy place," he said.

"That it is," Niall replied. "You had better take the dogs to the kitchen to dry. If they shake themselves in the house, Lady Alexandra will surely faint."

The men shared another smile, then Alan called to the dogs and, upon Niall's command, they turned and followed obediently after his foster brother. Niall turned back to Alexandra.

She was staring at him with a very strange expression on her face.

"Alan took Fergus and Flora for a swim," he explained. "He is going to make certain they are dry before he lets them into the house."

A faint line creased her perfect brow. She nodded.

Niall sighed. "What does Taylor want now?"

"He wouldn't tell me. He wanted to speak to us both."

Her voice sounded oddly subdued.

"Very well. Then let us go and find out what this is about."

"He is in the Blue Drawing Room," she said, and turned to lead the way.

*   *   *

As they entered the drawing room, Alexandra was still reeling from the effects of Niall's smile. It changed his whole face, she thought. He didn't look arrogant at all when he smiled. He looked young, and . . . and brilliantly happy. It was an astonishing transformation.

He was not smiling at the moment, however. Instead, he was staring intimidatingly at James Taylor, who had risen from his chair when they came in. "What is it now, Mr. Taylor?" Niall demanded.

The solicitor's expression was very grave. "I am sorry to disturb you, my lord, but I have received a communication that requires a response from you and Lady Alexandra."

Without answering, Niall strode to one of the windows and opened it. Chilly air rushed into the room, blowing the fragile Jacobean draperies.

"Those draperies are very old and very precious, my lord," Alexandra said, her voice as cold as the wind that was pouring into the room. "It is not good for them to be blown about in such a fashion."

"Everything in this house is old and precious," Niall muttered. "It's like a museum."

Alexandra was incensed, as she always was at any hint that Gayles was not perfect. "It is the house of a gentleman," she said grittily. "Perhaps you are not accustomed to such an abode."

"I am certainly not accustomed to living in a house that is so armored against fresh air," he returned.

"It's April, not July, for God's sake," Alexandra snapped.

"At home we keep the windows open all year round," Niall informed her. "That is the healthy way to live."

Alexandra opened her mouth to reply when a cough from Taylor stopped her. She turned angry eyes on the solicitor.

"If you would sit down my lord, my lady, I will tell you about the communication I had this morning from the treasurer of the Jockey Club."

The words *Jockey Club* were sufficiently ominous to cause Alexandra and Niall to take seats facing James Taylor.

The window remained open.

"All right," Niall said. "What is this urgent communication, Mr. Taylor?"

The solicitor cleared his throat. "Shortly after the late earl's death, I notified the Jockey Club about the conditions in his will. Since the club figured in the will in such a prominent manner, it was its legal right to be so informed."

Niall and Alexandra said nothing.

Taylor went on, "I also notified the club that the conditions of the will were going to be met by Lady Alexandra and the new earl, who we supposed at the time to be Mr. Geoffrey Wilton. I undertook to inform the club when the marriage between Lady Alexander and Mr. Geoffrey Wilton had actually taken place."

The solicitor nervously smoothed his fingers along the edge of the envelope he was holding. "As soon as my partner learned from me about the existence of a new heir, he informed the Jockey Club of the change. In response, we received this communication from the Jockey Club's treasurer."

The solicitor held up the envelope.

"There is no need to be so dramatic, Mr. Taylor," Alexandra said crisply. "What precisely is in this communication?"

"The Jockey Club wishes to know if the conditions of your father's will are still going to be met, my lady," Taylor said with obvious embarrassment.

The only sound in the drawing room was the ripple of the drapes blowing at the window Niall had opened.

At last Niall spoke. "How long do we have to make up our minds about this?"

"His Lordship will be dead eight months in May," the solicitor returned. "Eight months was the time stipulated in his will. If Lady Alexandra has not married the seventh earl within that time period, the money and the stud farm will go to the Jockey Club."

Alexandra closed her eyes and leaned her head against the blue-silk back of her chair. "This is like a nightmare," she said drearily.

"I am terribly sorry to distress you, my lady," Taylor said. He really did look upset. "But I must make some reply to Lord Chisholm."

His use of this name produced an almost volcanic effect in Niall. "Did you say *Chisholm*?" he demanded.

Taylor and Alexandra looked at him in alarm.

"W . . . Why, yes, my l . . . lord," Taylor stuttered. "Lord Chisholm is the treasurer of the Jockey Club."

"Chisholm of Strathglass?" The words sounded as if they were shot from a cannon.

"I . . . I believe so, my lord. He is married to the daughter of the Earl of Bentham."

"What do you know about Lord Chisholm?" Alexandra asked the thundercloud that was her cousin.

"I know that he is one of the most evil men ever to taint the earth with his footsteps," Niall replied fiercely. "He is the man who evicted his people, his clan who had lived in Strathglass since the beginning of time, from the land of their ancestors. And for what reason did he do this heinous deed? So he could bring in sheep. He could get more money from sheep than he could from his people, so he evicted them and forced them to emigrate to Nova Scotia."

Oddly, these emotional words did not seem overly dramatic.

"I have heard of the Highland Clearances," Alexandra said slowly.

Niall looked at Taylor. "Do you remember the glens that surround Glen Alpin and how desolate they were?"

"Yes," Taylor returned soberly.

"They belong to Chisholm."

Taylor let out his breath in a long, hissing sigh.

"Men like Chisholm are not fit to live," Niall said with deadly seriousness. "They are worse than the English."

Taylor and Alexandra looked at each other, but so violent was Niall's emotion that neither of them dared to utter a protest.

Niall got to his feet. "Come with me," he commanded Alexandra. "This is a matter to be discussed in private."

Without even a thought of objecting, she rose from her chair. Taylor rose with her.

"Remain here," Niall commanded the solicitor. "I will speak with you shortly."

"Yes, my lord," Taylor said, and sat down.

Niall gestured for Alexandra to precede him out of the room. Once they were in the hall, he said, "Let us go outdoors. I think better when I am outside."

Rather to her own annoyance, Alexandra found herself docilely following him out the front door and around to the garden, a twenty-acre expanse on the south side of the house. As in so many great house gardens, the trees and shrubs and flowers had been planted in such a way that each season had its own cascade of color. What made Gayles's garden different, however, was the way it had been arranged into a series of enclosures, each separated from the other by hedges of box, yew, holly, hornbeam, and beech. Some of these hedges were low, mere borders to planted beds, while others formed solid walls of green too tall to look over, giving the impression that one was in a room. Many were clipped into various topiary shapes.

The garden looked lovely in the April sunshine, but Alexandra was still wearing her thin morning dress, and the air was chilly on her bare arms. She led Niall to an enclosure that was surrounded by English yews clipped in the shape of elongated cones. The yews sheltered the enclosure from the brisk spring breeze.

Inside the yew enclosure there was a stone fountain and a single stone garden bench. Neither Niall nor Alexandra made any move toward sitting down. Both knew, instinctively, that the bench was too small to allow them the distance they needed from each other.

They faced each other, rather like two combatants before the start of a duel. They were both bareheaded, and the sun glinted off the pale gold of Alexandra's hair and drew glints of deep mahogany from Niall's.

His hair is not truly black, she thought irrelevantly.

Niall said, "I will do anything to keep that money from getting into the hands of Chisholm."

"It is not Lord Chisholm who will get the money," she replied. "It is the Jockey Club."

His face was as hard as granite. He didn't answer.

She said, "What did you discuss with Mr. Mason this morning?"

"He showed me the books for all of the properties."

"Then you must realize the extent of the responsibilities that have fallen upon you," she replied. "You speak with disgust of Lord Chisholm because he neglected his responsibilities to his people. If you steal money from my people to help yours, you will be guilty of the same crime."

He lifted an ironic eyebrow. "I can find little pity in my

heart for the plight of your people. Most of them live like princes in comparison to the clan back home in Glen Alpin."

"I am sure they do," she snapped. "We despised English take care of our people."

He stared at her for a long moment, then suddenly it seemed as if the anger drained out of him. "I am sorry," he said.

She, who was usually so socially adept, felt awkward and did not know how to reply. She nodded.

"Alexandra," he said. It was the first time he had used her name, and for some reason she felt color stain her cheeks. He went on, "I am thinking that we should marry. It is the best solution to both our problems. It will give me enough money to revitalize Glen Alpin and it will give you enough money for yourself and for Gayles."

The air felt suddenly colder and she rubbed her hands up and down her arms for warmth. "It will not solve one problem," she said steadily. "We neither of us will ever have a child to follow after us."

He frowned and then, as she watched in surprise, he unbuttoned his coat and slipped out of it. Then he stepped closer to hang it around her shoulders. It was huge, reaching almost to her ankles.

"You have only that little dress on," he said. "I should not have brought you out here without a shawl."

She could feel the warmth of his body in his coat. It seemed somehow a very intimate thing that he had done, and she thought suddenly that it might be difficult in more ways than one to be married to Niall MacDonald.

He said, "The problem of an heir is a situation that will affect you and Gayles more than it will me. In the Highlands we are not bound by laws that give away our property to strangers."

"In that respect, I must agree that your laws are more sensible than ours," she said tartly. The lining of his coat was smooth and warm against her arms. She bit her lip. "Perhaps we could divorce."

"I don't think that would solve the problem of an heir," he said smoothly. "If you remarried, would your son be the next in line to inherit Gayles?"

She glared at him and didn't answer. They both knew the answer to that question.

"I suggest that we hurdle one obstacle at a time," he said pleasantly. "Right now we need to deal with the problem of how to keep your father's money from going to the Jockey Club." He lifted one of those slashing eyebrows. "Besides, you do not seem to be much attracted to the married state. My understanding is that you have refused numerous offers for your hand."

She folded her arms. "I have always intended to get married someday."

Abruptly, his agreeable manner vanished. He said, "If you expect me to sympathize with you, you are looking at the wrong man. You are a strong and healthy girl, and you have never in your life had to dirty your hands with work or wonder where your next meal was coming from. That dress you are wearing would probably feed a Highland family for a year. If you marry me and inherit your father's money, you will have wealth beyond the imagination of anyone I have ever known. You can continue to live here at Gayles and queen it over the countryside. It seems to me that for you the benefits of marriage to me far outweigh the single drawback."

She was so furious that she couldn't speak. She spun around so that her back was to him and blinked back the angry tears that were stinging her eyes.

The only sound in the garden was the dripping of water into the stone basin of the fountain.

She heard him say stiffly, "I did not mean to hurt your feelings."

The tears were gone, and she turned back to him. "You are the most obnoxious man I have ever met in my life."

He didn't reply.

Water continued to drip into the fountain.

"Let us be certain that we understand each other," she said, each syllable dropping with crystal clarity from her lips. "If we do marry, it is only a formality. I have no intention of moving into the earl's bedroom with you. I will continue to live my life the way I always have. Separate from you."

He nodded gravely. "That is my undertstanding of the arrangement."

"Very well." She lifted her chin and said bravely, "Then— under those conditions—I will marry you."

"There is no need to look like Joan of Arc going to the stake," he said irritably. "You may believe me when I say that I have no designs upon your person. Spoiled English girls do not appeal to me."

She took off his coat and dropped it on the ground. "How long will it take you to find your bloody cattle?"

"Not too long, I hope," he replied, looking at his coat lying in a heap at her feet.

"Good," she said. "Now, if you will excuse me, I have things to do." She turned and began to walk toward the opening in the yews.

He called after her, "Do you want me to tell Taylor that we have decided to wed?"

She paused. "Yes," she said over her shoulder, as she swept out of the garden enclosure, and marched, straight-backed, toward the house.

Chapter Eight

Alexandra stood in front of the fireplace in the Blue Drawing Room, looking up at the portrait of the fair-haired young man that hung beside it. It was almost time to dress for dinner, but for some reason she had felt the need to go in there to look at the portrait of her brother.

Marcus gazed serenely back, nothing in the cerulean blue of his eyes to indicate the desperation that would drive him to take his own life only three years after this portrait was painted.

If Marcus had lived, he would have succeeded their father and none of this nightmare would be happening to her. But the gambling addiction that had tainted so many of her family had got a stranglehold on Marcus. At age twenty-one he had been in so deep that he had despaired of ever digging his way out.

He had shot himself one month before Alexandra turned eighteen. She had been grief-stricken. Her father, on the other hand, had been coldly furious. He had paid his son's stupendous debts, the debts that had triggered Marcus's suicide, and taken his portrait down from its place of honor in the drawing room. Alexandra had replaced the picture shortly after her father himself had died in circumstances that were scarcely honorable.

Looking at her brother's portrait, Alexandra reflected that, in their differing ways, her father and her brother had both been men who thought only of themselves. Her mother had been the same. When she had died six years ago, Alexandra had scarcely missed her. The most time she had ever spent in her mother's company had been the late-afternoon hour that the countess had allotted to her children when she was at Gayles. When her mother was in London for the Season, Alexandra had not seen her at all.

The one person who had always loved her was Geoffrey. When they were growing up, he had spent most of his school holidays at Gayles, and over the years they had become a close-knit partnership. It was he who had stood beside her during the awful months after Marcus's death.

She loved Geoffrey more than anyone else in the world. She did not want to cause him pain.

How was she going to tell him that she had promised to marry Niall MacDonald? It was bad enough that Niall had robbed him of an inheritance he thought was his.

"Alex."

She turned and saw Geoffrey coming toward her. He looked very white.

He said her name again. "Alex. Is it true? Have you agreed to marry MacDonald?"

Her heart ached for him. She looked at him in distress and could not answer.

His full lips tightened. "It can't be true!" Panic sounded in his voice. "Alex, you don't know anything about this man."

She found her voice. "It's not what you think, Geoff. I have agreed to a marriage in name only, so that Papa's money will not go to the Jockey Club. After we are wed, Mr. MacDonald will return to Scotland, while I will remain here to manage Gayles."

He stepped closer to her. It was easy to look at Geoffrey, she thought. His eyes were only an inch above her own.

"You don't seriously believe that?" His voice was harsher than she had ever heard it.

Her brow puckered. "Believe what?"

"Believe his promise that it will be a marriage in name only."

"Yes, I believe it," she returned. She gave him a reassuring smile. "In fact, he has been kind enough to inform me that he is not attracted to spoiled English girls like myself."

"Well, he is lying." Geoffrey's light blue eyes were burningly bright in his pale face. Two patches of hectic color stained the fair skin over his cheekbones. "There does not exist on this earth a man who would not want you, Alex. Marry him, and you'll end up in his bed, whether you want to or not."

Out of the corner of her eye, Alexandra saw a footman pass by the door. She returned her attention to Geoffrey and lowered her voice.

"Darling Geoff," she said soothingly, "I promise you I will end up in no man's bed against my will. And I am even less attracted to that arrogant Scot than he is to me."

Geoffrey lifted his hands to grasp her shoulders. "Marry me, Alex," he said intensely. "The hell with the money. We will have enough to live on."

Slowly, regretfully, she shook her head. "You know how I feel, Geoff. I only promised to marry you before because of Papa's will. I love you, but not that way."

Suddenly she found herself crushed against him and his mouth was covering hers. He had never kissed her like that before, desperately, hungrily.

Everything in Alexandra cried out, *This is wrong*.

But she felt so terribly sorry for Geoffrey that she couldn't bring herself to push him away. So she stood passively in his embrace, not responding but not withdrawing either.

A voice with a faint, foreign lilt said, "Am I interrupting something?"

Alexandra jerked back against Geoffrey's imprisoning arms. After a moment he let her go, and she spun around to face her future husband.

He was looking at Geoffrey and his expression was not friendly. "Perhaps you have not heard," he said. "Lady Alexandra and I are to wed."

He pronounced her name *Aleksandra*. She found herself thinking irrelevantly that they must not have the sound of x in Gaelic.

"I have heard," Geoffrey replied. His voice was shaking.

Behind Niall, his two dogs were staring at Geoffrey in a manner as unfriendly as their master's.

Niall lifted one reckless, arrogant eyebrow. "Is it the English custom to maul newly engaged ladies?"

Blood suffused Geoffrey's pale skin, galvanizing Alexandra into action.

"Stop picking on him," she snapped at her fiancé. "He thought he was going to marry me. Of course he's upset."

"Well he is not going to marry you," Niall replied softly. "I am."

Something inside Alexandra stirred at that tone, that look.

Geoffrey said grittily, "I have been telling Alex that if her marriage, her *nominal* marriage, does not go as she thinks it will, she will find a friend in me."

Niall's dark blue eyes, which were so much more arresting than Geoffrey's paler gaze, narrowed dangerously. One of the dogs growled low in its throat.

Alexandra put a firm hand on Geoffrey's arm and began to propel him toward the door.

"Come along, Geoff. If we don't change immediately, we'll be late for dinner."

"No, Flora," Niall said to his dog in Gaelic.

He watched as Alexandra ushered Geoffrey out the door. He could hear her soothing voice as they began to ascend the stairs, although he could not make out what she was saying.

For the first time he realized that he had clenched his hands into fists.

What is the matter with me? he thought in annoyance, opening his fingers and flexing them. *What do I care who that damned Sassenach hussy chooses to kiss?*

Flora leaned against his legs, and he bent a little to pat and to reassure her. Fergus, who was larger but far less fierce than his sister, watched amiably.

I cannot become possessive about that woman, Niall told himself firmly. *She does not belong to me. This marriage is nothing but a sham.*

Flora gazed up at him adoringly, her tail waving back and forth in speechless joy.

"You are the only girl in my life," he told her, bestowing one final pat on her flank before turning to look at the door through which Alexandra had gone out.

The following morning, when Alexandra entered the family dining room, she found Niall at the breakfast table. He was alone.

She moved to the side table where chafing dishes filled with eggs and bacon and ham were laid out and helped herself to a plate. She returned to the table and took the seat directly across from him.

After his first, "Good morning," he had said nothing else. Alexandra thought once more that his manners were execrable. Determined not to allow herself to sink to his level, she said pleasantly, "What did you think of our horses, my lord?"

He put down his coffee cup and shrugged. "Those skinny, long-legged aristocrats would be useless in the Highlands. They are not built to cover rough ground."

Alexandra had never met anyone who could make her so instantly furious. "I'll have you know that my hunters have been known to get over some very rough ground indeed," she informed him haughtily.

Niall's eyes flicked to his faithful deerhounds. "Do you hunt deer on horseback then?" he asked in surprise.

She swallowed her eggs. "We don't hunt deer, we hunt foxes."

"Oh," he said. "Foxes."

He was clearly unimpressed.

She put down her fork and asked sweetly, "What do you hunt in the Highlands? Wolves?"

His blue gaze was steady. "Stag and deer, mostly," he returned. "There are not many wolves left, and we do not have many foxes either."

"And you hunt on foot?"

"Yes. With deerhounds."

He pushed back his chair and went over to the side table to refill his plate. Silence fell as he worked his way through a pile of eggs and ham.

"What do people who live in the Highlands do to earn

money?" Alexandra asked curiously when he finally put down his fork.

He lifted his coffee cup. "We do what Highlanders have always done. We are a pastoral people, Lady Alexandra. We have always tended our cattle, moving them from pasture to pasture for grazing and driving them to market in the fall. We grow our own vegetables and hunt for our own meat. It is a simple life."

Alexandra thought *primitive* would be a more appropriate description.

"What do you do for entertainment in the evening?" she asked.

"The Gaels are a very musical people," he replied. He leaned his shoulders against the back of his chair and regarded her over the low flower arrangement in the middle of the table. "We love to gather and listen to the songs of our *seanachaidhs*." He frowned, searching his mind for a word. "Bards, I believe you would call them," he said at last.

Despite herself, Alexandra was fascinated. "Are these bards like traveling minstrels?" she asked, trying and failing to picture a troubadour in a kilt.

He shook his head. "The *seanachaidhs* is a very high-ranking member of the chief's household. It is a hereditary position, passed down in one family from generation to generation. The Glen Alpin *seanachaidhs* go back five hundred years."

Alexandra was amazed. "And are these songs played on the bagpipes?"

He gave her a look of scorn. "The bagpipe is an instrument of war. It is not played indoors. Indoors our instrument is the harp."

Alexandra poured herself more coffee. "Besides a bard, what are the other members of a chief's household?"

He shrugged. "Today? Today most of the chiefs live in London and have butlers and footmen." His voice was corrosive with bitterness.

She dropped her gaze to the Wedgwood plate in front of her. "Well, what was it like when the chiefs were still in the Highlands?"

For a moment she thought he wasn't going to answer her, but then he said, "Before Culloden, when the clans were at their full strength, each chief would have a *seanachaidhs,* a standard-bearer, a piper, a sword-bearer, and henchmen, who remained close to the chief to protect him. Besides the henchmen there was the bodyguard, who were the pick of the warriors. They would accompany the chief on all ceremonial occasions."

He narrowed his eyes. "That is not how it is now, however. Now the clans are scattered, pushed out of the glens by their own chiefs, to Canada and to the cities of the Lowlands."

His expression was forbidding, and she dropped her gaze from his face.

"Chiefs like Chisholm," he added grimly.

Privately, Alexandra thought that the Highlanders might be better off in the more modern economies of Canada and the Lowlands, but she was sensible enough not to utter this inflammatory statement out loud.

A little silence fell. Then he said matter-of-factly, "I am to go on a visit to Coke of Norfolk this afternoon. Taylor has told me that he is an expert on the breeding of cattle. I will most likely be away for a few days. When I return, I am thinking we should get married."

Alexandra's heart began to thump more loudly.

"We have to have the banns called first," she said, and was annoyed to hear how breathless her voice sounded.

"Taylor tells me that it is possible to get a special license that makes calling the banns unnecessary." He looked down his arrogant nose at her. "Before I can return to Scotland, there will be legal matters to arrange. The sooner we are wed, the sooner I will be free to go home."

"Well that is certainly 'a consummation devoutly to be wished,'" Alexandra muttered.

He lifted one of those infuriating eyebrows and continued to look down his nose at her.

"It's Shakespeare," she informed him with lethal kindness. "*Hamlet*."

"I have read *Hamlet*," he returned pleasantly. "And the consummation he was referring to was death, I believe. Not marriage."

She stood up so she could look down her nose at him and announced, "You are the rudest man I have ever met."

She had done her hair in a careless knot at the back of her head, with a few ringlets allowed to escape and trickle over her shoulders. Her primrose-colored morning gown outlined her figure with deceptive simplicity. She looked gorgeous, but she was so accustomed to looking gorgeous that she usually never thought about it. She thought about it now, however, as she stared at Niall's indifferent expression.

As she watched, he leaned back in his chair and flicked his eyes up and down over her person. He did not appear impressed with what he saw. Her eyes glittered.

He said easily, "Well, you won't have to put up with me for long. Would you care to set a date, my lady?"

"A week from today?" Alexandra said recklessly.

He nodded. "A week from today it is."

Then, to her amazement, he picked up the newspaper lying next to his plate and began to read it with absorbed attention.

Forcibly restraining an impulse to pull the paper out of his hands and tear it up, she swung on her heel and stalked out of the room.

In the hallway she almost bumped into a footman, who was standing near the door. "I am sorry, my lady," he apologized as he jumped back out of her way.

Alexandra shot a quick look at the liveried servant. With his sandy hair and ordinary face he was certainly not memorable, but Alexandra knew all of her staff, right down to the youngest undergardener.

"Who are you?" she said. "I don't believe I have seen you before."

"My name is Harvey, my lady," the young man replied respectfully. "I was taken on a few days ago by Mr. Stokes."

"I see. Well, welcome to Gayles, Harvey. I believe you will like working for Stokes."

"He seems a very fine man, my lady," the young man replied. He lifted the silver salver he was holding in his hand. "I was bringing the post to the breakfast room, my lady. There is a letter for Lord Hartford."

"You will find His Lordship still at table," Alexandra said. "He is reading the newspaper."

"Thank you, my lady," the footman replied.

As he opened the door to the family dining room, Alexandra decided to go upstairs and change into her riding clothes. She would go down to the stables, where, she thought with a flash of temper, her horses would be glad to see her.

Chapter Nine

An hour later, Alexandra was standing in front of the stall of her beloved old gelding, rubbing his ear while he hung his head in bliss, when she heard Niall's voice coming from the stableyard.

"I am driving to Norfolk, Graham, so I will need a carriage and probably a pair of horses."

"Aye, my lord," she heard the head groom reply. "We can certainly do that for ye. What would ye like to drive?"

Alexandra's hand stilled.

"What have you got?" Niall asked.

Pendleton nudged her hand to remind her to resume rubbing.

Graham said, "There's the trap ye drove yesterday, but that isna' appropriate to take on a visit. We have a phaeton and a curricle, if ye wish to drive yerself. Or ye can take the chaise and the coachman will drive."

"What would be the most appropriate vehicle for a Sassenach earl to drive on such a visit?" Niall asked.

"The curricle, my lord." Graham sounded very positive.

Alexandra had been hoping he would recommend the chaise.

"Very well," Niall replied briskly. "Harness two horses to the curricle."

"You can have the grays, my lord, or the bays."

"Which are easier to drive?"

"The bays, my lord."

"I'll take them then. I don't believe I've ever driven a curricle."

To Alexandra's amazement her head groom, who was usually as protective of his horses as a mother tiger with a threatened cub, said, "Ye'll do just fine, my lord. I'll have one of the grooms go along with ye."

A moment later, Graham was coming into the stable and calling out to a groom, "Timmy, harness the bays to the curricle."

He saw Alexandra standing in front of Pendleton's stall and stopped in surprise. "I beg yer pardon, Lady Alexandra. I did not know ye were there."

"Have you ever seen His Lordship drive, Graham?" she demanded. "He himself just admitted that he has never driven a curricle, and it is a long way to Norfolk."

She kept her voice low as she did not want Niall to hear her.

"His Lordship will do just fine," Graham assured her. "He drove around the estate yesterday without a mishap."

"There is a big difference between driving on country roads and driving on highways," Alexandra snapped. "He is from the Highlands, Graham! They don't drive anything there except cattle. He could kill himself—and the horses, too."

Graham said soothingly, "There is naught to fret about,

my lady. I knew his father when he were a lad. Mr. Edward could do anything with a horse."

"Mr. Edward was taught," Alexandra pointed out. "His Lordship has learned different skills."

The old groom said, "He is a MacDonald, Lady Alexandra. They are a single-minded clan. He will do fine."

He stepped closer to Alexandra to allow the grooms leading the two bay carriage horses to pass.

Alexandra stared into her head groom's weather-beaten face. "I didn't know you were Scottish, Graham."

He was looking critically after the polished dark brown rumps of the two bays. After a moment he returned his gaze to Alexandra, and answered, "My folks moved to Derby from Perthshire before I were born, my lady, but the Grahams are surely Scots. And it was the clan MacDonald that rallied to support the greatest Graham of them all—the Great Montrose." Graham seemed to grow two feet taller as he pronounced the sacred name. "That is something that no Graham will ever forget."

Alexandra couldn't believe she had heard correctly. "Are you saying that you think His Lordship is adequately equipped to drive a curricle to Norfolk because his father was good with horses and his ancestors supported your ancestor in a war?"

Graham gave her a pitying look. "If you will excuse me, Lady Alexandra, I will go and make certain that the bays are being harnessed correctly."

Alexandra rolled her eyes in disbelief as the head groom departed. After giving Pendleton a final pat, she followed Graham out into the stableyard to confront Niall herself.

He was standing at a little distance from the curricle, watching as the bays were put into harness.

She marched up to him, and said, "I think you should have the coachman drive you to Norfolk."

Up went one eyebrow. "Why is that?"

"Because English highways can be highly trafficked and dangerous, and you have never driven on one."

He gave the shrug that was becoming irritatingly familiar to her. "I will manage."

She crossed her arms and narrowed her eyes. "My lord, would you care to tell me just how much driving experience you *have* had? If the Highlands are too rough for horses, I cannot imagine that you do much driving."

He regarded her thoughtfully. "I am thinking that if we are to be married, we should call each other by our given names."

Her eyes widened, and she blinked, thrown off stride by this change of topic.

"My name is Niall," he went on amiably. "It is spelled N-i-a-l-l but pronounced *Nee-il*."

She uncrossed her arms. "Just what does this have to do with your driving the curricle?"

He looked amused. "Nothing, I suppose, *Aleksandra*."

She opened her mouth to correct his pronunciation, then changed her mind. Assuming her sternest expression, she said, "I am quite serious . . . Niall. You could have an accident."

"Do not fret yourself," he returned easily. "I have often driven through the streets of Edinburgh. I shall be fine."

"It is not you I am concerned about," she retorted. "It is the horses."

"They will be fine, too." For the first time since they had met, he smiled at her. It was the kind of smile a man might give if he had just been told that he was cured of a long and agonizing illness. Alexandra actually felt her head spin and her knees buckle.

After a confusing moment, one coherent thought materialized. *The bastard. He is perfectly aware of the power of that smile.*

She inhaled to steady herself. Then, slowly and deliberately, she smiled back. She gave him her very best: a dazzling sparkle of brilliant gray eyes and very white, very straight teeth.

Their eyes locked, and the air between them suddenly sizzled with what Alexandra told herself was antagonism.

The charged moment was broken by Graham as he called to tell Niall that the curricle was ready.

Niall turned to answer the old groom and, without another word, Alexandra started up the path to the house.

The news that there was indeed going to be a marriage between the new earl and Lady Alexandra had sent a wave of relief throughout the household. All of the servants had been worried about what would happen to them with the accession of this Scottish stranger, and their fears were allayed by the news that their own Lady Alexandra would be the new countess. Lady Alexandra could be counted on to take care of them. There wasn't an inhabitant of the big house, or the farms or the villages that depended upon it, who did not firmly believe that.

Geoffrey, on the other hand, was grim-faced and silent. His mother tried to convince him to leave Gayles, but he steadfastly refused.

"I have to be here in case Alex needs me," he said when Mrs. Wilton approached him once again on the afternoon that Niall had left for Norfolk.

"*I* will be here," his mother pointed out. "You may safely rely upon me to make certain that Alexandra is not forced into this marriage against her wishes. There is no reason for you to remain at Gayles, Geoffrey. You are only torturing yourself by doing so."

The face Geoffrey showed his mother was tortured-looking indeed. "I can't leave, Mama. You know how I feel about Alex . . ." He swallowed and fought to regain his composure. "Until she is actually married, I can only hope that she will come to her senses and change her mind." He made a ghastly attempt to smile. "God knows, she has changed her mind often enough in the past."

"She is not going to change her mind this time," Mrs. Wilton said soberly. "Accept that, Geoffrey."

"I can't," he replied wretchedly. When she started to say something else, he held up his hand. "Don't, Mama. No more, please. I am not going to leave Gayles, and that is that." He strode out of the room.

Mrs. Wilton stared after her distraught son, her usually pleasant-looking face set and hard. "Damn, Alexandra," she muttered under her breath. "She has been breaking Geoffrey's heart for years. Why the devil didn't she marry him when that wretched will was first read? Then he would have been spared the anguish of having thought he had her only to see her snatched away at the last minute like this."

She got to her feet and stood there, her small figure rigid, her hands clenched. "If only the dratted girl had been born plain."

Three days before the date set for the wedding, her house-keeper approached Alexandra about beginning to move some of her clothing and belongings into the wardrobe in the count-ess's dressing room.

Alexandra had given some thought to that problem, and if the earl's apartment at Gayles had had separate bedrooms for husband and wife, perhaps she would have considered avoiding household gossip and moving. But the apartment consisted of one bedroom with attached but separate dressing rooms.

There was no way on earth that she was going to share a bedroom with Niall MacDonald.

So she put on her most serene expression, and said, "I will not be moving into the earl's apartment, Mrs. Moreton. His Lordship and I have decided that it will be more pleasant for both of us if I retain my old room."

"Oh," replied a clearly astounded Mrs. Moreton. "I see."

Alexandra watched her housekeeper's back as she walked in the direction of the servants' quarters and stifled a sigh. Within an hour, the news would be the talk of the household. She hated to be the object of discussion among her servants, but there was nothing else to be done. Unfortunately, it was not a situation that could be disguised.

Niall returned to Gayles on Monday afternoon with the special license in his pocket. Alexandra was just behind him on the drive, returning from a visit to one of her tenants who had recently given birth to a new son, and she watched the curricle critically as the bays trotted smoothly up the drive.

The horses appear to be unharmed, she thought with relief. Evidently Niall had managed to get to Norfolk and back without an accident.

Niall brought the curricle to a halt in front of the doorway, handed the reins to the groom who sat beside him, and jumped athletically to the ground. Two footmen came down the stairs to remove his luggage and bring it into the house.

Two rust-colored blurs came racing around the side of the house and flung themselves at the legs of their master. Flora and Fergus had been left at Gayles in the custody of Alan, and they were clearly ecstatic to be reunited with the chief object of their adoration.

Alexandra had stopped her mare a hundred feet down the

drive and, as she watched, the figure of Alan MacDonald followed in the wake of the hounds.

"Ailein!" Niall called, and then he began to speak in Gaelic. His voice sounded full of enthusiasm.

Alan came up to him and, still talking, Niall put his hand upon his foster brother's shoulder and began to walk up the stairs to the house.

Alexandra took her mare down to the stables and dawdled there until it was time to dress for dinner.

All Niall could talk about at dinner was the North Devon cattle he had seen at Holkham.

"Coke swears that they are the best breed he has ever seen for poor land," he informed the other three at the table. "The soil in Norfolk is not good, he said, and the North Devons are thriving."

Both Geoffrey and Mrs. Wilton looked politely bored with this information, but Alexandra was interested. The sooner Niall got his cattle, the sooner he would be going back to Scotland.

"Have you thought about the difference in the climate?" she asked him. "I'm sure the Highlands are colder than Norfolk."

He was expertly carving the lamb roast, and his knife didn't pause as he replied, "The average temperature in Glen Alpin in January is forty-eight degrees and the average temperature in July is fifty-eight. It rains a lot and the grass grows ten months of the year. The climate is actually milder than Norfolk."

This was a surprise to Alexandra, who had thought the Highlands must be freezing cold. "You must get snow?" she said.

"There is snow on the mountaintops, but not in the glens." He was efficiently piling the lamb onto their individual plates.

"In the spring, when the snow begins to melt, it fills the streams and the lochs with cold fresh water."

"Mountains and glens," Alexandra repeated. She gave him a gracious smile. "It sounds very pretty."

He lifted his arrogant nose. "England is pretty," he said. "The Highlands are beautiful."

Alexandra's eyes narrowed.

Mrs. Wilton sniffed.

A footman passed around the plates of lamb that Niall had carved.

In frigid silence, Alexandra helped herself to some green peas and apricot fritters.

Niall gave each of his dogs a piece of lamb.

When the silence became uncomfortable, Alexandra said stiffly, "Will you be able to purchase a herd of these cattle from Mr. Coke?"

Niall was eating as if he hadn't seen food in a month. "He can't sell me as many as I want," he replied after he had swallowed. He took a sip of wine. It was still his first glass, Alexandra noted. He was an abstemious drinker. "I shall have to go down to Devon myself to purchase the rest."

Alexandra cut herself a small piece of lamb and conveyed it to her mouth. *Good news and bad news,* she thought as she chewed. The bad news was that he would have to remain in England longer; the good news was that he would be in Devon, not Derbyshire.

For the first time since they had sat down, Geoffrey spoke to Niall. "Just how do you plan to get these cattle to the Highlands, my lord?"

"We'll have to drive them," Niall replied. He helped himself to more potatoes. "It should be quite an adventure."

He sounded pleased at the thought.

Alexandra stared. "*You* certainly don't plan to take part in a cattle drive?"

He looked genuinely surprised by the question. "The cattle are my investment. Of course I shall go along."

"English earls don't drive cattle," Geoffrey said flatly.

"Scottish chiefs don't normally drive cattle either," Niall retorted, "But these particular cattle are more valuable to me than gold. There are not so many of them in existence that I will be able to purchase such a number two times over. They must get to Glen Alpin safely."

Alexandra decided that she didn't care what he did as long as he did it somewhere other than Gayles. To keep them from falling into dead silence once more, she asked, "Are these large cattle, my lord?"

His face lit with enthusiasm, making him look almost boyish. "They are rather small, actually," he said. "But Coke tells me that their beef is of a particularly high quality . . ."

Alexandra listened as he waxed ever more lyrical about the virtues of the North Devon cattle, asking pertinent questions which kept him going until dessert.

At last dinner was over, and she was able to stand up and announce, "Mrs. Wilton and I will leave you gentlemen to your port."

Niall did not look enthusiasic about being left alone with Geoffrey. He stood up himself. "I do not understand this Sassenach custom of separating the sexes after dinner," he said. "In the Highlands we follow the French way. Let us all go into the drawing room together."

"Good idea," said Geoffrey with more vivacity than he had shown for anything all evening.

Alexandra, who realized that there was absolutely nothing the two men would be able to talk about, acquiesced. "Very well. We'll go upstairs to the Great Chamber."

The four of them, followed by the ubiquitous dogs, proceeded up the stairs to the room that had once been Gayles's state chamber.

As soon as she entered the room, Alexandra went to the piano. The less opportunity the four of them had for conversation, the better, she thought.

"Is there anything in particular you would like to hear, my lord?" she asked courteously.

"I am thinking that you would not know any of my music," he replied.

"Sing something for us, Alex," Geoffrey urged.

Niall gave Geoffrey a long, thoughtful look.

Alexandra struck the first notes of "Greensleeves," which was one of her favorite songs. Her voice was an untrained but true soprano.

"That was very pretty, Alex," Niall said after she had finished. Only he pronounced her name *Alec*.

Geoffrey glared at him.

"I actually do know several Scottish songs," Alexandra said hastily.

Niall was sitting in one of the room's tapestry chairs, with the dogs lying on either side of him. He inclined his head toward her, and said politely, "Will you play one?"

With minimal accompaniment, she sang the achingly sad lament, "The Flowers of the Forest."

After the last note had died away, she turned around on her seat and looked at him. He nodded amiably. "I remember hearing that song when I was at school in Edinburgh. It is about the Battle of Flodden, I believe."

Alexandra had expected a more enthusiastic response. "I am sorry it did not please you," she said stiffly.

He threw her a quick smile. "It was very well done. But all of my own songs are in the Gaelic."

Even though she distrusted his smile, still it disarmed her. Her voice softened. "I am afraid that I don't know any of those."

To her amazement, he said, "Shall I play one for you?"

Everyone stared at him.

"Do you play the piano, Niall?" Alexandra asked incredulously.

As she pronounced his name, she caught him throwing a triumphant look at Geoffrey.

"I play a little," he replied. "We do not have a piano at Eilean Darrach, but I took some lessons on the piano when I was at school in Edinburgh."

Alexandra blinked. "Eilean Darrach?" she said.

He was approaching the piano. "That is the name of our castle," he said matter-of-factly.

Castle? Alexandra thought in amazement. *Is there actually a castle in Glen Alpin?*

She slid off the piano bench and let him take her place. She did not sit down herself, but remained standing next to the instrument.

He placed his fingers carefully on the keys. They were long, well-shaped fingers, she noticed, with short, neatly cut nails. His face looked very serious.

He struck a few notes and then he began to sing:

> *O chi, chi mi na mor-bheana*
> *O chi, chi ma na corr-bheana*
> *O chi, chi mi n coreachon*
> *Chi mi no sgoron fo cheo*

His voice was a deep, clear baritone. Wonder sounded in his voice as he continued to sing, and reverence and joy. Listening to him, Alexandra almost forgot to breathe.

When he finished, he looked up at her. "It sounds best when it is played upon the harp."

"What do the words mean?" Alexandra asked.

"It is just a song about the beauty of the Highlands," he said. "It was made by my great-grandfather's harper. In English it would go something like this:

> O I will see, see the great mountains
> O I will see, see the great mountains
> O I will see, see the corries
> I will see the misty peaks . . .

And then it goes on to name all the beauties of the glen."

"I believe you once told me that Gaelic was a very musical language," Alexandra said. "I see now that it is."

He nodded, stood up, and looked down at her. "If you will excuse me, I am thinking that I should take the dogs for a walk."

Alexandra was surprised to feel a twinge of disappointment that he was going away. Annoyed at herself, she frowned.

"Certainly," she said.

He looked directly into her eyes. "Good night," he said. "Alec."

She looked back, and replied coolly, "Good night."

He looked amused.

"Good night, ma'am," he said politely to Mrs. Wilton.

Geoffrey got a nod.

Then he was gone, his dogs at his heels.

Chapter Ten

Alexandra spent Tuesday morning in her office, doing the household and stable accounts. She was toting up the farrier's bill when her butler knocked to inform her that Mr. Taylor and Lord Chisholm had requested to see His Lordship.

Alexandra immediately recognized the name of the treasurer of the Jockey Club. She also remembered Niall's reaction to that name. "Did they ask to see me as well?" she asked.

"No, my lady, but I thought you would wish to know of their arrival. His Lordship is out somewhere on the estate with Mr. Mason."

"Serve Mr. Taylor and Lord Chisholm some madeira, Stokes, and tell them I shall be with them directly."

"Yes, my lady."

"They are in the Blue Drawing Room?"

"Yes, my lady."

"Very well."

Alexandra waited until her butler had departed before she

made a dash for the back stairs. She would just take the time to wash her hands and then, with luck, she could get rid of Chisholm before Niall returned.

She was back downstairs in five minutes. During that time she had been cudgeling her brain to come up with a possible motive for Chisholm's visit, but no reasonable explanation had occurred to her. She stepped into the drawing room with the conviction that whatever the reason was, it was probably not going to be beneficial to her or Niall.

Both men, wineglasses in hand, were standing in the pool of sunshine that was coming in through the French doors. Taylor saw her first and said her name.

"Good morning, Mr. Taylor," she replied.

The solicitor did not look happy. "May I present Lord Chisholm, my lady," he said. "We have come to see His Lordship on a matter of business."

He laid very faint stress on the words *His Lordship*.

"How do you do, Lord Chisholm," Alexandra said. She crossed the room into the sunlight and held out her hand.

Chisholm looked into her face and his eyes widened. As Alexandra shook his hand she took a quick inventory of this man whom Niall had spoken of with such loathing.

The Jockey Club treasurer was a nice-looking man of about forty years of age. He had olive-colored skin, dark eyes, and black hair that was just beginning to turn gray. He was tall, although not as tall as Niall.

"How do you do, Lady Alexandra," Chisholm said. He looked faintly dazzled.

Alexandra removed her hand from his and returned her eyes to Mr. Taylor. "His Lordship is not at home," she said. "Perhaps I can be of help to you."

"I think it would be best if we spoke to His Lordship first, my lady," the attorney replied firmly.

Facing the men as she was, the sun was in her face, and she narrowed her eyes a little against it.

"If this is in regard to my father's will, then I believe I am entitled to know about it as well," she replied with equal firmness. "I assume that is why you are here, Mr. Taylor? Lord Chisholm is the treasurer of the Jockey Club, I believe."

"I am, Lady Alexandra," Chisholm replied.

She noticed that his English had no Gaelic lilt to it.

"Shall we sit down?" Alexandra said pleasantly. She had every intention of finding out what was going on before Niall returned.

There was a grouping of delicate French chairs close by, and Alexandra moved to one of them and seated herself, effectively forcing the two men to join her.

When all three were seated on the fragile-looking gilt chairs, Alexandra gave Chisholm an inquiring lift of her smoky eyebrows. "Well, my lord?"

Chisholm became all business. "You know the terms of your father's will, Lady Alexandra," he said. " In order for you to inherit your father's money, you must marry the seventh earl, who is Niall MacDonald. If you do not marry him, then the money is to go to the Jockey Club."

Alexandra placed her hands on the gilt arms of her chair. "That is correct, my lord," she replied calmly. "And, as I am sure Mr. Taylor has told you, Niall MacDonald and I have plans to wed. The marriage is to take place tomorrow, in fact."

Chisholm was looking at her with speculation in his eyes. He said, "Are you aware, my lady, that in order for a marriage to be legal, it must be consummated?"

Alexandra's eyes flew to Taylor, who was looking horribly embarrassed. "What does Lord Chisholm mean?" she demanded.

The attorney shifted on his seat. His voice was gruffer than usual when he replied. "It means, my lady, that a marriage in name only, a marriage that does not include physical consummation, may not legally be a marriage. If this is the arrangement you have made with Niall MacDonald, then Lord Chisholm has informed me that the Jockey Club is prepared to challenge you in court as not fulfilling the conditions of your father's will."

Alexandra's fingers tightened their grip on the arms of her chair. She stared at Lord Chisholm. "Why would you think we have made such an arrangement?" she demanded.

"I have it on very good authority that you and MacDonald plan to occupy separate bedrooms," Chisholm returned.

How on earth did he find that out? Alexandra thought in astonishment.

"Husbands and wives frequently occupy separate bedrooms," she flashed back.

"My information is that you are not planning to move into the earl's apartment at all," Chisholm said evenly. "You are planning to remain in your old room. In fact, nothing in your relationship with MacDonald is going to change except for a piece of paper that says you are married. Well, that was not the intent of your father's will, my lady. Your father most certainly intended that the seventh earl should have heirs of your body, which he will not have if the marriage remains unconsummated. And I repeat, if that is the situation, then I suggest you call off the marriage right now, because I am not going to allow you to get away with such a fraud."

Alexandra glared at him, her eyes glittering with fury. "I have every intention of moving into the earl's apartment," she said. "I cannot imagine how you ever heard otherwise."

Chisholm's jaw jutted forward. "It is common gossip among your servants that you are keeping your old bedroom, Lady Alexandra."

Alexandra jumped to her feet. She was so angry that her heart was thudding. "You are mistaken, Lord Chisholm. But that is what happens when you listen to servants' gossip. I can assure you that Niall and I have every intention of making a real marriage . . ."

A step sounded on the uncovered floor just inside the drawing room, and she spun around to see her fiancé striding into the room. He was looking at Chisholm, and the expression on his face should have turned the other Scot into stone.

"Chisholm," he said. Loathing dripped from every syllable.

"*An Siosalach* to you," the other returned with some hauteur.

"You are no chief," Niall replied with bitter scorn. "Chiefs are the guardians of their people. You are their destroyer."

He came to stand next to Alexandra.

Chisholm and Taylor had both risen and now Chisholm's dark face flushed with anger. "You are as ill-mannered and arrogant as your grandfather."

"What are you doing here in my house?" Niall demanded.

Alexandra put a warning hand on his arm. "He has come because he heard a servants' rumor that our marriage is not going to be a real one," she said. "He threatened to take us to court for fraud, but I have assured him that the rumor was false."

He looked at her hand on his arm. Then he looked into her face. Slowly he nodded that he understood.

Alexandra dropped her hand.

Chisholm said, "It is my duty to represent the interests of the Jockey Club in this matter."

"You don't give a damn about the Jockey Club," Niall replied. "What you want is to keep me from getting my hands on enough money to bring cattle into Glen Alpin."

Chisholm removed an imaginary speck from his immaculate blue coat sleeve. "That is ridiculous. Why should I want to do that?"

The far less elegantly dressed Niall narrowed his eyes dangerously. "Because you want to buy Glen Alpin from my grandfather so you can run more sheep," he returned.

Chisholm abandoned his coat sleeve. "I may have offered to buy Glen Alpin once or twice, but I can assure you, MacDonald, there is plenty of other Highland property I can buy if I want to run more sheep. There is nothing so extraordinary about Glen Alpin."

"You have offered to buy it more than once or twice," Niall said grimly.

"It is on the boundaries of Strathglass," came the reply. "It would be a convenient enlargement of my own property."

Alexandra said defiantly, "My father was a lifelong member of the Jockey Club, Lord Chisholm, and I cannot believe that the other men in the club would stoop to dragging his daughter into court over the intimacies of her marriage."

"It is the lack of intimacy that the Jockey Club is concerned with, Lady Alexandra," Chisholm replied tartly.

"Just how do you plan to investigate this matter, Chisholm?" Niall asked with deadly sarcasm. "Do you plan to have a member of the Jockey Club stationed in our bedroom as a witness?"

Alexandra could feel herself turning pale.

"They can't do that," she said. She looked at Taylor and demanded, "Can they?"

The young attorney looked almost as horrified as she did. "No, Lady Alexandra, they most certainly cannot. But I'm afraid that the Jockey Club can bring suit if all of the external evidence suggests that the marriage between you and His Lordship is a fraud perpetrated to rob the Jockey Club of its rightful legacy."

"This is outrageous," Alexandra said angrily. "The will only stated that we had to marry, and we are going to do that."

"The court might consider the issue of heirs a valid one," Taylor replied uncomfortably.

The sound of dog nails on bare floor sounded behind them, and then the two deerhounds were beside Niall, their mouths open in happy grins.

A voice from the doorway said, in accents of unmistakable loathing, *"An Siosalach."*

"Yes, Alan," Niall said without turning around. "The vulture has come calling."

Chisholm was staring over Niall's shoulder at Alan. "I see you have brought your foster brother with you."

"Get out of my house," Niall said. "I do not want your stench in any of my rooms."

Alexandra stiffened. This was the second time Niall had referred to Gayles as his.

"I will be watching you, MacDonald," Chisholm said. "If I think I have enough evidence to prove a fraud, I will not hesitate to go to court—the sensibilities of the lady notwithstanding."

"Get out, you spying toad," Alexandra said furiously.

Without another word, Lord Chisholm, *An Siosalach*, Chief of Strathglass, strode to the door. Alan moved away from him as if afraid of contamination.

Tense silence reigned in the Blue Drawing Room. Then Alexandra said to Taylor, "Can he really take us to court?"

The solicitor nodded miserably. "I am not saying that he would win the suit, Lady Alexandra, but you do not wish to find yourself testifying in court as to the state of your marriage."

Alexandra shuddered at the thought.

"What a nasty man," she said. "It is not as if the Jockey Club is in desperate need of money."

"It is Glen Alpin," Niall said grimly. "For the last six months Chisholm has been trying to buy Glen Alpin from my grandfather. He knows that if I introduce a profitable cattle-raising operation into the glen, then he will have no chance at all of buying the land. That is the reason he does not want me to have the money."

"How lovely that such a man should turn out to be the treasurer of the Jockey Club," Alexandra remarked.

Niall said to the attorney, "If Lady Alexandra and I share the earl's apartment, will that be enough evidence that our marriage is a valid one?"

"I should think so, my lord," Taylor replied. "I cannot tell you how distasteful this whole matter is to me, but apparently Lord Chisholm has a spy among your household."

Alexandra thought of the new footman whom she had run into on several occasions. She opened her mouth to say something, then changed her mind.

She felt Niall's eyes on her and looked up at him. He said, "You and I must talk."

She nodded.

"Is the wedding still set for tomorrow?" the solicitor asked.

"I picked up the license on my way home from Holkham," Niall replied. Once again he turned to her. "Have you spoken to the rector?"

"Yes. He invited us to be married in the church, and I said I would speak to you about it. Under the circumstances, it might be a good idea. It would make our marriage look more . . . serious."

Niall shrugged. "I don't care where we do it, as long as we get it done."

My prince, Alexandra thought with a mixture of sarcasm and despair.

"Can we do it in the afternoon?" he asked next. "I have a few things I want to take care of in the morning."

"I don't care when we do it as long as we get it done," she returned expressionlessly.

He shot her a quick, assessing look, then said to the attorney, "Be at the church at two."

Taylor nodded and walked to the door.

Niall said to his foster brother, "Take the dogs outside, will you, Alan?"

Alan whistled, and the hounds rose and trotted to join him.

In a moment, Niall and Alexandra were alone.

Niall went to one of the windows and opened it.

"Can't you be in a room without opening a window?" she asked testily.

"I don't like the feeling that I am breathing stale air," he replied. He gestured to the French chairs. "Sit down and let us discuss this situation."

They sat. He looked ridiculous in the delicate gilt chair, she thought inconsequently. He was just too big for it.

"How did Chisholm learn about our keeping separate apartments?" he asked.

"I think Mr. Taylor is right and that he has inserted a spy

into the household," she returned, and she proceeded to tell him about the new footman she seemed to keep tripping over.

"Well the first thing we do is fire the damn spy," Niall said when she had finished.

"I don't know." She tapped her fingers on the chair arm. "Perhaps we could use him. You know . . . stage a few charming little scenes that would convince him we are truly married. Then he would be reporting to Chisholm in our favor."

"That is an excellent idea, Alec," he said, and she was annoyed at the rush of pleasure she felt at his approving words.

He was going on, "Also, it appears that we are going to have to share the earl's apartment."

She had been thinking about that. "You can sleep in your dressing room," she said. "There is a daybed in there."

"That is where Alan sleeps," he objected.

"Well, Alan will have to sleep on the floor," she snapped.

"The servants will know I am not sleeping with you."

"How will they know that?"

His look was ironic. "They will know by the condition of your bed," he replied.

Color burned in her cheeks. "I will thrash around and dishevel it."

His look of irony deepened, but he did not reply.

"It is not a ruse we will have to sustain for long," she said a little defensively. "You are going into Devon shortly, are you not?"

Someone came in the door, and said, "I did not realize you were here, my lord. I just came to remove the wineglasses."

Alex turned her head sharply and saw the placid, ordinary face of the new footman.

"That is quite all right, Harvey," she said pleasantly. "His Lordship and I were just going for a stroll in the garden." She stood up and went to lay a hand on a startled Niall's shoulder. "I don't believe I have ever shown you our rose garden, have I Niall?"

He understood instantly what had happened.

"I don't believe you have, " he replied, and bent his head to lightly touch his lips to her fingers, which were still lying on his shoulder.

To her shock, she felt the touch of his mouth all the way down in her stomach.

He stood and smiled down at her. Even though she knew he was pretending, her heart began to hurry. "Let us go, Alec," he said. His voice caressed her with its lyricism.

This is terrible, Alexandra thought in dismay as she allowed him to escort her out through the French doors. She had never reacted like this to any other man.

Why couldn't I have felt like this about Ashcroft or Barrington, or any of the other men who wanted to marry me? she thought with dismay. *Why does it have to be this man I don't even like?*

They were walking across the grass when he said in his normal tone, "I assume that is the spying footman?"

"I think so," she replied. "He keeps appearing at particularly opportune moments."

He nodded, stopped walking, and turned to look down at her. His mouth was set in a grim line, but there was a look in his eyes that caused Alexandra's heartbeat to accelerate.

He said, "All of this would be very much easier if you weren't so bloody beautiful." And he turned and strode away, leaving her staring after him, her eyes wide with surprise.

Chapter Eleven

What to wear to her wedding? Alexandra contemplated this question as she stood in front of the large oak wardrobe that contained her clothes. Her eyes fell on one of the black mourning dresses she had worn for six months after her father died.

Perhaps I should wear that, she thought with morbid humor. *It certainly would reflect my feelings.*

Unfortunately, she had little doubt that the dreadful Chisholm would have one of his spies in position to report back to him all the minute details of the ceremony. Such an outfit would scarcely conduce to the idea that she was taking the marriage seriously.

Her maid said, "It is a pity that you did not have a wedding dress made, my lady."

Meg had been after Alexandra ever since her engagement to Geoffrey to think about a wedding dress. Alexandra had not been receptive to the idea.

"I'm sure we can find something perfectly adequate in my present wardrobe," she said now.

"All of your dresses are from last Season," the fashion-conscious Meg complained.

"I rather suspect that His Lordship will not notice if my dress is a trifle out-of-date," Alexandra responded drily. She reached into the wardrobe and put her hand upon a frock. "What about this Pomona green muslin?"

Meg shook her head decisively. "Green is unlucky for brides."

Alexandra, who thought she was going to need all the luck she could get, discarded the Pomona green.

"I saw the prettiest dress in the *Lady's Magazine* the other day," Meg said wistfully. "It was a white French muslin with a pleated ruff and tiny pleats above the hemline. Pleats are quite the newest style."

"Well I don't have anything with pleats," Alexandra said. Her eyes lit on a simple long-sleeved day dress of pale blue muslin. It had no frills other than the satin ribbon banding at the bottom of the skirt. "I'll wear this," she said, taking it out of the wardrobe.

Meg was dismayed. "But it is so plain, my lady."

"I'll wear it with the silk-embroidered shawl," she said. "It will look just fine."

Meg sighed. She was a small, plump pigeon of a girl who had lived all of Alexandra's London Seasons vicariously through her employer. "Yes, my lady," she said resignedly. "Will you wear the matching straw bonnet as well?"

Alexandra had an impish impulse. "His Lordship comes from a very traditional society," she said. "I am sure all Highland brides wear their hair down."

Meg looked scandalized. "You cannot mean to let your hair hang loose?"

Alexandra was not prepared to go as far as that. "No, but

I think I shall wear it in a braid." Further inspiration struck. "Entwined with flowers."

Meg's face lit with sudden enthusiasm. "You could carry a basket of matching flowers, my lady. That would be a pretty touch."

Privately, Alexandra thought it would make her look as if she were going out to bring in the May. But, "Why not?" she replied airily.

"You might even start a new fashion for brides," said her enthusiastic maid.

"I hope not," Alexandra replied with sudden soberness. "I devoutly hope not, Meg."

Her maid looked at her, indecision in her eyes.

"What is it?" Alexandra said.

Meg's eyes dropped. "Nothing, my lady. It is just . . ." Her round china-blue eyes lifted again. "Everyone on the staff wishes you well, my lady."

They probably all envisoned her as a sacrificial lamb being fed to the Scottish lion, Alexandra thought. She felt a twinge of irritation. She did not care at all for the role of sacrificial lamb.

She lifted her chin, and said crisply, "Thank you, Meg. Now you had better help me get dressed."

Up until the very morning of the wedding, Geoffrey had fully expected Alexandra to back out of it. He simply could not imagine that she, who previously had refused so many suitable men who adored her, would actually marry that eagle-faced stranger from the Highlands. It was not until she rose from the luncheon table and went upstairs to change into her wedding dress that he fully realized it was going to happen.

"I can't let her do this," he said to his mother.

Mrs. Wilton put down her teacup. "There is nothing you can do to stop her."

Geoffrey stood up.

"Sit down," his mother said sharply. "Alexandra does not care about you, Geoffrey. Can't you see that? All she cares about is her precious Gayles. She would have married you when it seemed you owned Gayles, and now she will marry this new earl. Nothing you say to her will change her mind. She wants Gayles."

Geoffrey's face was white and pinched-looking. "Perhaps that is true, Mother, but Alex thinks that this marriage is merely a nominal ceremony necessary to free up her father's money. She doesn't understand what she is getting into."

"It has always seemed to me that Alexandra understands her own self-interest better than most people," Mrs. Wilton replied bitterly. "She knows exactly what she is doing, Geoffrey. Why can't you see that? She threw you away when you were no longer of use to her, and she will do the same with Niall MacDonald. No matter the circumstances, you can be certain that Alexandra will always come out ahead."

"That's not true!" Geoffrey stared angrily across the luncheon-strewn table at his mother. "I thought you liked Alex, Mother!"

"She has been hurting you for years, Geoffrey," Mrs. Wilton replied. "Under those circumstances, it is a little difficult for me to like her."

Geoffrey threw down the napkin he was holding. "It isn't Alex's fault that she doesn't love me," he said. "Or . . . she does love me, but not the way I love her."

"If that is so, then give her up!" Mrs. Wilton leaned across the table toward her son. "She is being married today and no longer needs me as a chaperone. There is nothing to stop us from packing our bags right this minute and going home."

"I am not leaving Alex alone with that man," Geoffrey's voice cracked with emotion. "She thinks she is safe from him, but she's not. I've seen the way he looks at her when he thinks no one is watching him. I know what he is feeling. I am going to talk to her, Mother. She simply cannot marry Niall MacDonald."

Geoffrey turned sharply and strode out of the room.

Mrs. Wilton looked after her son, a hard, set look upon her usually pretty, doll-like features.

Alexandra answered Geoffrey's knock herself. She stared at him in obvious alarm, and his heart turned over the way it always did when he saw her.

"Geoff!" she said. "What has happened? Is someone hurt?"

"I have to talk to you," he said tensely.

She bit her lip in indecision, then stepped outside into the gallery. Her maid had obviously been brushing her hair because it floated loose around her shoulders, a silky mass of palest gold. He had to forcibly restrain himself from reaching out to touch it.

"You cannot do this, Alex," he said. "You simply cannot marry that man."

She sighed. "Geoff, this is hard enough for me as it is. Please don't make it any worse."

He felt as if he were being ripped apart.

He said harshly, "If you think that MacDonald will leave you alone, you are wrong. Keeping your old bedroom is not going to save you."

She flicked him a look. Then she said quietly, "Geoff, be reasonable. You really do not think that Niall MacDonald would rape me, do you?"

He stared back at her in anguish. It had been bad enough before her father's death, he thought. But to have been her affianced husband for months, and then to lose her like this . . .

He answered in a suffocated voice, "If he should try to seduce you, think of this. MacDonald is your first cousin. If you think it would be wrong to sleep with me, it would be even more wrong to sleep with him."

Color stained the lines of her beautiful cheekbones. Her eyes darkened to the color of storm clouds. "Believe me, Geoff, I have no intention of ever sleeping with Niall MacDonald. You can get that thought right out of your mind."

She meant it. He knew Alex too well for her to lie to him successfully. She was not attracted to Niall MacDonald.

He felt a slight measure of relief.

Somehow he managed to smile. "I'm sorry. It's just . . . well, you know how I feel about you . . ."

She looked straight into his eyes, and hers were deadly serious. "Geoff, you are going to have to stop feeling that way about me and start looking for someone else."

He didn't reply.

"Are you listening to me?" she demanded.

"Yes."

"I mean it, Geoff. I don't want to talk about this with you anymore. What I choose to do with my life is not your concern. Do I make myself clear?"

"It isn't as easy as that, Alex."

She shook her head. "What is it that Hamlet says? 'I must be cruel only to be kind'? Well that is how it is, Geoff. For your own good you have got to drop this obsession you have with me and find another girl. If I have to forbid you to see me, I will. I don't want to do that, but I will."

At the thought that she might really sever any relationship between them, he panicked. "All right, Alex," he said hastily. "All right. I'll try. I really will."

She took a few steps away from the door, toward the large expanse of windows that ended the Long Gallery. Without looking at him, she said, "I am going to settle some money on you, enough so that you can support a wife and family comfortably."

He went rigid. "I don't want your money!"

She turned to face him. The window behind her lit her hair like a golden nimbus. "For three years you have thought it was going to be your money," she said. "My father made you an allowance because you were his heir. You gave up your idea of being a clergyman because you thought you were going to be an earl. You are owed some of this money, Geoff, and I am going to make certain that you get it."

In a flat voice he said, "So I can marry someone else."

"Eventually, yes."

Bleakly, Geoffrey realized that she wanted him to have the money so she would feel less guilty about him. In a low voice he said, "All right."

She came forward to kiss him on the cheek. A cousinly kiss.

"Don't worry about me," she said. "As soon as Niall has the money in his hand he is going to buy a herd of cattle and go home to Scotland. I shall probably never see him again."

He nodded. He was simply incapable of speech.

She smiled. "Don't worry about me," she repeated, turned away, and went back into her bedroom.

Niall and Alan got to the church first. Niall was dressed in one of his two blue morning coats, and Alan wore his brown wool jacket. James Taylor, who was to witness the ceremony personally so he could report back to Lord Chisholm, was standing outside the front door when the two Scots arrived.

The three men greeted each other in subdued voices and

entered the small stone church. The rector was lighting the altar candles, and they moved up the aisle to join him at the communion rail.

Niall looked around the church, which looked and smelled very much like the church he sometimes attended in Fort Augustus, and for the first time in his life he found himself wondering about the marriage of his parents. He had been born thirteen months after they wed, so the marriage had not been for the obvious reason.

In all these years, he had never asked his grandfather anything about his father. Thinking about it now, he realized that, without directly saying anything, his grandfather had managed somehow to make it clear that such an inquiry would not be welcome.

Did they love each other, I wonder?

As soon as the thought materialized in his mind, he scowled. What kind of an idiot was he, to be thinking about such a thing? His own marriage was a business arrangment, and that was how he wanted it to stay. The last thing in the world he wanted was to find himself in thrall to the charms of a spoiled Sassenach beauty.

There was a sound behind him, and he turned to see Alexandra coming in the door. As she walked slowly up the aisle to join him in front of the altar, something twisted in his gut.

Dhé, he thought angrily. *Why could she not have been homely?*

She wore a high-waisted pale blue dress that outlined her breasts and then fell in straight soft folds to her ankles. It was a style that did not flatter many women, but on Alexandra's long-legged slimness, it looked wonderful. Her glorious hair reached halfway down her back in a thick, flower-entwined braid. Her beautiful face, with its sweetly curving cheekbones, was grave. For a brief moment her gray eyes met his.

Niall's own face was set into its harshest expression. He knew what he was feeling for this girl who was about to become his wife, and he didn't like it at all.

The rector said, "Good afternoon, my dear. You are looking very lovely."

"Thank you, Reverend Thackery," she replied.

Niall tore his eyes away from her and turned to the rector. "Let's get on with it, then," he said tersely.

She came to stand at his side. The scent of the flowers in her hair floated to his nostrils. A muscle jumped in his jaw.

The rector began to read from *The Book of Common Prayer* which was followed by both the Scottish Episcopal Church and the Church of England.

"Dearly beloved, we are gathered together here in the sight of God, and in the face of this congregation, to join together this Man and this Woman in holy Matrimony . . ."

There was absolute silence in the empty church as the rector continued with the words of the traditional wedding ceremony. Alan was next to Niall and on Alan's other side stood Taylor. A woman whom Niall did not know was standing beside Alexandra.

The rector turned to Niall. "Wilt thou, Niall Ian Alistair, have this Woman to thy wedded wife, to live together after God's ordinance in the holy estate of Matrimony? Wilt thou love her, comfort her, honor, and keep her in sickness and in health; and, forsaking all others, keep thee only unto her, so long as ye both shall live?"

"I will," Niall said in a voice that was almost brusque.

The rector turned to the girl at his side. "Wilt thou, Alexandra Maria Elizabeth, have this Man to thy wedded husband to live together after God's ordinance in the holy estate of Matrimony? Wilt thou obey him, and serve him, love, honor, and keep him in sickness and in health; and, forsaking all others, keep thee only unto him, so long as ye both shall live?"

Silence reverberated throughout the church.

Niall clenched his teeth.

Finally, when it seemed the weight of the silence would become unbearable, Alexandra said in a voice that was no more than a whisper, "I will."

Niall was in a vile mood for the rest of the day. It had not been a good idea to hold the marriage in the church, he thought. It had made it seem much too solemn, much too . . . real. It made him distinctly uncomfortable to think that he had promised, in the presence of God, to forsake all others and keep only unto Alexandra for as long as they both should live.

He sat at the head of the dinner table, in the black long-tailed dinner coat he had hastily acquired in Glasgow on James Taylor's urgent suggestion. He could go out to dinner anywhere in Scotland in his scarlet kilt and black-velvet jacket, but apparently that would have caused a sensation at Gayles, and Niall had not wished to cause a sensation. He had wanted to collect his inheritance, buy some cattle, and return home as soon as possible.

He most certainly had not wanted to get married.

He looked at his wife, who was sitting at the opposite end of the table, and scowled. Her low-cut blue-silk dinner gown showed far too much breast for any man's comfort. She had got rid of the flowery braid and swept her hair up on the top of her head, a style which revealed the satiny skin of her long, elegant neck.

There was far too much of Alexandra on display, Niall decided in annoyance. Was she trying to seduce him?

"Is there anything wrong, my lord?"

Niall turned to the woman who was seated next to him. She was a Mrs. Richardson, a widow who lived not far from Gayles and was apparently a friend of Alexandra's. He noticed that Mrs. Richardson also wore a low-cut gown and upswept hair. She, however, did not give the appearance of being half-naked.

"No, nothing is wrong, ma'am," he said, making an effort to affix a pleasant expression to his face.

She looked dubious.

Dhé, he thought. *If I go about with this hangman's look, I will only be giving ammunition to Chisholm.*

"I am sorry if I looked surly," he said to Mrs. Richardson. "I was distracted." Deliberately, he smiled at her.

She glowed in response. "Not at all, my lord."

He asked her an innocuous question about the neighborhood and pretended to listen attentively as she responded.

At the other end of the table, Alexandra was pretending to eat while she watched her husband from beneath her lashes. She saw him smile at Nora Richardson and saw Nora's response.

A shiver ran down her back.

This was the man she had just promised to live with "after God's ordinance in the holy estate of Matrimony."

She had almost not done it. The solemn words, the rector, the church where she had been baptized and confirmed, all of this had combined to make her realize the magnitude of what she was doing. She had actually opened her mouth to say *I cannot do this.* What had come out, however, was *I will.*

She glanced surreptitiously around the dinner table.

Geoffrey looked like death. Mrs. Wilton looked stern. James Taylor looked uncomfortable. The only two people who looked as if they were enjoying themselves were Niall and Nora.

Suddenly Niall glanced her way, and their eyes met across the length of the table.

Alexandra's heart gave a very unwelcome thud, and she hastily looked back down at the uneaten food on her plate. That glance had made it quite clear that Niall was not having a good time.

She had a feeling that he was experiencing the same unease she was. A man who always prayed before his meals was not a man who took promises made in front of God lightly.

The meal dragged on. Finally, Alexandra was able to stand and shepherd the women out of the room. This time Niall remained behind to drink port with James Taylor and Geoffrey.

Nora Richardson was going home, and Alexandra accompanied her to the door and saw her into her chaise. Then she returned to the Great Chamber, where Mrs. Wilton pleaded a headache and went to her room.

It did not take Alexandra very long to decide that she would retire as well. She would have given a great deal if she could have gone to her old room, but, because of the wretched Chisholm, that plan had changed. She went out into the corridor, turned right, went past the stairs, opened the first door she came to, and stepped into the bedroom that had belonged first to John Wilton and then, over the course of two centuries, to all of his eldest male descendants.

The bedroom walls were covered with massive Flemish tapestries. The great carved four-poster had been made in 1629 for John Wilton's eldest son. The embroidery on the eighteenth-century bed hangings had been done with real pearls.

It was a magnificent room, and her mother had enhanced its period splendor by adding some splendid pieces of seventeenth-century furniture. At the moment, however, Alexandra regarded its grandeur with dismay and thought longingly of her own cozy room upstairs.

She turned and went though the door that led into the countess's dressing room.

Her mother had decorated it in a more comfortable fashion. The walls were hung with straw-colored silk and the chaise longue and padded chairs were a cheerful apple green. The windows, which looked out on the west front of the house as well as over the side lawn, were hung with the same yellow silk that covered the walls.

The room was empty. She could ring for Meg, but it was ridiculously early to think of going to bed.

I wish I had a book, Alexandra thought.

She let out a long, melancholy sigh and went to stand in front of the window, which looked out over the side lawn. The sky was still light, and the bronze fountain glittered in the distance. Summer was coming, she thought. The days were getting longer and longer.

Her life stretched before her with bleak monotony.

Is this what it is going to be like? she thought. *Am I always going to be alone?*

Someday her love would come. She had always believed that. She had refused numerous splendid suitors and jilted a perfectly lovely man, all because they had not been the one she was waiting for. Now there was this man, this man she had married. Something in her responded to him as she had never responded to the other men in her life. But he was arrogant and narrow-minded and chauvinistic, and she didn't like him.

The thought that he would be sleeping right next door made her exceedingly uncomfortable.

She had been surprised when Geoffrey had reminded her that Niall was her cousin. She didn't think of him that way. She would never think of him that way. She had grown up with Geoff. This man was a stranger.

And she was going to keep it that way.

Chapter Twelve

Niall's wedding night was as unpleasant as his wife's. The bed in the earl's dressing room was narrower and less comfortable than the big four-poster where he had passed his last few nights, but it was not the bed that kept him awake. He could have slept as peacefully as Alan was sleeping on the floor if his mind had been at rest.

He couldn't get the picture of Alexandra in her low-cut gown out of his mind. The thought that he was married to her and that she was sleeping right next door did not help.

She was a Sassenach, and he didn't like her, but she was also very beautiful and, lying sleepless in his narrow bed, he admitted that he wanted her. This was not a situation that made him happy with himself.

He had opened the window before retiring, and moonlight was pouring into the dressing room. On an impulse, he got out of bed and went to the wardrobe to find some clothes.

"What is it?" Alan asked, sitting up. Like most Highlanders, he had the gift of coming instantly awake.

"I cannot sleep, Ailein," Niall replied. "I am going to go for a walk."

"Do you want me to come with you?"

"Na. Go back to sleep. I am thinking I will be better off alone."

Alan lay back down on the floor and Niall reached into the wardrobe for the only kilt that he had brought with him. He put it on, along with an old white shirt that tied at the neck. He left the tie undone, pushed his bare feet into a pair of soft shoes, and went out the door.

He went downstairs soundlessly, unlocked the French doors in the Blue Drawing Room, and let himself out of the house.

The evening air was damp and chilly, and Niall inhaled it deeply into his lungs. He looked up at the bright three-quarter moon, which lighted the hedges and lawn in front of him. It was a lovely sight and totally different from the view of loch and mountains that he had grown up with.

He started briskly along the path that led across the lawn to the great bronze fountain about a quarter of a mile away.

Dhé, but it felt good to be back in his own clothes. The kilt hung loosely around his legs, allowing him to stride out strongly. The soft, unstarched collar of his shirt was a great improvement over the stiff high collar and cravat he had been wearing since he came to England. The cool night air felt wonderful on his bare legs and neck.

He stopped in front of the great fountain, which featured an array of sea gods blowing water through trumpets at a figure of Atlas carrying the world on his shoulders. The spray of water shone in the moonlight. Niall turned away from the fountain and looked back at the house.

It felt very strange to think that half of him had originated in this place. He wondered what it had been like for his father, growing up here. He wondered how his father had ended up in Scotland married to his mother.

His grandfather had never wanted to acknowledge that Niall was anything other than a MacDonald. But the other half of his heritage had brought him to this place, had given him Gayles.

The magnificent glass windows of the house glittered in the moonlight. As he regarded the beauty of glass and stone that lay before him, the possessiveness that was so deeply a part of Niall's nature stirred.

Mine, he thought. *All of this is mine.*

The woman is mine, too.

The minute that thought surfaced, he tried to banish it. It was folly to think that way. It would be folly to let himself become involved with Alexandra.

Too complicated, he thought. *Best to finish my business and get out of here as soon as possible.*

He tried not to think about the church ceremony that had made such an unwelcome impression upon him that afternoon, but the words he had spoken, and Alexandra's long delay in answering, kept coming back to him.

After a while, he slowly made his way back to the house.

At two-thirty in the morning Alexandra gave up trying to sleep and decided she would go to the library to get a book. She put a silk robe over her nightdress, took a candle, and, barefoot, went out the bedroom door into the passageway. She had almost reached the top of the stairs when she saw a figure looming ahead of her in the darkness.

She jumped in surprise and almost dropped her candle.

"It's just me," Niall said.

She righted the candle in its holder and held it so she could see him.

"I'm sorry I startled you," he said. "I just went out for some air."

She stared at him in shocked surprise. In the flickering light of the candle his shoulders looked enormous. His throat was bared by his open shirt, and a pleated kilt hung from his narrow hips. His dark hair was tousled and fell forward over his forehead.

Alexandra was suddenly intensely conscious of her own long, tangled hair, thin nightclothes, and bare feet. She wet suddenly dry lips with her tongue, and said nervously, "I was just going to the library for a book."

He lifted an eyebrow. "Couldn't sleep, eh?"

She tried to collect her scattered poise. "Apparently you suffered from the same problem."

He looked at her broodingly and didn't reply. He was blocking her path to the library. She considered retreating to her room, but somehow that seemed cowardly.

Finally, he spoke. "I didn't think you were going to answer the rector today."

She hesitated, then spoke the truth. "I almost didn't. It all seemed so . . . so solemn. So religious. I felt like a cheat."

His brooding look hadn't changed. "I know. I felt the same way."

She tried for lightness. "Well, there's nothing we can do about it now. It's done."

"Perhaps there is," he replied.

She gave him a puzzled look. "Perhaps there is what?"

"Something we can do about it."

She read what was on his face, and her heart began to hammer so hard she thought it might possibly break one of her ribs. The candle trembled in her hand. "W . . . what is that?"

He took the candle from her trembling hand and put it on

a small table. "We could go ahead and consummate the marriage," he said. "Then it wouldn't be a cheat."

She opened her lips to refuse, and found them crushed under his.

Alexandra had been kissed before. In fact, she had made a point of kissing all of her suitors, hoping against hope that something in her would flame up into a bonfire of passion at their touch.

It hadn't happened with any of her suitors, but it happened with Niall. His mouth was hard on her mouth and his hands were hard on her back, pressing her against him so that she felt the solidity of his body against her own. Fire flickered in her veins, and her mouth opened under his.

She had never felt such intense, such dizzying passion before, and when he lifted his mouth from hers she would have fallen if his hands had not been there to hold her up.

"Let's go into the bedroom," he said. His eyes were narrow slits of midnight blue.

Everything in her wanted to go with him. It was the very urgency of her desire that terrified her into backing away.

"No," she said. "No." And before he could reply she spun around and bolted back to her bedroom, locking the door behind her.

She did not sleep for the rest of the night. She was shaken to the core by her response to Niall's kiss.

I don't even like him, she kept telling herself. *How is it that I could be so indifferent to the kisses of men I genuinely liked, yet feel this for someone I dislike?*

He was the last man in the world for her. She did not approve of him, and he certainly did not approve of her.

He wanted her, though. He was as physically attracted to her as she was to him. He might not like her, but he would very much like to get her into bed with him.

I can't do it, she told herself as she lay in the huge four-poster staring into the dark. *If I want to keep my self-respect, I can't do it. I don't love Niall MacDonald, I only want to go to bed with him.* Her body tingled at the very thought of what that would be like.

I ought to be ashamed of myself. I am ashamed of myself. The thing to do is to keep as far away from that treacherous Scot as I possibly can. This is just a temporary aberration. Once he leaves Gayles, I shall be myself again.

At six o'clock in the morning, Niall collected his dogs and went down to the stables. The house had barely been stirring, but the stables were full of activity as the horses were fed their breakfasts.

The head groom came to meet him.

"Did ye want to ride, my lord?" The old groom's eyes looked anxious. "Next time ye want to ride so early, ye should send me a message the night before, and I won't grain one of the horses."

"Sorry, Graham," Niall said abruptly. "I wasn't thinking."

"I could give ye Ajax," Graham said doubtfully. "He was one of the first to get his grain."

Niall shook his head. The early sun was bright in the eastern sky. He thought that he had never seen such a run of good weather in his life. "I'll wait," he told the groom. "How long do you like to give them?"

"I like to wait an hour before putting on a saddle, my lord."

"Fine."

Graham looked grateful that his advice was being heeded. He asked hesitantly, "Would ye like a cuppa tea while ye wait, my lord? I have some in the stable office."

Niall smiled. "Tea sounds grand."

The old groom grinned back, and said, "Come along wi' me."

Niall followed Graham along a perfectly manicured path to the door at the end of the stable that led into the office. The top part of the stall doors were open, and as he passed in front of them, Niall was able to look in and see each occupant industriously finishing breakfast.

They truly were beautiful horses, he thought. And they looked very fit.

The head groom's office was about as large as one of the horse stalls and held a desk, two chairs, and a wall lined from floor to ceiling with shelves. Bloodstock and racing books figured most prominently, but there was also a beautiful bronze figure of a thoroughbred with a very Arabian-looking face.

"Who rides most of these horses, Graham?" Niall asked as he took the seat that faced the desk. "There appears to be quite a lot of them."

"There are too many of them at the moment," Graham said sorrowfully. "Mr. Geoffrey has been riding His Lordship's horses, but once he leaves there will only be Lady Alexandra, and she has four of her own horses to keep fit." The groom handed Niall a cup of tea. "Unless you are planning to remain at Gayles, my lord?" he added hopefully.

Niall shook his head. "I don't belong here, Graham."

"Of course you belong here," the groom replied. "No one who knew your father could doubt that you are his son. You have his eyes—and his smile, too." The groom shook his balding gray head. "He could get you to do anything in the world for him, could Mr. Edward, with that smile."

Niall took a sip of the strong tea Graham had poured for him, and regarded the groom over the rim of his cup. "I don't know anything at all about my father," he said. "He died before I was born."

Graham took the other seat that was behind his rather battered-looking desk. "He was quiet, was Mr. Edward, but he was deep. And he was magic with horses. His Lordship liked the excitement of owning and racing horses, but Mr. Edward loved the individual animal." He looked at the two perfectly behaved deerhounds that were curled up on either side of Niall's chair. "Looks like you inherited that love, my lord."

"I am good with dogs, Graham, but I am not much of a rider," Niall replied.

"You never had the opportunity to learn correctly," Graham said. "Give me a few months, and I'll have you riding almost as well as Lady Alexandra."

Niall sipped his tea, and said in a noncommittal voice, "Lady Alexandra is a good rider?"

"Aye." Graham nodded vigorously. "She loves the individual animal, like your father did."

Niall's eyes dropped to the heap of rust-colored fur that was Flora. "Well, she may love horses, but she certainly doesn't love dogs."

"What makes you think that, my lord?" Graham sounded astonished.

"Her comments about Fergus and Flora have scarcely been encouraging," Niall returned drily.

"That is surprising," Graham said. "She used to have a spaniel she loved very much. He died right around the time Mr. Marcus killed himself. I thought for sure she would get another dog, but she never has."

Niall lowered his cup and stared at Graham. "Marcus Wilton killed himself?"

"Aye, my lord." The groom's faded blue eyes regarded him curiously. "Didn't you know?"

"No."

"It was a terrible thing. Mr. Marcus lost a tremendous amount of money in a card game and His Lordship refused to pay the debt. It was not the first time that Mr. Marcus had lost money gambling, and I think His Lordship wanted to teach him a lesson. But Mr. Marcus killed himself instead."

"That certainly solved his problem," Niall said ironically.

"Mr. Marcus was charming but weak," Graham said with regret. "Lady Alexandra was always the strong one. I have often thought it was too bad that she was not a boy."

Niall gave a sudden grin. "I'll wager that you must be the only man in the world to have had that thought, Graham."

The groom chuckled. "That is so." He sobered. "But it is a thousand pities that Lady Alexandra could not inherit Gayles. She would have made a better lord than either her brother or Mr. Geoffrey."

Niall stretched his long legs in front of him. "Or me?"

Graham looked his employer in the eye. "Or you, my lord, if you are going to be an absentee landlord."

Niall leaned forward and plunked his teacup down on Graham's desk. His face looked grim. "I have a prior responsibility, Graham, as well you know. The clan at home has far more need of my attention than do the well-fed Sassenach of Gayles."

Graham dropped his eyes.

"Besides, I am leaving you Lady Alexandra," Niall said. "As you have pointed out, she will be a far better lord than I."

"So that is the way it will be." The head groom looked very somber. "It is not my business, my lord," he went on, "but I have known Lady Alexandra since she was a little lass, and I care for her. She should not have to live her life alone. It is not fair to her."

Niall stood up, making the office look even smaller.

"Lady Alexandra and I understand each other perfectly, Graham." He glanced at the clock that reposed on the book-shelf next to a pile of racing journals. "The horses must have digested their breakfasts by now. I will wait in the stableyard for you to have one saddled up."

"Aye, my lord."

Niall returned along the immaculate stable pathway, his brows knit in a ferocious frown. The grooms, who had been chatting as they went about their work, took one look at him and fell silent. Finally, a groom leading a large glossy bay thoroughbred came out into the yard.

"This is Jacob, my lord," the groom said respectfully.

Niall nodded, put his foot into the stirrup, and swung into the saddle. Jacob was quite the tallest horse he had ever sat on, and as he picked up the reins and nudged the horse forward with his calves, he hoped he was not going to disgrace himself and get thrown.

He waited until he was well out of sight of the stable before he asked the horse for a trot. Niall was accustomed to the bone-jarring trot of Highland ponies, and he had not experienced much smoother paces on the horses he had occasionally ridden in Edinburgh. So he was prepared to grip with his legs and stay on when Jacob moved off.

He was astonished by the response he got. Jacob's trot was forward and powerful but it was also the smoothest gait Niall had ever experienced. It was not at all difficult to sit on.

Niall grinned.

I wonder what his canter is like.

Niall squeezed his legs and felt the horse lift under him.

Then they were leaping along, covering huge amounts of ground with every stride. It was no harder than sitting on a rocking horse.

"*Dhé*," Niall said in excitement. He squeezed harder, and Jacob lengthened into a gallop. The wind blew Niall's hair and stung tears from his eyes and the ground flew by beneath him and Fergus and Flora raced behind him. Niall laughed out loud. He could get used to riding a horse like this!

The path ahead looked as if it were narrowing, and Niall took back a little on the reins. Jacob slowed obediently, to a canter, to a trot and finally to a walk. Niall patted his neck enthusiastically. "I am tempted to take you home with me, Jacob," he told the horse in Gaelic. "I am thinking you would like grazing on the green grass of Glen Alpin."

He let out his reins so Jacob could stretch his neck, inhaled the fresh morning air, and let his mind contemplate the conversation he had just had with Graham.

I did not know that her brother killed himself.

Even if they had not been close, it must have been a dreadful shock for Alexandra, he thought. Then her father had left her with that dreadful will.

It seemed as if the beautiful Alexandra had not been treated well by her family. If she seemed cold and uncaring, then perhaps she had a reason.

She was not cold when I kissed her.

Just thinking about that kiss was arousing.

A girl who kisses like that cannot be a virgin, Niall told himself. *She knows what she is doing, that one.*

Niall, the Scot, was not at all horrified by this thought. In England the sexual code was that unmarried girls should be virgins. Wives, on the other hand, were given a much wider license. As long as she was discreet, a wife's sexual life was her own business. In the Highlands, the sexual code was just the opposite. Unmarried girls were allowed to "try out" potential husbands before making their final choice. Once the vows were spoken, however, both parties were expected to be faithful.

So it was not strange that Niall should think Alexandra experienced, particularly considering her history of engagements and almost-engagements.

He thought back again to his conversation with Graham.

If we should have a son, then the future of Gayles would be assured, he thought. *And taking care of a child would give her something to do with herself.*

By the time he returned to the stable, Niall had convinced himself that it was in Alexandra's best interests to sleep with him.

Chapter Thirteen

Alexandra finally fell asleep a little after dawn and she slept until almost eleven o'clock. This unusual behavior caused a great deal of speculation among the staff as to what kind of a wedding night poor Lady Alexandra must have experienced.

Niall had requested James Taylor to call at noon so that he and his new wife could sign the papers that the attorney had drawn up in regard to her legacy. At exactly twelve o'clock, a footman opened the front door to admit Taylor.

"Good," said Niall, who had been crossing the hall on his way to the estate office. "You're on time."

Unlike most of his fellow Highlanders, Niall himself was always on time. He thought fleetingly that he must have inherited this tendency from his English father. Promptness was definitely not one of the Celtic virtues.

"I have the papers, my lord," Taylor said, lifting the leather case he was holding in his left hand.

"Excellent." Niall caught sight of the housekeeper at the far end of the hall and called her over.

"Yes, my lord," Mrs. Moreton said, coming up to stand before him.

"Would you please ask Lady Alexandra to join Mr. Taylor and me in the estate office?" Niall said.

"I will ask *Her Ladyship*," the housekeeper replied in a tone of icy disapproval. She bestowed a scorching look upon Niall and marched off toward the stairs.

Niall stared after her in surprise, wondering what on earth he had done to earn such censure from his housekeeper.

The two men repaired to the estate office, where Taylor spread his documents on the desk so that Niall could read them. After fifteen minutes, as Niall was putting down the last paper, Alexandra came into the office looking pale and big-eyed and fragile.

Dhé, Nial thought as he got to his feet. *She looks as if she is about to be carted off to the guillotine. No wonder the housekeeper glared at me so.*

He scowled at his bride, and said, "Come and sit down and we can get this business done with."

"Good morning, Mr. Taylor," Alexandra said as she approached the table.

"Good morning, my lady," the solicitor replied gently. He gave Niall a reproachful look.

I did not touch the girl, Niall wanted to shout. Then he remembered the kiss and realized that this was not exactly true. However, he most certainly had done nothing to make Alexandra look like such a martyr.

"Are you not feeling well, my lady?" he asked his wife in a grim voice. "You look pale."

"I did not sleep very well," she replied. A beautiful rose-pink color stained her cheeks as she realized what she had said. She bit her lip and took one of the empty chairs at the table.

Well at least no one in the household will doubt that the marriage has been consummated, Niall thought with morbid humor. *If we're lucky, the news will fly back to Chisholm.*

Taylor looked at Niall as if he were Attila the Hun.

Niall sat down and waved to Taylor to do the same. "Get on with it," he said.

The attorney made a neat pile of his papers. Then he looked at Alexandra, who was sitting across the table from the two men, and addressed her in the soft, gentle voice one would use to a frightened child.

"Now that you and His Lordship have wed, my lady, I am free to release your father's money." He tapped his fingers on the pile of papers in front of him. "As you know, your father's private fortune was willed to you, but since you are now married, by law the control of your money has passed to your husband."

"What?" Alexandra's back straightened, and she glared across the table at Niall. "I thought we had a bargain . . ." she began hotly.

He held up his hand. "And we still do. Just listen, will you?"

Her gray eyes were dark with anger and she looked considerably less fragile than she had when she first came in. "All right," she said tensely. "I'm listening."

Taylor said, "The arrangements His Lordship asked me to draw up are thus, my lady. One half of your father's assets are to be put in a trust fund for you. The income from the trust fund is yours for life, to do with as you like. You may not touch the principal, however, without the consent of His Lordship."

"That is not what we agreed upon," Alexandra flared, once more glaring at Niall. "We said half of the money was to go to you and half to me. If you think you can affix strings to my half, you are mistaken."

"Will you go on, Mr. Taylor?" Niall said impassively.

"His Lordship has made a similar disposition for his half of the money, my lady," Taylor told Alexandra. "His half of your father's assets are to go into a trust fund with the income to be his for the rest of his life. He can only touch his principal with your consent."

Alexandra blinked. "Why did you do that?" she asked her husband in a more moderate tone.

"There is one more thing," Niall said. "Taylor?"

"The stud farm is to be yours, my lady, free and clear."

Alexandra looked at Taylor then back again to Niall. "Why?" she repeated.

He shrugged. "What would I do with a stud farm?"

"I don't understand," Alexandra said slowly. Her gray eyes were steady on his face. "Why did you tie up the money like that?"

He didn't want to have to explain himself to her. He wasn't sure he could find the right words. He said, "There will be ample money available to each of us from the interest," and he named a sum that was ample indeed. "There is no reason to touch the principal."

A single line dented her clear brow. "I still don't understand your reasoning."

"This way, neither of us will be able to gamble away Gayles's future," he said lightly. "I should think you would approve of that."

Taylor cleared his throat. "I assure you that His Lordship is acting very responsibly, my lady."

Alexandra ignored the solicitor and continued to confront Niall. "I thought you wanted the money so you could spend it in Scotland."

He looked irritated. "I will have the interest from my portion of the money to spend on Glen Alpin, and you will have the interest from your half to spend on Gayles. I don't understand why you are making such an issue of what is a perfectly sensible disposition of the inheritance."

"I don't like the idea that I have to consult you if I should want to spend some of the principal of my own money," she retorted. "That is what I am making an issue of."

"That is the way I want it," he said implacably, "and that is the way it is going to be."

She looked furious.

Silence fell as they stared at each other across the polished mahogany table where, once a month, Mr. Mason collected the tenants' rents.

At last Taylor said nervously, "I do believe that this is the wisest way to secure the future for your children, my lady."

Alexandra looked nonplussed.

Niall's mouth quirked with amusement. "Exactly so, Mr. Taylor."

Alexandra opened her lips, then closed them again as if she could find no words.

Niall's brief amusement vanished. "Now, my lady," he asked, "are you going to sign these papers?"

"Oh all right," she replied crossly. "I suppose I will sign them."

"I will be happy to go over them with you, my lady," Taylor said.

"I would appreciate that," she replied.

Niall leaned back in his chair and gazed out the window at the sun shining on one of the Elizabethan pavilions and listened with half an ear to the drone of the solicitor's voice and the lighter tones of Alexandra's as she asked questions.

At last the final document had been explained and she had signed it. Niall prepared to rise.

"I have a disposition of my own that I would like to make," Alexandra said. 'If you have a few moments, Mr. Taylor, perhaps we could attend to it now."

"Certainly," the attorney said.

Niall sank back into his chair.

"I want to settle some money on Geoffrey," she said.

Taylor and Niall looked at each other.

"That is not necessary, Lady Alexandra," Taylor said. "You don't owe anything to Mr. Wilton."

"Yes, I do. He fully expected to be the next earl, and I think he deserves to be compensated in some way for his loss."

"He only became your father's heir upon the death of your brother three years ago," Taylor pointed out quietly.

"He thought he was the earl, and he thought he was going to marry me. Now he has nothing. It's not fair, and I want him to have enough money to enable him to live comfortably."

"Doesn't Wilton have any money of his own?" Niall asked.

"He inherited a small property from his father, but I believe it is heavily mortgaged," Taylor said.

Alexandra nodded in agreement. Niall thought to himself that her hair looked like spun gold in the morning light.

She said, "Highgate is mortgaged, and Geoffrey needs enough money to pay off the mortgage and make repairs on the property. I had planned to take a sum out of the money I inherited and give it to Geoffrey, but it seems I cannot do that without His Lordship's agreement."

"That is so," Taylor returned.

She looked directly across the table at Niall. "Well then, I am asking for your agreement, my lord. I would like to give Geoffrey twenty thousand pounds so that he can redeem his mortgage and repair his property."

Niall looked back at her as if she were insane. "You want to give away twenty thousand pounds of my money to a perfectly healthy young man because you feel sorry for him?"

Alexandra's hands, which had been folded on the table in front of her, clenched into fists. "It is not your money, it is my money! You have more than enough to buy your precious cattle. Why should you care what I do with my half of the inheritance?"

"I care because you are taking away money that rightfully belongs to Gayles," Niall replied coldly.

"You don't care about Gayles," she flung back at him. "You once told me you would beggar Gayles if you had to. You just don't want Geoffrey to get any money, and I think it's beastly of you."

Niall made a tremendous effort to contain his anger. "I may not have grown up here at Gayles, as you did, but I have inherited it, and I have the responsibility for it. I was content to leave the administration of Gayles to you, because I thought you cared for the place and the people. But now . . ." The rein he was holding on his temper slipped slightly. "*Dhé*, how can you wish to steal from Gayles in order to enrich a useless young Sassenach like Wilton!"

Alexandra leaned forward, and said slowly and distinctly, "I don't want to enrich Geoffrey. I want him to have enough money to enable him to live as a gentleman."

"Let him earn his own money," Niall said brutally. "Or, if he cannot do that, then let him marry it. But he will not get a penny of mine."

Alexandra was flushed with anger. "And just what do you

think *would* constitute a reason for allowing me to dip into my principal?" she challenged him.

He looked at her roused face and his blood stirred.

Not now, he thought angrily, forcing his mind to concentrate on the matter at hand.

"If you wanted to make a large improvement on the property, such as building a canal, I would consider it," he said. "I would consider an investment in the type of up-to-date farm equipment I saw at Holkham to be worthwhile. But none of my money is to go to Geoffrey Wilton."

"Fine," Alexandra flashed back. She leaned back in her chair and crossed her arms over her breasts.

He looked at them, then compelled his eyes to return to her face.

"Then I will sell the stud farm and give Geoffrey the money from that," she said.

"I don't care what you do with the stud farm. It is not mine, and I am not responsible for it. But I am responsible for Gayles." His eyes narrowed. "I may not have been brought up to be an earl, Alec, but I *was* brought up to be a chief. I know how to take care of what is mine."

He paused a moment to let his words sink in, then he pushed back his chair and stood up. He looked at the attorney. "I hope I have made myself clear, Taylor."

"Very clear, my lord," Taylor replied.

"Good." Niall's eyes returned to his wife. "One more thing. I want Geoffrey Wilton gone from Gayles by the end of the day."

She stared at him in stunned amazement. "But why?"

"He's in my way," Niall said, strode to the door, and went out.

Silence reigned between the two he had left behind.

Taylor looked at Alexandra, whose face had gone from

rosy pink to white. He understood that her intentions were good, and he felt sorry for her, but he also thought that Niall was right.

Geoffrey Wilton could fend for himself.

"How much is the stud farm worth?" Alexandra asked him in a voice that sounded choked.

"The horses alone are worth half a million guineas, my lady."

She looked startled by this large sum. "Did His Lordship know that when he agreed to give me the farm?"

"He did, my lady."

Her gray eyes narrowed. "Whose idea was it to give me the stud farm? Yours or His Lordship's?"

"It was His Lordship's idea, my lady," Taylor replied truthfully. "He said that you loved horses."

Alexandra put her elbows on the table and rested her forehead in her hands. "I want to do something for Geoffrey," she said in a muffled voice.

Taylor hoped desperately that she was not crying.

"If that is what you wish, my lady, then I will draw something up for you."

Her golden head nodded.

"Do you want to sell the stud farm?"

Another nod.

"Very well. I will do that and once you know how much money you have realized, you can decide what to do about Mr. Wilton."

"All right."

"Is . . . is there anything else, my lady?"

At last she looked up. Taylor was vastly relieved to see that there was no sign of tears on her flawless face.

"What does His Lordship know about canals?" she demanded.

"I believe he was discussing them with Mr. Mason," the solicitor replied cautiously. "Mr. Mason has been recommending a canal to your father for years."

"Yes," Alexandra said. "I know."

Silence.

"If that will be all, my lady . . ."

It was evident from his poised position that Taylor was eager to be gone.

Alexandra was not ready to release him yet. "Did you report to Lord Chisholm that our marriage had taken place?"

"I did, my lady."

"And do you think he was satisfied?"

"He was satisfied that the ceremony did in fact take place. As you know, however, he is going to want evidence that the marriage is more than nominal."

Alexandra looked at the leather case into which Taylor had returned the signed papers. "You've already released my father's money to us, though. Surely that means you are satisfied that the terms of his will have been met."

"*I* am satisfied, my lady," Taylor said quietly. "I was present at the ceremony and that is sufficient for me to feel I can release your money. I cannot guarantee what Lord Chisholm will do, however."

"Is it possible he could still try to take the money away from us?"

"It is a possibility. I do not think it will come to pass, but it is a possibility. I think it would be wise for you and His Lordship to make an effort to convince Lord Chisholm that he has no cause to bring a suit against you."

Alexandra looked at the ceiling as if she were calling upon divine intervention. "And just how do you suggest we do that?"

"I know that His Lordship is anxious to purchase some

cattle for his Scottish lands, but I have suggested to him that he postpone his buying trip for a few weeks. I do not think it would give a good appearance for him to leave you too quickly."

Alexandra slowly lowered her eyes from the ceiling to Taylor, who flinched at the expression on her face.

"And what did His Lordship say to this helpful suggestion?" she inquired.

"He agreed, my lady."

"How nice."

Taylor looked down at the leather case lying before him on the table.

After a moment he heard her draw a deep breath, then she said, "Thank you, Mr. Taylor. I will not detain you any longer."

The solicitor got hurriedly to his feet.

"Good day, my lady. If you should have any further need of me, just send a message."

"Thank you," Alexandra said again.

She remained sitting alone at the table until the door had closed behind the young attorney. Then, very calmly, she stood up, looked at the empty chair where Niall had sat, and said, "I hate you."

The empty chair did not reply.

"How am I supposed to tell Geoff and Cousin Louisa that they are no longer welcome at Gayles?"

No answer came from the chair.

Alexandra thought of the worst swear words that she knew, and said them. Loudly.

It didn't make her feel any better.

The undeniable relief she felt at the thought that she would no longer have to endure endless meals trying to make conversation with Geoffrey and Mrs. Wilton did not make her feel any better either.

On the other hand, she certainly did not relish being left alone with her husband. She had been expecting that he would leave Gayles within the next few days. Now it appeared she would have to put up with him for weeks.

She swore again, even more loudly than before.

It didn't help the second time either.

Chapter Fourteen

Luncheon at Gayles was an informal meal, where platters of cold food were set upon a side table for the family to serve themselves. Alexandra, Geoffrey, and Mrs. Wilton sat down together, and Alexandra seized the opportunity to inform her guests of Niall's desire that they vacate the premises.

Geoffrey went chalk white. "I am not leaving you alone with him," he stated categorically.

Alexandra didn't answer.

"My dear," Mrs. Wilton said, "you have no choice in the matter. Gayles is no longer your house."

Alexandra looked at Geoffrey's mother. "I am so sorry, Cousin Louisa. You have been very kind to me, and this sounds so horribly ungrateful."

Mrs. Wilton looked as if she agreed, but she said politely, "I quite understand the situation, my dear."

"I know this is not my house," Geoffrey said "It is Alex's house." He turned to Alexandra, who was sitting at the head of the table with mother and son on either side of her. "And I am not leaving here unless *you* ask me to."

They had all helped themselves to cold meat and fruit, but no one had eaten anything.

Alexandra cursed Niall under her breath for putting her in such a horrible situation, "I *am* asking you, Geoff," she said.

He shook his head in denial. "You are asking me on the orders of MacDonald. I meant that you must ask me of your own free will."

She forced herself to meet his pain-filled blue gaze. In a careful, steady voice she said, "I am asking you of my own free will. We have discussed this before, Geoff. I have no need of your protection. Niall MacDonald and I understand each other very well. You must leave here and begin to live your own life." She paused, then added firmly, "Without me."

"Alexandra is right, Geoffrey," Mrs. Wilton said. "What has happened here may be grossly unfair, but it has happened, and you must live with it. We should return to Highgate immediately."

Alexandra looked gratefully at Mrs. Wilton. "I should tell you, Cousin Louisa, that I have made arrangements to sell the stud farm and I plan to turn half of the proceeds over to Geoffrey. The money will be enough to enable him to refurbish Highgate and clear it of its mortgages."

Mrs. Wilton looked stunned. It was a moment before she said, "That is kind of you, my dear."

Geoffrey said harshly, "I don't want MacDonald's money."

"It is not his money, it is mine," Alexandra said. "The stud farm was given to me, free and clear, to do with as I choose. And this is what I choose to do with it."

Geoffrey looked at Alexandra, his face a mask of anguish. "It isn't the money, Alex. It's that . . . I just can't . . ."

Mrs. Wilton said briskly, "We will pack and be gone in an hour, my dear."

"Thank you, Cousin Louisa," Alexandra said. "I truly appreciate all that you have done for me. I know it was not easy for you to remain here after Geoff was displaced."

Mrs. Wilton nodded and stood up. "Geoffrey, I think we should go and pack."

Alexandra had never heard Geoffrey's mother's voice sound so hard and authoritative.

He didn't get up. "I will come in a minute, Mama," he said. "I want just a moment alone with Alex."

The two women looked at each other.

"Please," Geoffrey said.

Alexandra had hoped to avoid this, but she did not have the heart to deny him.

"Go along, Cousin Louisa," she said. "It will be all right."

Mrs. Wilton frowned, then turned and went slowly out the door, leaving Alexandra and Geoffrey alone at the table.

She said quietly, "What is it that you wish to say to me, Geoff?"

He didn't answer, just stared at her with desperate hunger in his eyes.

She couldn't bear to look at him, and gazed down at the single slice of ham she had put on her plate.

He said in a strangled voice, "I . . . I just want to say that if anything should happen, send and I will come to you immediately."

"Thank you, but that will not be necessary," she said to the ham.

He leaned toward her. "Alex, please promise you will call

on me if you need me. Highgate is only a few miles away. I can be here in less than an hour."

She assumed the sternest expression she could manage and lifted her eyes to meet his. "Geoffrey, go to London for the Season. Do not sit at Highgate waiting for me to send you a message. I shall be perfectly fine, I assure you."

Their gazes held, and she saw the refusal in his. He set his jaw. "I am not moving one step out of this neighborhood until MacDonald has gone back to Scotland."

She did not know what other arguments she could advance. His obdurance made her angry, but his unhappiness crippled her with guilt. At last she said helplessly, "Your mother will be waiting for you."

"All right." At last he stood. "I meant every word that I said, Alex. I will be at Highgate if you need me."

"I wish you would go to London."

He shook his head, turned and went out the door.

Fifteen minutes later, Alexandra was still sitting at the table, staring at her untouched plate, when Niall came in with his dogs.

"Is it too late to get something to eat?" he asked.

"Of course not." She looked at the platters still reposing on the side table. "Will this do, or do you want something fresh?"

"This is fine," he said and went to the table, picked up a plate, and began to fill it with ham, roast beef, and cold potatoes. When he had finished he came to take the seat Geoffrey had just vacated. Fergus and Flora lay down behind him.

"I saw Wilton in the hallway," he said. "He looked even more dismal than usual. Did you tell him he had to go?"

"Yes."

"Good." He opened his napkin. "I am thinking that if I

had to sit through another dinner looking at his doleful face, I might have done something violent."

Alexandra, who felt the same way, nevertheless leaped to Geoffrey's defense. "This has been very painful for Geoff."

Niall smeared mustard on his ham and horseradish on his beef. He added a few pieces of bread from the basket on the table.

He said, "I do believe he is more unhappy about losing you than he is about losing the earldom."

Alexandra didn't reply.

He picked up his knife and fork and looked at her. "Are you unhappy about losing him?"

She blinked at the unexpected question.

"What do you mean?" she parried.

His blue eyes were unreadable. "I think what I meant was perfectly clear. Are you unhappy because you could not marry Geoffrey Wilton? Do you love him?"

She avoided that blue stare by looking down. "Geoff and I grew up together. He was more a brother to me than Marcus was. I love him very much."

He was chewing on a piece of beef. When he had finished he asked, "But not as a husband?"

She shook her head, her eyes still on her untouched plate.

He said, "Apparently he does not regard you as a sister."

"No." She sighed. "He doesn't. Unfortunately."

In the sardonic tone she had come to dislike intensely, he said, "My, my, my. You have certainly left a quantity of disappointed suitors scattered in your wake, haven't you?"

Her head shot up, and she glared him. "My suitors are none of your business."

He looked back at her, and there was something in his eyes that made her stomach clench. He didn't answer.

"Don't tell me that there aren't plenty of girls in Scotland who are mourning the fact that you are married," she flung at him.

He shrugged and ate a piece of ham.

"I suppose there will be a few," he said after the ham was swallowed.

It took her a moment to register the tense.

"Will be?" She narrowed her eyes. "Surely you have informed your family in Scotland that you are married?"

For the briefest moment she had a glimpse of what he must have looked like when he was a boy. Then he glanced away. "My grandfather will not be at all happy to learn I have married a Sassenach," he said casually. "It will be best if I bring him the news in person."

The little-boy-caught-with-his-hand-in-the-sweets look had vanished almost as quickly as it had come. Alexandra stared thoughtfully at the self-contained arrogant face of her husband and said, "Could it be that you don't plan to tell him at all? Perhaps you will just go home and take a second wife and forget that I ever existed."

He scowled at her.

"Well, my lord?" she demanded. "Is that what you plan to do?"

He held her eyes. "I might have thought about such a plan once, but that was before I made those promises in the church."

She could not pull her eyes away from his.

"Alec," he said, his deep voice more husky than usual, "what do you think? Perhaps we should make this a real marriage, after all."

She swallowed. "It isn't a real marriage."

"It would be if we consummated it."

She couldn't answer. She just shook her head.

"Wouldn't you like to give Gayles an heir?"

Her heart was thumping so loudly she was afraid that he could hear it.

"Gayles already has an heir," she managed to say. "Geoffrey."

His mouth thinned. "I do not want what is mine to go to Geoffrey."

"There is nothing wrong with Geoffrey!"

"He is a mouse, not a man," he replied contemptuously.

"That's not fair. You hardly know him."

"I know what I have seen, and what I have seen is that he drips his misery over you until you must feel suffocated by it."

The fact that he was echoing her own thoughts made her even more furious. "Geoffrey loves me," she said. "Of course it is hard for him to see me married to another man."

"Under those circumstances, a man has two choices," Niall replied, "and neither of them involves hanging around you and making you feel guilty."

Once again he had hit too close to home. She glared at him. "What two choices do *you* see that he has?"

"He should either kill me or he should go away and leave you in peace," Niall replied, and ate his last piece of ham.

Alexandra stared in astonishment. "Kill you?"

"Yes." He cut off a piece of his roast beef and ate it.

"Geoff is not a barbarian," she managed to say.

He raised an eyebrow at her and continued to eat his luncheon.

Silence fell.

She took a sip of the lemonade that she had not yet touched.

"Why aren't you eating?" he said.

"I'm not hungry."

"It is a sin to waste good food," he replied, reached over, took her ham, split it in half, and fed it to the dogs.

She said stiffly, "Mr. Taylor told me that you are remaining here at Gayles for a few more weeks."

"Yes. He thinks that we should give an appearance of living together."

She frowned down at her plate. For luncheon they used a set of plain white china trimmed in gold with the Wilton coat of arms monogrammed in the center in green and gold. The monogram was completely visible now that the slice of ham was gone.

In a deepened voice, he said, "Alec. We would deal very well together, you and I."

Her eyes flew to his.

"I am thinking that you know it, too."

She swallowed, pushed her chair back, and stood up. "If you will excuse me, I have things I must do," she said, and made a great effort to exit with some semblance of dignity.

Where could she go to get away from him?

Gayles was a large house, but somehow Niall had managed to establish his presence in a way she would not have believed possible a short week ago. Even her own bedroom wasn't off-limits to him, she thought resentfully. He had a right to come into it anytime he wanted.

He wouldn't come into her old bedroom, though.

With a decisive move, she swung around and climbed the stairs to the third floor. She passed through the Long Gallery to the corner room that had been hers ever since she left the nursery. She let herself in and closed the door behind her.

Safe.

It was outrageous that she should feel so insecure in her own house, she thought angrily. This man had come in and filled it up with his arrogance and his dogs, and she was reduced to hiding out in her girlhood bedroom in order to avoid him.

I hate him, she told herself as she walked to the window seat and sat down. It occurred to her that she had never felt quite so violently about any other person in her entire life. She had both liked and disliked people, but this jumble of intense emotion evoked by Niall MacDonald was something she had never experienced before.

I have always wanted to feel passionately about a man, she thought as she gazed out at the west court. *But not this man. This man is heartless and arrogant and overbearing. I want nothing to do with a man like him.*

She stood up restlessly and crossed the floor to look out the windows that opened onto the gardens on the south side of the house. Her eye was caught by the anomaly of a figure in livery walking down the garden path.

There was no reason for a footman in livery to go into the garden. On their day off some of the staff cut through the garden to get to the village road, but if this man was headed for the village, he would not be wearing his livery.

Alexandra had excellent eyesight, and she stared intently at the footman's back as he went down the garden path.

I'll bet it's that man Harvey, she thought, and in the very next instant she was at her bedroom door.

She raced down the stairs to the second floor and on the flight between the second and the first floors she nearly bumped into Niall, who was on his way upstairs.

"Whoa," he said, catching her by the shoulders. "Where are you running to?"

"I just saw that spy of a footman taking off through the garden," she informed him breathlessly. "I'm going to follow him and see what he is up to."

He removed his hands from her shoulders, and said calmly, "He is going to report to Chisholm, I imagine."

She quivered like a foxhound that has caught the scent of its quarry. "That's what I think. Come along and we can catch them together."

For a moment she thought he was going to refuse, then he shrugged. "Why not?"

"I saw him going down the garden path," she said. "There is a wood beyond the garden, and after the wood is the road. I bet he is going to meet Chisholm there."

"All right," he said, turning around. "Let's go."

By the time they emerged on the south side of the house, the footman had disappeared into the acres of trees, shrubs, and flowers that composed the garden. Alexandra and Niall followed the main path, which wound in and out among the various hedges that separated the garden into individual rooms. The afternoon sun, high above in a deeply blue sky, felt warm on Alexandra's bare arms as she hurried along beside Niall, throwing in an occasional running step to keep up with his long stride.

Beyond the trimmed hedges and borders of the garden lay a copse of woods that had been left to grow wild. Niall stopped at the edge of the garden, looked down into Alexandra's flushed face, and asked, "Where is the road?"

"Just beyond the wood," she said. "There is a path of sorts that goes through the trees. Some of the servants use the garden and wood as a shortcut when they are walking into the village. If we hurry, we may be able to see Harvey meeting with Chisholm."

He was still looking down at her, and she was surprised to see amusement in his dark blue gaze. She was about to ask him what he found so entertaining, when he said agreeably, "All right," and began to walk into the woods.

The path was too narrow for two people to walk side by side, so Niall went first. Alexandra followed, still imbued with the thrill of the hunt.

In front of her, Niall stopped so suddenly that she bumped into his back. He turned, put a finger to his lips, and motioned her off the path into the trees.

Alexandra followed close behind him, trying to keep her skirt from becoming tangled in the undergrowth. She wished she were wearing boots and not thin slippers. But she forged on valiantly and made no complaint.

Niall stopped before they had reached the edge of the copse and, bending so that his lips were close to her ear, said, "Stay out of sight."

She nodded impatiently and moved a few steps forward to peer between the trees. A phaeton was pulled up on the road some twenty feet away from them, and its driver was deep in conversation with the liveried footman. Alexandra recognized the driver as Lord Chisholm.

I knew it, she thought triumphantly.

She stood on tiptoe, and whispered to Niall, "Let's go and confront the wretches."

He didn't move, just lifted his brows and inquired in a puzzled voice, "Why should we do that?"

"So we can tell Chisholm we know what he is up to and dismiss his spy, of course," she replied impatiently.

He said in the same puzzled manner, "But I thought your plan was to keep Harvey in place and use him for our own ends."

Her eyes widened. In the excitement of the hunt, she had completely forgotten about that plan.

"Oh," she said weakly. "That's true."

The footman turned away from the phaeton and began to return to the woods where the two of them were hiding.

Niall put his hand on Alexandra's arm and drew her deeper into the cover of the trees.

As they waited for Harvey to pass, Alexandra fumed in silence. She felt like a complete fool.

It was my idea to use Harvey in the first place, she thought. *I just got so excited when I saw him sneaking away that I forgot all about it. What an idiot Niall must think me.*

"I think it's safe to go back to the path now," he said.

She nodded glumly.

He began to thrust his way through the underbrush, and she followed, still brooding about her own rashness. Suddenly she tripped and would have fallen to her knees if she hadn't grabbed on to Niall who was directly in front of her.

"Are you all right?" he asked, turning to face her.

Some thorns had snagged the hem of her dress.

"How delightful," she said crossly, looking down at the needles that had impaled the thin white muslin of her skirt. She bent and tried to disengage it without lifting her skirt too high.

"Don't," he said. "You'll make it worse." And he pushed a bush out of his way, sat on his heels, and methodically began to unhook her dress from the briars.

She looked at his long fingers working on her dress and felt the oddest sensation of light-headedness.

"There." He began to straighten up and the bush he had pushed out of his way suddenly swung loose and whacked him in the face.

"*Dhé,*" he exclaimed, putting his hand to his cheek.

"Are you all right?" she asked with concern.

"It's nothing." He turned around to go ahead of her once again. "Let us get back to the path before anything else attacks us."

She followed behind him on the narrow path until they

reached the end of the wood. He stopped then and turned to look down at her and for the first time she saw that the briars had torn a deep cut into his left cheek right over the cheekbone.

"Niall," she said, "you're bleeding."

He put his hand up to his cheek, and his fingers came away stained with blood. With his other hand he searched inside his coat and pulled out a handkerchief.

"Give it to me," Alexandra said. "There is a fountain close by, and I'll wet it with some cold water."

He handed her his handkerchief and followed her into a small shrubbery-guarded arbor that contained a stone figurine of a woman in Roman dress bearing a pitcher on her shoulder. Water poured from the pitcher in a steady stream into a shell-shaped fountain.

Alexandra dampened the handkerchief in the fountain and came back to Niall. "Sit down," she said, "and I'll try to stop the bleeding."

Without argument, he sat on the stone bench that was situated to give a view of the fountain. She tilted his face up to her with one hand and applied the cold compress with the other. He closed his eyes.

Alexandra looked down at the long lashes that lay upon those hard masculine cheeks. He was very still under her hand. Her pulses began to race.

This was not a good idea, she thought.

"You can probably hold this handkerchief more easily yourself," she said.

He didn't open his eyes. "You're doing just fine," he said.

She swallowed.

The water trickled into the fountain behind her. The sun drew sparks of deep mahogany brown from his hair. She cleared her throat. "It was silly of me to go running after

Harvey that way. I was so angry when I saw him that I completely forgot about my plan."

"I wondered why you were so anxious to catch him," he murmured.

"Well why didn't you say something?" she asked in annoyance. "You could have saved us both from tearing around in the woods like idiots."

He didn't answer.

"Why didn't you say something?" she repeated.

His eyes opened, and he looked up at her. "I thought it might be fun to tear around in the woods with you," he said.

She felt herself begin to tremble.

"Alec," he said, and reached up to draw her down beside him on the bench.

She went, her knees giving way as she came to rest in the curve of his arm. He bent his head and kissed her.

The sun was still hot on her head, but she no longer heard the sound of water falling from the Roman maiden's pitcher. The only sound she could hear was the beating of her heart. They were enclosed behind a wall of tall yews, as perfectly alone as if they had been in their bedroom.

He tightened his grip on her, and her body yielded, submitted and blended into his. Her head fell back on his shoulder, and her mouth opened under the urgency of his. For a long, mindless moment, she surrendered to the force in him that called so strongly to something deep within her.

Something was pushing at her legs, but she ignored it until the dog actually barked at her. She pulled away from Niall and looked down at Flora, who glared fiercely back.

Niall said something in a voice that was so husky she scarcely recognized it.

Flora took advantage of the space that had opened up between Niall and Alexandra and wedged herself into it. The fierceness in her glare turned to triumph as she rested her chin on Niall's knee.

"I think Flora is jealous," Alexandra managed to say.

"What the hell are these hounds doing loose in the garden?" Niall asked in ominous tones.

Then they heard Alan calling the dogs' names.

Niall said something in Gaelic that Alexandra was certain was a curse.

She had moved to the edge of the bench and now she looked over at him as she struggled to regain her composure. His hair was hanging over his forehead, and he was glaring at Flora as if he would like to kill her. She pressed her head under his hand and whined pitifully.

"You are a bad girl," he told her. But his voice was gentle.

She moved her head up and down, indicating that she wanted to be petted. He obliged.

Alexandra swallowed.

He looked at her. "Now you know my secret," he said as his hand continued to caress his dog. "I am a fool for beautiful females."

Alexandra looked down at Flora's blissful face. Then she looked up again at Niall.

He smiled at her. And her heart turned over.

He raised his voice, and called, "We are here, Alan."

Alexandra clasped her trembling hands together and tried very hard to keep her face expressionless.

In a moment Alan MacDonald was entering their previously secluded arbor.

"They must have got a scent of you," he told Niall. "All of a sudden they took off, and they would not come back when I called."

Niall sighed and stood up. "Come along, Alec," he said. "We had best be going."

She stood up.

Fergus came to her and gazed up into her face. She looked down into the hound's brown eyes and could have sworn his expression was sympathetic. She smiled and caressed his head.

Niall said with amusement, "Fergus has an eye for a beautiful female also."

Pull yourself together, Alexandra, she commanded herself. Trying to compose herself, she petted the dog a few more times. Then she looked up and said lightly, "I am going to return to the house and change my dress. I'll leave you gentlemen to go about your own business."

She could feel Niall's blue gaze burning into her back as she walked away.

Chapter Fifteen

When Alexandra arrived back at the house, Stokes met her with the news that Lord Chisholm had called to see Niall. She stared at the butler in stunned amazement.

"Lord Chisholm?" she said.

"Yes, my lady. Do you happen to know where His Lordship is?"

"His Lordship was in the garden when last I saw him, Stokes," she replied. "You might send someone to look for him there."

"Thank you, my lady. I will do so immediately."

Alexandra had every intention of joining Niall and the perifidious Chisholm as soon as she changed her torn dress and filthy shoes. She hastened upstairs to her bedroom and prodded Meg to dress her as quickly as possible. She had reached the second floor on her way to the first when she was intercepted by Mrs. Moreton, who had a problem with one of the chambermaids she needed to consult Alexandra about immediately.

Alexandra did her best to listen patiently to her housekeeper and respond to the problem. At last she was free to descend to the first floor and ask one of the footmen where she could find Niall.

"I believe he is in the office, my lady," the footman replied. "Lord Chisholm was with him."

Alexandra smiled an abstracted thank-you to the young footman and turned toward the family dining room, which would lead her to the estate office.

The door was closed. Drawing a deep breath, Alexandra thrust the door open and walked in.

Niall was standing at one of the windows with his back to the room. He was alone.

He heard the door open and swung around, a frown on his face. "Alec," he said in surprise. His frown lifted.

The scratch on his cheek looked red and angry. She made a mental note to make sure he had it properly cleaned and anointed.

She closed the door behind her. "Stokes told me that Chisholm was here. What did he want, Niall?"

The line between his brows came back.

"What did he learn from Harvey?" she went on. "Is he still threatening to take us to court about the marriage?"

He said, "Chisholm came here to make me an offer to buy Glen Alpin."

Alexandra felt her mouth drop open. That was the last thing she had expected to hear. "He wanted to buy your lands in *Scotland*?"

Niall's frown deepened. "Yes. He was so kind as to tell me that since I was now a rich English lord, I should be glad to rid myself of Glen Alpin."

Alexandra realized that Niall was furious.

She asked slowly, "Did he say anything about the Jockey Club's claim to my father's money?"

Niall lifted an ironic eyebrow. "Oh yes. He said that if I agreed to sell him Glen Alpin, he would drop the Jockey Club claim."

"What did you say to him?" Alexandra asked.

"I threw him out of the house," Niall replied.

Alexandra stared at her husband in bewilderment. "This doesn't make any sense," she finally said.

"It doesn't make any sense to me either," he returned grimly. He moved away from the window in the direction of the desk. "Come and sit down. Perhaps between us we can figure out what is going on in Chisholm's warped mind."

He crossed to the chair behind the mahogany desk, and she moved to take the chair facing it. In silence they regarded each other over the big leather ledger in which Mason kept the estate's rent records.

Alexandra spoke first. "I did not realize that Glen Alpin was yours to sell."

"It isn't," he replied. He leaned back in the chair and stretched his legs out in front of him. "It belongs to my grandfather, but it will come to me upon his death."

She looked puzzled. "Then how can Chisholm expect you to sell it, if it is not yet yours?"

His expression became even grimmer. "Oh, he made me a very creative proposal. He is willing to pay me part of the money for Glen Alpin right now in return for my written promise to turn the property over to him when I inherit it."

"The man is outrageous." Alexandra said indignantly. "First he tried to cheat us out of my father's money, and now he is trying to buy something from you that isn't yours to sell. Why he's . . . he's . . . dishonorable!"

Niall's angry expression disappeared, and he broke into genuine laughter. "You sound as if you have never known a dishonorable person in your entire life."

She felt a treacherous stab of delight at having provoked his laughter. Then she was annoyed with herself for feeling that way. She lifted her chin, and said with dignity, "I am accustomed to dealing with gentlemen. It seems that Lord Chisholm does not fit into that category."

"It seems not," he replied. He was still smiling.

She drummed her fingers on the arm of her chair. "He didn't say anything about what he might have learned from speaking to Harvey?"

His smile disappeared. "He said that he feels he still has a case, that the fact that we are sharing the same apartment is not enough proof that our marriage is a real one."

"The man is a toad," she said furiously.

His eyes gleamed. "I gave him something to think about, though."

She regarded him cautiously. That gleam looked dangerous. "What was that?"

"I asked him if he really thought he could convince a judge that I was the sort of man who would keep his hands to himself if he shared a bedroom with a tasty morsel like you."

She half jumped out of her chair in shock. *"What?"*

"I thought it was rather clever of me to think of that," he said modestly.

She glared. "Did you really call me a tasty morsel to that hateful man?"

He was not completely successful in smothering a smile. "I am afraid that I did."

She rose to her feet and directed a haughty look at the sprawling figure on the other side of the desk. "Well, my lord, allow me to inform you that this is one morsel you are not going to taste."

He lifted an eyebrow. "No?"

"No."

His eyebrow went down, his eyes narrowed, and he said softly, "That would be a great pity."

Her insides quivered at the expression she saw in his eyes.

"Sadder things than that have happened," she informed him, and turned to depart for safer regions.

She had taken one step toward the door when he said, "Don't go, Alec. Help me try to figure out a reason why Chisholm should be so anxious to get his hands on Glen Alpin."

Slowly she turned to face him once more. He was still leaning back in his chair, his long legs stretched under the desk. She was surprised to see that he actually looked worried. She said a little unwillingly, "I thought it had something to do with sheep."

"There are plenty of other landlords who would be willing to sell Chisholm land upon which to graze sheep," he replied. He looked directly into her eyes. "Why is he so determined to have Glen Alpin?"

She came around the chair and sat down once again so that she was facing him. "Perhaps the grazing is better in Glen Alpin than it is elsewhere."

He shook his head. "There is good grazing in all of the Western Highlands because of the mildness of the climate and the rainfall."

A little silence fell.

"It *is* strange," she said at last. "Glen Alpin must be very important to him. Not only is he willing to pay you for the land before you can legally turn it over to him, but apparently he is willing to relinquish the Jockey Club claim to Papa's money as well."

"I know. And I cannot understand it."

"Perhaps he wants to keep you from bringing in cattle,"

she suggested. "I know that sheep and cattle can't graze on the same pastures."

He looked at her with interest. "How on earth did you know that?"

"I grew up in the country," she replied with dignity. "In the course of my life, I have managed to acquire some rudimentary knowledge about farming."

He said with approval, "There is more to you, Alec, than I thought there was."

A delighted thrill went through her at that mild compliment. She looked down at the ledger so he would not be able to read her eyes.

He said, "It is true that cattle cannot graze upon sheep pasture because sheep cut the grass almost to the root. Sheep can graze upon cattle pasture, however. I don't think that my bringing in cattle has anything to do with Chisholm's offer."

A comfortable silence fell as they mulled the matter over in their minds. Then Alexandra said, "Perhaps he doesn't want you to bring in cattle for another reason."

"And what reason would that be?"

"Perhaps he thinks it would make him look bad."

He frowned. "I am not following you."

She put one hand on the desk and tapped her forefinger. "You are bringing in cattle so that your clan may stay in Glen Alpin and earn a livelihood, is that not so?"

He nodded. "That is so."

"On the other hand, Chisholm has evicted all of his clansmen and put in sheep."

He nodded once more, his face suddenly grim.

She lifted her hand. "Well, ask yourself, Niall, who looks like the better chief? Him or you?"

For a long time he was silent, looking at her with the same grim face. Then he said. 'You don't understand, Alec.

Chisholm and his ilk have no interest in being chiefs; nor do they care what their fellow Highlanders might think of them. The only people they wish to impress are the Sassenach among whom they have chosen to live. And the Sassenach think that bringing in sheep is an excellent way to 'improve' one's property."

She looked down at her lap, and said quietly, "Niall, why do you say the word *Sassenach* with such hatred? What have the English ever done to harm you?"

She looked up at him again to find him regarding her bleakly. "How can you ask such a question? After Culloden, the English set out quite deliberately to destroy us. Not only did they put to the sword every man woman or child that they could find, but they enacted a series of laws designed to totally obliterate Gaelic culture. Weapons were banned, and the bagpipes, and the wearing of tartan. The chiefs were forced into exile, and the people at home were left leaderless in the face of brutal English repression." His eyes glittered. "Even your own people called the man your king put in charge of the Highlands a 'butcher.'"

"All of that was very terrible, certainly," she agreed. "But it happened a long time ago, Niall."

"Long ago to you, perhaps, but not to us," he replied curtly. "My grandfather was born in France. He did not see his own country until he was twenty-five years of age." His blue eyes were fierce. "My grandfather was not yet born when Culloden was fought, yet the Sassenach forced him to grow up in a foreign land. Is it any wonder that he has no love for the English?"

Very softly, she replied, "Yet his only daughter married an Englishman. You yourself, Niall, are half-English by blood."

"I never think of that," he said. His nostrils were white with tension.

Still softly, she said, "Perhaps you never thought of it before, but you can't ignore it now. It is your English blood that is allowing you to rebuild Glen Alpin." She smiled faintly. "Perhaps that is justice, after all."

He did not smile back. "I was reared a MacDonald, Alec, and that is what I am. I can never turn myself into an English earl. And when a cur like Chisholm tells me that I should sell off my Scottish lands and turn Sassenach, I want to take out my dirk and kill him where he stands."

There was a moment of charged silence. Then Alexandra said quietly, "But you didn't."

At that moment the door opened, and Mason came into the room, a pile of papers in his hand. He stopped when he saw Alexandra. "I am sorry, my lady. I did not realize that you were here."

"Mason and I had an appointment," Niall said.

Alexandra stood up. "I was just leaving, Mason. Please don't go away on my behalf."

Neither she nor Niall said another word to each other as she walked out the door.

At about two in the morning, Alexandra was aroused from sleep by the sound of a door closing. It was so soft a sound that if she had not been sleeping lightly she probably would not have heard it at all.

She sat up in bed and looked toward the door that connected her bedroom to Niall's dressing room, fully expecting to see his tall figure approaching her. She had been half expecting him to try to come in earlier, and she had actually prepared a scorching speech in which she rejected his advances.

The door was closed, and there was no sign of Niall.

Alexandra frowned. Then she sniffed. Was that smoke she smelled?

Suddenly the space in front of the bedroom door that opened on the passageway was a wall of orange flame. Alexandra leaped out of bed and ran for her husband's dressing room. She pushed the door open and cried into the darkness within, "Niall! The bedroom is on fire!"

"Dhé!"

He leaped out of the narrow bed he had been sleeping in and she saw Alan jumping up from his blanket on the floor.

"Shut the dressing-room door," Niall commanded her. "Air will only feed it."

She obeyed him and turned to close the door behind her, at the same time registering with her dark-adjusted eyes that neither man was wearing any clothes.

When she turned back, Niall was fastening a kilt around his bare waist. The dressing-room window was wide-open, and the room was freezing.

Niall said to her, "Go and rouse the servants to bring buckets of water. Alan and I will see what we can do to contain it now."

She hesitated for a moment, and he said forcefully, "Alec, go."

She nodded, went out the corridor door, and ran for the stairs and the servants' quarters.

It seemed forever to Alexandra before half-dressed footmen were racing up the stairs carrying buckets of water. The smell of smoke was acrid in the air. She wanted to follow the men but knew her presence would only be a distraction, so she made certain all of the female staff were accounted for and moved them into the family dining room, where they could evacuate the house quickly if it became necessary.

Footmen ran down and then back up the stairs with buckets of water. One of the upstairs maids was crying.

The smell of smoke was pronounced even in the family dining room.

Dear God, don't let anything happen to him, Alexandra found herself praying. *Please, please don't let anything happen to him.*

When she realized what she was thinking, she almost stopped breathing.

Someone said, "My lady, perhaps we should send to the neighboring farms for help."

Alexandra looked a little dazedly at her housekeeper. "We'll wait until we hear from His Lordship," she said. "I'm sure he will know what to do."

It was five more minutes before one of the footmen brought her a message that the fire was almost out. "His Lordship and Mr. MacDonald were fighting it with wet blankets when we arrived with more water," he reported. "It is a good thing that they were so quick, my lady; otherwise, I fear t'would have spread."

"Can the servants return to their rooms?" she asked.

"Aye, my lady. His Lordship says it is safe."

Alexandra looked at the group of frightened women and girls who were gathered with her in the family dining room. Like herself, they all wore white nightgowns, and their long hair was either loose or plaited. She smiled at them. "You heard James. It is safe to return to your rooms now. Everyone may sleep an hour later tomorrow."

The pretty upstairs maid who had been crying looked at James with stars in her eyes. The young man smiled at her before he turned to leave.

Chattering excitedly among themselves, the women were

slowly making their way to the door that led into the servants part of the house.

"Thank you, my lady," they chorused as they departed. "Good night, my lady."

At last Alexandra was free slowly to make her own way upstairs to the second floor. The tight, frightened feeling in the pit of her stomach had nothing to do with the fire.

I prayed for him. What can that mean?

She knew what it meant as soon as she saw him. He was standing in the passageway in front of his dressing-room door talking to Alan and one of the footmen. Someone had lit a lamp, and in the dim light she saw that he was still wearing a kilt and nothing else.

His face and bare arms and shoulders were smudged and dirty. She thought he looked magnificent.

"Get someone to give you some ice to put on that burn," Niall was saying to the footman, who was holding a towel to his upper arm. "Then cover it with some kind of a salve."

"I will, my lord," the footman replied.

"Are you all right, Roger?" Alexandra heard herself asking.

The young footman turned to her. "Yes, thank you, my lady. It is just a little burn."

Three more footmen came out of the bedroom.

"It's naught but ashes now, my lord," one of them said.

Niall smiled at the men around him. "You did a grand job, lads. Let's all go down to the kitchen and have a dram together."

The men's smoke-blackened faces lit with grins.

Niall's eyes fell upon Alexandra. As the footmen went down the corridor toward the stairs, he said, "You can't sleep in there tonight. Perhaps you had better go back to your old room."

"What started the fire, Niall?" she asked in a voice that shook a little. "I awoke because I thought I heard something, and all of a sudden the door burst into flames."

In the dim light of the passage she saw his face harden.

"What did you hear?" His voice was sharp.

"I thought I heard the door close. I was sleeping lightly, and it woke me."

He regarded her for a moment in silence, as if debating what answer he should give her.

"Was the fire set?" she asked, and this time her voice was steady.

He nodded briefly. "It looks that way. Do you want to talk about this tonight or do you want to wait until tomorrow?"

"Tonight," she replied instantly.

"All right. I must spend a little time with the brave lads who helped to put it out, then I will come to you."

The bottom dropped out of her stomach.

"All right," she managed to reply.

Without another word he turned to go down to the kitchen. She stood in silence and watched him go.

Chapter Sixteen

Alexandra stood alone in the passage and thought that her prayer had been answered. Niall was safe. He was safe and in a short time he would be coming to her bedroom.

She lifted her candle and slowly climbed the stairs to the third floor. The candle's flame was reflected in the windows of the Long Gallery as she traversed it on the way to her old bedroom. She found herself hoping pragmatically that Mrs. Moreton hadn't ordered the bed stripped of its sheets.

At last she had reached the door of her beloved sanctuary. She went inside, lit the lamp on the bedside table, then pulled down the bedcovers. The sheets were still there.

The room was cold, and Alexandra was barefoot and in her nightdress, but she did not want to be in bed when Niall arrived. She went to the wardrobe, opened the door, and looked in. A few of her oldest clothes were still hanging there and she pulled out a dark green riding jacket and put it on over her nightdress. A large chair upholstered in worn moss green velvet faced the fireplace, and she curled up in its familar comfort, tucking her feet under her to warm them up.

She thought about the many times she had sat in this chair, staring at the fire and dreaming of the man she could love. She had thought once before that she had found him, in Nigel Butler, Earl of Ashcroft. She had hoped so hard that he was the one that she had even let herself get engaged to him.

He had been an extremely nice man, and they had had a great deal in common. She had liked his family. She had liked his home. She had liked him.

There had been an uproar of titanic proportions when she called off the wedding. It had been one of the hardest things she had ever done. She had hurt Nigel terribly, and she had not wanted to do that. He did not deserve it.

But she had finally come to the realization that she did not love him, could not love him. She found his kisses to be pleasant, and she supposed his lovemaking would be pleasant also. But something in her knew that pleasant was not good enough. Something in her was waiting for more. Was waiting for Niall.

Her heart had known from the first what her mind had refused to accept. This Scottish stranger was the man for her.

He shouldn't be. He was not of her world, and he had made it clear that he did not want to be of her world. He wanted to go home to Scotland and raise cattle.

He did not want her.

Oh, he wanted her in bed with him. He had made that clear enough. But he did not want her as a wife to live with. She was a Sassenach, an enemy, someone he would never trust.

What to do?

A knock sounded on the bedroom door, and a deep voice said, "Alec?"

She smiled wryly. Her heart turned over at the mere sound of his voice. She had no idea how their marriage might turn out, but now that she had found her man, she had no intention of giving him up without a fight.

"Come in, Niall," she called.

The back of her chair was to the door, but she heard it open. He came up behind her silently, with his hunter's walk, and gave her a brief pat on the head before crossing to the window. He pulled up the blinds and opened the window halfway.

"Isn't it already cold enough in this room?" she said.

"Fresh air is good for you," he replied, and turned to look at her.

He had washed his face and tucked an open-necked white shirt into his kilt. On his bare feet he wore a pair of soft shoes. In the dim light of the single lamp his hair looked perfectly black. The cut on his cheek was in shadow.

He leaned his shoulders against the wall beside the window, and said without preamble, "Someone put an oil-covered rag inside your door along with a few sticks of oil-soaked wood. If you had not awakened so quickly, the whole room would have caught on fire."

She swallowed. It was one thing to suspect that someone had tried to set fire to her room and quite another thing to know that it was true.

"Who would do such a thing?" she almost whispered. "And why?"

His voice was perfectly level as he answered, "I am thinking that someone tried to kill whoever he thought was sleeping in that room."

She stared at him. "Everyone thought that we were both sleeping in that room."

He nodded slowly. She wanted him to gather her into his arms and comfort her, but he didn't move from his station by the window. At last she said, "It doesn't make any sense. There is no reason for anyone to want either of us dead."

He regarded her steadily. "I am thinking there may be a reason for someone to want *me* dead."

She tried to overcome the fear that was lodged like a lump in her chest and think clearly. "Lord Chisholm?" she guessed.

He shook his head. "No, I do not think Chisholm is responsible for the fire. He wants Glen Alpin, true, but there is no advantage to him in killing me. My grandfather is even less likely than I am to sell."

She thought out loud. "If you were dead, then there would be no money to bring cattle into Glen Alpin. Under those circumstances, perhaps your grandfather *would* sell it."

He said curtly, "There are no circumstances under which my grandfather would sell Glen Alpin."

She had already thought of something else. "What about the person who would inherit Glen Alpin if both you and your grandfather died? Perhaps that heir would sell it to Chisholm. Perhaps that is his scheme."

"I can assure you that there is nothing in Glen Alpin that is worth murdering for," Niall said sardonically. "On the other hand, I can name someone right here in England who stands to gain a great deal if something should happen to me."

"And who might that be?" she said in her chilliest voice. She did not like the sarcastic way he had dismissed her theory about Chisholm.

"The man whom I displaced as earl," came the grim reply.

At that, she sat up straight, her bare feet touching the rug in front of her chair. "You can't possibly mean Geoffrey?"

"I surely do mean Geoffrey," he replied in the same grim voice.

"That is a ridiculous suggestion," she snapped. "Geoffrey is not a murderer."

"You would be amazed at what men can do murder for," he replied.

Her feet were cold again and she scrambled so that she was half-kneeling in the chair, with her cold feet tucked under her. "No matter how he might feel about you, Geoffrey would never set fire to a room if he knew that I was in it," she said with the same finality with which he had told her his grandfather would never sell Glen Alpin.

"I think you are right about that," he agreed. "But did Geoffrey know that you would be in that room? Or did he think you would still be sleeping in this room"—he gestured to his present surroundings—"as was our original plan."

For a moment, Alexandra's heart plummeted. Niall was right. She had not let Geoffrey know about the change in plans necessitated by Chisholm's threat.

Then she was furious, furious with Niall for blaming Geoffrey and furious with herself for entertaining for one second the idea that Geoffrey might be guilty.

"It was not Geoffrey!" she said heatedly.

He was still leaning his shoulders against the wall, and he folded his arms across his chest, and said with the same infuriating sarcasm with which he had spoken before, "Well then, perhaps another one of your spurned suitors is the guilty party."

She shot out of her chair and faced him. "Contrary to your belief, the world is not littered with my 'spurned suitors,'" she said. "Furthermore, let me remind you that the only person who has made threats to us is that miserable Chisholm. He, not Geoffrey, is the one who planted a spy in our house." She glared into his inscrutable face. "Speaking of spies, do you happen to know what Harvey was doing when the bedroom was set on fire?"

"I asked. According to the footman who shares a room with him, Harvey was in bed asleep."

A lock of hair that had pulled loose from her bedtime plait drifted across her cheek, and she lifted a hand to push it back. Her feet were like ice. She looked at the open window next to Niall, and said in annoyance, "I wish you would close that window. I am freezing."

"I have a better idea," he returned. "Let me warm you up." And he started to cross the floor in her direction.

Alexandra stood as if she were truly frozen and watched him come. She didn't say a word as his hands gripped her shoulders. She could feel through the thin fabric of her nightgown that he had calluses on his palms.

His face was shadowy in the flickering light of the lamp. His hard, intent face looked like a hawk's, she thought, a hawk that was about to swoop down on its prey.

The last thought she knew before his mouth closed on hers was, *I have waited all my life for this.*

Then all coherent thought stopped.

Niall was surprised when she didn't push him away. He was even more surprised when her lips parted under the pressure of his and her mouth opened to him. She had to know that she couldn't kiss him like that without expecting him to take her to bed.

He moved his hands from her shoulders to her waist. It was so slim, like the stem of a flower. He bent her back a little and caressed her breast with light fingers. He could feel her nipple stand up under the thin cotton of her nightdress.

I shouldn't do this, he thought as he felt her slender body quiver under his touch. *She is frightened about the fire, and I am taking advantage of her. She will be furious in the morning.*

But he knew he wasn't going to stop. He didn't think he could stop. He didn't think he had ever wanted anything as much as he wanted Alexandra right at that minute.

He swung her up into his arms and carried her to the bed. He kissed her as he laid her down, not wanting to give her a chance to change her mind. He undid the buttons on her nightdress as he kissed her, then slid his hand under the soft cotton to touch her bare flesh.

It felt like satin under his rough fingers.

She whimpered, and that little sound was enough to release all of his brakes. He had wanted her from the moment he first saw her, and now that he had her under him all his need was to get inside.

He pulled at her nightdress, trying to get it out of his way. She lifted herself up to help him. When he had it up around her waist, he stopped for a moment, poised above her, and looked down into her face.

He had never seen anything more beautiful in his life.

"All right?" he asked hoarsely.

She nodded. There was a look in her eyes he did not understand, but he was not about to stop and chat with her about her feelings. He raised her hips and plunged.

She cried out sharply.

"*Dhé!*" He heard the shock in his own voice.

He froze, struggling with every ounce of his will to deny the imperative of his body.

Too late, he understood what that look in her eyes had meant.

"Alec, are you all right? Did I hurt you too much?"

"No." Her voice sounded very husky. "I am fine, Niall. Don't worry about me."

Thank God.

Nothing in his life had ever felt as good as this. He tried desperately to move slowly, to court her not to hammer her, and at last he was rewarded by another cry, this time not of pain but of pleasure.

Thank you, Alec, he thought, and allowed himself to find his own release.

He held her close to his thundering heart and thought in surprise, *She has never belonged to anyone else.*

Every cell in his possessive nature thrilled to this thought. He touched his lips to her beautiful hair and whispered, "I am sorry if I hurt you, *m'eudail.*"

Her sleepy voice drifted up to him. "It only hurt a little."

He remembered the sharpness of her cry and knew that she lied.

"It won't hurt like that again, I promise."

He felt her lips touch his bare throat. His reaction was immediate.

I could take her again, he thought in amazement.

"Go to sleep," he told her gently, smoothing the silky hair back from her brow.

"Hold me," she said.

And he did.

When Alexandra woke in the morning, she was alone. She looked at the pillow next to hers where his head had lain and was filled with an intense feeling of loneliness. She wanted him there. He should be there. And he wasn't.

She thought of what had happened between them last night. He had hurt her, true, but he had also given her a pleasure that had been astonishing in its intensity.

He wasn't there. Why hadn't he stayed? Why was he not here to make love to her again, to reassure her that everything was all right between them?

Was everything all right between them? He had been fierce last night, but he had also been tender. What would he be like this morning, now that he had got what he wanted from her?

She longed to see him but was afraid of what she might find in his eyes.

Niall, she thought. *Please please feel about me the way I feel about you.*

She heard the door open and her heart jerked almost painfully.

Meg's voice said, "Are you awake, my lady?"

She waited a moment to compose herself before she replied, "Yes, I am, Meg. Have you brought me some tea?"

"Indeed I have, my lady." Meg looked at the open window, and said disapprovingly, "It is freezing in here, my lady. Shall I close the window?"

Alexandra almost told her maid to leave it open. Somehow closing the window seemed an absurdly final act.

Don't be an idiot, she told herself. "Yes, close it, Meg," she said.

She was glad of the company of her maid. It kept her from thinking too much. They talked of the fire, and Alexandra realized that Meg did not know that it had been set.

It was probably best to keep that a secret, she thought. No sense in alarming the servants unnecessarily.

Meg had brought her a morning dress of pale blue muslin sprinkled with tiny yellow flowers. It had a scoop neck that was lined with lacy white cotton. After it was on, Meg brushed and arranged her hair, which had spilled out of its plait during the passionate encounter of the previous night.

Alexandra regarded herself in the pier glass and was shocked that she looked like the same person she had been yesterday. She did not feel like the same person. Yet there she was, as normal-looking as ever. It was unbelievable that one could be so changed inside yet show no sign of it on one's face.

It was time to leave the security of her room and go downstairs to breakfast.

Would Niall be there? If he looked at her with indifference, she would shrivel up and die.

She heard his voice before she saw him. Her heart began to hammer, but she kept her face serene as she entered the family dining room where her husband was talking with Alan MacDonald.

Both men looked at her as she came in.

"Good morning," she said. A quick glance at Niall's face told her nothing. She went to the side table and filled a plate with food she knew she couldn't eat. Then she looked at the dining table and hesitated.

Niall was sitting in his usual place at the head of the table, with Alan seated on his right. As she stood there indecisively, Niall turned to her, and said, "Come and sit next to me, Alec. We are discussing last night's adventure."

She crossed the floor, detoured behind Niall and his faithful hounds, and sat down.

"Shall I pour you some coffee?" Niall asked.

"Yes, thank you." She couldn't tell anything from his voice and was afraid to look at him.

She watched his hand as he poured coffee into a cup and passed it to her.

Alan said, as if continuing a conversation, "According to Roger, John sleeps like the dead."

She swallowed some coffee. "Who is John?" she asked.

"The footman who shares a room with Harvey," Niall replied.

Her eyes widened and she looked at him. "So that means we can't be certain of Harvey's whereabouts when the fire was set."

He was drinking his coffee and frowning at the empty plate in front of him. "So it seems," he replied.

A little silence fell. Alexandra forced herself to take a tiny bite of her eggs. She said, "Meg did not seem to know that the fire was set. Are we keeping that a secret?"

"I'd like to," he replied.

"I agree," she said. "There is no point in alarming the servants unnecessarily."

He shot her an enigmatic look. "True."

Alexandra had never felt this unsure of herself in her life. Nervously, she took another small bite of the eggs. Her stomach heaved as she forced the food down.

Alan stood up. "Well, I will be on my way then," he said.

"Good," said Niall. "We will meet later."

"Good-bye, my lady," the clansman said politely.

"Good-bye, Alan," she managed to return.

Alan went out, leaving husband and wife alone together.

Niall turned to her and smiled. "So, my lady, how are you feeling this morning?"

All her doubts fled in the radiance of that smile.

"I am very well, thank you," she replied demurely.

"Are you up to sitting on a horse?"

Demureness turned to indignation. "Of course I am!"

"Well then, perhaps you will accompany me on a riding tour of the tenant farms this morning."

"I would be happy to," she replied.

"An hour from now, then, in the stables?"

"Fine," she replied.

He reached over and took the coffee cup out of her hand. Then he raised her fingers to his lips and kissed them. Hard.

"In an hour," he said, stood up, and went out the door.

Chapter Seventeen

Alexandra was at the stables half an hour early in order to discuss with Graham which horse they should give Niall to ride.

"His Lordship rode out on Jacob yesterday morning, my lady," the head groom informed her. "I was thinking to put him on Jacob again today."

Alexandra had not known that Niall had ridden yesterday. However, as Jacob was the exact horse she was going to suggest, she nodded approvingly at Graham and agreed with his choice.

Jacob had been one of her father's horses, a sixteen-year-old bay thoroughbred gelding with impeccable manners and marvelously smooth gaits. Unfortunately, when the groom took Jacob out of his stall to brush him and saddle him up, the gelding was lame.

Graham was irate. "What happened?" he stormed at the hapless groom. "He was fine yesterday when His Lordship brought him back."

"He was shod yesterday afternoon, Mr. Graham," the

groom reminded him. "Could be the farrier caught him with a nail."

Graham stared piercingly at Jacob, who was holding his near front hoof off the ground.

"Get the farrier back here immediately to take that shoe off," he ordered.

"Yes, Mr. Graham. Do you want me to soak the foot in a bucket of water?"

"After the shoe has come off."

While Jacob was being tended to, Alexandra fretted about what horse she should give to Niall. All of the horses in the stable were thoroughbreds and, with the exception of the extremely sensible Jacob, they had the nervous temperaments so characteristic of the breed.

Alexandra loved thoroughbreds for their beauty and great hearts, but they were not the kind of horse one gave to an inexperienced rider.

"Perhaps we ought to give His Lordship Pen," she said to Graham. The dark bay gelding was hanging his head over the bottom part of his door, allowing her to rub his ears. "He is certainly the safest horse in the stable."

"You retired him because he was unsound, my lady," the head groom reminded her. "Put weight on his back, and he'll go lame again."

Alexandra bent her head and kissed the soft black muzzle of the first horse she had ridden that had not been a pony. Then she turned back to Graham and sighed. "What do you think? Have you actually seen His Lordship ride?"

"Only at the walk, my lady. He looked just fine."

"How about Cassandra?" she said, naming one of her own mares.

"She's not big enough," came the ready reply. "And you

know how fussy she becomes if anyone bounces on her back."

They looked at one another.

"I suppose it will have to be Czar," she said resignedly.

"I think so, my lady. He is big enough, and if His Lordship leaves his mouth alone, he should be all right."

Czar had a very effective way of dealing with heavy-handed riders. He bucked them off.

When Niall arrived in the stableyard, he found Alexandra already in the saddle. "*Dhé*," he said as he looked up at the enormous dark red horse that was saddled and waiting for him. "He is even bigger than the one I had yesterday."

"Jacob is sore from yesterday's shoeing, my lord," the groom said politely. "This is Czar."

Alexandra looked at her husband appraisingly. He was dressed appropriately enough in high black boots and a brown riding jacket, but he was eyeing Czar with a definitely dubious expression on his face.

She thought in wonderment, *How can I possibly love a man who doesn't ride?*

The groom said, "I will lead him to the mounting block for you, my lord."

"That won't be necessary. It's not the getting on him that I'm worried about," Niall said humorously. "It's the coming off."

He put his foot into the stirrup and swung up into the saddle. As Czar was almost seventeen hands high, this was not an easy feat. Alexandra felt a little better.

Niall looked down at her as she sat on her under-sixteen-hand dappled gray mare. "You are the rider," he said. "Why aren't you on the big horse?"

She thought of what Portia would do if an inexperienced rider ever sat on her and shuddered.

"Czar is more . . . er . . . tolerant," she said diplomatically. "Portia likes things done the same way all the time."

He picked up his reins. "All right. Let's go."

Alexandra moved first and Czar followed right alongside. His ears were pricked, and he snorted as they left the stable-yard. He recognized an unfamiliar rider on his back and began to jig.

"Ignore the jigging and keep that little loop in your reins," she instructed Niall. "Czar adores Portia and will keep right alongside of her if you don't pull on his mouth."

"All right," he replied.

After they had gone a half a mile, Czar finally decided that he could trust his rider not to hurt his mouth and began to walk normally.

"How much riding have you done?" Alexandra asked her husband as the two horses went side by side along the wide ride that wound through the park.

"I learned to ride on Highland ponies," he replied. "That is all we have in Glen Alpin. I rode full-sized horses a few times while I lived in Edinburgh, but that is all. I have never ridden a horse like this until I rode Jacob yesterday." He flashed her a grin. "It was grand."

"Czar's paces are not quite as smooth as Jacob's, but I think you will find them more comfortable than those of your Highland ponies," she said. "Do you want to trot?"

"Surely."

She tapped Portia with the long whip she carried on the off side of her side saddle and the mare broke into a brisk, forward trot. Czar followed.

To Alexandra's relief, Niall's seat was secure enough for him to hold the reins steadily and not jerk on Czar's mouth. In fact, he sat very well, with his legs hanging under him as if he were standing on the ground.

She complimented him on his seat.

"This is like sitting on a cloud compared to our ponies at home," he said. "And the saddle and stirrups are a help."

She lifted her eyebrows. "You rode bareback?"

"Of course."

"In a kilt?"

He grinned. "You soon learned to sit on your thighs."

As he was doing now, easily following the movement of Czar's trot.

Alexandra began to feel much better.

"How about a canter?"

He nodded enthusiastically.

They went from a canter to a full gallop, the two horses thundering beside each other along the wide ride. When at last they pulled up, Alexandra looked at her husband and laughed.

His eyes were brilliantly blue. His teeth looked very white as he laughed back at her.

"I could get used to horses like these," he said.

"I thought you couldn't ride!"

"Well," he said thoughtfully, "I am thinking that if you can ride a Highland pony bareback over the mountains, then perhaps you can ride anything."

"I am thinking that perhaps you are right," Alexandra replied with a smile.

They had a pleasant and productive morning going from farm to farm and speaking to their tenants. Niall had met most of the farmers before, in the company of Mason, but the welcome he received was far warmer when he came in company with Alexandra.

Niall had been brought up to believe that a chief was a father to his people, not just a landlord, and this was the way he approached his new responsibility as Earl of Hartford. Alexandra watched him in amazement and admiration as he dealt with the people of Gayles. He had exactly the right touch, she thought. His authority was unquestionable, yet he was easy and approachable and genuinely interested in a way she had never seen in any of the men of her own family.

The children looked at him with awe, the women with a certain gleam in their eyes, and the men with respect. Alexandra felt herself falling more in love with every passing minute.

It was a perfect day until, on their way home, a gun went off close by and spooked Czar.

Niall's riding had so impressed her that Alexandra had decided to go home by way of a shortcut she knew, which involved descending a rather steep hill. They arrived at the hill, a limestone outcrop of rock with a narrow path etched into it that the horses could follow. She said, "I'll go first. Wait until I get to the bottom before you start."

Niall nodded that he understood.

Portia picked her dainty way downhill, while Czar snorted in frustration at being left behind. Alexandra reached the bottom of the hill, turned and waved to Niall to follow. Czar started downward.

Suddenly the air was shattered by an explosion of sound.

Czar let out a high piercing whinny and plunged forward on the downward slope, frantic to escape the danger he was certain was threatening him. His hooves slipped on the rock, and he pitched forward onto his knees. The momentum of his huge body caused him to flip over in a complete somersault. He landed heavily on his side, with Niall under him.

Alexandra threw Portia's reins around her neck and raced up the slope to where Czar was struggling to get up. As she reached him, the horse managed to regain his feet. He shook his head and stood still, trembling violently. Alexandra dropped to her knees next to the man on the ground.

"Niall! Are you all right?"

His eyes were closed, and he didn't answer.

She didn't know where he had been hurt and was afraid to touch him. She prayed that he had not smashed his head against the rock. "Niall," she said again, urgently.

His long lashes fluttered, then slowly lifted. He looked at her, and said something in Gaelic.

She thought perhaps he didn't know her. "It's Alec, Niall. Where are you hurt?"

"Everywhere," he grunted.

"Do you want me to go for help?"

"No." He closed his eyes again. "Just let me catch my breath."

Czar decided to join Portia at the bottom of the hill and began to descend cautiously.

Alexandra waited fearfully until Niall's eyes finally opened again. "All right," he said, his voice stronger than it had been before. "Let's see how I am."

She scrambled up. "Take my hand."

He took her hand to steady himself, but he got to his feet on his own power. "I'm all right," he said. "Just bruised and shaken up."

She couldn't believe he had emerged unscathed from such a horrendous fall.

"Are you sure?"

"Yes." He inhaled cautiously, winced in pain and scowled. "Who the devil was shooting so close to us?"

"I don't know. The woods around here belong to Gayles. Someone must have been poaching." She regarded him anxiously. "Do you think you've broken your ribs?"

He shook his head and said, "It's a damn strange place to be poaching."

"Yes," Alexandra agreed. "It is." Anger began to replace the terror that had consumed her when she saw Niall caught under Czar. "I will have Mason make inquiries into this," she said. "I want whoever shot that gun held responsible."

Niall's face was inscrutable. "I doubt if you'll find him. Whoever shot off that gun knew what he was doing. He was most certainly close enough to us to hear us talking."

He began to brush dust and gravel from his clothes.

Alexandra stared at him, struggling to assimilate what he had just said. At last she said incredulously, "Do you think someone was deliberately shooting at you?"

Without answering, he began to walk down the hill toward the horses. She scrambled after him.

"Don't turn away from me," she said furiously to his back. "I asked you a question. Do you think someone was shooting at you?"

"No." He threw the word over his shoulder.

"Well, what *do* you think then?"

Her foot slipped on some loose gravel, and she lost her balance. He heard the noise, turned, and caught her before she fell, pulling her against his chest. She felt him wince as her weight came against his rib cage.

He *had* hurt his ribs, she thought grimly. But she had been warned off once and had enough sense not to say anything else about his injuries. She stepped away from him and looked up into his face.

He returned her look soberly and answered her question. "I don't know what I think, Alec. If it weren't for last night, I would have dismissed the gunshot as an accident. But there are enough suspicious circumstances about that shot to make me wonder. It went off just as Czar was starting down-hill, the worst possible time."

Fear knifed through her. Instinctively, her hand went up to her mouth. "Dear God, Niall," she said. "Dear God." She made an effort to think clearly. "If someone truly wanted to harm you, wouldn't they have just gone ahead and shot you?"

"A death from a fall is an accident," he replied grimly. "A death from a gunshot wound is less easy to explain."

She kept staring at him and didn't answer. Didn't know what to answer.

He turned to continue on down the hill. "Keep behind me so that if you trip again, I can catch you."

She couldn't even summon enough indignation to protest his insulting assumption that she was not surefooted. They descended to the bottom of the hill, retrieved their grazing horses, and returned home far less lighthearted than they had been when they set out.

As she walked in the back door of Gayles, Stokes met Alexandra with the news that Geoffrey had called to see her.

Alexandra stared at her butler in dismay. "Mr. Wilton is here?"

"Yes, my lady, in the Blue Drawing Room."

"How long has he been here, Stokes?"

"He arrived a few minutes ago, my lady."

At that reply, a distinctly nasty shock jolted through Alexandra.

"I see," she said impassively. She stripped off her tan-leather riding gloves as she went toward the Blue Drawing Room. Geoffrey was sitting on the sofa under the great ta-pestry, but he leaped to his feet when he saw her and came across the floor to greet her.

"Alex!" He smiled a little nervously. "I know you said to stay away from Gayles, but I was in the neighborhood and I thought I would just stop by to say hello."

She looked somberly into the fair-skinned face of her cousin and friend and could not bring herself to believe that he was capable of harming anyone. He had just come to check up on her.

She folded her arms across her chest and did not return his smile. "Exactly what is it that brought you into this neighborhood, Geoff?" she asked ominously.

He hesitated, started to reply, then stopped. "Well," he said at last, with a charmingly contrite look. "You did."

Alexandra was thinking hard. *I have to get Geoffrey away from Gayles before Niall finds out he's here,* she decided. *He is sure to take Geoff's presence as proof that he was the gunman on the hill.*

She said implacably, "Well now that you have seen me, you can go away again. Immediately."

He started to protest, but she overrode him. "How did you get here? By hack or by carriage?"

"I rode," he replied a little sulkily.

"Where is your horse?"

"At the stable, of course."

It might be all right, she thought. She could ask Stokes not to mention Geoffrey's visit to Niall, and there was certainly no reason for any of the grooms to mention it. If she could only get Geoffrey away immediately, all might be well.

"I want you to leave here right away," she instructed Geoffrey in a no-nonsense tone. "Go down to the stables, collect your horse, go home to Highgate, and do not come back. Do I make myself clear?"

A lethally pleasant voice said from behind her, "I will be happy to second that request, *m'eudail*."

She shut her eyes. Too late. He was here.

She half turned toward her husband, and said, "Geoffrey called to say hello, Niall. He is just leaving."

Niall came into the room and she noticed immediately that his always fluid stride was stiffer than usual. With the ugly scratch on his cheek and his dirt-stained riding clothes and scuffed-up boots, he was a complete contrast to Geoffrey's immaculate elegance. Yet of the two, it was Niall who dominated the room.

He stopped beside her and fixed Geoffrey with a dangerous blue stare. "Where were you about forty minutes ago?" he asked in a voice that was as dangerous as his eyes.

Geoffrey looked courageously back. "I was riding here from Highgate," he said in a voice that was pitched slightly higher than usual. "Not that it is any of your business."

"Can you prove that?" Niall said. "Did someone see you?"

"My mother saw me leave," Geoffrey replied. He looked at Alexandra. "Why should I have to prove such a thing anyway?"

Alexandra said hastily, "No reason at all, Geoff."

But Niall was relentless. "How about last night? Can you tell me where you were last night?"

By now Geoffrey was getting angry. "I was at home," he said huffily.

"All night?"

"I say, what is going on here?" Geoffrey demanded. "Why are you cross-examining me like this?"

Through the French doors Alexandra could see a gardener moving about on the terrace, watering the plants.

Niall answered Geoffrey's question. "We had a fire last

night." He was standing next to Alexandra, and he raised his hand and rested it on the bare nape of her neck. "In our bedroom."

At those words, Geoffrey went so white that she was afraid he was going to faint. She tried to move away from Niall, but his hand on her neck tightened and held her where she was.

"What bedroom was that?" Geoffrey said in a strangled voice.

"The bedroom in the earl's apartment, of course," Niall replied. "Fortunately, Alexandra woke me in time and we put it out."

He was deliberately making it sound as if the two of them had been sharing the earl's bedroom, Alexandra thought with annoyance. She intervened with a quick explanation. "I had to move into the earl's apartment, Geoff. Lord Chisholm threatened to claim in court that our marriage was a fraud and that Papa's money should go to the Jockey Club. You can understand that we had to be careful not to give him any evidence that would back up his claim."

She was terribly conscious of the feel of Niall's hard hand on the softness of her unprotected nape. He was standing so close to her that she could feel the heat from his body. She knew what he was doing, knew he was showing Geoffrey that he was the man in possession, and she also knew that she ought to be angry with him for such chauvinistic behavior. However, the fact of the matter was that she wanted to turn into his arms and kiss him passionately.

Geoffrey stared at Niall, and Alexandra was shocked at what she saw for a moment in his eyes.

Niall said, "I don't want you anywhere in the vicinity of this house, Wilton. I don't want you on my land."

Geoffrey's face went from white to fiery red, and he looked to Alexandra for support.

She said softly, "I'm sorry, Geoff, but Niall is right. It would be best for you if you stayed away from Gayles. Go to London. Please."

Geoffrey opened his lips, as if he was going to answer, then closed them again. Without another word, he turned and walked steadily out the door.

As soon as Geoffrey was gone, Alexandra pulled away from Niall. She swung around to face him and said, "He didn't know anything about the fire! You saw how horrified he looked when you mentioned it."

"What horrified him was the discovery that *you* were sleeping in that bedroom," Niall replied grimly. "He thought you were safe somewhere else."

She accused him, "You deliberately led him to believe that we were *both* in that bedroom. That is really why Geoffrey looked the way he did. He thought we were sleeping together. And we weren't!"

"We weren't," he agreed. His voice deepened, and his eyes narrowed and turned an even darker blue. "Then."

At the look in his eyes, an urgent pulse began to throb between her legs. She put her hand up to her throat, as if she needed air. She didn't know what to say.

He bent his dark head and kissed her mouth.

The pulse throbbed more strongly.

He lifted his head and looked into her eyes, his face hard and concentrated. He said just one word: "*Tonight*." Then he left her alone.

Chapter Eighteen

The fire in the earl's bedroom had been contained, but at least two of the priceless Flemish tapestries were irrevocably damaged. The entire apartment reeked of smoke, rendering it uninhabitable. Alexandra instructed her housekeeper to move Niall's belongings from his dressing room into the bedroom across the gallery from hers. It would be a few days at least until they could use the earl's apartment again.

The sky had become progressively more overcast as the day went on, and that evening, as Alexandra prepared for bed, she could hear the sound of rain beating against the window glass.

"The farmers will be glad of the rain," she said to Meg as she sat at her dressing table while her maid brushed her hair. "It has been unusually dry this spring."

"That is so, my lady," Meg returned. She put the silver brush down and deftly began to plait the long silky mass of Alexandra's hair into a single braid. She secured the braid with a pink ribbon, and said, "Will there be anything else, my lady?"

"No, Meg, thank you. I will see you in the morning."

"Good night, then, my lady."

"Good night, Meg."

After the door closed behind her maid, Alexandra went to stand in front of the cozy fire that was burning in her pretty white-wood fireplace. She looked at the leaping flames and thought contentedly how snug and secure her room was in contrast to the chill rain that was pouring down outside. She curled up in the comfortable chair that faced the fireplace, wrapped her velvet robe around her, and prepared to wait for Niall.

Half an hour later, he came. As she heard the door behind her open, her lips curled, and she smiled into the flames.

He said, an incredulous note in his voice, "A fire? Are you ill?"

Alexandra's smile disappeared. She turned her head to glare at her husband, who was standing in front of the closed door wearing only an open-necked white evening shirt and black trousers.

She said with asperity, "Perhaps you haven't noticed, but it is raining out. This room was damp and chilly before the fire was lit, and now it is cozy and warm."

"It's stifling in here," he grumbled, went to the window on the side of the house where the wind wasn't blowing, and opened it.

Alexandra jumped to her feet. "Niall MacDonald, shut that window instantly. This is my room, and I feel the cold."

"You have the fire to keep you warm," he pointed out reasonably.

"Yes, and now that you have opened the window, the fire is dragging a freezing cold draft right across the room onto me," she retorted. To make her point more emphatically, she crossed her arms over her chest and shivered.

He looked puzzled. "Are you truly cold, Alec?"

"Yes," she said. "I am."

She waited to see what he would do.

Still looking puzzled, he turned back to the window and closed it.

"Thank you, Niall," she said, and this time her voice was very soft.

He came across the floor to where she was standing next to the chair, picked her up in his arms, and carried her to the bed. He laid her down and stood there for a moment, looking at her. In a voice so deep and dark it made her shiver, he said, "You may be a frail little Sassenach, but, *Dhé*, you are beautiful."

He leaned over her and kissed her.

It was a lover's kiss, passionate but sweet, asking for her surrender, not demanding it. He put one knee on the bed beside her and his hands cupped her face as delicately as if he were holding a flower. Alexandra circled his wrists with her fingers, feeling the tensile strength that was being so gentle with her, and yielded to him.

He took her mouth, surging into her with his tongue, and she opened her lips and let him come. His big body came down next to hers in the bed and she turned to him, stretching out so she could feel him against every inch of her. A delicious throbbing began to spread through her loins.

She made no complaint about the cold when he removed her robe. She didn't even make any complaint when he removed her nightgown. If the room was chilly, she didn't feel it, nor did she hear the rain beating against the window. All she felt was the heat radiating from Niall's body, and the heat rising within her own.

Moment by moment, touch by touch, he built her need for him until it was of such urgency that she couldn't stand it, and her hips lifted, a wordless offering of her sheathing place. A hot drenching swell of sensation surged through her when he entered her, causing her to lift herself even more so he could come in deeper.

He groaned and said something in Gaelic.

She couldn't believe the intensity of the sensations she was feeling. She locked her arms around his neck and hung on to him, surrendering to him, letting him do what he wanted to do, feeling him inside of her, stretching her, giving her such an intense mounting pleasure that she thought she would scream if the culimination didn't happen soon.

Then, at last, she reached it, the climax moving up through her, its fiercely explosive pleasure causing her whole body to convulse violently, again and again and again.

When it was over, he didn't move, nor did she. She lay pressed against him listening to the thunder of his heartbeat as it gradually slowed. She felt his lips on her hair. At last he said, his voice huskier than usual, "Did I hurt you this time?"

She shook her head, which was buried in his shoulder. "No."

He let out a long breath, and his heartbeat slowed a little more.

"Alec," he said, "that was amazing."

She pulled back a little so she could look up into his face. What she saw there reassured her, and her lips curved in a slow, satisfied smile.

In the light of the bedside lamp, his eyes looked almost black. "Ach," he said, running a gentle finger along the curve of her neck where it connected with her shoulder.

"Look what I have done. My beard has made your lovely soft skin all red."

"I don't mind," she said.

He smiled down at her. "You are too good to be true."

I love you, she thought as she gazed up into the eagle face that was poised over hers. *That's why I don't mind, Niall. I love you.*

She wanted to speak the words out loud, but some instinct told her not to. She said instead, "It isn't always like this?"

The smile disappeared from his lips, leaving him with an expression that was almost severe. "No," he said. "It is not always like this."

"I'm glad," she whispered, and once more snuggled her head into his shoulder.

She fell asleep and dreamed she was making love to Niall in a meadow of sweet-smelling grass. She felt the thrilling tension beginning to swell in her loins and she whimpered a little and opened her eyes.

He was there beside her and his hand was caressing her.

"Alec?" he whispered. "Are you awake?"

The room was redolent with the smell of wet grass. The sound of the rain had stopped.

"Did you open that window?" she whispered back.

"It was stuffy in here." His mouth descended onto hers, pressing her head back into the pillow.

Her body arched up, responding to the urgency she felt in his kiss. His fingers touched her and a spasm of intense pleasure washed through her. She whimpered once more.

Then he was entering her again. He felt so good inside her, so right, the only thing capable of releasing her from the fierce, throbbing need that was making all her pulses pound. He drove into her, again and again, until at last the unbearable tension peaked and shattered and the excruciating plea-sure of climax rolled through her once more.

When she woke again, he was no longer beside her. She opened her eyes and saw him standing at one of the win-dows, which had been opened to admit the early-morning air and light. He was naked except for the black evening trousers he had pulled on, but he did not appear to be at all cold. He stood looking out the window for what seemed to her a very long time. Finally, he turned and came back to the bed, stooping to retrieve his shirt from the floor beside it.

The same instinct that had caused her to hold her tongue last night caused her to close her eyes, lie still, and pretend to be asleep. For a long time she felt him looking at her. Then he touched a lock of her hair. It was a gossamer touch, as gentle as the kiss of an angel. A moment later she heard the bedroom door close.

Alexandra opened her eyes and stared at the door. In the midst of last night's passion they had neither of them said a word about love. But she could still feel the gentle touch of his hand on her hair, and suddenly she was very happy.

They had three days of comfortable companionship and three nights of increasingly erotic passion. Alexandra had not known it was possible to be so happy. She had not known it was possible to love someone as much as she loved Niall.

On the fourth day, Niall received a visit from James Tay-lor, who came to Gayles accompanied once again by Lord Chisholm. Stokes hurried to inform Alexandra of this visit the moment she came into the house, telling her that the two men were presently closeted in the library with His Lord-ship. Alexandra went to join them.

When she reached the second floor, the smell of smoke

from the fire assaulted her nose. The stench had spread and could be detected even in the Great Chamber. She wrinkled her nose in disgust and crossed the chamber to the library. The door had been left open a crack and she paused for a moment, listening as Niall said sarcastically, "What precisely has brought about this miraculous change of heart?"

"Apparently I don't have a case," Chisholm returned. "It seems you have been successful in getting the lady into your bed."

Alexandra stiffened in anger and reached out a hand to push the door all the way open.

Niall's voice hardened, "May I ask how you reached that particular conclusion?"

Alexandra had the sudden conviction that the men would speak more frankly if she was not present, so she dropped her hand and prepared to listen shamelessly from the other side of the door.

"It doesn't matter how I know, what matters is that I am going to relinquish the Jockey Club's claim to the inheritance," Chisholm said. "Congratulations, MacDonald. She is a famous beauty."

Niall said in the same hard voice, "Why did you bring him here?"

James Taylor replied, "I thought it might be wise to have Lord Chisholm's release in writing, my lord. And I thought you might wish to witness it."

Hallelujah, Alexandra thought in triumph. *We have won.*

Niall said coldly, "Very well."

"I have taken the liberty of drawing up a document," Taylor said. "It states that you, my lord, swear that you and Her Ladyship have fulfilled the terms of the late Lord Hartford's will. Lord Chisholm will then state that, in consequence of your marriage, the Jockey Club has relinquished all claim to Lord Hartford's money."

"Let me read the document," Niall said.

Silence fell. On the other side of the door, Alexandra had a smile on her face.

Then, "Do I sign it here?" Niall said.

"Yes, my lord."

Another short silence. Alexandra didn't move.

"Now, Lord Chisholm," Taylor said. "If you would sign here, please."

After a moment there was a rustling sound, as if a paper were being folded. Then Chisholm said, "Congratulations, MacDonald. As well as an earl's title, you have wealth and the most sought after woman in England as your wife. Surely you cannot intend to return to Scotland now."

"Why would you think that?" Niall said. There was no discernible emotion in his level voice.

Chisolm's laugh sounded forced. "The answer to that is obvious, I should think. You have everything a man can desire right here in England: power; money; a beautiful woman. You have no reason to return to a poverty-stricken glen in Scotland."

"I have the best reason in the world," Niall returned in the same level voice as before. "Glen Alpin is my home."

"You can't mean that." Chisholm sounded incredulous. "You cannot seriously imagine Lady Alexandra Wilton living in a place like Glen Alpin?"

Alexandra stopped breathing, waiting for Niall's answer.

"My wife will remain at Gayles, but I have every intention of returning to Scotland," he said.

Slowly, the happiness that had filled Alexandra for the previous three days began to drain away.

Chisholm said, "Be sensible, MacDonald, and sell Glen

Alpin to me. It can only be a nuisance to you. I promise I will not try to take possession while your grandfather lives."

A little silence fell before Niall replied slowly, "I cannot help but wonder why you want this poverty-stricken glen so badly."

"I have already told you why I want it." Chisholm sounded impatient. "I want to run more sheep, and Glen Alpin is contiguous to my own lands."

"And I have already told you that there are other glens with chiefs more willing to take your silver than I am," Niall replied. "I repeat: Why are you so insistent on acquiring Glen Alpin?"

Alexandra listened intently for Chisholm's answer to this key question.

"I *will* go elsewhere if you refuse my offer this time," Chisholm said. "But you will be a fool if you do that, Mac-Donald—or *Hartford*, as I suppose I should call you now. Let me say again that I understand that you can do nothing while your grandfather is still alive. All I ask is that you agree to sell to me after he is dead."

Niall said, "I have no intention of selling my Scottish lands."

Chisholm burst out angrily, "Damn it, man, don't you understand? With the title and the wife that you have, you can be one of the most important men in England. You are no longer just the impoverished heir to an impoverished Highland chiefdom. You are an earl! You don't ever need to go back to Glen Alpin."

Niall said with icy contempt, "It is impossible to explain my feelings to such a one as you. Get out of my sight, you traitor to your own people."

There was a moment of silence. Then Chisholm said, "You are a fool, MacDonald."

Niall spoke some words in Gaelic, and Alexandra could hear the sharp intake of Chisholm's breath. Then Niall said in English, "The ghost of my grandfather will never return to see strangers in Glen Alpin, Chisholm. I will make very sure of that."

Taylor said hastily, "I think it's time we were going," and at those words Alexandra turned away from the library door.

She crossed the Great Chamber on silent feet and mounted the stairs to the next floor. A chambermaid was dusting the furniture in her room, and Alexandra sent her away. As soon as the door had closed behind the maid, she went to stand at the window, with her forehead pressed against the glass.

The ghost of my grandfather will never return to see strangers in Glen Alpin. The words reverberated again and again in her mind. He was going home, and he was going without her.

Why?

She thought of all the passion and tenderness that had passed between them these last few days, and she didn't understand. Did he perhaps think she wouldn't want to go to Scotland with him?

She had always understood that Niall could never live permanently at Gayles. The essence of the man was completely different from that of anyone else she had ever known, and she knew that this was because he was a Highlander. Whatever it was that bound him to that wild and beautiful land up north, it was what made him the person he was. And that person was the man she loved.

She had always thought that she would know her true love by her willingness to leave Gayles for his sake. And she knew now, as she felt the cold glass of the window that looked out upon Gayles's beauty pressing upon her forehead, she knew that, if necessary, she would follow Niall MacDonald to the ends of the earth. Where she lived did not matter. What mattered was that she lived with him.

So, she thought, *it is clear what I must do. I must convince Niall of my desire to go with him. I must convince him that I am willing to make a life for us both in Glen Alpin.*

Alexandra straightened to her full height and lifted her chin. She thought that she had a good chance to accomplish her goal—and not because of Niall's obvious desire for her body, but because of the gentle way he had touched her hair.

Chapter Nineteen

The following morning Niall and Alexandra were breakfasting together when Niall received a note from Mr. Coke of Holkham informing him that Coke had visiting him a man who might be willing to sell Niall some of his North Devon cattle. Coke suggested that Niall come to Holkham as soon as possible in order to speak to this cattle owner personally.

A delighted Niall decided to leave immediately.

Alexandra asked, "Would you like me to come with you?"

He looked at her, surprise stamped all over his face. "You would be bored to death talking about cattle, Alec. And I won't be away for long."

Alexandra struggled not to show how hurt she was by his dismissal. Instead she forced herself to smile, and say lightly, "I'll miss you."

He gave her an abstracted smile in return, finished the coffee in his cup, and stood up. "If you don't mind, I'll need to have a few words with Mason before I leave."

"Of course I don't mind," she replied steadily, and held up her face as he passed by her chair. He kissed her cheek lightly and said, "I'll let you know when to expect me back."

Then he walked out of the room. An hour later he was gone, driving the curricle; he didn't even take one of the grooms along to look after the horses.

Instead of dwelling upon the emptiness that his going had left in her heart, Alexandra decided she would embark upon her campaign to get Niall to take her with him to Glen Alpin by exerting herself to charm his foster brother. She sensed that Alan did not like her, and Alan had influence with Niall. So Alexandra decided it would be smart to change Alan from her enemy into her friend.

On the morning after Niall's departure, she caught up with Alan in the garden. "Do you mind if I walk with you and the dogs?" she asked with her best smile.

Not a muscle moved in Alan's narrow, Celtic face. "Of course not, Lady Alexandra," he replied.

She fell into step beside him and lifted her face to the warmth of the morning sun. "Such a lovely day."

"Aye."

Fergus came over to Alexandra, and she held out her hand for him to sniff. He gave her a friendly lick, and she laughed and stroked his magnificent head. Then he trotted off to join his sister, who was farther down the path.

"I think Fergus is beginning to like me," Alexandra said.

"Aye," said Alan.

"Flora, on the other hand, appears to regard me as a rival for Niall's attention."

This time Alan varied his reply. "That is so."

Flora is not the only one who is jealous of Niall's attention, Alexandra thought with a flash of irritation. It was the only explanation she could think of to account for Alan's distinctly unfriendly behavior.

She redoubled her efforts to charm. "Tell me, Alan, is Glen Alpin very beautiful?"

"Aye," Alan replied. "It is beautiful indeed."

"And the house?" she persisted. "Eilean Darrach? Is that beautiful also?"

"Aye. Very beautiful."

"Do you live at Eilean Darrach?"

He shook his head. "I am having a house to myself, with twenty acres to farm." For the first time, a recognizable emotion sounded in his voice. "The land has been in my family forever."

Alexandra tried to capitalize on the pride she heard in his voice. "Twenty acres," she said admiringly. "That must be one of the largest farms in Glen Alpin."

He shot her a scornful look, not at all taken in by her flattery. "It is large for Glen Alpin, but small in comparison to the farms here at Gayles."

Alexandra sighed and gave up on flattery. "I am not trying to patronize you, Alan," she said quietly. "I am just trying to be friendly."

He shot her a suspicious look and did not reply.

Good God, Alexandra thought in horror. *Does he think I am trying to seduce him?*

"I love Niall very much, you see," she said hurriedly. "And I would like to be friends with his foster brother." And she gave him a dazzling smile, the smile that had been known to bring strong men to their knees.

The dogs had gotten out of their sight and Alan whistled to them. In a moment they came cantering into view. His face was completely shuttered, as he said, "It takes deeds to make a friend, not just words."

Alexandra felt as if she had been slapped in the face. She slowed her steps and let him walk on without her. Standing there on the garden path, looking after Alan's slender back, she thought, *I hope to God not everyone in Glen Alpin is like that.*

On Friday, after Niall had been gone for two days, Alexandra received a letter informing her that he would be back at Gayles on Saturday. The missive was most unloverlike:

> *My Dear Alec, I have had a very successful visit here at Holkham. I managed to buy twenty-five head of cattle from this North Devon farmer Coke knows. Tell Alan the good news. I plan to be back at Gayles sometime Saturday afternoon. Your Husband, Niall MacDonald*

Alexandra read the letter over three times, trying to extract something personal from it.

He had called her *Alec*, she thought. That was something. And he had signed himself *Your Husband.*

Still, it was a most unsatisfactory letter.

He could have said he missed her.

Perhaps he didn't miss her, though. Perhaps he was so caught up in the purchase of his beloved cattle that he hadn't even noticed her absence.

This is ridiculous, she scolded herself as she sat over luncheon with Niall's letter in her hand. *I am acting like Flora, whining for a crumb of his attention.*

Have some pride, Alexandra, she continued to admonish herself as she refolded the note. *You will see him tomorrow. He may not be very loverlike in his letters, but you know that there is one way he is not indifferent to you.*

She saw his face in her mind's eye, his blue eyes narrow with passion, and her breath began to hurry.

"My lady." It was her housekeeper. "I am sorry to disturb your luncheon, but may I speak to you when you are finished?"

"Certainly," Alexandra replied, looking with surprise at Mrs. Moreton's grim face. She stood up. "I am finished now. Shall we go into my office?"

"Thank you, my lady."

Alexandra led the way to the small, pretty room where she attended to household affairs. As soon as the door had been closed behind them, the housekeeper said, "The problem is Maria, one of the chambermaids, my lady. I have discovered that she is increasing."

"Oh dear," Alexandra replied. Maria was a very pretty girl with luxuriant brown hair and big brown eyes.

"I have come to you because I thought you should know that the man responsible is one of our own footmen." Mrs. Moreton's lips pinched together as she contemplated in disgust the thought of this sinful duo cohabiting under her own roof.

Alexandra had a sudden memory of the starry-eyed look Maria had cast at one of the footmen on the night of the fire.

"Is it James?" she asked.

Mrs. Moreton looked astonished. "Why, yes, my lady. It is."

Alexandra sighed. "How did you discover Maria's condition?"

"She has been ill in the mornings." Mrs. Moreton's lips tightened even more. "I confronted her with my suspicions, and she confessed."

Alexandra understood that the housekeeper fully expected her to dismiss Maria. Nor was Mrs. Moreton's an unreasonable expectation. It was standard practice in most great houses to summarily dismiss a female servant who was found to be with child.

Alexandra herself had had personal experience of this practice. When she was thirteen years old, one of the upstairs maids, a pretty, lively girl whom Alexandra had liked very much, was discovered to be increasing, and Alexandra's mother had discharged her on the spot. Alexandra could still remember the look of stark terror on the maid's face as she was escorted down the back stairs, carrying her meager belongings in a pillowcase.

It had not taken Alexandra long to find out what the entire household already knew: The man responsible for the unwanted child was Alexandra's father.

For a long time Alexandra had had nightmares about the terrible things that might be happening to her baby half brother or sister.

So now she looked at her housekeeper's pinched face, and said crisply, "Have Maria and James come to see me."

The housekeeper gave a satisfied smile. "Immediately, my lady?"

"Immediately. I will wait for them here in the office."

"Certainly, my lady," said Mrs. Moreton, whose title of *Mrs.* was one of courtesy as she had never been married.

While she waited, Alexandra looked out the window at the rain pooling on the terrace and thought about how best to deal with this situation.

Maria appeared in the office doorway first. In a subdued voice, she said, "You wished to see me, my lady?"

"Yes, Maria," Alexandra said pleasantly. "Come in."

She looked at Maria's reddened eyes as the maid stepped timidly forward. It was obvious that she had been crying.

Alexandra said, "Mrs. Moreton tells me that you find yourself in some trouble."

The girl's full lower lip quivered. "Y . . . yes, my lady."

"And the father of your child is James?"

The lip quivered even more. Maria nodded.

"Do you love him, Maria?" Alexandra asked gently.

The great brown eyes swam with tears. "Oh yes, my lady. I do!"

A male voice said, "Did you wish to see me, my lady?"

Alexandra looked at the door. "Yes, come in, James."

The young footman was very pale, but Alexandra noted approvingly that he came to stand right next to Maria. She looked up at him, and whispered, "I'm sorry, James."

He took her hand into his. "Don't be daft, lass." He met Alexandra's eyes, and said steadily, "This is my fault, my lady, not Maria's. I took advantage of her affection for me."

Alexandra replied, "I am glad to hear you taking responsibility, James."

"It wasn't just James," Maria said shakily.

"I realize that, Maria," Alexandra returned with humor. "It takes two people to make a baby."

The boy and girl, who were about her own age, looked at the ground.

Outside the rain continued to pour down.

"Well, I suppose we shall just have to get you married," Alexandra said.

Two pairs of eyes jerked up.

"Married?" James said.

"Don't you want to marry Maria?" Alexandra asked.

"Of course I do, my lady, but . . ." His voice trailed away.

Alexandra waited. "Well?"

Maria blurted, "Are you going to dismiss us, my lady?"

"If I did that, how would you support the baby?" Alexandra asked practically.

Their faces told her that they didn't know the answer to that question. Maria cupped her hand protectively over her stomach and moved a little closer to James.

Alexandra said, "Nanny's cottage has been empty since she died last year. You can live there."

The boy and girl looked thunderstruck.

Then James said incredulously, "Do you mean to let us live in Mrs. Petrie's cottage, my lady?"

"I believe that is what I just said," Alexandra replied. "James will continue with his employment here, but Maria will have to stay at home." She raised an eyebrow. "I'm afraid that Mrs. Moreton would be scandalized if I let you keep your position, Maria."

The two criminals were looking at her dazedly.

She concluded, "I will tell Mr. Mason to raise your wages, James, now that you are to be a family man."

Maria started to cry.

James said, "My lady . . . I don't know how to thank you . . ."

Alexandra shook her head. "Take the rest of the day off and go to look at the cottage. It hasn't been opened up in over a year and it may be in need of some repairs. If it is, let Mr. Mason know and he will see that they are taken care of."

Maria smiled radiantly through her tears.

James opened his mouth, and Alexandra said, "There is no need to thank me again. Go along, and I will deal with Mrs. Moreton." She waved them to the door.

I hope this does not start a trend among the younger servants, she thought with rueful amusement as the young couple went out. *If it does, all the cottages we have built for our retired servants will end up being filled by growing families.*

* * *

Left alone in the study, Alexandra decided that the rainy day was a perfect opportunity for her to catch up on her household accounts. She spent the next few hours at her desk, entering the amounts she had paid for a variety of household items, from flour and sugar for the kitchen, to oil for the lamps, to coal for the fires and the kitchen stove. She was just entering the last bill when Stokes came hurriedly into the room, and said, "My lady, I regret to inform you that His Lordship has apparently been in a carriage accident."

Alexandra's heart leaped into her throat, and she jumped to her feet. "Is he all right?"

"James came upon his curricle overturned in a ditch on the river road," Stokes replied. "His Lordship was lying unconscious next to it."

"But he was alive?"

"Yes, my lady."

Alexandra closed her eyes. *Thank you, God.*

She opened her eyes again, and said, "Send someone for Dr. Adams immediately. Where is James?"

"Waiting at the back door, my lady."

As Alexandra hurried toward the back of the house, she kept thinking, *I should have gone with him. I knew he shouldn't drive that curricle. He was lucky the last time, but he really doesn't know how to drive. I should have gone with him.*

A rain-sodden James was standing just inside the back door.

"What happened, James?" she demanded.

"I didn't see the accident happen, my lady, but I heard it." Water dripped from James's hair onto his nose and he wiped it away. "Maria and I were coming from the cottage when we heard a crashing sound and then the scream of horses.

We raced down the road, around the turn by the mill, and we saw His Lordship's curricle lying on its side in the ditch. The horses were struggling to get to their feet but they were all tangled up in the harness. Maria and I ran to see what we could do, and we found His Lordship lying unconscious at a little distance from the curricle. I told Maria to stay with him while I ran for help. I left her the umbrella so she could keep the rain off him."

The river road was the road Niall would have traveled on his way back from Norfolk.

"You're sure he was alive?" Alexandra said urgently.

"Aye, my lady. He was breathing."

Alexandra forced herself to think logically. "We will need a carriage to bring him home."

"I have already sent John to the stables to have a carriage made ready, my lady," James said reassuringly. "He and I will bring His Lordship back home."

"I'm going with you," Alexandra said.

He gestured to his drenched clothing. "It is raining hard, my lady."

She ignored this comment. "Was His Lordship bleeding?"

"Not that I could see, my lady. But I did not examine him too closely. I thought it was more important to go for help."

Alexandra nodded, and said, "Let us go down to the stables and see if the carriage is ready."

Stokes came up to her carrying a cloak, which she took from him. She flung it around her shoulders and, followed by James, went out into the rain.

By the time they reached the stableyard, a horse had been hitched to the fourgon, the carriage that was primarily used to transport baggage whenever the family traveled. Its flat bed would make transporting an injured man relatively easy.

When Graham saw Alexandra, he came out of the shelter

of the stable to tell her that a groom had ridden off ten minutes earlier for the doctor.

Alexandra nodded, walked to the fourgon, lifted her skirt, and stepped up into the front seat, which had a folding hood open to protect her from the rain. "Get in," she said to James as she picked up the reins.

"Ye had better take another lad in case His Lordship needs to be lifted," Graham said.

Alexandra, who had been at the point of driving off, lowered her hands.

At this moment, Alan MacDonald came pounding into the stableyard. "They told me Niall was hurt," he said to Alexandra.

"Get in," she replied tersely.

A pale and rain-drenched Alan scrambled up into the front seat next to James. Alexandra lifted the reins, and the gray horse moved off. In a moment Alexandra had put him into a canter.

Why was he coming home today? Alexandra thought as she urged the gray onward. *He wrote me he was coming tomorrow.* And then once again she sent up a prayer: *Please, God, let him be all right. Don't let him be dead. Please, please, please, I'll do anything You want, but let him be all right.*

Chapter Twenty

Niall! Niall!"

Someone was calling his name.

He struggled to fight clear of the fog of darkness that enveloped him.

"Niall, can you hear me, darling? Try to open your eyes."

The voice was speaking English, and he recognized it now. It was Alec.

He tried harder to push his way up through the darkness. Concentrating with painful intensity, he opened his eyes.

She was kneeling over him, and he could smell the fragrance of her hair.

His head hurt like hell.

A voice said in Gaelic, "Are you all right, Niall? What happened?"

It was Alan.

He struggled to remember. He had been driving the curricle and then . . .

He frowned. "My head hurts," he said to Alec.

"You must have struck your head when you landed in the ditch," she replied. "Do you hurt anywhere else?"

He moved a little and grunted in pain.

"Don't worry, we're going to get you home, darling," she said.

For the first time he realized that it was raining and someone was holding an umbrella over him. He could hear the rain thudding on it.

"Ailein," he said in Gaelic, "I am thinking you had better stay with me."

The grim set of his foster brother's face told him that Alan had understood.

"Help me get up," he said, and Alan squatted next to him and put a bracing arm around his waist.

Alec said something in a distressed voice, but Niall was working too fiercely to gain his feet to hear her words.

Pain knifed through him as Alan boosted him to his feet. He would have fallen if Alan had not been holding him up.

"What is it? Your ribs?" Alan asked.

He nodded. He had broken his ribs before and knew what it felt like. He was no longer sheltered by the umbrella, and the rain beat steadily on his bare head. He tried to breathe shallowly to spare his ribs.

He heard Alec say distressfully, "How are we going to get him into the carriage without hurting him?"

Niall didn't know the answer to that question himself.

"The lad and I will lift him into the back," Alan said.

"Be very gentle," Alec commanded.

Niall appreciated the sentiment.

Alan said, "Can you walk?"

"I think so," he replied.

"Come along then," and, with his arm still around Niall, Alan took a step forward.

Still slightly bent over, breathing carefully, Niall stepped with him. Finally, they were at the luggage carrier. Then Alan and James boosted him into the back of the carriage. He sprawled flat on his back on the bare boards. The rain fell on his upturned face as he struggled not to lose consciousness again.

Alan got into the carriage beside him.

The fourgon began to move forward, and every jolt hurt like hell.

He looked up into Alan's somber face and said in Gaelic, "Someone forced me off the road."

"Dhé!"

"Don't say anything to anyone else yet."

Alan nodded grimly. "I will not leave you alone," he promised.

His head hurt so badly he thought his skull would split open. He closed his eyes and gritted his teeth and prayed it would not be long before he could get out of the bumpy carriage.

At long last the carriage stopped, and he heard Alec's voice asking if the doctor had arrived.

"Not yet, my lady," came the response.

"My lady," someone else said. "I have had the chair brought up that we used for your father the time he broke his leg."

"Stokes, you are a genius," Alec said. "That is just what we need."

Then she was standing at the back of the carriage talking to him. "Niall, we have a chair we can use to carry you upstairs. If you can just get out of the carriage, darling, we'll have you warm and dry and in bed in a trice."

"Of course I can get out of the carriage," he heard himself say.

Alan's arm went around him and supported him as he slid to the back of the carriage. Pain knifed through his ribs as his feet hit the ground, and he couldn't stop himself from wincing.

"Here's the chair, darling," Alec said. "All you have to do now is sit down."

It was a wooden chair with four carry poles held by four of Gayles's largest footmen. They had indeed positioned the chair so that all Niall had to do was sit down. Once he had done that, the footmen lifted the chair poles and carried him into the house.

In such fashion he was carried up two flights of stairs and down the Long Gallery to the bedroom he had been using since the fire. As he was in the process of being transported, Dr. Adams arrived. He followed Niall up the stairs and came into the bedroom after the footmen had lowered the chair to the floor and exited.

"Get him out of those wet clothes before he catches pneumonia," the doctor said to Alec, who was in the bedroom along with Alan.

Niall scowled with annoyance and started to inform the doctor that he wasn't some dainty Sassenach who wilted in the rain.

"Be quiet," Alec ordered. "Alan, get him out of those clothes while I get some dry things from the wardrobe."

"You will get the bedclothes all wet unless you take off these wet things," Alan said in English as he carefully pulled Niall's coat off his shoulders and slid it down his arms.

From her station in front of the wardrobe, Alec said, "If you slept in a nightshirt like decent people, you would have something to cover you. As it is, you will have to make do with drawers and a shirt."

By this time, Niall's head was pounding so hard he

could scarcely focus his eyes let alone resist Alan's skillful hands. Indeed, though he tried not to show it, he was very grateful finally to lie down in the bed and rest his head on a soft pillow.

The doctor's diagnosis was uncomplicated. Niall had three broken ribs, a badly bruised right hip, and a concussion, as well as a multitude of bruises and abrasions.

"He was very fortunate that it wasn't worse, my lady," the doctor said to Alec.

Niall leaned back against his pillows and closed his eyes. Once again he saw the carriage that had pulled out to go by him on the road, saw how it had suddenly swerved into his horses, crowding them toward the ditch. He heard himself yelling to the bloody fool of a driver to be careful, then he watched in horror as the other carriage moved over even farther until it quite literally pushed his horses off the road.

The next thing he remembered was waking up in a ditch.

He opened his eyes and looked up into his wife's face. "You're going to be fine, darling," she said. "You just need to rest."

He didn't answer. His headache was getting worse, not better.

"I'll be on my way, my lady," the doctor said from the far end of the room. "I've done all I can do here for the moment."

Alec turned away from him to thank the doctor. "Won't you have some tea and something to eat before you go out into that rain again?" she offered.

"That would be very welcome, my lady," the doctor replied, and Niall could hear the special note in his voice that men got whenever they talked to Alec. "You are very kind."

"Alan," Alec said, "will you stay with His Lordship in case he needs anything?"

"I was planning to do just that," Alan replied a little grimly.

Niall heard the click of the latch as the door closed.

Alan pulled up a chair next to Niall's bed and said, "Go to sleep, Niall. I will stand guard, never fear."

Niall didn't think he would ever be able to sleep with such agony pounding in his head.

The next thing he heard was Alan's voice saying urgently, *"Niall! Niall! Wake up. Come on, man, open your eyes and look at me."*

Niall didn't want to wake up, but he heard the urgency in Alan's voice and opened his eyes. The face that he saw leaning over him was not Alan's, however, it was his wife's.

"Alec?" he said. "What are you doing here?"

She looked like an angel, he thought confusedly. Perhaps he had died and was waking up in heaven.

"The doctor said we had to wake you at intervals for the first twenty-four hours," she said. "You took a nasty blow on the head, darling."

The two deerhounds had come to the side of his bed when they heard his voice. Flora whined and pushed her muzzle against his shoulder. He winced, and said, "What are the dogs doing here?"

"Alan insisted on bringing them," Alec said. From the tone of her voice he understood that she was not in agreement with Alan's decision.

"I thought it was best for them to be with you, Niall," Alan said in an uncompromising tone of voice.

"What time is it?" Niall asked.

"Eight o'clock," Alec answered. "We just finished dinner."

It was one of the few times in his life that the mention of food did not make Niall hungry.

"Well, now that you have been successful in awakening me, can I go back to sleep again?" he grumbled.

"Yes." She leaned down and lightly kissed his forehead. He caught the delicate scent of spring flowers that always clung to her hair and closed his eyes and inhaled it.

"I'll stay with His Lordship for a while, Alan," he heard her say. "Why don't you go and get some dinner for yourself?"

"That is all right, my lady," Alan replied. "I am not hungry."

"Nonsense," Alec said. "Go ahead and eat."

Her voice made it quite clear that she was not asking Alan to leave, she was commanding him.

Speaking with his eyes closed, Niall said, "It's all right, Alan. The dogs are here."

There was a pause. Then Alan said, "Are you sure?"

"Yes. Go ahead and get something to eat."

"Very well," Alan said abruptly.

After a moment, Niall heard the door close.

"What did you mean, 'the dogs are here'?" Alec asked in a puzzled voice.

"Do you think I could have a drink of water?" he asked plaintively.

"Of course."

He lifted his head a little and took a few sips of water from the glass she was holding to his lips. Then he rested his head once more on his pillow and closed his eyes.

He heard the swish of Alec's skirts as she sat down in the chair that Alan had pulled up beside his bed. He breathed in her faint, delicious scent as he once more drifted off into the deep sleep of the badly concussed.

* * *

It was two days before Niall awoke to find that his headache had become bearable. Alan, as usual, was sitting in the chair by his bedside.

"Ailein," Niall said. Cautiously, holding his head as still as he could, he sat up in bed. He winced as his ribs protested.

"Are you better?" Alan asked.

"My head is better," he replied. "The ribs will just take time."

"Thank you, God," Alan said simply.

Niall lifted his hand to rub his face and felt the roughness of his beard. "I think I could manage a bath," he said. "And then I will eat."

"Good," said Alan. "I will go and have the tub brought."

"Tell me first, has anything unusual happened here?"

"Nothing that I know of," Alan replied. "But I have been with you almost the whole time."

"All right. Go ahead and order the tub."

"There is a gun in the drawer of the bedside table," Alan said calmly before he closed the door behind him.

Setting his teeth against the knifing pain from his ribs, Niall swung his legs over the side of the bed. He sat there for a moment, bracing himself to stand up.

The door opened and his wife came in.

"Niall!" she said. "Alan told me you were awake and feeling better. Thank God."

He gave her a sketchy smile and slowly stood up. His knees felt like water and he staggered. In a flash she was at his side, her arm around his waist to steady him.

"Are you all right?" she asked urgently. "I think you had better sit back down."

"No." He breathed deeply and evenly. "I will be fine. Just give me a moment."

He straightened up and took a few steps in the direction of the open window. Unfortunately, his movement brought him into line with the long pier glass that was part of the room's furniture. He stopped and stared in horror at the grisly sight that met his eyes.

His hair looked as if it had grown two inches, and his beard had progressed well beyond a stubble. Under the beard and the hair his skin looked pasty white. There was a great purple bruise on his temple. His soft, collarless Highland shirt came almost to the bottom of his gray-flannel drawers. His legs and feet were bare.

"*Dhé!*" he said. "That is a sight to scare small children."

"You have looked more dapper," Alec agreed with amusement.

He turned to look at her. She wore her glorious hair braided on the top of her regal little head like a crown. Her sprigged muslin dress was fresh and fell from beneath her breasts, over the long line of her beautiful waist, to skim her slim hips and long legs and end in a beribboned hem on her high-arched instep.

He looked at her and, aching and pain-wracked as he was, he was stirred. Abruptly, he asked the question that had been on his mind ever since the accident.

"Alec, why did you write and ask me to come home on Friday?"

She looked back at him in bewilderment. "I never wrote you to come home on Friday. In fact, I got a letter from you saying that you would be home on Saturday."

He frowned, as if he were confused by her reply. "You didn't send me a letter?"

She shook her head. "No, I did not." The lovely color drained from her face as she realized the implications of his question. "Niall, did someone send you a letter saying it was from me?"

"Yes," he replied.

"Do you still have it?"

He thought back. "No. I saw no need to save it." He thrust a hand through his matted hair. "Damn," he said mildly.

Her hands were tightly clasped together at her waist. "Did the letter say *why* I wanted you to return Friday?"

"It said that something urgent had arisen, and you needed me."

"Just how did your accident occur?" she asked sharply. "I have been assuming that you drove too close to the ditch and the carriage tipped in. Was that what happened?"

"No," he said. "Someone forced me off the road."

She went so pale he was afraid she would faint. He started toward her, saying, "Sit down, Alec."

She backed up to the bed and sat on its edge. He reached her and put a hand on the back of her head, gently pushing it down. "Let your head hang between your knees," he said.

Her braids felt like woven silk under his fingers.

Obediently, she lowered her head. He sat next to her on the bed and waited.

Finally, the golden crown was upright once more. She turned to look at him, her gray eyes dark with fear. "Tell me what happened."

"A carriage came up behind me on the road and pulled out to pass me. There was plenty of room for it to go by; the road is quite wide there. But as soon as the other carriage drew abreast of my horses, it swerved into them and forced them off the road into the ditch. The curricle, of course, followed."

"Dear God, Niall," she breathed. "Do you think that whoever sent you that message to return to Gayles on Friday was lying in wait for you?"

"That would seem the obvious explanation. If James had not been so quick on the scene, who knows what might have happened while I lay there helpless?"

Her hands were pressed to her mouth. "This is like a nightmare," she breathed.

"It is not very pleasant," he agreed.

"It must have been Chisholm," she said. "If you remember, Niall, the very day before you left for Holkham, you once again refused to sell him Glen Alpin."

"That is so," Niall agreed. She was sitting so close to him that he could smell the scent of her hair. "But how would Chisholm learn that I was at Holkham?"

"His handy spy, of course." She moved away from him a little so that she could turn to face him. Her eyes were bright with anger. "We had better get rid of Harvey immediately. He has become dangerous."

He wanted to believe that she hadn't written that letter, that she was genuinely concerned for him, but he wasn't sure. The thought had occurred to him that there was one other person who would benefit from his death besides Geoffrey: Alec herself. Having already followed the dictates of her father's will and married the seventh earl, his death would free her to claim her inheritance and to marry whomever she chose. There could be no doubt that Geoffrey Wilton would make a more satisfactory earl in her eyes than he would.

"What about Geoffrey Wilton?" he asked. "Might not he also have learned that I was at Holkham? It certainly was no secret among the household."

"I wish you would stop trying to implicate Geoffrey!" she said. "I keep telling you that he would never try to hurt you.

Nor does he have any monetary reason to wish you ill. I have told him that I am going to give him half of the proceeds of the sale of the stud farm."

She was always so passionate in her defense of Geoffrey. Niall did not like to contemplate the possibility that his wife and Geoffrey might be partners together in a plan to get rid of him, but the thought would not go away.

She said abruptly, "Does Alan know about this?"

"Yes."

"So that is why he has been sticking to you like glue these last few days."

"Yes."

Sudden color flushed into her cheeks. "You thought I wrote that letter," she said accusingly. "You have been thinking that I arranged to have you pushed off the road!"

"I never thought that," he said.

She looked up into his face searchingly and he met her gaze with steady eyes. "I would never ever want to hurt you," she said. "You must believe that."

His instinct was that she was telling him the truth. But, when it came to Alec, he didn't trust his own feelings. She affected him so intensely, in a way no woman had affected him before, that he couldn't rely on his own objectivity.

He wanted her. Even now, beaten-up as he was, he wanted her. And it was not just her beauty. There was a kernel of wild sweetness in her that filled some profound inner need of his own.

He would have to be careful. Until he knew for certain who was responsible for the attacks against him, he would have to keep up his guard. Even against his wife.

Chapter Twenty-one

Five days after Niall's carriage accident, a letter from Glen Alpin arrived from Ewan MacDonald, one of Niall's cousins and a principal landholder of Niall's grandfather, the chief. Alexandra was at breakfast with Niall and his foster brother when Niall opened the letter to read it. From the expression on his face, she knew immediately that the news was bad. She waited tensely to see whom he would turn to first, herself or Alan.

He looked at Alan and said something in Gaelic.

Alan reached out a hand and grasped Niall's forearm, a gesture of male solidarity that Niall acknowledged by an infinitessimal lowering of his lashes. Then he turned to Alexandra, and said, "My grandfather is very ill. I must go home."

"Oh, Niall," she said with quick sympathy.

"Something is wrong with his heart."

He looked white around the mouth.

She said helplessly, "I am so sorry."

His brow furrowed, and he turned back to Alan. "It will

be fastest to drive straight through to Scotland and get a boat there."

Alan nodded agreement, and Niall looked at Alexandra. "I'll need a carriage."

"You can have the chaise and the grays," she said immediately. "The grays are our fastest team."

"Thank you," he said somberly. He stood up, and said to Alan, "Go get us packed while I have a word with Mason."

Alan stood as well and both men walked out of the room together, leaving Alexandra sitting next to Niall's empty seat.

He turned to Alan first.

Alexandra had been struggling with her jealous feelings about Niall's closeness to his foster brother ever since the accident. She had never been jealous in her life, and she did not like the feeling one little bit, but she could not seem to help herself.

The relationship between the two men had not bothered her before the accident. Then, her intense physical intimacy with Niall had made her feel close to him in every way. She had felt that she was important to him, and she had not begrudged in the slightest Alan's devotion to him or his to Alan.

The accident had changed all that. It had been a mind-numbing shock to realize that Niall had actually suspected her of trying to harm him.

I have the dogs. That is what he had said to Alan the one time she had insisted on being left alone with him. Once Alexandra had understood what he meant, the words had scalded themselves on her heart.

She kept telling herself that he had reason to doubt her. After all, the letter that had lured him to the river road had supposedly come from her. If their situations had been reversed, perhaps she would have doubted him.

Her heart was wounded by his distrust, but her brain understood that he had had reason for it. What really haunted her, however, was the fear that he hadn't believed her when she had denied sending such a letter.

There was a distance between them that had not been there before the accident, and it was more than the lack of sexual intimacy that Niall's injuries imposed. He had made no gesture of affection toward her at all since the accident. He had not touched her hair, or kissed her cheek, or done any of the small things that, for three blissful days, had let her know how he felt about her.

He was polite, but he kept his distance, he in his room and she in hers. The person to whom he turned now was not her but Alan MacDonald.

At dinner the previous evening she had said something casual about what a good friend Alan was to him, and Niall's reply had not made her feel any better. "To a Highlander a man's foster brother is as the lifeblood of his heart," he had told her gravely.

The jealousy she was striving to keep in check had flamed up at those words. That was what *she* wanted to be, the lifeblood of his heart. That was what he was to her.

He had not said a word about her accompanying him on his journey home to Scotland. He was taking Alan, not her. She stared at the remains of her half-eaten breakfast and knew with absolute certainty that if she let Niall go back to the Highlands without her, she would lose him forever.

The solemn words of the marriage ceremony came back to her now:

Wilt thou have this Man to thy wedded husband, to live together after God's ordinance in the holy estate of Matri-

mony? Wilt thou obey him and serve him, love, honor, and keep him in sickness and in health; and, forsaking all others, keep thee only unto him, so long as ye both shall live?

She had said yes to that wedding vow, and Niall had made the same pledge to her. She was damned if she was going to let him get away now.

She rang the bell imperiously and Stokes himself answered her summons.

"Stokes," she said, "send a message to the stables to harness the grays to the chaise. His Lordship and I and Mr. MacDonald will be leaving immediately for Scotland. His Lordship's grandfather is very ill."

Stokes was so surprised that he actually questioned her. "You are going, too, my lady?"

"Yes, Stokes," she replied evenly. "I am going, too."

The surprise on Stokes's face was replaced by its usual gravity. "Very good, my lady. I will have the message taken to the stables immediately."

Alexandra pushed back her chair and stood up. "Thank you. Tell Meg to come to my room. I need to pack."

"But what should I pack, my lady?" Meg wailed. "What kind of clothing will you need in Scotland?" She made it sound as if Scotland was as far away and alien as China.

Alexandra had already removed her fragile muslin morning frock and was now in the process of fastening the frogged front of a light gray wool driving dress. "Boots," she told Meg briefly. "Warm dresses. My heaviest pelisse."

Meg was piling clothing on the bed next to the open portmanteau when there came a knock upon the door.

"Come in," Alexandra called.

The door opened and Niall stood upon the threshold.

"May I speak to you, Alec? There are a few things we should settle before . . ."

His voice died away as his eyes rested upon the open portmanteau and the bed heaped with clothes.

"What is this?" he asked.

"I am going with you," she replied, her calm voice in direct contrast to the hammering of her heart.

His face wore its most hawklike look. "You will do no such thing. You are needed here at Gayles."

Alexandra turned, randomly picked up a pile of underwear, and dumped it into the portmanteau. Over her shoulder, she said, "Mr. Mason is perfectly competent to see to things here. He doesn't need me."

In a grim voice, Niall said to Meg, "Leave us, girl."

Meg hastened out of the room, closing the door behind her.

As soon as the door had latched, Niall said ominously, "Now, what is this all about?"

She turned around to face him, determined not to let him see how nervous she was. "It's about the fact that I am going with you," she replied. "Is that so difficult to understand?"

"You can't go with me," he said again.

She felt a healthy spark of anger at his dismissive tone of voice. "Why not?" she demanded.

A lock of dark hair was hanging over his brow and he pushed it back with impatient fingers. "My grandfather is very ill, and I am going to travel as if the hounds of hell are at my heels," he replied roughly. "And speaking of hounds, I am taking Flora and Fergus, so there will be no room for you in the chaise. Nor do I plan to stop overnight at comfortable inns with nice meals and clean sheets on the beds. We'll change horses and keep on going. Then, when we reach Troon, we'll get the first boat we can find and head up the west coast. It will probably be raining, and the sea will be rough. It is not a journey for the likes of you."

This speech was all Alexandra needed to ignite the spark of anger into a real temper. She narrowed her eyes and closed the distance between them, pointing her index finger at his chest. "Let me tell you something that may surprise you, Niall MacDonald, but I am every bit as tough as you are. If you can make this trip with broken ribs, I can make it, too. I have stayed in the saddle for seven hours at a time on hunting days, and I think I can manage to sit in a chaise for a few days and nights of travel. I don't get seasick, and I don't dissolve in the rain. And I am going with you."

His face looked very hard. He shook his head.

She folded her arms. "Very well, if you won't take me, then I shall just have to follow you by myself."

Now *he* was angry. "What is the matter with you?" he demanded. "You don't want to go to the Highlands!"

"That is your assumption," she informed him. "I have never said such a thing myself."

"I don't want you to go," he said brutally. "You will be in my way."

She was struck to the heart but refused to give in.

"I promised God that I would forsake all others and keep only to you," she said. "And I always keep my promises to God. If you won't take me with you, I shall follow you. You can't stop me."

His scowl would have backed off a regiment, but Alexandra's blood was up. She stared back and held her ground. He had to let her come. He had to.

Don't you understand? her heart cried in silence. *I love you. That is why I want to go with you. Because I love you.*

But she was afraid to say the words, afraid of his reaction. She made a swift decision to change tactics and moved to stand directly in front of him. Resting her palms lightly on his chest, she said softly, "Please, Niall. Please let me go."

He looked down into her face and she saw a muscle twitch in his jaw. She leaned a little closer to him, so that her breasts just touched him. The muscle in his jaw twitched again.

He was not indifferent to her. She felt a flood of relief as she recognized his physical reaction.

"All right." His voice was harsh, and he reached up to remove her hands from his chest, but he had given in. "All right, Alec, you can go. But I don't want to hear any complaints from you. Is that clear?"

"Perfectly," she replied meekly.

He glared at her in baffled fury. Clearly he did not know how he had allowed himself to be backed into this corner.

"If you will go away, I will get Meg to finish packing for me," she suggested.

"I am leaving in half an hour," he said.

"I will be ready."

He looked as if he might say something else, then didn't. He turned his back and left the room.

Alexandra shut her eyes. She had done it. She had been so frightened that she was actually shaking, but she had done it. She was going with him.

After a moment she went out into the gallery to summon the banished Meg.

At precisely ten-thirty in the morning, the Earl of Hartford's chaise departed from the Gayles stableyard. Inside the well-sprung carriage rode the earl himself, his wife, his foster brother, and his two large deerhounds. A minimal amount of luggage was strapped to the top of the carriage and the Gayles coachman was in the driver's seat.

The chaise's brisk departure down the front drive was followed with interest by the footman who called himself Harvey, who was looking out the window of the family dining room where he had been tidying up after breakfast. When the chaise was completely out of sight, Harvey went to seek out someone who might be able to give him some information about the earl's sudden journey.

"They was sure bowling along," he said to James when he found the other footman replenishing coal in the fireplace of the Blue Drawing Room. "Do you know where the earl is going that he is in such a hurry?"

So it would not look as if he had come into the room just to pump James, Harvey busied himself trimming the lamps.

"Scotland," James replied. He finished emptying the coal scuttle, stood up, and brushed his knees. "His Lordship's grandda is sick."

"Really?" Harvey murmured softly. He finished with the lamp he was trimming and went to deal with another one.

"So Mr. Stokes said." James bent down and picked up the empty coal scuttle.

"Did he get a letter?" Harvey asked.

James stoppped on his way to the door and turned to look at Harvey. "Aye," he said.

"And Her Ladyship went with him?" Harvey said.

"Why are you so interested in where the earl is going?" James asked suspiciously.

Harvey gave him an innocent look. "I was just trying to talk nice to you, James."

A grunt was the only reply James accorded this remark as he turned his back on Harvey and left the room.

It was over an hour before Harvey was able to slip out of the house, but finally he found his chance. He cut through the garden to the road that led either west to the village or east to the Hartly Arms, a small inn that was patronized mainly by local people. It had been patronized for the last week by the burly-looking man called Ruggles who was Harvey's contact with his employer, Lord Chisholm.

It was over an hour's walk from Gayles to the inn, and Harvey was slightly out of breath as he came into the taproom. The burly courier was sitting at a corner table by himself, a flagon of ale in front of him.

It took five minutes for Harvey to report his news and leave. It took fifteen more minutes for Ruggles to mount his sturdy brown cob and turn toward Doncaster, where Lord Chisholm was staying for the races.

At one o'clock that afternoon, Mrs. Wilton's chaise pulled up at the front door of Gayles, and Geoffrey's mother got out. She was not happy to be paying a call upon Alexandra, but Geoffrey had become so anxious that she had given in to his begging and come to see how Alexandra was faring.

Stokes himself opened the door and invited her into the anteroom, where he informed her that the earl and countess had left but a few hours earlier for Scotland.

Mrs. Wilton was stunned. "Her Ladyship has gone to Scotland?"

"Yes, Mrs. Wilton," the butler replied. "His Lordship left us the address, if you would care to write to her."

Mrs. Wilton took the card Stokes handed her and looked at it. Written on it in black ink, in a strong slanting hand, were the words: Eilean Darrach Castle, Glen Alpin, Scotland.

"Good God," Mrs. Wilton said faintly.

"His Lordship just learned this morning that his grandfather is very ill, and they left in a hurry, Mrs. Wilton," the helpful Stokes explained.

Mrs. Wilton stared blankly at Gayles's butler and thought, *How am I going to tell Geoffrey that Alexandra has gone to Scotland with that man?*

"May I offer you some refreshment, Mrs. Wilton?" Stokes inquired kindly.

"Oh . . . no, thank you Stokes. I had better be getting on home."

She walked slowly down the stone steps and, assisted by a footman, stepped into her chaise. During the hour-long drive home, she stared blindly out the window and turned over in her mind all the implications of Alexandra's departure.

When she reached home and confronted Geoffrey with the news, he did not take it well. He stood in the drawing room of the charming old pink-brick house that was Highgate and stared at his mother incredulously.

"Alex has gone to *Scotland*?"

"I am afraid that she has, dear," Mrs. Wilton replied.

"She can't have."

"Geoffrey, dear, she has. I had the news directly from Stokes."

"He forced her, then," Geoffrey said. "There is no way in this world that Alex would have left Gayles under her own willpower."

"Don't be ridiculous," Mrs. Wilton said sharply. "If there is one thing Alexandra has, it's a will of her own. Believe me, Geoffrey, if she did not wish to go to Scotland with her husband, she would not have gone."

Geoffrey began to pace up and down the room. "I have to do something," he said, a note of near hysteria in his voice. "I can't let her get away from me like this."

Mrs. Wilton went over to her son, took his lapels in her hands, and stared up at him commandingly. "She already has got away from you! She is married, Geoffrey. You must forget her. For your own sake, you must forget her."

Geoffrey was shaking his head back and forth, back and forth. When finally she released him, he stepped back. "I will never forget Alex, Mother," he said. "Nor will I desert her in her hour of need."

"What are you going to do?" his mother asked apprehensively.

"I am going to follow her to Scotland," Geoffrey replied decisively, and walked out of the room.

Tears blurred Mrs. Wilton's eyes as she watched him go. If only Niall MacDonald had never been born, she thought with deep bitterness. If Niall did not exist, Geoffrey would be the Earl of Hartford and married to Alexandra. He would have been as happy as he deserved to be.

Mrs. Wilton heartily wished that it was Niall and not his grandfather that was lying near death in that barbarous country to the north of England.

Chapter Twenty-two

Niall sat grimly in his corner of the chaise and held on to the strap to brace his sore body against the jolting induced by the horses' speed. Alexandra sat across from him and did not try to make conversation. Fergus was stretched out next to her, taking up most of the seat, and after a while he put his head in her lap. She did not push him away, but gently stroked the deerhound's great shaggy head.

Flora was curled up next to Niall, and on the other side of Flora, crammed uncomfortably against the door, was Alan.

They changed the grays after the first fifty miles, picking up a fresh team at a coaching inn and continuing on through the night. The full moon was out, lighting the road almost as clearly as daylight. Alexandra dozed restlessly, waking every twenty minutes or so to peer out at the ribbon of moon-lit highway.

At seven in the morning they stopped at another coaching inn to change horses and take on a new driver to relieve the exhausted coachman. Alexandra was so grateful to be out of the chaise that she even ate the overcooked breakfast.

It seemed a matter of minutes before Niall was beside her, telling her that the chaise was ready to go again. He himself was looking haggard. Alexandra wanted to tell him that this kind of traveling was dangerous for a man recovering from a serious concussion and broken ribs, but she held her tongue. Such a comment would only succeed in annoying him; it would not make him slow their pace.

"All right," she said. "I'm coming."

It took over two and a half days to reach Scotland. After the first twenty-four hours in the chaise, Alexandra lost all sense of time, dozing and waking only to doze again. She tried to eat when food was put in front of her, but the relentless movement of the carriage affected her stomach and her appetite. She was enormously grateful that they had the dogs with them, because it made Niall stop the coach periodically to let them out. Alexandra took those opportunities to walk briskly around the chaise and stretch her cramped legs as best she could.

She was asleep, her head pillowed on Fergus's flank, when their team of rented carriage horses finally trotted into Troon. Niall sent Alan to the waterfront to hire a boat while he made arrangements to leave the chaise at the Troon Inn.

Alexandra was still asleep in the chaise when he came back after paying the innkeeper. Niall looked down at his wife and marveled that she had endured the difficult journey with such grace. She had not complained once. In fact, he thought, she looked a hell of a lot better than either he or Alan. The coronet of pale gold braids that was pillowed on Fergus's auburn fur was still neat, and her long lashes lay on skin as fresh and fine as a baby's.

Women never became as unkempt-looking as men because they didn't grow beards, Niall thought reflectively as he rubbed his rough cheek. He and Alan both looked like un-pruned plants.

He put an inexorable hand on Alexandra's shoulder and woke her. Then he took her into the inn to have something to eat. Alan returned in time to join them, bringing with him the news that he had managed to make arrangements with the owner of a small fishing boat to take them all the way to Loch Linnhe.

The sky was overcast when Niall and his party boarded the small wooden boat that was tied up at the Troon dock. Niall saw Alexandra's nose wrinkle at the strong odor of fish, but she made no comment. There was a bench of sorts at the rear of the vessel, and that **is** where he installed her, along with the dogs.

It was foggy and overcast as they sailed out of Troon, and, ignoring the protest made by his ribs, Niall inhaled the mist and the smell of seawater deeply into his lungs. As the afternoon progressed, the small fishing vessel sailed out of the Firth of Clyde, rounded the Mull of Kintyre and turned north, the Isle of Kintyre to the east and open sea to the west.

Late in the afternoon it started to rain. It came down heavily and steadily, drenching the boat's occupants. None of the men minded getting wet; it was a state they were all well accustomed to. But Niall worried about Alexandra.

When the rain first began, the boat's owner, a MacDonald from Arran, had offered Alexandra the plaid that he himself used in bad weather. Unfortunately, the garment was very dirty and reeked of fish, and she had refused to take it. Consequently, she was as drenched as the men were. When Niall made his way to the back of the boat to ask her if he could do something for her, she shook her head, upon which she wore a fetching but soaked straw bonnet. "What about the dogs?" she said, looking down at the two wet fur balls that were curled at her feet. "The poor things are getting drenched."

Niall looked down as well and saw that Fergus had actually poked his face under her pelisse to keep out of the rain.

"The dogs are used to weather like this," he replied. "You aren't."

"I told you before we left Gayles that I don't dissolve in the rain, Niall," she returned composedly. "I shall be perfectly all right."

But the rain didn't let up, and as the water became rougher, the spray from the waves was added to the deluge from the sky. That time of year, it stayed light in the north for a long time, and Niall had planned to continue on until the light faded. But he was worried about his wife.

Once more he made his way to the back of the boat and this time he sat beside her, too close for her to hide the fact that she was shivering.

This was what he had been afraid of, he thought grimly. He had spent most of his life outdoors, and the weather rarely bothered him, but Alec was a Sassenach.

He cursed.

She jumped and turned to him. Her cheeks were wet and there were drops hanging from the ends of her long eyelashes.

"Why did you not tell me you were cold?" he demanded.

"I'm f-f-ine," she said, her teeth chattering.

He longed for something warm and dry to wrap her up in, but there was nothing.

"Come here," he said, and, reaching out, he gathered her into his arms.

"I'll h-h-urt your r-ribs," she said.

"Never mind my ribs."

He could feel that her whole body was shaking as she

huddled against him. If he didn't get her warm and dry soon, she would be ill.

He looked at the shore and saw only a stretch of beach with waves pounding against the shore.

"Wait here," he said to Alec, as if she had someplace else to go, and he made his way to where the boat's owner was steering his way through the waves. "Where is the nearest place we can put in and find shelter?" Niall asked.

Rory MacDonald turned to Niall in surprise. "We have four more hours of daylight at least. The boat can manage this weather."

"The boat may be able to manage, but my wife can't," Niall returned.

MacDonald looked back at Alexandra and nodded. "The next town along the west coast of Kintyre is Bellochantuy," he said. "There is sure to be an inn of sorts there."

"We'll pull in there and wait out the bad weather," Niall said, and returned to his seat next to Alexandra on the bench.

He bent his head and said into her ear, "How would you like to sleep in a real bed tonight?"

"I would l-love it," she replied.

"I would, too," he said and gathered her closer, trying to share some of his own body heat.

There was indeed an inn in the tiny town where Mac-Donald docked his boat. It was a small, dreary-looking wooden building, called in its English translation, Fisherman's Rest, and it was mainly a place for the local fishermen to meet and have a dram. It did offer two rooms for hire, however, and Niall engaged them for the night.

Niall's face was grim as he led Alexandra up the drafty narrow wooden stairs of the Fisherman's Rest. She was shivering convulsively, and he wanted very much to lift her in his arms and carry her, but he knew his ribs weren't up to such a feat. He opened the first door on the landing at the top of the stairs and motioned for her to go in.

The room was tiny, with most of it taken up by the bed. The roof was extremely low, only two inches above the top of Niall's head, which made the room seem even smaller. There was one candle on the single scuffed wooden table and one tiny window. The walls exuded a smell of damp and, faint but unmistakable, there was also the odor of fish.

Alexandra looked dazed as she stood in the two-foot space beside the bed and looked around.

Niall saw the room through her eyes and his face grew very grim. *I knew she should not have come,* he thought. *She lives in a different world; she can never fit in here.*

A knock sounded on the door and when Niall opened it, Alan was standing there with the dogs and Alexandra's portmanteau. As Niall took the bag, Flora shook herself vigorously, spraying both Niall and Alan with the water from her long coat.

"The innkeeper's wife is bringing some towels for the dogs and Her Ladyship," Alan said.

Behind Niall, Alexandra made an odd sound.

Niall thanked Alan, closed the door, and turned to his wife.

She said, "Do I g-get to use the towels b-before or after the dogs?"

Merriment was clearly stamped on her blue-tinged face, and the sound he had heard had been a giggle.

Niall stared at her in shock. She had taken off her water-logged bonnet and dropped it on the floor, and begun to unbutton her sodden pelisse. Her fingers were so stiff with cold that she fumbled with the buttons.

"I will do it," he said, and took the two strides necessary to get from the door to the bedside. She stood docilely in front of him and let him unbutton her pelisse and peel it off. The dress she wore underneath was wet as well, and he was beginning to unbutton that when a woman called in Gaelic from outside the door, "I have your towels."

Niall went to the door, opened it and received into his hands two almost threadbare towels of a grayish white color. He understood perfectly that these were the best the inn had to offer, and thanked the landlady, but he knew what Alexandra would think of them and wished they were better.

"Here are the towels," he said.

She looked at them and he thought of the soft, thick towels he had used at Gayles and winced.

"One for you and one for m-me," she said gravely.

"You can have them both. I don't need a towel."

"Thank you," she replied, took one of them and briskly dried her face. Then she looked at him.

He felt huge and horribly awkward standing next to her in this damp and tiny room. "I am thinking I will just go and see how Alan and the dogs are faring," he said.

She nodded.

Niall turned, took two steps to the door, and went out.

Alan was in the room next door, which was equally tiny and smelled more of wet dogs than of fish.

"How is Her Ladyship?" he asked courteously.

"Very well," Niall replied.

Niall was perfectly aware that Alan distrusted his Sassenach wife, but, with his usual delicacy, Alan had understood from the first that the subject of Alexandra was taboo between them.

In silence, he and Alan peeled off their wet clothes and made do with a single towel between them. Alan had brought their bags in from the boat and both men changed into dry clothes, Niall choosing his kilt and smiling with pleasure as he felt the familiar pleats swinging around his knees. He borrowed a pair of wool socks from Alan, put on a clean shirt, rolling down the ridiculous high collar he had been forced to wear for the last month or so, and went downstairs for a dram.

With the whiskey warming his insides, Niall returned upstairs bearing a pot of tea and some bread and butter for Alexandra. He opened the bedroom door and looked cautiously inside, not sure what he was going to find.

She was sitting cross-legged in the middle of the bed, a blanket draped around her, drying her hair with a towel. She had unbraided the drenched coronet and was briskly rubbing the long, darkened strands. She saw him and her face lit with a radiant smile.

"Tea!" she said. "Please tell me that it's hot."

"It's hot," he replied, and went to lay the tray carefully on the bed in front of her.

"Will you pour me a cup? If I don't get the knots out of my hair immediately I will have to cut it all off." She picked up a brush and began to drag it through her still-damp hair.

"That would be a tragedy," he said gravely. The only table in the room was on the other side of the bed, and he picked up the tray, brought it to the table, and put it down. Without looking at Alexandra, he poured the tea into a substantial-looking pottery cup. He poured another cup for himself, said, "It's ready when you want it," and looked up.

Her hair was beginning to dry as she brushed it and some of the ends had already turned gold. She put down the brush and reached for the teacup he was holding out to her. As she took it, their fingers brushed.

The heat that jolted through him at that touch was much more intense than the jolt he had gotten earlier from the whiskey. He watched as she raised the cup to her lips and drank greedily. She closed her eyes and sighed.

"That tastes wonderful," she said.

He sipped his own tea and found it to be far weaker than what he liked. But it was hot.

"Are you hungry?" he asked. "I brought you some bread and butter."

She took another drink of the tea. "Let me finish this wonderful tea first."

He didn't say anything else, just watched her out of hooded eyes as she drank her tea. When the cup was empty, she held it between her two hands and looked at him solemnly. "I am sorry that you had to stop because of me," she said.

He looked at her sitting there in the middle of her glorious hair and felt something inside him give way. He had just put her through a hellish journey, and she had not complained once. He had almost made her ill with cold and wet, and here she was, apologizing to him.

"It is not your fault, Alec," he said haltingly. "The fault is mine for subjecting you to such an ordeal."

"Do you mean you wish you had left me home?" she asked.

Niall knew he was treading on treacherous ground. "I did not say that," he returned cautiously.

To his horror, her gray eyes filled with tears. She blinked them away determinedly and shoved her teacup at him. As he took it, she flopped back on the bed, the blanket slipping away and revealing her bare shoulders and arms. "Go away," she said. "You can spend the night with Alan."

He had had every intention of spending the night with Alan, but he told himself that he did not want to leave her while she was so upset.

"I only meant that I knew how difficult our traveling would be, and I should not have let you come . . ."

His voice trailed off as he realized he was making bad worse.

"You have been very courageous," he offered.

A single drop slid from the side of her eye and rolled down her cheek toward her ear.

He plunked the teacups down on the table, leaned over her so he could see her face, and said desperately, "Alec, please don't cry."

She looked up at him, her gray eyes shimmering with tears. "I'm n-not crying," she said. Her lower lip quivered and she sank white teeth into it to quiet it. He stared at her mouth for a moment, as if mesmerized, then lowered his own mouth and touched it to that soft, trembling lip.

She did not push him away.

Before he could think about the wisdom of his actions, he was kissing her frantically, opening her mouth with his mouth, his hands tearing the veiling blanket away to reveal her nearly naked body clad only in a thin white lawn chemise. She arched toward him and he tore the chemise away from her breast and took her perfect pink nipple into his mouth.

Slowly, slowly, he told himself through the pounding of his blood. *Be careful, don't hurt her. Go slowly.*

But he was possessed by an all-consuming need such as he had never known before. He felt as if he could tear the universe apart to get at her . . . as if he could devour her. . . .

He heard her whimper, and he clenched his teeth. "Kiss me, Alec," he said. "Kiss me."

She kissed him the way a man dreams of being kissed. So deep, so hot . . . he was trembling, all of his muscles clenched in a heroic effort not to be brutal. He shoved at her chemise, trying not to tear it but just to get it out of his way. Then he was touching her, and when he felt her wetness his mouth opened in a wordless groan of gratitude.

She pushed against his hand and whimpered again.

"Niall," she panted. "Oh my God."

"Just a minute, just a minute . . ." He lifted himself over her, held himself poised for a moment, and then plunged. As he drove into her that first time, they both shuddered, holding on to each other as to an anchor in the maelstrom of passion that was pounding through the both of them.

He shut his eyes tightly. He was buried deep within her, exactly where he wanted to be.

Then she spread to take him even farther in, her long legs coming up to circle his waist. He moved inside her, felt her softening around him. He thought he heard her sobbing. Then he felt her body jerk and she cried out, high and sharp, and he let his own body go, let his life pump into her, fill her, make her his.

Afterward, he held her in his arms while a dark and endless peacefulness welled up within his soul. Out of the soft darkness her voice came drifting to his ears, "Niall, your ribs . . . are they all right?"

He blinked. Vaguely he felt the familiar pain in his torso, then he banished it from his mind. He bent his head and kissed the soft hair on the top of her head. "They're fine."

The rain was beating hard on the roof above them. He felt a deep gratitude to her, that she had given him this fulfillment. He would do anything in the world for her, he thought sleepily. He turned a little, so that he was not lying on his sore ribs, and went to sleep.

Chapter Twenty-three

Alexandra awoke the following morning in the tiny, fishy-smelling room under the eaves. She felt wonderful. A single ray peeking through the miniscule window signaled that even the sun was out.

Niall was already up, but the pillow next to hers was still dented from his head. She stretched luxuriously, got out of bed, grimaced as her bare feet touched the cold, stained floor, and lifted her portmanteau up on the bed so she could search through it for something to wear. She climbed back on the bed to dress in order to come into as little contact with the floor as possible. She managed to brush the tangles out of her salt-stiffened hair, braided it and went downstairs to find Niall.

He was having breakfast with Alan and Rory MacDonald. The food smelled wonderful, and for the first time she realized that she was ravenous.

All three men stood up as she approached them and Fergus actually came to greet her and escort her to the table. She bent to pat him, and his tail wagged ferociously in response. She laughed and looked up to share the moment with her husband.

He said, "Sit down, Alec, and have something to eat."

Alexandra blinked. His voice sounded impatient, as if he was annoyed that she had kept him waiting. There was no tenderness or warmth in his eyes as he looked at her. It was as if last night had never happened.

She felt as if he had slapped her across the face.

She replied mechanically to the greetings of Alan and Rory and took the empty chair at the table. The three men resumed their seats and a middle-aged woman wearing a brown homespun dress put a bowl of porridge in front of her.

Alexandra picked up her spoon and sipped the porridge. Her stomach contracted as the hot stuff went down and for a moment she was horribly afraid she was going to retch.

She knew her stomach had reacted because she was upset; the porridge was not that dreadful. But she could not eat it. She could not eat anything.

What was the matter with Niall?

He said to her, "If all goes well, we should make it to the head of Loch Linnhe by dark. We'll spend the night there, rent a carriage, and travel up the Great Glen to Fort Augustus. From Fort Augustus it is only a matter of hours to Glen Alpin."

Alexandra pushed away her porridge. "I'm not hungry. I'll be ready to leave whenever you want."

He scowled. "You ate scarcely anything yesterday."

"I'm not hungry," she repeated.

"I am sorry the porridge is not to your taste," he said stiffly.

With the two MacDonalds looking on, she was not going

to attempt to explain to him why she had lost her appetite. She said nothing.

Niall stood up. "Is your portmanteau packed?"

"Yes."

"I'll go and get it then," he said. "If you are determined to starve yourself, we can leave immediately."

The sun was indeed shining, but to Alexandra, the day was even more miserable than the previous day had been. She sat by herself in the rear of the fishing boat, the deerhounds sleeping next to her on the deck, and tried to understand what was happening between herself and Niall.

How could the fiercely tender lover of last night have turned into the indifferent man of today? It was as if she had been caught for a while in an enchanted dream only to have awakened to bleak reality. She had never felt so forlorn in all her life. Not even the magnificent scenery around Loch Linnhe could distract her from her unhappiness.

When at last they arrived at the inn at the head of Loch Linnhe, she was sunburned and windblown and determined to confront Niall as soon as they were alone so she could demand an explanation for his behavior.

He had scarcely exchanged five sentences with her all day.

She was standing with the dogs in the main room of the inn, thinking of all the things she was going to say to him, when he appeared with the innkeeper at his side.

"There are no rooms available, Alec," he said. "Mr. Campbell has asked an elderly lady who is staying the night if you may have the second bed in her room and she has agreed." He shrugged. "I am sorry, but that is the best I can do."

She stared at him, completely aghast. "But where are you going to sleep?"

"On one of the benches in the taproom, I suppose," he replied impatiently. "It doesn't matter, I can sleep anywhere, but you must have a bed."

She would rather sleep on a bench with him, but she could hardly say this with the innkeeper standing there.

"All right," she said weakly.

"If you will come with me, my lady, I will show you to your bedroom," Mr. Campbell said.

Alexandra looked appealingly at Niall, hoping he would say something tender to her.

He said, "Campbell will have some food brought upstairs to you. You will not want to eat with the crowd down here."

All of a sudden, Alexandra was angry. She felt color burn in her cheeks and, if she had had something in her hands, she would have thrown it at him. "Please don't worry yourself about me, my lord," she snapped. "I shall be perfectly fine without you."

And she turned her back on him and went up the stairs with the innkeeper.

A maid brought her a dinner plate of perfectly cooked salmon, but Alexandra couldn't eat it. The elderly widow whose chamber she was sharing was enormously curious about her roommate, and asked Alexandra dozens of questions. When finally they went to bed, the widow snored loudly for the entire night, keeping Alexandra awake.

By the time she joined the men the following morning, Alexandra felt as if she would sell her soul for a bath and a hair wash. She managed to eat some bread for breakfast before she climbed into the ancient coach that Niall had hired to take them to Fort Augustus. She lay down on one side of the carriage seats for part of the afternoon and slept. That was possible because Alan kept the two dogs on his side of the coach while Niall sat outside with the driver.

She woke as the coach was driving into Fort Augustus. She sat up, smoothed her skirt, and prayed that there would be a private room at the inn. She felt as if her skin was caked with grime and her hair . . . she didn't even want to think about her hair.

The coach rolled to a stop in front of an inn, and after a moment Niall opened the door and helped her to alight. She stumbled a little when her feet touched the ground and in catching her his hand brushed against her breast.

She looked up at him but he did not meet her eyes. His mouth was set in a grim line, and he said, "Come inside and have something to eat."

Alexandra did not want to eat, what she wanted was a bath. But she did not want to listen to his comments about her lack of appetite, so she followed him to a table and sat down.

The dining room was empty except for a group of men who were speaking in English. Alan said to Niall, "No one has heard news of Mac-Mhic-Donnail."

"That is a good sign," Niall replied.

Alan nodded somberly.

Niall said, "What would you like to eat, Alec?"

Suddenly she couldn't face the thought of sitting here for one more minute in all her filth. "What I want is a bath," she said. "Do you think the inn is capable of arranging that?"

He looked at her in silence.

Good God, she thought. *He's going to tell me that they don't have bathtubs!*

He said, "I wasn't planning to remain in Fort Augustus. We have hours of daylight left. I was going to go on to Glen Alpin."

Alexandra's temper flickered. "Why on earth can't we stay the night here and set off for Glen Alpin tomorrow?" she demanded.

His formidable black brows drew together. "My grandfather is dying. Every moment may count if I wish to see him while he is still alive. If you don't want to make the trip to Glen Alpin with me today, then I will leave Alan with you here in Fort Augustus, and he will bring you on tomorrow."

It was as if he had dumped a barrel of cold water on her anger, thoroughly extinguishing it. She felt ashamed of herself. He was right, she thought. If his grandfather should die while he was staying the night at Fort Augustus, he would never forgive himself.

Even worse, he would never forgive *her.*

"I'm sorry, Niall, I wasn't thinking," she said quietly. "Of course we must go on."

"I meant what I said. If you are too tired, you can remain here in Fort Augustus," he replied.

She thought with resentment that he sounded as if he wanted her to stay behind.

"I slept in the coach," she said evenly. "I will be ready to leave whenever you are."

"Very well," he said. "I shall see about hiring some ponies." And he got up from the table, leaving her with an expressionless Alan and the dogs.

As the miles were eaten up by his long, hillman's stride, and the magnificent, towering beauty of home surrounded him, Niall felt his heart cramp with love, and with another emotion he did not wish to think about. He looked around at the high, green slopes, at the carpets of fern and of heather, at the rushing little burns and the still clearnesses of the lochs, and thought how much he had missed the sight and the smells of home.

He had been walking in the forefront of their party, and he stopped now at the top of a hill to give the others a chance to catch up to him. As he waited, his eyes rested on his wife, who was seated incongruously on a shaggy Highland pony, and he wondered bleakly how he was ever going to tell his grandfather that he had married a Sassenach girl.

She looked like a displaced queen upon the sturdy pony, he thought. He recalled the splendid thoroughbreds she was accustomed to riding along the wide rides that ran through Gayles's magnificent, perfectly tended park, and he wondered what she was thinking.

Niall's feelings about Alexandra were very conflicted, and that conflict was closely tied to the confusion he was experiencing about himself and who he was. For the first time in his life, he was being forced to face the fact that part of him, half of him, was Sassenach.

Since birth, Niall MacDonald had been reared to regard the English as the assassins of his people. He had gone south to claim his English inheritance with the sole idea that he would take the Sassenach earl's money and use it for the betterment of Glen Alpin. When he had left for England, he had been a MacDonald to his fingertips.

He had not been prepared for the surge of recognition and possessiveness that had overcome him as he rode across the extensive property that was his birthright from his father. He had not been prepared for the intensity of his feeling for Alexandra, who was the very sort of Sassenach lady he had been reared to despise.

He had coped with this unwelcome internal division by separating the two worlds in his mind. Gayles and England and Alexandra were an entirely separate entity from Glen Alpin, and subconsciously he felt that as long as he kept the two places completely distinct, he would not have to face the confusion that lurked so dangerously inside him.

Then Alexandra had insisted on accompanying him to Scotland. The world of his father was invading the world of his mother, and the crutch Niall had constructed in his mind to deal with his crisis of identity was being shattered.

When he had awakened beside Alexandra in the inn on Kintyre, he had been terrified by the feelings that had swept over him. He had never felt like this about a woman before. He desired her desperately, but it was more than that. She gave him something he had never gotten from anyone else. Somehow—he did not know how it had happened—but somehow she had managed to get her slim, elegant fingers around his heart.

Even while he lived in England, he had found it difficult to acknowledge his feelings for his wife. His brain had told him not to trust her, had even suggested that she might be cooperating with Geoffrey Wilton to try to do away with him. But his heart knew otherwise.

He was trying very hard not to listen to his heart.

He told himself that his home and his life were in Glen Alpin, and Alec could never be a part of that world. He told himself that he wished she had never come.

Alexandra's pony reached the top of the grass-covered hill, and Niall immediately moved off, following the path that led down the other side. It was growing late, but the long Highland day was still bright, and when they passed the first MacDonald *clachan* he could see children playing outdoors in the evening sunshine.

"They are the first people I have seen," Alexandra said, much as the attorney, Taylor, had remarked months before.

"Now we are in the lands of Glen Alpin," Niall replied proudly. "Now you will see people instead of sheep."

His long legs lengthened their stride. *Please, dear God,* he prayed silently. *Please let me be in time.*

At long last he was standing on top of the last steep hill and looking down into the beautiful glen that was his home.

He stared hungrily at the sunset-tinted waters of the loch, at the surrounding, snow-covered peaks, and his heart lifted.

It was a scene he would never tire of looking at, he thought, as he turned to his wife to gauge her reaction.

She was staring at the magnificent view, her lips slightly parted. The perfect skin of her cheeks was flushed from the long ride and a few strands of gold hair had come loose from her braid to curl behind the delicate shell of her ear.

He said gruffly, "The castle that you see is my home. It is called Eilean Darrach."

"Oh my," she said softly. "Oh my." She looked at him, her gray eyes wide with awe. "Niall, it is so beautiful."

He nodded. He had known that she would find it beautiful. It was impossible not to. But living here . . . that was something altogether different.

"Come on," he said abruptly, and led the way to the narrow path that would take them down into the glen.

They were met on the road that led around the loch by two clansmen.

"Dougal and Ian," Niall greeted them in Gaelic. He felt his whole body tense as he asked the crucial question. "How is Mac-Mhic-Donnail?"

"He is very ill," Ian MacDonald replied. "It is good that you have come."

Thank God, Niall thought. *I am in time.*

Both men looked at Alexandra.

Tension tightened the muscles in Niall's neck and shoulders, and he said more brusquely than he had intended, "This is my wife."

Ian and Dougal could not have looked more shocked if he had introduced her as the daughter of Satan.

Niall turned to Alexandra and said in English, "These are two of my clansmen, Ian and Dougal MacDonald."

"How do you do," she said regally to the two men.

They stared at her, then turned to look at Niall.

He said grimly, "Let us be on our way."

In silence the five of them, followed by the hounds and two pack ponies, followed the path around the loch until, after saying farewell to Niall, Alan turned off to go on to his own home, followed a few minutes later by the clansmen. Niall and Alexandra were alone when they reached the causeway that led to the castle.

They were met in the courtyard by a dark-eyed woman with gray streaks in her brown hair. "Niall," she called, and came to envelop him in a warm embrace. "I am so sorry that you had to come home to such ill news, my dear," his foster mother said to him in Gaelic.

"How is he?" Niall said.

"I think he has been waiting for you," she replied. "You will find him . . . much changed."

"I'll go to him immediately."

He turned as if to leave, but the woman put a restraining hand on his arm. "And the lassie?" she said gently.

"Oh." Niall looked at Alexandra as if surprised to find her there, and switched to English, "This is Margaret MacDonald, my foster mother," he told her. Then, to Margaret, "This is my wife."

Margaret's eyes flew wide open. "Your wife?"

"Yes," Niall said, still speaking English. "I will tell you all about it later. In the meanwhile, will you show her to a room? We have been traveling since dawn, and she is exhausted."

"Of course," Margaret MacDonald said. "I will settle Lady MacDonald just fine. Go you along to Mac-Mhic-Donnail."

Niall nodded gravely and walked out of the room.

Chapter Twenty-four

Left alone with Niall's foster mother, Alexandra tried not to feel as if she had been abandoned.

"Do you have baggage with you, Lady MacDonald?" Margaret MacDonald asked in an expressionless voice.

"Yes," Alexandra replied. "The brown-leather portmanteau is mine."

"I will have one of the lads bring it. Come along with me, and I will take you upstairs."

Alexandra followed Margaret to the dark, narrow stone staircase at the far end of the hall and climbed behind Niall's foster mother up three steep flights. When they reached the third floor, Margaret turned left and went along a narrow, dark passageway. Alexandra followed her past four closed doors, then they went up another small staircase that led to a large, scarred oak door. Margaret MacDonald opened the door and went into the room. Alexandra followed.

She knew as soon as she stepped inside that she was in Niall's bedroom. It was furnished with a heavy oak bedstead and armoire; a bookcase, crammed untidily with books of varying sizes; a washstand with a shaving mirror set upon it; two tables with fat candles in dishes; and, at the foot of the bed, a wooden chest. There was a straight wooden chair in front of the washstand and the stone fireplace did not contain either coal or wood.

On the wall, directly over the empty fireplace, was a painting of Loch Alpin that looked as if it had been done from atop one of the surrounding hills. The other walls held a formidable collection of the small daggerlike knives the Highlanders called dirks as well as pictures of a dog and a magnificently antlered buck.

Margaret MacDonald went to the casement window and pushed it open, letting a draft of chilly air into the room along with the soft luminous light of the Highland evening.

"I will have your baggage brought upstairs," Niall's foster mother said in the same expressionless voice as before. "Is there anything else I can get you, Lady MacDonald?"

Alexandra turned and looked into the other woman's wary brown eyes. "I gather that Niall did not write to inform you of our marriage," she said.

"No, he did not," Margaret returned flatly.

Alexandra summoned up one of her most winning smiles. "Well, I will leave it to him to explain to you just how our union came to be."

Margaret MacDonald did not return the smile. "I will have some hot water brought up to you," she said.

Alexandra felt thoroughly rebuffed. Her smile died.

"That would be wonderful," she said. "I feel as if I have not washed in a year."

Margaret MacDonald favored her with a long, level look. "Would you like to have a bath?" She offered the bath as if she felt she had to cater to this milksop Englishwoman her foster son had married.

Alexandra gave up caring what Margaret MacDonald might think of her. At the moment all she could think about was the bliss of sinking into a tubful of hot water and washing her hair. "I would adore to have a bath," she said fervently.

"I will see to it." Margaret looked at Alexandra with distinct disapproval and went out.

Ten minutes later, as Alexandra was standing by the window looking out at the truly spectacular view, two men knocked on the door and came in carrying a tin tub, which looked both ancient and blessedly large. They set it in the middle of the floor, not in front of the fireplace as Alexandra had expected.

It was then that she realized that no one was going to light the fire, that she was expected to bathe in the unheated room, with the draft from the open window blowing on her.

"Is it possible to start a fire?" she asked the men as they were on the point of departing.

They turned and looked at her as if she had three heads.

"A fire?" one said. "But it is April."

"Yes," Alexandra replied pleasantly. "I realize that it is April. But I am English, you see, and in England we always bathe in front of fires." She looked at the open window. "And close the window, please."

The two Scots exchanged a look that was patently disgusted. Then one of the men said, "I will go and bring some wood."

"Thank you," Alexandra returned firmly.

Eventually the window was closed, the fire was lit, and the tub was filled with hot water. A pretty red-haired girl named Bridget was appointed to help Alexandra bathe and wash her hair. Bridget proved efficient, and Alexandra was soon wrapped in a warm robe and sitting in the single hard chair in front of the delightful fire. Bridget was brushing out her hair when Niall walked into the room.

He stopped dead when he saw his wife. "What are you doing here?"

"This is where Mrs. MacDonald brought me," she replied.

"Oh." He looked confusedly from the fire to the still-filled tub.

Alexandra thought he looked exhausted and on impulse she said, "Would you like to bathe, Niall? The water is still warm."

He looked at her blankly.

"Bring some dry towels," Alexandra said to Bridget.

The girl went out, leaving husband and wife alone.

Alexandra went to Niall and matter-of-factly began to pull his coat off his shoulders. He stood docilely and let her do it.

By the time Bridget returned with more towels, Alexandra had stripped Niall down to his trousers. She went to the door when Bridget knocked, took the towels, and went back to her husband.

"Sit down," she said, pushing him toward the chair. Then she knelt in front of him and pulled off his boots. In the same matter-of-fact way, she stood him up and stripped off his trousers.

"Now," she said. "Get into the water."

He nodded and went mechanically to the tub, stepped in, and sat down. She followed him, bent down to wet a sponge, and began to wash his back.

He didn't say a word, even when she dumped water over his head and soaped his hair and rinsed it.

Her own robe was patched with wet by the time she had finished.

"All right, darling, you can get out now," she said.

She handed him a towel and he dried himself, knotted it around his waist and stepped out of the tub. He stood there, looking down at her as if he was seeing her for the first time.

"He's dying, Alec," he said. "I don't think I believed it until I saw him."

"I am so sorry, Niall," she said.

"He looks . . . all sunken in."

"Has there been a doctor to see him?" she asked softly.

He nodded. "Ewan MacDonald got a doctor from Fort William. His heart is badly damaged, the doctor said. He could go anytime."

She felt so helpless. She didn't know his grandfather, and there was nothing she could find to say that might comfort him. Never had she felt more a stranger in his life.

She wanted very much to know if he had told his grandfather about her, but she was afraid to ask.

He walked to the bed as if he were very weary and sat down on the edge. After a moment's hesitation, she joined him.

"Would you like me to rub your shoulders?" she asked.

He looked at her in puzzlement.

Without further explanation, she knelt on the bed behind him and dug her fingers into his taut flesh. He let out a long breath. "That feels good."

He was so strong. He hung his head a little and let her do what she wanted, and it was amazing to her to feel such power and strength under her kneading fingers.

When at last her fingers were too tired to work any further, he turned around to where she still knelt behind him. "Thank you, Alec, that felt very good." He lifted his hand and brushed a silky tress of loose hair off of her temple. Then he leaned forward, cupped his hand around the back of her head, and gently kissed her mouth.

She remained perfectly still, scarcely breathing.

His kiss hardened, deepened, and he pulled her against him. Desire, liquid and sweet, rippled through her in undulating waves.

"Alec," he said, "God help me, but I can't resist you."

He bent her back onto the bed, then followed her down. He kissed her again and again, caressing her with his hands until she was dizzy, until all of the wanting was centered in one trembling, vulnerable place.

"Yes," he said hoarsely as, helplessly, she lifted her hips toward him in silent invitation. "Open for me."

A distant voice in her brain was telling her not to do this, that he couldn't ignore her as he had and then turn around and expect her to go to bed with him. But his hand moved up between her legs and the thrilling sensation that followed his touch swept the distant, protesting voice into oblivion.

She locked her arms around his neck and felt him enter her. The feel of him inside her was so good and she closed her legs around his waist. She arched her neck and her back, surrendering herself totally to his pounding possession as, one after another, the intense convulsions of orgasm washed through her.

After his own release was accomplished, he let his weight collapse on top of her briefly, but then he rolled on his side to spare her, all the while still keeping them connected.

They lay clasped together, heartbeats gradually slowing, the perspiration drying on their cooling skin.

"My God," he said after a while, "I can't believe that it gets better every time."

"You don't deserve this," she murmured softly against his ear. "You have been perfectly beastly to me these last few days."

He didn't answer immediately. Then he said, "I'm sorry. It's just . . . I've been worried about my grandfather."

She didn't think that was the reason for his standoffish behavior, but, now that she had him in her arms again, she didn't want to spoil the moment.

She had enough confidence now to ask, "Did you tell him about me?"

"Yes."

"And was he . . . upset?"

"Yes."

She said with genuine indignation, "You know, Niall, I have never done the slightest harm to a single person named MacDonald, yet everyone here seems to regard me as a sworn enemy."

He sighed, kissed her temple, and reluctantly withdrew. "I know, Alec. I tried to tell you. The past is still very present in Glen Alpin."

He swung his legs over the edge of the bed and got up.

She lay back against the pillows and regarded him broodingly as he went to the armoire and pulled out some clothes.

"Do you know something, Niall? It isn't the English who are responsible for destroying the Highlands. It is your own people who have done that."

He had pulled a long shirt over his head, and now his head came up and he stared at her. "That is a ridiculous statement."

"Oh, the English behaved reprehensibly after Culloden, I will not dispute that. But as you told me yourself, the clans supported their chiefs while they were in exile, and eventually all of the chiefs returned. But it seems to me that as soon as they returned, they started selling off their land. If all the Highland chiefs were like your grandfather, there would still be a living culture in these hills. It is your own chiefs who have betrayed your people, Niall, not the English."

A very bleak look settled over his face. He picked up the kilt he had laid on the chair and began to fasten it around his waist. "I am not going to dispute with you," he said.

Just stop blaming me! The words hovered on the tip of her tongue, but she did not say them.

"If you will get dressed, Alec," he said, "my grandfather would like to meet you."

Alistair MacDonald, Chief of Glen Alpin, lay against the pillows in his massive four-poster and breathed with difficulty. Looking down into his grandfather's face, Niall wanted to weep. The cheeks and temples had sunk inward, and only his formidable nose remained what it had been.

"Mac-Mhic-Donnail," Niall said steadily, "I have brought you my wife."

The dark eyes opened and Alexandra stepped closer to the bed so that he could see her.

"I am so sorry that you are ill," she said in her cool, English voice.

The old man looked at her.

If anyone could bring him to accept an English girl as his grandson's wife, it would be Alec, Niall thought. She looked like an angel as she bent over and lightly kissed the sunken cheek of the dying chief.

Alistair said, "Do not take my grandson away from his land and his people." The words, which once would have been spoken fiercely, now only sounded breathless.

"I would never do that," Alexandra replied clearly. "I could not do it, even if I wished to. Niall belongs here. I know that and I will not try to change it."

Niall looked at his wife in surprise. She did not look back, but suddenly she bent over and whispered something into his grandfather's ear.

The old man's face relaxed infinitesimally, and for a moment his eyes closed. Then they opened, and he looked at Niall. "Stay for a while," he said in Gaelic.

"I have no intention of going anywhere else," Niall replied in the same language. The chair that he had used earlier was still pulled up to the bed and he went to sit in it.

"I will leave the two of you alone," Alexandra said softly.

Niall looked at her, grateful for her understanding but guilty that he was leaving her on her own in a strange house.

"I shall be fine," she said, seeming to read his thoughts. "Don't worry about me."

He nodded gravely and watched her leave. Then he turned back to his grandfather and put his warm, strong hand upon the old man's where it lay upon the coverlet.

Alistair appeared to have fallen into a doze. Niall looked at him and tried to imagine a life without his grandfather in it.

He has always been there, he thought. *Ever since I can remember. However am I to go on without him?*

Minutes turned to hours as Niall sat keeping watch by the deathbed of the chief. At three-thirty in the morning, Alistair opened his eyes. "I am away on my journey," he said.

Niall stood up.

"Never forget that you are the chief," Alistair said. Then his eyes closed again. At four o'clock, his breathing stopped.

For the rest of the night, Niall stayed in the empty room from which his grandfather's spirit had gone, keeping the watch for the dead.

He was the last of the great chiefs, Niall thought, as his eyes rested on the sunken face and still-magnificent nose of his grandfather. *He kept all the ancient loyalties burning bright, and all the ancient enmities as well.*

It was men like his grandfather who had raised the clans for Charles Stuart against the German usurper who had stolen his throne. That rising had ended in Culloden, the death knell of the Highland way of life.

As he sat alone in the profound silence of the room, for the first time Niall considered the possibility that it was not just the English who were responsible for what had happened to the Highlands.

It is your own chiefs, not the English, who have betrayed your people.

In some ways perhaps Alec was right, Niall thought, as he sat looking broodingly at his grandfather's peaceful face. It was too easy to blame the English for the sheep that were displacing the clans in so many Highland glens. The greatest betrayal of all had come from within. No longer did the chiefs regard themselves as guardians of the land and the clan. They had become landlords; property, not people, was their concern; profit, not the well-being of the clan, was their goal.

He would not be like that. He would bring in cattle to graze upon the rich green grass of Glen Alpin, and his people would thrive. As chief, he would oversee the renaissance of the Glen Alpin MacDonalds.

And Alec? How did she fit into this future he envisioned?

She didn't. She couldn't. She was English. She belonged at Gayles.

When Margaret MacDonald came into the room at seven o'clock, Niall was standing at the window, his forehead pressed against the glass.

Chapter Twenty-five

Niall was composed when he came to tell Alexandra the news that his grandfather had died during the night. She was still in bed when he came into the room, and he rested his fingers lightly on the wooden footboard, and said, "He went peacefully and knew that I was with him. There are worse ways to start off on your journey."

Alexandra listened with an ache in her heart. She longed to get out of bed, go to him and take him in her arms, but his face told her not to.

"I am so sorry," she said. It seemed to her that he must be sick of hearing her repeat that useless phrase, but she didn't know what else to say.

"Thank you," he replied.

"You will miss him, I know."

Not a muscle moved in his face. He nodded.

"Where will you bury him?" she asked.

"The family graveyard is away down the loch. We will carry him there in two days time and put him in the earth." She saw his fingers tighten on the footboard so that his fingernails went white, but his face never changed. "I have given the word for runners to go out to all of the clan bearing the news. It will take a while for everyone to assemble."

"Surely it will not take that long to send word around the glen," Alexandra protested, thinking it would be best for Niall not to have the funeral prolonged.

He shook his head impatiently. "Those who live in the glen itself are easily reached, but several of the *ceann-tigh* live on the other side of the mountains. It will take most of the day to reach them with the news, and then they must gather their people and come back across the mountains to get here."

Alexandra had been under the impression that all of the clan lived in the area of the glen itself. "Who are these *ceann-tigh*?" she asked in bewilderment.

"They are cousins, the heads of various branches of the family who oversee large pieces of land for the chief," he replied. "It is the *ceann-tigh* who will carry the coffin of Mac-Mhic-Donnail to the grave."

Almost the full length of the bed was between them, but he had made no move to come closer.

"Will women be coming to the funeral as well as men?" she asked.

He nodded. "The wives of the *ceann-tigh* will keep the death watch, and they will follow the funeral procession with us to the grave."

Alexandra searched his strictly controlled face. "I will be happy to keep the death watch with you, Niall," she offered quietly.

His brows drew together, and he gave her his most formidable stare. "It is not one of your customs."

She smoothed her fingers along the top of her blanket. "I

know that." She kept her voice very soft. "But I will be happy to share this custom with you."

He shook his head dismissively. "There is little point in sitting up all night with someone you did not know."

I know you, her heart cried. *I want to do this for you.*

But, as so often happened, she was afraid to speak her heart's feelings out loud.

He must have seen from her face that he had hurt her because he said abruptly, "You may come with us to the graveyard if you wish."

"I would like that."

He nodded, said stiffly, "I will leave you to get dressed," and departed.

No one came to bring her tea or to help her dress, so Alexandra dressed herself and even managed to knot her hair tidily at the back of her head. Then she went downstairs.

Already there were strangers in the house. Alexandra could hear the deep sounds of men's voices speaking Gaelic as she stepped into the dining room in search of breakfast. Niall was there, sitting at the table with Alan MacDonald and four other men whom she did not know.

As Alexandra stood hesitating in the doorway, Margaret MacDonald said from behind her, "I have set out some breakfast for you in the library, Lady MacDonald."

Alexandra was a little taken back. Did Highland ladies not breakfast with their men? She hesitated, and looked at Niall, but he was deep in conversation and did not look back. Finally, "Thank you," she said to his foster mother, and followed Margaret out of the dining room.

She had her solitary breakfast in the library and by the time she finished, other mourners had started to arrive. They were welcomed by either Niall or Margaret MacDonald, who assumed the role of hostess with such naturalness that

Alexandra realized it had never occurred to the woman that such a position should belong to Niall's wife.

Alexandra was not completely forgotten, however. Either Niall or Margaret punctiliously introduced her to the arriving family, all of whom, men and women, looked at the Sassenach bride with horrified shock.

Never in her life had Alexandra felt such an outsider. The fact that everyone was speaking Gaelic only increased her sense of isolation. For almost the entire morning, she sat silently in the castle's beautiful drawing room, surrounded by people who were speaking a language she did not understand.

The only living creature who paid attention to her was Fergus, who spent an hour curled up next to her skirts. Then Niall looked in, called for him, and Alexandra was left alone once more.

With the departure of Fergus, Alexandra was suddenly angry. She was Niall's *wife*, she thought furiously, not some pariah who had appeared on the doorstep and been taken in for the sake of charity. This was *her* house, and it was extremely rude of these women to speak Gaelic in front of her when she suspected they all spoke English perfectly well.

She got to her feet and walked to the door. Behind her the conversation faltered, but she kept on going, her head held high, her back straight as a lance. Once outside, she went in search of Niall's foster mother, whom she discovered coming down the main staircase.

"Lady MacDonald," Margaret said with surprise when Alexandra hailed her, "is there aught that you need?"

Alexandra waited until the woman had reached the bottom of the stairs and was standing next to her. Then she said, "I would like to help you, Mrs. MacDonald. Tell me what I can do."

"That is not necessary," Niall's foster mother said with calm dismissal. She looked up into Alexandra's face with the cool brown eyes of her son, Alan. "But thank you for your offer."

Alexandra's simmering temper abruptly flared. She had run Gayles for six years and knew full well that the influx of so many people caused a great deal of work for the household. And Eilean Darrach did not seem to have an over-abundance of staff.

She looked back at Margaret MacDonald and made a great effort to clamp down on her anger. It would do no good to insult this woman. So she drew a deep, steadying breath, and said, "I know well that this is not my grief, but I have lost a father and a brother, and I believe I can appreciate what Niall and the rest of you are feeling. I have had the running of a household and I know how pressured you must be to feed and house all of these people. Of course you need help. Tell me what I can do."

Margaret eyed her warily. "What is it that you wish to do?"

"Do you need help in the kitchen?" Alexandra asked practically. "I can peel potatoes, if that is what you need."

Margaret's mouth actually dropped open. "Do you know how to peel potatoes?"

"Yes," Alexandra replied.

The two women looked at each other steadily, and after a moment Margaret's face relaxed infinitesimally. "All right then," she said. "Come along with me. We are going mad, and I am sure there will be something that you can do."

Alexandra spent the rest of the afternoon helping Margaret MacDonald. It was Alexandra who set the dining-room table with the lovely china and crystal that Margaret showed her, and it was Alexandra who checked all of the guest rooms to make certain there were sheets on the beds, water in the jugs, and firestarters for the candles. She actually ended up putting linens on a few of the beds herself, as well as doing some dusting and sweeping of rooms that had clearly been unused for quite some time. It was she who checked the larder and decided that they would need more meat for the following day, and it was she who arranged to get it.

By the end of the second day of the wake, the ice between Niall's foster mother and Alexandra was thoroughly broken. Alexandra was no longer "Lady MacDonald," but "lassie," and the two women worked in efficient harmony to keep the hospitality of Eilean Darrach flowing smoothly. The castle was filled to capacity, with the *ceann-tigh* and their families, Niall's cousins, and the traditional officers of the clan. The night before the funeral, Alexandra went to bed, exhausted but satisfied that she had done a good job and been a help to her husband in this trying time.

She was alone when she awoke the following morning. Once again Niall had spent the night keeping watch over the coffin of his grandfather, this time with the mourners who had arrived yesterday. He had had scarcely any sleep in the last three days, and Alexandra thought that he must be incredibly weary.

Suddenly a high, wailing sound assaulted her ears, and she realized that it was this sound that had awakened her. She got out of bed and went to the window. The day was bleak and gray, and mist hung in the air. Alexandra looked across the expanse of dark, cold water and her eyes widened with shock.

The meadow on the far side of the causeway was filled with over a thousand kilted men. As Alexandra watched, more and more of them poured off the hillside to join those already lined up. The newcomers were accompanied by the skirling of the pipes.

Goose bumps that were not from the cold came out on Alexandra's skin as she stood by the window and watched the Glen Alpin MacDonalds line up in the meadow. At last she turned away to dress. She was putting the last pins in the simple knot she had made of her hair when Niall came into the bedroom.

"Are you ready, Alec?" he asked.

Weariness was imprinted in all the lineaments of his face. Impulsively, she went to him and put her arms around him, offering comfort.

He was stiff and resistant within her embrace.

"I am all right," he said. "You needn't worry about me."

Rebuffed, she dropped her arms and stepped back.

In a low voice, she said, "I am ready."

They went down the stairs to where the coffin awaited them in the front hall. It made an eerie sight, Alexandra thought with a shiver, as she walked beside Niall under the candles that had been fixed between the enormous antlers of the stags' heads that surrounded the hall.

The room was utterly silent. Four men bearing flaming torches stood at each of the coffin's corners, and several of the *ceann-tigh* stood against the wall, looking somber.

In silence, Alexandra walked beside Niall through the hall and out into the courtyard, where a crowd of people awaited them. Alexandra saw Margaret MacDonald with Alan, and the older woman gave her a sober nod.

In front of the mourners stood an immense clansman bearing the great yellow banner of the clan. The sky was filled with racing gray clouds and the wind whipped the flag into wild folds. The sound of the blowing flag was the only noise. All of the pipes had fallen silent.

Then, slowly, the castle door swung open, revealing the eerily lit hall within. As Alexandra watched, the *ceann-tigh* bent and lifted the coffin to their shoulders. Then they walked slowly forward, bearing Alistair MacDonald, Chief of Glen Alpin, out of his castle for the last time.

Behind the coffin paced his piper and his bard.

The mourners in the courtyard moved aside to let the coffin go before them. As the *ceann-tigh* reached the causeway and began to cross the loch, the piper gave voice to his pipes.

For as long as she lived, Alexandra knew she would never forget the funeral of Alistair MacDonald. The weather deteriorated as they followed the loch west, toward the ancient graveyard of the Glen Alpin MacDonalds, and soon it began to rain. The long line of MacDonalds—afterward she would estimate that there had to have been two thousand of them—continued onward in the wake of their dead chief, accompanied by the high-pitched wailing of the pipes.

Alexandra walked next to Niall, her long legs easily keeping up with the somber march of the mourners. As the rain began to fall more heavily, Niall looked down at her.

"Are you all right?"

"I'm fine, darling," she replied.

He gave her a shadowy smile and returned his gaze to the coffin-bearers in front of them.

The graveyard was set on a grassy hillside with a splendid view of both loch and castle. Some of the men had dug the grave the previous day, and now the bearers brought the coffin up beside the open hole and laid it on the ground.

Then Niall stepped forward and took a piece of paper from inside his jacket. Holding one hand so that it shielded the writing from the rain, he read aloud from the Ninetieth

Psalm. Then he lowered the paper, looked directly at the coffin of his grandfather, and said clearly:

"I am the resurrection and the life, saith the Lord: he that believeth in me, though he were dead, yet shall he live: and whosoever liveth and believeth in me shall never die."

Slowly he stepped back to stand once more beside Alexandra.

As the rain beat relentlessly down, the bard reached his arms to the heavens and broke into a wild lament. Then, as the coffin was slowly lowered into its last resting place, the words of the bard were taken up by all of the watching clan, a chorus of grief flung into the stormy skies,

Alexandra shivered and looked up at her husband. His face was wet and she thought that not all the drops were from the rain. Tentatively, she slipped her gloved hand into his bare one, and his fingers closed around hers.

Niall stood like a rock as the pipes skirled and the dirt was flung over the grave. He never once looked down at her, but the pressure of his hand was so tight that it hurt her bones.

Most of the clansmen left for home directly from the graveyard. Only the *ceann-tigh* returned to the castle for the funeral meal, and they would leave Eilean Darrach on the following morning. Niall presided over the ample dinner and watched his wife, who was seated at the far end of the table, direct the service with easy competence.

He looked at his foster mother, who was seated halfway down the table, to see if she showed any signs of resenting Alexandra's assumption of command. Margaret's face was perfectly serene.

After dessert had been served, Niall and the men retired to the library to share a bottle of brandy and discuss the new cattle venture upon which the clan would be embarking. It was a cheerful conversation, and a welcome one after the mourning of the past few days.

Niall had uncharacteristically embarked upon his third glass of brandy when he heard Ewan MacDonald say with a chuckle, "I am thinking that An Siosalach will be furious when he hears about the cattle. He has been hoping to bring his sheep into Glen Alpin."

Niall stared at his cousin, who was sitting across from him at the big library table where he had been taught his lessons as a child. He put his brandy glass down, and said, "How do you know that?"

Ewan shrugged. "Would you believe it? He came to see me a while back and wanted to know what my thoughts would be about selling Glen Alpin to him."

"He came to see *you*?" Archibald MacDonald asked in astonishment.

Ewan tilted his head and finished the brandy in his glass. "He did, weasly thing that he is."

"What did you answer him?" Niall demanded.

Ewan looked amazed. "What do you think I said? I told him that I did not have the selling of Glen Alpin in my hands, and that the hands that did hold it would never sell it. I told him that hell would freeze over before he would put sheep in Glen Alpin."

The rest of the men loudly expressed their approval of this rousing reply.

Then Alexander MacDonald said, "I still do not understand why An Siosalach would talk to Ewan about the selling of Glen Alpin."

Niall looked around the table at the faces of his kinsmen. He leaned back in his chair, stretched his legs in front of him, and said soberly, "Ewan is not the only one An Siosalach has talked to about selling Glen Alpin." And he related the sequence of events that had occurred in England, leaving out for the moment the attempts on his life.

Enlightened, Ewan said, "So that is why you married a Sassenach."

"Aye," Niall replied a little grimly.

"But why should An Siosalach desire Glen Alpin so dearly?" one of the other men said in bewilderment. "There are plenty of other chiefs willing to sell off their hereditary lands, lands which are close to Strathglass, too."

Niall contemplated his half-full glass of brandy, as if looking for an answer. At last he shook his head. "That is a question I cannot answer."

Ian MacDonald leaned forward, his eyes intent on Niall. "Here is an odd thing," he said. "One of my own men, Donald Dhu, came to me a few weeks back with a story that he had run into two men at the west end of Loch Alpin. They told him that they were fishing, but he had been watching them for a while and he did not think that was what they were doing. He told them that they were on property that belonged to Mac-Mhic-Donnail and that they would have to find somewhere else to fish. He waited until they had packed up their gear before he left them."

"What is so odd about that?" Ewan said. "There have been strangers in the glen before this."

"Donald thought he recognized one of the men—he thought he was a Chisholm from Strathglass." Ian paused, narrowed his eyes, and continued to look at Niall. "In fact, he thought he was the foster brother of the chief."

Niall's eyebrows lifted.

Ian nodded.

A weighty silence fell upon the room.

"*Dhé*," Ewan said at last. "What can An Siosalach be wishing to do with Glen Alpin?"

Niall made up his mind. "I don't know, but I would like to take a look at the place where Donald Dhu found those men." He turned to Ian MacDonald. "Was Donald specific about the place?"

"He was. He said it was at the head of the loch, near where the Gley comes in."

Niall got to his feet. "It will be light for many hours yet," he said. "Who wants to go with me?"

To a man, the *ceann-tigh* rose to join him.

Chapter Twenty-six

The late northern light was slowly dying from the sky when at last the men returned to Eilean Darrach. Alexandra and the wives of the *ceann-tigh* were gathered in the drawing room, where they had been waiting for their husbands.

To Alexandra's relief, the women had taken their cue from Margaret MacDonald and changed the language they were speaking to English. She was thus ennabled to join in the conversation, the main topic of which was the men's decision to go off on this mysterious trek up the loch.

Alexandra was pleased to note that every wife present was annoyed that her husband had not confided in her the reason for his sudden departure. She thought that it spoke well of these Highland marriages that the women apparently considered themselves their husbands' usual confidants and were bothered by not knowing what was going on.

The men were close-mouthed when they returned, but it was evident from the expression on every wife's face that she was only waiting for the moment when she could get her man alone to begin the inquisition. Consequently the drawing room soon cleared as people went upstairs to bed.

"Come along," Niall said to Alexandra, and they joined the procession to the stairs. When the door to their bedroom closed behind them, Niall yawned, stretched his arms high over his head, and said, "I have not slept in a bed for three nights. That looks very good."

"I am sure that it must," Alexandra replied. She stood beneath one of the wildlife pictures on the wall and watched in silence as he began to undress.

First he took off the short jacket that was so unlike the long, swallow-tailed coats he had worn in England. Next came his shoes and socks. He removed the dirk that he wore in his belt and then took off the belt itself. He tugged his long white shirt out of his kilt and pulled it over his head. Finally, when he was standing there in only his kilt, he seemed to realize that he was the only one who was undressing.

He looked at her, one black eyebrow raised. "Is something wrong?"

His bare torso glimmered in the light from the candles on the mantel, and the thought crossed her mind that a sculptor would love to have him for a model. What she said was: "Where on earth did you and the other men go for all those hours?"

He let out his breath slowly. "Alec, I'm tired. Can't this wait until tomorrow?"

She didn't answer, just regarded him steadily out of dark gray eyes.

"Oh, all right," he said with weary resignation. "Get into your nightgown, and I will tell you."

Unconcernedly, he stripped off his kilt and walked naked to the window to open it. He lifted the casement, stopped, glanced over his shoulder at her, then turned back and closed it again. He went to the bed, got in under the blankets, crossed his arms behind his head, and looked at the ceiling.

Alexandra undressed as quickly as she could, pulled her nightdress over her head, and went to join him.

By the time she got there his eyes were closed and he was breathing slowly. She was torn between the desire to shake him awake so he could talk to her and the desire to let him get the sleep he so sorely needed. She had just decided on the latter course when his eyes opened, and he looked up at her.

"It seems you were right, and it is Chisholm after all who is responsible for my accidents," he said.

Her eyes widened. This was the last thing she had expected to hear. "What do you mean?"

"I learned this afternoon that Chisholm also approached my cousin Ewan, who is next in line after me. He wanted to know if Ewan would consider selling him Glen Alpin."

She had been sitting up, but the room was cold even with the window closed, so now she scooted down in the bed and pulled the blankets up to her chin. He leaned up on his elbow so he could look at her. "I still don't know why Chisholm wants Glen Alpin, but I'm sure it isn't to run sheep. A few weeks ago, Donald Dhu saw Chisholm's foster brother with another man out at the head of the loch. That is where we just went, to see if the men were still there."

"And were they?"

"No, but there are a number of caves in the region and in one of them we found shovels and other digging tools. There was also evidence of digging in two of the other caves."

"Good heavens," Alexandra said in wonder. "But the men were gone?"

"Temporarily, at least. They left their tools behind, as well as a considerable collection of provisions."

"That is very interesting," Alexandra said slowly.

"It is interesting indeed," Niall returned. He was still leaning on his elbow looking down at her. "What in the name of God can they be doing?"

"It sounds as if they are looking for some kind of buried treasure," she said.

Niall looked skeptical. "There is no treasure buried in those caves."

"There is no treasure that *you* know of," Alexandra corrected him. "But what if Chisholm has discovered something that you don't know about—a map or something? It may sound far-fetched, but look at the facts, Niall. First Chisholm tries to buy the glen from you, and now you find his men digging in your caves. What other way can you explain these things other than that Chisholm thinks there is a treasure buried in Glen Alpin? That is the reason why he has been trying to purchase the land. It must be a great treasure indeed if he is willing to kill for it as well."

Niall lowered himself to his back, folded his hands on his chest and once more regarded the ceiling. Alexandra was quiet, letting him think.

"Treasure," he said after a while. "I wonder . . ."

His voice trailed off, and Alexandra could keep silent no longer. "Yes?" she prompted.

"I wonder if he thinks he has located the French gold," Niall said.

Alexandra sat up with a bounce. "What do you mean? What French gold?"

He moved his eyes from the ceiling to her face and explained.

"England and France were at war when the clans rose for Prince Charlie in 1745. The French king would not go so far as to send troops to support the Stuart rebellion, but he did send money. It came too late to help the clans, however. Two ships carrying seven barrels of gold landed in Scotland exactly three weeks after Culloden. The prince was in hiding, and the clan representatives who received the gold decided that the best way to keep it safe was to bury it, which they did near Loch Arkaig. A few years later, after the prince had escaped to the Continent, the treasure was dug up and reburied against the time when he should return. Unfortunately, the men who buried the gold the second time died before they passed along the secret of where it was concealed. To this day, the gold has never been found."

Alexandra said triumphantly, "I'll wager that Chisholm thinks it is buried in Glen Alpin!"

Niall frowned. "There has never been any indication that Glen Alpin was the place where the gold was buried."

"You just said that no one knows where it was buried," Alexandra pointed out.

"I know, but the general belief is that it was taken west, to Morar perhaps."

"Have people looked for it before now?" she asked.

"Of course," he replied. "We are talking about seven barrels of gold louis d'or, Alec. Many people have looked for it."

Alexandra was getting more and more excited. "Suppose that Chisholm came across something that made him think it was buried here in Glen Alpin. He tried to buy the glen so he would have the freedom to search for the gold. Even if he couldn't find the treasure, he still would be able to turn a profit on his purchase by running sheep on the land." She blew a strand of hair away from her face, and concluded forcefully, "Anyway you look at it, Niall, it was to Chisholm's advantage to acquire Glen Alpin—by any means he could."

Their eyes held.

"I am thinking that you may be right," he said slowly.

At his words, all of Alexandra's jubilation died away. "If I am right, then you are still in danger," she said.

"I am safe here. Chisholm is in England."

She smoothed his hair back from his brow. "He was in England. How do we know that he has not followed us north?"

Silence fell as he contemplated that idea.

"If An Siosalach has come north, he will have gone to his home in Strathglass," he said at last. "Perhaps I should take a trip north to see if he is there. If he is, then we have things we need to discuss."

"You cannot go alone," she said instantly.

"I was not intending to. I will take the *ceann-tigh* with me."

"Well . . ." She frowned worriedly. "If you must go, make sure you are all armed."

He gave her his wonderful smile. "Are you concerned about me, Alec?"

"Yes," she said.

His eyes glinted. "That is nice."

All of a sudden, his smile mutated into a jaw-cracking yawn, and she laughed. "Go to sleep, Niall. You are exhausted."

The glint in his eyes turned rueful. "I am afraid that I am."

She leaned over to blow out the candle on her nightstand, then curled up on her side, pulled up her blankets and snuggled her head into her pillow. "I'm tired too. We can talk some more in the morning."

There was no answer. In the time it had taken her to blow out the candle, he had fallen asleep.

Alexandra did not see her husband the following morning until he came into the dining room as she was eating a late breakfast. After that first day, she had no longer been banished to the library.

He sat next to her at the table and poured himself a cup of tea.

"I have told the *ceann-tigh* of our discussion last night," he said, "and they are in agreement that it is possible that Chisholm believes the French gold is hidden in Glen Alpin. We have decided that some of us will go to Strathglass to see if Chisholm is there, while the others will keep watch at the head of the glen, in case the diggers return."

She looked at him gravely. "Be very careful, Niall. You will be a target the whole time you are on the road."

He looked at her in amusement. "There is no road, Alec, unless you want to count the sheep tracks. We are going across the mountains. I shall be perfectly safe."

She bit her lip. "What will you do if you find Chisholm in Strathglass?"

"Confront him with my suspicions about the gold. If he knows that we have tumbled to his scheme, he may well decide to be honest." His tone turned ironic. "He will probably offer to make a deal with me."

She gave him a stare that was every bit as formidable as his own could be. "You must make certain that Chisholm understands that under no circumstances will he be able to get his hands on Glen Alpin. *That* is what will keep you safe—his knowledge that no MacDonald will sell him the land."

"Yes, ma'am," he said meekly.

She narrowed her eyes, and he laughed. "Don't worry," he repeated. "I shall be fine."

He was about to get up from the table when she stopped him by putting a hand on his sleeve. "What will you do if you should find the gold?"

"To be honest, Alec, I don't think it is buried in Glen Alpin," he replied. "The clansmen would have wanted to get it as far away as possible from the English bastions of Fort Augustus and Fort William. I am sure that they took it west."

"But what if they didn't?" she persisted. "What if it really is buried right here? What would you do with it?"

"The gold was meant to aid all the clans," he said. "And that is how I would use it—for the welfare of all the Highland people."

She smiled at him.

He reached out and touched her cheek with his forefinger. "I am sorry that I must leave you alone here. I'm afraid I won't be back until the day after tomorrow."

Her cheek tingled from his touch.

"I won't be bored," she assured him. "Margaret and I will have plenty to do keeping all of the wives you are leaving with us fed and entertained."

There was an odd expression on his face, and a hint of amazement in his voice as he said, "You and my foster mother seem to be getting along rather well."

"We are getting along just fine," Alexandra replied serenely, and went back to her breakfast.

After the men had left, Alexandra went around the house, inspecting each room to see if it was in order. As she stood in the drawing room, with the morning sun pouring in through its large windows, she looked with appreciation upon the beautiful things in front of her. There were oriental rugs, glass-fronted china cabinets, Louis XIV chairs, and portraits of Niall's ancestors hanging upon the walls. The women in the portraits wore pale blue satin or creamy lace, scarlet velvet or green taffeta, while the hawk-nosed men were uniformly dressed in tartan kilts with blue velvet hats, and pistols and dirks at their belts. The hands of both men and women rested upon the heads of dogs that might have been the ancestors of Fergus and Flora, and the background for all the portraits was the familiar outline of mountains and loch that could still be seen out all the windows of Eilean Darrach.

Alexandra had been surprised to find so many valuable things tucked away in this isolated Highland castle. Mixed in with the stag heads and the landscapes of Highland scenery that hung upon the walls were paintings by Titian and Caravaggio and Poussin. The oriental rugs in the drawing room were magnificent, as was the Flemish tapestry in the small drawing room on the first floor.

There was nothing English in the castle. The china was French Sèvres, the sculptures were Italian. There was no piano, but there was a splendid Italian harp in the small drawing room. Clearly this was a family that historically had looked across the Channel for its culture, not to the country that lay just to its south.

She and Margaret shared a cup of tea late in the morning, and Alexandra pumped Niall's foster mother for stories about his childhood. Margaret was delighted to oblige, and it was clear to Alexandra, from the way Margaret talked, that her love for her foster son was deep and real.

"I wish I had a foster mother," she said a little wistfully. "My own mother was much too busy to have time for us."

"Busy with what?" Margaret asked. She had put on a pair of spectacles to read a letter that Niall had written her years before, and now she peered at Niall's wife over the top of them.

"She was a great power in society, my mother," Alexandra explained. "That is what she liked. She spent most of her time in London, and when she was at Gayles—that is the name of our country home—she was usually entertaining. She had no interest in my brother or me."

Margaret took off her spectacles.

"You have a brother? I thought that the reason Niall inherited was because your father did not have a son."

"My brother died," Alexandra said. She looked at her half-empty teacup.

"Ach, I am sorry," Margaret said with warm sympathy.

With shock, Alexandra heard herself saying, "He killed himself."

As soon as she said the words, she scowled. Why had she told that to Niall's foster mother? She took a sip of her tea, which had turned cold.

"He killed himself?" Margaret sounded horrified.

"Yes." Alexandra put down her cup. "He had lost a great deal of money gambling and he had no way to pay the debt."

"That is a terrible story," Margaret said.

At last, Alexandra looked at the older woman. "Yes," she said quietly, "it is."

"Men," said Margaret resignedly, meeting her eyes with rueful forbearance. "They do such foolish things. And young men are the worst."

"Has Niall ever done a foolish thing?" Alexandra asked curiously.

"If I told you some of the things that he and my Alan got up to, it would curdle your blood," Margaret said.

Alexandra smiled with delight. "Tell me."

"Ach," said Margaret comfortably. "Why not?" And she settled back and began to talk.

Chapter Twenty-seven

James Taylor stood on the crest of a Highland hill and looked down at the shining dark water of Loch Alpin as it wound its way up the glen and out of sight around the curve of a mountain. A golden eagle rose from its craggy nest and soared out over the glen, sailing on the air as easily as a great ship would sail on the sea. Sunlight reflected off the weathered gray stone of Eilean Darrach, although it looked as if it might be raining farther up the loch.

Not for the first time since he had left England, the thought occurred to Taylor that he must have been insane to allow Geoffrey Wilton to convince him to come to Scotland. His eyes followed the flight of the eagle as he thought back on the meeting with Geoffrey that had precipitated this rash Highland journey.

"He kidnapped her," Geoffrey had said with convincing intensity. "He forced her into a coach and drove off to Scotland with her. I have to rescue her, Taylor, and you have to help me. You know how to get to Glen Alpin. You *have* to come."

If anyone had told James Taylor that one day he would act like Sir Lancelot dashing to the rescue of a lady in distress, he would have snorted in disbelief. Yet here he was, about to confront the most formidable man he knew and demand that he turn over his legal wife.

I must be insane, he thought again. *Under law, it is impossible for a man to kidnap his own wife.*

But Taylor had never been impervious to Alexandra's beauty and charm, and the thought of her being constrained against her will—even if it was by her husband—ignited a fire he had not known he possessed. Ignoring the counsel of his cool, legal brain, he had agreed to accompany Geoffrey to Glen Alpin.

Now he turned away from the loch and looked at his companions, who were standing a few paces behind. Besides Geoffrey there was Tim Abbott, a large, silent man who had been Mrs. Wilton's groom for years and whom she had insisted accompany her son as a bodyguard, as well as the Highland guide they had acquired in Fort Augustus. Taylor said to Geoffrey, "Remember now, our plan is to get Lady Hartford alone so we can discover the truth of her situation. If we find that she does indeed wish to return to England, then we will have to discuss how best to accomplish that goal."

Geoffrey looked at the compact, muscular figure of Tim Abbott, who said expressionlessly, "We'll figure sumthin' out."

"Yes," James Taylor said nervously. "Well, we had better be on our way." And he gestured to the guide, who began to move off down the steep hillside.

Alexandra sat in the drawing room of Eilean Darrach, with the four women guests who remained, waiting for dinner to be announced.

"Margaret tells me that we are having mutton stew for dinner," Ewan MacDonald's wife said to Alexandra.

"Why, yes," Alexandra returned with a little surprise. "I hope that mutton stew is to your taste?"

"I like it very well," Lady Ewan returned with a mischievous smile.

"I enjoy it also," the tall, black-haired, dignified woman who was Archibald MacDonald's wife said. "Almost as much as I enjoyed the roast lamb we had yesterday."

Alexandra's brow furrowed. Until the present moment she had been impressed by the beautiful manners of these Highland women. It surprised her that they would complain about a lack of variety in their meals—especially since they must be well aware of the strain that entertaining so many guests placed on the larder.

"I am sorry I have not been able to offer you a greater variety of meat," she said stiffly, "but with the men so occupied, it has been impossible to send out a hunting party for venison."

Lady Ewan said merrily, "We are not criticizing your menu, Lady MacDonald. We think you have gone about solving the food problem in excellent Highland fashion."

Alexandra looked around cautiously. All of the women were smiling broadly.

"I thought for certain that Margaret MacDonald must have been responsible for procuring the sheep, but when I asked her she told me that it was you," Lady Ewan said.

Understanding dawned, and Alexandra smiled back. "Chisholm is a toad," she said. "He deserves to lose some of his sheep."

"I could not agree with you more," the dignified Lady Archibald replied regally. "It was well done of you to send a few of the lads to—ah—"

"Acquire," Alexandra prompted.

Lady Archibald continued, "'*Acquire* some sheep.'"

Lady Ian said soberly, "An Siosalach is a wicked man."

All of the women, Alexandra included, agreed fervently with this assessment. They were in the process of tearing Lord Chisholm's character to shreds when the drawing-room door opened and Bridget looked in. "There are some gentlemen here to see you, Lady MacDonald." She added ominously, "From England."

Alexandra's eyes widened in surprise. "Will you excuse me for a moment?" she said, and stood up.

"Certainly," Lady Ewan returned, her face alive with curiosity. The four Highland wives exchanged mystified looks as Alexandra walked out of the room.

Geoffrey's yellow head was the brightest spot in the gloomy hall, and she spotted it instantly as she came down the stairs. "*Geoffrey*," she said in a voice that was equal parts astonishment and anger, "what on earth are you doing here?"

She reached the landing and Geoffrey came toward her, his blue eyes glittering in his pale face. "Don't worry, Alex," he said. His voice was shaking. "I am here to take you home."

She stared at him in alarm and her voice sharpened. "Take me home? What are you talking about? Has something happened?"

"I know that you have been brought to Scotland against your will," he replied in the same unsteady voice. "But I am here to rescue you."

A small silence fell as Alexandra stared into the overly bright eyes of her cousin. Finally, "Are you mad, Geoffrey?" she demanded. "What on earth are you talking about? I came to Scotland with my husband. I have no desire to go home."

Taylor let out a stifled groan, and her eyes turned in his direction. She looked amazed when she recognized him. "Mr. Taylor! How came *you* to be involved in this wild-goose chase?"

From the look on his face, Taylor was wondering the same thing. "Mr. Wilton thought you had been kidnapped, my lady. He asked me to accompany him because I knew the way to Glen Alpin."

"Kidnapped!" Alexandra looked stunned. "What can you be talking of? Who would kidnap me?"

"You don't have to pretend to me, Alex," Geoffrey said. "I know you never planned to come to the Highlands, and when I heard that you had been taken by MacDonald, I determined to rescue you."

Alexandra's astonishment turned to disgust. She crossed her arms over her breasts and glared at her cousin. "I am sorry to have to tell you this, Geoffrey, but your journey has been in vain. I most definitely was not kidnapped by my husband. In fact, he didn't want me to come. It was I who insisted upon accompanying him!"

Geoffrey began to shake his head in denial, and Alexandra's gray eyes flashed. "Listen to me, Geoff! I have no idea how you acquired this mad notion that I was kidnapped, but I assure you that I accompanied my husband of my own free will." She looked beyond Geoffrey to where Taylor stood, with Tim Abbott slightly behind him. The Highland guide had already found his way to the kitchen. "See what you have done. You have dragged poor Mr. Taylor all this long way, and for nothing." She paused, but Geoffrey did not reply; he just continued to stare at her out of burning blue eyes. She said in a slightly kinder voice, "I am married,

Geoff, and I go where my husband goes. Will you please get that through your head?"

Geoffrey was so pale that his skin glimmered ghostlike in the dimness of the hall. "You can't have wanted to come here," he said.

"I did want to come here," she replied emphatically. "I love Niall MacDonald, and where he is, that is where I want to be."

Taylor said, "I am dreadfully sorry, Lady Hartford. This has all been a terrible mistake."

"I thought better of you, Mr. Taylor," she said severely. "How could you allow yourself to be so taken in?"

"You see, Mr. Wilton was so upset . . . so sure . . ." Taylor looked at his feet, unable to meet her eyes.

Her gaze alighted on the third member of the group. "And who is this?"

When it became clear that Geoffrey was not going to answer, Taylor said, "This is Mrs. Wilton's groom, Tim. He . . . er . . . accompanied us."

Alexandra rolled her eyes. "All right, since you are here, I suppose I will have to offer you our hospitality. We were just about to go in to dinner. I'm sure you and Mr. Taylor are hungry after your long journey, Geoff. I will take you upstairs so you can wash and tidy up, then you may join us in the drawing room." She looked at Tim Abbott. "You may wait here, and I will send someone to show you where to go."

"Yes, my lady," the groom replied in a voice that sounded rusty from lack of use.

Alexandra turned toward the stairs, followed in uncomfortable silence by Geoffrey and James Taylor.

*   *   *

James Taylor was furious with Geoffrey Wilton, but he was even more furious with himself. How could he have been such an idiot? He was a middle-class English solicitor, not a knight-errant.

"It seems you were mistaken about Lady Hartford, Mr. Wilton," he said coldly when she had left him and Geoffrey alone together in a freezing bedroom, after promising to have water sent so they could wash.

"She's lying," Geoffrey said. His eyes had the same bright, burning look they had taken on the moment he saw Alexandra. "Can't you see that she's afraid of him?"

"She said she loved him," Taylor said.

Geoffrey shook his head. "She was coerced into marrying him, and now she has been coerced into living in Scotland. We have to get her away from here, Taylor."

Taylor regarded Geoffrey out of narrowed eyes, and said slowly and clearly, "I don't think she's lying, Wilton. I think she does love him."

"She doesn't love him," Geoffrey shouted. With a visible effort, he moderated his tone. "She can't love him. It's impossible for a sweet, gentle girl like Alexandra to love a barbarian like MacDonald." He clenched his teeth and repeated, "It's impossible."

Taylor didn't reply. It was becoming clear to him that, in regard to Alexandra, Geoffrey saw only what he wanted to see.

What the devil is Niall MacDonald going to say to us when we meet him at dinner? Taylor thought unhappily as he washed his hands and face in a basin of blessedly warm water. He was enormously relieved when he walked into the drawing room and saw only women.

"You must let me make you known to my husband's cousins," Alexandra said. "Lady Archibald, this is Mr.

Wilton, who is *my* cousin, and Mr. Taylor, who is my solicitor."

A tall, black-haired woman with a strongly featured face nodded pleasantly. Alexandra introduced the other three women who were present and then announced that they could go into the dining room.

Taylor had been to Eilean Darrach before, so he was not surprised by the elegance of the dining-room table, but he could see Geoffrey Wilton staring at the Sèvres china and heavy silver serving dishes in open astonishment.

The women at the table all wore white dresses with sashes of MacDonald tartan draped so that they fell from one shoulder to the opposite hip. Only Alexandra was dressed differently, in a black dress he remembered she had worn when she was in mourning for her father.

The uniform white worn by the other women must be French mourning, the solicitor realized. That is when he understood that Alistair MacDonald must have died.

"His Lordship's grandfather?" he asked Alexandra, speaking softly across Lady Archibald to where his hostess sat at the head of the table.

"We buried him two days ago," she replied.

"I am sorry."

She nodded, and said gravely, "Niall is not here because he and his cousins have gone on a mourning retreat. It is a custom here in the Highlands."

The women at the table all looked at her.

"I see. When do you expect them back?" Taylor asked.

"Perhaps tomorrow, perhaps the day after."

"Mourning retreats do not have any set amount of time, Mr. Taylor," Lady Archibald said.

She and Alexandra exchanged a glance, and Taylor could have sworn that they looked amused.

"Where did they go for this retreat?" Geoffrey asked suddenly.

"To the mountains, Mr. Wilton," another one of the women answered. "As the psalmist wrote, *'I will lift up mine eyes unto the hills.'* We in the Highlands take those words to heart and seek for our comfort in the splendor of our hills."

By then Taylor was certain that the women were amusing themselves at his and Geoffrey's expense.

I suppose I deserve this, he thought gloomily. *I should never have let Wilton talk me into coming here.*

He looked at Alexandra, who was sitting gracefully and assuredly at the head of the table, talking to the impressive-looking Lady Archibald.

If we leave here tomorrow morning, perhaps we can avoid meeting Niall MacDonald, he thought hopefully. *I shall talk to Wilton after dinner. If he is fool enough to want to stay, I think I might just leave without him.*

They were waiting for dessert to be brought when one of the kilted young men who had served them came into the room empty-handed and went to stand beside Alexandra. "An Siosalach is here, Lady MacDonald," he said. "He has asked to see Mac-Mhic-Donnail."

Alexandra looked appalled, and the woman seated next to Taylor caught her breath audibly. The attorney frowned in an effort to remember where he had heard the phrase An Siosalach before.

Alexandra's next words enlightened him. "Lord Chisholm is here at Eilean Darrach?" She sounded as if she couldn't believe her ears.

Chisholm, Taylor thought. *That is who An Siosalach is.*

"That is so, Lady MacDonald," the kilted young man returned.

Geoffrey said, "What the devil is Chisholm doing in Scotland? I thought he lived in England now."

Alexandra was looking with something close to panic at Lady Archibald, the oldest woman present, and Lady Archibald said reassuringly, "If An Siosalach is looking for Niall, then he thinks Niall is here. Do not worry, my dear, I am certain that your husband is safe."

Safe? Taylor thought in mystification. *Why shouldn't he be safe?*

Alexandra drew in a long, steadying breath. Then she nodded at the older woman, and said, "I suppose I had better find out what he wants."

"By all means."

Alexandra excused herself and left the table.

There was silence in the dining room after she had gone. Then the young woman who had been introduced as Lady Ewan said, "If An Siosalach is coming from Strathglass, he must have passed our men somewhere in the mountains."

"There is more than one way across," Lady Archibald agreed. "Two parties could easily pass each other without knowing the other was there."

"I wonder why he has come to Glen Alpin," said Lady Ewan worriedly.

Geoffrey Wilton voiced the question Taylor longed to ask, "What is going on here? Why are you so perturbed by Chisholm's visit? And why *is* Chisholm here? He relinquished the Jockey Club's claim to the earl's money." Geoffrey looked at the solicitor. "Isn't that right, Taylor? Didn't Chisholm sign a document relinquishing his claim?"

"He did," Taylor replied.

"An Siosalach is here on Highland, not Sassenach, business," Lady Archibald said somberly.

"What business is that?" Geoffrey demanded.

Lady Archibald's dark eyes regarded him steadily. "I believe I said that it was not Sassenach business," she replied.

Geoffrey flushed angrily.

At that moment Alexandra walked back into the room, followed by Lord Chisholm, whom she invited to take a place at the table.

"The most vexing thing has happened," she said. "Lord Chisholm has come to Glen Alpin to see Niall, and Niall has gone to Strathglass to see Lord Chisholm. They must have passed each other in the mountains."

"That is vexing indeed," Lady Archibald agreed.

So much for the mourning retreat, Taylor thought ironically.

Alexandra said, "I have invited Lord Chisholm to remain with us until the men return from Strathglass. If he returns home, there is a good chance that the same thing will happen again."

The women looked suspiciously at Chisholm, but murmured agreement with their hostess.

Geoffrey stared at Alexandra, and said belligerently, "I thought you said MacDonald went on a mourning retreat!"

For the first time Chisholm noticed the presence of Geoffrey and Taylor. "What the devil are you two doing here?" he demanded.

When Geoffrey didn't reply, Taylor said lamely, "We are here on a visit to Lord and Lady Hartford."

"Why are *you* here, Chisholm?" Geoffrey shot back. "Surely you are not still trying to weasel that inheritance for the Jockey Club?"

"I am here on Highland business," Chisholm said, in unconscious repetition of Lady Archibald's earlier words.

The kilted young man entered carrying a plate, which he placed in front of Lord Chisholm. Taylor looked at it and saw that it was filled with an assortment of food left over from their own dinner.

Chisholm picked up his fork and began to eat hungrily.

A large apple pie was carried in next, and as it was served, Alexandra talked fluently about the weather, enthusiastically supported by every woman at the table.

At ten o'clock that night, Niall and the *ceann-tigh* arrived back at Eilean Darrach. The last rays of Highland light were fading from the sky when they strode into the drawing room of the castle to meet their wives, Lord Chisholm, and the two unexpected guests from England.

"Niall!" Alexandra jumped to her feet and hurried across the floor. "We didn't expect to see you until tomorrow."

He put an arm around her shoulders, but his eyes were on Chisholm. "It appears we missed each other," he said to the other chief.

"So I understand. They told you at Strathglass that I had come here to see you?"

"Yes. We set out immediately to return home. You and I have things to talk about."

"So it seems," Chisholm said.

For the first time, Niall noticed the presence of Geoffrey Wilton and James Taylor.

"Dhé," he said. "What are you two doing here?"

His hand was still on Alexandra's shoulder, as if he had forgotten that it was there.

"We have come to bring my cousin home to England," Geoffrey said. "If you refuse to let her go, I shall bring charges of kidnapping against you."

Niall looked with astonishment at his wife.

She said, "Geoff has this ridiculous idea that I am here

against my will, Niall. I have told him repeatedly that this isn't so, but he doesn't seem to believe me."

Niall looked back at Geoffrey, and said flatly, "A man cannot kidnap his own wife."

Taylor rushed into words. "This has all been a dreadful mistake, my lord. Mr. Wilton and I are very sorry that we misunderstood the situation and will leave your house the first thing tomorrow."

"Thank you, Mr. Taylor," Alexandra said firmly.

Geoffrey's mouth set in a bitter line, but he said nothing.

Chisholm said impatiently, "Is there somewhere private where we may talk?"

Niall dropped his hand from Alexandra's shoulder, and said, "Come with me to the library."

There was absolute silence as the two men left the room.

Chapter Twenty-eight

Geoffrey Wilton sat fully dressed on the edge of his bed at Eilean Darrach and stared sightlessly at the Highland landscape that hung upon the wall.

She can't love him, he thought in rising panic. *I don't believe that she loves him. He's her first cousin! Her father and his father were brothers. How can she even think of . . .*

His mind shyed away from picturing Alexandra in any position of intimacy with Niall and instead returned to its most recent refrain. *He must have some kind of a hold over her.*

Although Geoffrey would not admit it to himself, his belief in that idea had been shaken by his encounter with Alexandra, who certainly had not looked intimidated.

The thought that truly terrorized Geoffrey finally broke through to the surface of his mind. *If I leave her here with him, I might never see her again.*

Raw anguish swept through him and he pressed his knuckles to his mouth to keep from crying aloud. It was all Niall MacDonald's fault, he thought. If it weren't for Niall,

Geoffrey would be Alexandra's husband. He and Alex would be living together at Gayles, and she would have been happy. He knew she would have been happy.

He clenched his fists, and said through clenched teeth, "God, how I hate him."

Alexandra was still awake when Niall came into their room after his conversation with Lord Chisholm.

"What did Chisholm want?" she demanded from the bed as soon as he closed the door behind him.

He put his night candle down. "It's late," he said. "You should be asleep."

"Yes, well if *you* want to get any sleep, you are going to have to tell me what Chisholm wanted," she retorted.

He groaned. "You are a relentless woman."

"Yes," she replied. "I am."

"All right, just give me a chance to get into bed, will you? I am exhausted even if you are not."

She was quiet while he undressed, blew out his candle, and got into the big bed next to her. Then she said, "Did Chisholm tell you why his men were digging in Glen Alpin?"

"Yes, he did." Their heads were lying side by side upon their respective pillows, and he linked his hands behind his head and looked into the darkness above him as he replied, "You were right—he was indeed looking for a treasure. That is why he was so eager to buy Glen Alpin."

"Was it the French gold?" she asked excitedly.

"Amazingly enough, it was." In contrast to hers, his voice was perfectly calm. "It seems that Chisholm recently came across an old diary of his grandfather's where his grandfather claimed to be one of the men who dug up the gold from Loch Arkaig and reburied it."

"Niall!" Alexandra's voice bubbled with suppressed excitement as she strained to see his expression in the dark. All she could see, unfortunately, was the shadow of his hawk-like profile. "Did his grandfather say it was buried in Glen Alpin?"

"He did," replied that irritatingly calm voice.

"Did he say where?"

"According to Chisholm, he did. Chisholm said that he would tell me where to look if I agreed to give him half of the gold when I found it."

"The toad," Alexandra said indignantly.

"It seemed a fair enough offer to me." He sounded amused.

"You should have it all because you will use it to help people," Alexandra said passionately. "Chisholm will only use it to enrich himself."

"That may be true, but Glen Alpin is a big place, Alec." All the amusement had disappeared from his voice. "I am thinking that half the gold is better than none."

"Yes, but you already know that Chisholm was looking in the caves," she said triumphantly. "That must be where the diary said the gold was buried."

"Perhaps." He sounded more weary than triumphant. "But even if it is buried somewhere in the caves, we could waste years looking for it. There are more than a dozen caves at the head of Loch Alpin."

"Look where Chisholm's men were digging."

"If Chisholm knew exactly where that gold was buried, you can be certain that he would have dug it up by now."

A little silence fell, then she said with some dismay, "You're not going to look for it at all?"

"What I will do is give Chisholm permission to continue to look himself, and I'll claim my half if he is successful.

The men of Glen Alpin have better things to do than waste their days digging in caves."

She didn't reply.

He turned his face so he was looking directly into hers. "The real gold is the cattle that I am going to bring into the glen. *They* will be the salvation of the Glen Alpin MacDonalds, not some elusive buried treasure."

It was still too dark for her to see his expression. "But suppose Chisholm finds the gold and does not share it?" she said worriedly.

"Oh, we will keep an eye on his digging operations," Niall said. "There is no way that Chisholm will be able to haul seven barrels of French gold out of Glen Alpin without our knowing about it."

"I suppose that is so," she said, although she did not sound certain.

He unlinked his hands from behind his head, pulled the blanket up over his bare shoulders, and turned over on his side, so that his back was to her. "Good night, Alec," he said firmly, and settled down to sleep.

She sat up. "Wait! Did you say anything to him about the fire and the accidents?"

"I'll tell you tomorrow." He sounded very sleepy.

"Niall!" She reached out and shook his shoulder.

He groaned. "Alec, I have traveled over the mountains to Strathglass and back today. I am dead. Can't this wait until the morning?"

"No, it cannot," she said.

The only reply she got was a gentle snore.

There was clearly no point in trying to rouse him again, she thought crossly. He wasn't too exhausted to stay awake, he just didn't want to talk to her anymore. Apparently he didn't want to make love to her, either.

She stared at the imposing bulk of him next to her in the bed. He knew something he was not telling her.

She lay awake, thinking hard.

Everything seemed all right. She couldn't see any reason for Chisholm to wish to harm Niall now. They would get James Taylor to draw up a legal document awarding half of the French gold to Chisholm should he find it, and that should be enough to satisfy him.

Everything wasn't all right, though, she thought. Niall had gone to sleep in order to avoid her.

I will find out tomorrow, she vowed as she finally drifted off to sleep herself.

To Alexandra's annoyance, Niall was already gone by the time she awoke the following morning.

That man is as quiet as a cat, she fumed as she dressed with the help of Bridget. She had been planning to talk to him before he went downstairs to breakfast, knowing that once he was absorbed into the busy household, her chances of getting him alone again would be slim.

The dining room was filled with MacDonalds, all of whom were talking about leaving for their respective homes.

Thank goodness, Alexandra thought, as she smiled and listened and ate her breakfast of oatmeal and scones. She was almost finished when Bridget came to tell her that Mac-Mhic-Donnail wished to see her in the library.

Mystified, Alexandra excused herself and made her way up the stairs to the castle library, which was on the second floor of the newer addition.

Two things had struck Alexandra about the library at Eilean Darrach when first she saw it. The first was amazement that so many books lined the walls of this remote Highland castle. The second was surprise that so many of those books were in French. Niall had been educated at the University of Edinburgh, but the earlier chiefs had all been sent to Paris for their education, and the library reflected that fact.

The first person Alexandra saw when she walked through the library door was Geoffrey, who was sitting with visible tenseness in one of the chairs that flanked the large rectangular table in front of the fireplace.

She stopped short in the doorway, and Niall said, "Come in, Alec, and close the door behind you."

She looked toward the window, where her husband was standing, then turned and slowly closed the library door.

"Come and sit down," Niall said, moving toward the table himself. "The three of us have some things that need to be discussed."

Geoffrey was sitting in a chair at the end of the long side of the table, and Niall held out the chair opposite Geoffrey's for Alexandra. After she was seated, Niall took the chair at the head of the table, between them.

They sat for a moment in strained silence, Alexandra looking worriedly from Niall to Geoffrey then back again to Niall. What could this be about? she wondered.

Geoffrey cleared his throat and articulated her own silent question. "What did you wish to see me about, MacDonald?"

"I want to know what you are doing here in Glen Alpin," Niall replied. His voice was calm, but there was a chill in his eyes that frightened Alexandra. She could feel her neck muscles tighten.

Geoffrey lifted his chin in a gesture of challenge and looked defiantly back into Niall's cold blue eyes. "I came to take Alex home with me."

Niall's flinty gaze didn't waver. "Because you think I kidnapped her?"

"Yes," Geoffrey replied, defiance ringing in the single syllable.

Alexandra looked at her cousin in exasperation. "I don't know where you got this mad notion that I was kidnapped, Geoffrey! I came to Scotland with Niall because I wanted to be with him, and that is all there is to it. There was no reason for you to come after me—and to drag poor Mr. Taylor along with you! It's insane."

"I think there was every reason," Geoffrey replied. He leaned across the table and his eyes pleaded with her. "You were forced to marry this man against your will. No one knows that better than I, Alex. And no one knows better than I how you feel about marriage to a cousin. What do you expect me to believe? That you have fallen passionately in love with a man who is closer in blood to you than I am? I'm sorry, but I don't believe it." He slammed his hand down on the table. "I can't believe it." His blue eyes glittered feverishly. "I won't believe it."

Annoyed as she was by Geoffrey's obduracy, Alexandra also felt a twinge of guilt. By his lights, what he had said was perfectly reasonable. She said in a milder voice, "Well, you must believe it, Geoff, because it's true."

The two of them looked at each other across the heavy wooden table. Then Geoffrey turned to Niall, and said tightly, "I don't know what it is, but you have some kind of a hold over her, MacDonald. Go out of the room and leave us alone so that she can talk to me without fear of you overhearing her."

"I will be happy to do that," Niall said.

"Don't." Alexandra reached out and put a hand on her husband's sleeve. Leaving her hand where it was, she turned back to Geoffrey. "I would tell you the same thing with Niall out of the room that I have told you in his presence," she said. "I am married, Geoff, and I am happy in my marriage. You must stop thinking about me and look for another girl to love."

Two spots of bright hectic color appeared in Geoffrey's cheeks. "He's your first cousin, Alex!" he cried. "You wouldn't marry me because we were cousins, but you'll go to bed with him?"

Pain and anger sounded in the shrillness of his voice.

Alexandra felt dreadful. She looked at her hand on Niall's arm, took it away, and put it in her lap. She said to Geoffrey, as quietly and reasonably as she could, "I have already explained my feelings to you. Niall and I met as adults and as strangers. We did not grow up together as brother and sister, the way you and I did. For God's sake, Geoff, they used to give us a bath in the same tub when we were little! How I feel about you is colored by many years of sisterly affection. I don't have those years of shared affection with Niall."

Geoffrey's eyes fell away from her earnest gaze. He stared at the table in front of him, and his mouth set into a stubborn line.

From between them, Niall said, "If something should happen to me, would you marry Wilton, Alec?"

Slowly she turned her head to look at her husband. "No," she said. "I would not."

Geoffrey said, "You were ready enough to marry me before MacDonald came upon the scene!"

Alexandra felt the dull throb of a headache beginning behind her eyes. She said wearily, "Geoff, we have been over this a thousand times. You know I didn't want to marry you. I was going to do it simply because it was the only way to save Gayles."

Geoffrey shook his head sharply, as if denying her words.

Niall said in a voice as hard as his eyes, "Do you understand what is being said here, Wilton? If I die without leaving a son, you might get the earldom, but you will not get Alexandra."

Suddenly Alexandra felt very cold. "W-what are you implying, Niall?" she asked, looking fearfully at her husband's implacable, hawklike face.

He turned his cold eyes on her. "Geoffrey Wilton has tried to kill me three times, Alec, and I would prefer him not to try again."

"That isn't true!" she cried passionately.

"Oh, but it is," Niall returned. His mouth was thin and hard as he regarded her impassively.

Geoffrey said nothing.

"I thought we had agreed that it was Chisholm who was trying to hurt you," she said to her husband. "Chisholm is the one with the motive, Niall. Geoffrey may be a little overprotective of me, but he would never stoop to anything as base as murder!"

Niall leaned back in his chair and regarded Geoffrey with what looked like irony in his eyes. "As you can see, she does not really understand your feelings." He lifted one black eyebrow. "I, on the other hand, do."

The spots of color had faded from Geoffrey's cheeks, leaving him very pale. He stared back at Niall and said nothing.

"You thought that I was sleeping in the earl's bedroom when you had someone set it on fire," Niall said. "You must have been horrified when you learned that it was not I but Alec who was sleeping in that room."

Geoffrey continued to stare at him in silence.

"I'm not sure how you managed the second episode,

spooking my horse on the hillside," Niall went on, "but I know how you managed the third. You learned from your household spy that I had gone to Holkham, and you sent me a letter, supposedly from Alexandra, asking me to come back a day early. Then you waited for me on the river road."

"You are mistaken," Geoffrey said in a colorless voice.

"No, I'm not." Niall looked at Alexandra. "Chisholm had no reason to wish me dead, Alec. He wanted to buy Glen Alpin from me, true, but killing me wouldn't have brought him any closer to ownership of the land."

"He would have tried to buy it from your heir," she cried. "Chisholm wanted the treasure for himself, that is why he tried to kill you, Niall. It wasn't Geoffrey."

Slowly Niall shook his head. "It's much too far-fetched, Alec."

"It is just as far-fetched to think that Geoffrey would kill you so that he could become the earl," she shot back.

He said gently, "This isn't about the earldom or the money, Alec. It's about you."

It was the gentleness in his voice that frightened her most. She looked at her cousin, and he did not look back. "Geoff?" she said in a wavering voice. "It's not true, is it?"

Slowly his blue eyes lifted, and she read her answer in their pain-filled depths.

"Oh my God." Her hands went to her mouth. *"How could you do such a thing?"*

He closed his eyes, as if he could not bear to look at her any longer. "I don't know," he said numbly. "I think I must have been a little mad."

"You tried to kill Niall." She spoke the words as if she was trying to fix the reality of them in her mind.

"Yes," Geoffrey said, and slumped in his chair.

She looked at her husband. "It was never Chisholm?"

He shook his head.

She looked back at the drooping figure of her cousin. He didn't look capable of harming anyone.

"Dear God," she whispered. Her fingers twisted restlessly in her lap. "This is all my fault."

"Don't be ridiculous, Alec," Niall said sharply. "How can this be your fault?"

She didn't answer her husband, but said to Geoffrey, "I should never have agreed to marry you."

He was white to the lips. "It made things . . . difficult."

"I love Niall, Geoff," she said. "It's true that I didn't want to marry him at first, but I love him now. I'm sorry if that hurts you, but you must believe that I am telling you the truth."

He nodded speechlessly. Then, straightening slightly in his chair, he turned to Niall. "What are you going to do?"

"I think that the best thing to do is to pretend that none of this has happened," Niall replied grimly. "My wife and I will spend the summer and autumn here in Glen Alpin, then we will come south to pass the winter at Gayles. If you feel that you can associate with Alexandra as her cousin and childhood friend, you will be welcome to visit us. If you cannot do that, then I suggest that you stay away."

Alexandra stared at Niall in astonishment. This was the first she had heard of them spending the winter at Gayles.

Geoffrey nodded, said, "I'm sorry, Alex," and stood up.

Niall said, "One thing more. Who in my household acted as your spy?"

Geoffrey shook his head. "Leave it alone, MacDonald."

Niall said implacably, "Someone in my house set fire to my wife's room, and I want to know who it was."

Geoffrey rubbed his eyes. "I'll remove him from your staff and take him on myself. Will that do?"

"Yes," Alexandra said.

"Taylor and I will leave this morning," Geoffrey said.

There was silence as Alexandra and Geoffrey looked at Niall, waiting for his judgment. "All right," he said at last.

Geoffrey turned and shuffled toward the door like an old man. He stopped in front of it and looked back to say, "One other thing. You said there were three attempts on your life. I was only responsible for two."

Niall frowned. "Which two?"

"The fire and the carriage accident. I don't know of any other incident."

After a moment, "I suppose the third accident could have been just that—an accident," Niall said.

Geoffrey nodded, turned and shuffled out the door. As soon as it closed behind him, Alexandra began to cry.

"Don't, *m'eudail*," Niall said. He came around to her chair, lifted her out of it and held her in his arms. "It isn't your fault," he said, his lips against her hair.

"I should be angry with him," she sobbed. "He tried to kill you, and I should be furious. But I'm just so . . . so sad."

"He will learn to live without you."

"You don't think he will try to hurt you again?"

"No. I don't think he will do that."

She leaned against him, feeling the length and hardness of his body pressed against hers, and after a while her tears slowed. She sniffed and stepped away from him so she could look up into his face. It wore an expression she could not read.

"This is what you wouldn't tell me last night, wasn't it?" she said. "You wanted to make Geoff admit his guilt to me directly."

He nodded, took out a handkerchief, tilted up her chin,

and began to dry her cheeks. "I knew you would not believe me. You had to hear it from him."

She sniffed again. "I still find it hard to believe."

He released her chin and gave her his handkerchief so she could blow her nose. When she had finished he said, his voice as grave as she had ever heard it, "I am sorry, Alec, for the way I have treated you. I hope very much that you can find it in your heart to forgive me."

She stared in astonishment at his grim face as he went on, "I know my behavior was unforgivable, but I ask for your forgiveness nonetheless."

She struggled to find words. "Your mind was on your grandfather," she said at last.

He looked into her eyes. "We both know it was more than that."

She did know that, and a spark of righteous anger kindled in her breast as she brought out his worst sin. "I can't believe that you actually suspected *me* of trying to kill you!" Her eyes flashed indignantly, "Did you think I was in partnership with Geoffrey?"

"I tried to think that," he replied in the same grave manner as before. "It was a way of . . . defending myself against you."

She didn't respond, just stood there looking at him, and after a moment he lifted her hand and held it cradled in both of his. "Did you mean it when you told Wilton that you loved me?"

"Yes," she replied. The sparkle of temper had not quite left her eyes.

His mouth quirked. "You are so sweet," he said deeply, "and I have been such an idiot."

At those words, all of Alexandra's anger drained away,

and her heart lifted with joy. "You have been an idiot," she said. "You don't deserve my love."

He drew her into his arms and rested his cheek on the smooth silkiness of her hair. "I don't," he said huskily. "I surely don't."

Blissfully, she inhaled the wonderful autumnlike smell that was his alone. The scratchiness of his wool jacket felt wonderful againt her cheek. "But what was it, Niall?" she murmured. "Why did you feel you had to defend yourself against me?"

She felt him inhale, then he replied haltingly, "It was all mixed up with the idea I had of the Sassenach."

"Ahhh," she breathed into his jacket. "The English enemy."

"That is what I was brought up to believe." He had buried his lips in her hair, and his voice sounded muffled. "Then I discovered that I was half-Sassenach myself. Of course I had always known that my father was English, but I had never *felt* it before." She could feel his body tense. "Can you possibly understand what I am struggling so hard to explain to you? Or does it just sound mad?"

She let her cheek continue to rest against his shoulder while she thought. At last she answered, "I think I can understand. You were beginning to feel blood ties to Gayles, and you thought that such feelings were a betrayal of your grandfather. The only way you could deal with how you felt was to separate the English part of you from the Scottish part. And I belonged to the English part."

"*Dhé*, you understand better than I do," he said shakily. "I could cope with my feelings for you as long as you were in England, but when you came with me to Scotland, I did not know what to do."

She removed her cheek from his shoulder and tilted her

head so that she could lightly kiss the underneath part of his chin. "It's all right, darling," she said.

"I thought you would hate it here," he said. "I thought you would be cold and bored and miserable."

"I have been cold," she said. "I will never understand why Scots have such an aversion to fires."

He looked down into her upturned face with a smile in his eyes and did not reply.

"But I've been far too busy to be either bored or miserable."

"So I have seen."

She searched his eyes, then said softly, "Niall, if you dwell too much on the past, it can cloud your vision of the future."

Slowly he nodded. "I did a lot of thinking during the hours that I kept the death watch for my grandfather, and that is the conclusion that I reached." His mouth smiled now as well as his eyes. "Although I did not phrase it so elegantly."

She smiled back.

He said, "I treated you abominably, and the only demand you made on that terrible trip north was that you wanted to wash your hair."

She laughed. Then, sobering, she asked the most important question of all. "Do you love me, Niall?"

"I am thinking there is not a woman more loved in the whole of our two countries," he replied, and bent his head to kiss her.

She felt dizzy with happiness, and when he lifted her in his arms and took her to sit on his lap in one of the old leather chairs, she slid her arms around his neck and rested her cheek on his shoulder.

"Did you mean what you said to Geoffrey about spending he winter at Gayles?" she asked.

"Yes. That is one of the things I thought about during hose long hours of the death watch. I thought it would be oolish of me to go on hating the English when one half of ny own blood is English and three-quarters of the blood of ny children will be English as well. I thought, too, that you vere right when you said the biggest enemy of the clans oday is not England but our own chiefs. I thought that I did ot have to turn my back on Gayles in order to be a good hief for Glen Alpin."

Alexandra sat up so she could see his face. She was so appy she thought she might start to cry again.

He said slowly, "I have a seat in the English Parliament. Vhy not use it to call attention to what is being done in the lighlands? At least there will be one voice to say that arowing people out of their homes in order to bring in sheep ; wrong."

Tears prickled behind her eyes. "Oh, Niall," she said a lit- e thickly. "I think that is a wonderful idea."

He frowned in alarm. "You aren't going to cry again, are ou?"

"They are happy tears," she explained, and tried to blink hem away.

With his finger he gently blotted away the single drop that ad fallen on her cheek. Then he said, "I am sorry about ieoffrey, *m'eudail*."

She bit her lip and nodded. "I just feel so awful about im." She sniffed. "I thought I knew him, Niall. I never in a uillion years thought he would be capable of this."

It was a long moment before he answered. At last, he said, I understand him very well. I can't say I like him very uuch, but I understand him."

She looked into her husband's fierce, hawklike face and thought that he looked so implacable when he was not smiling. She said, "Did you mean what you said about letting him visit us?"

"Yes, I did." His expression did not soften.

She gave him a tentative smile. "He will get over his feelings for me, Niall, and then we can go back to the way we were as children. You'll see."

He looked as if he might be going to disagree with her, but then his face relaxed into its wonderful smile. "All I want is for you to be happy," he said.

She smiled back before once more laying her head on his shoulder. "I am," she said, closing her eyes and nestling as close as she could get. "I am."

Epilogue

Two years later

Newlywed Clarissa Wilton let a footman hand her out of the carriage in front of Gayles and tried not to look too awestruck by the sight of the magnificent house. She turned to say something to her husband, who had alighted after her, and surprised a look of strain on his face.

Poor Geoffrey, she thought in quick sympathy. *It must be very difficult for him to come here as a visitor when he was so close to being the master.*

She walked beside her silent husband across the stone terrace and through the front door into the Great Hall. The footman was just saying, "I will inform Her Ladyship that you have arrived," when a feminine voice called, "Is that really you, Geoff?"

The owner of the voice ran down the hall, threw her arms around Geoffrey and hugged him hard. His own hands touched her arms briefly, then she stepped back and said with a laugh, "It's so good to see you! Now, introduce me to your wife."

Clarissa's eyes widened in astonishment as Geoffrey's cousin Alexandra, for it must be she, turned to look at her.

Clarissa had never seen a more beautiful face.

She heard Geoffrey say, "Alex, may I present my wife, Clarissa. Clarissa, this is my cousin, Lady Hartford."

Geoffrey's cousin gave her a radiant smile and came to envelop her in a warm embrace. "Never mind the Lady Hartford," she said. "My name is Alexandra, and I am so pleased to meet you."

She was at least three inches taller than Clarissa.

"Thank you, my . . . ah, thank you," Clarissa replied breathlessly. "I am very pleased to meet you also."

Alexandra released her and turned her radiant smile on Geoffrey. Linking her arm with his, she said, "Come along into the drawing room and I will have some tea brought. Then you must tell me all about what you have been up to, Geoff. It's been two years! We have quite a bit of catching-up to do."

Clarissa walked on Geoffrey's other side, feeling distinctly overwhelmed by the magnificence of the house and by the beauty and warm friendliness of the countess.

She had not known that Geoffrey was this close to his cousin. She knew that he had been the earl for almost six months, until a closer heir had been discovered, but it was not a period of his life that he ever talked about. In fact, Geoffrey hardly ever talked about any part of his life before the two of them had met.

Clarissa was a warm-hearted girl, and she had thought she understood how painful it must be for him to contemplate the power and riches he had lost, so she had never pursued the subject. But now she began to wonder.

When they reached the drawing room, the countess charmingly arranged them according to her wishes, she and

Clarissa on a sofa and Geoffrey in a chair facing them across a polished rosewood tea table.

Clarissa gazed at the magnificent tapestry on the wall, then at the portrait of a beautiful young man that hung beside the fireplace.

Alexandra saw where she was looking and said quietly, "That is my brother, Marcus. He died when he was very young."

Clarissa, who knew from Geoffrey's mother how Marcus had died, said with genuine sympathy, "How tragic."

"Yes. It was." Alexandra's voice lightened. "I'm sorry my husband was not here to greet you, but he has been thinking about building a bridge closer to the mill to make it easier to access, and the engineer arrived today, so they went to look at it." She smiled at Clarissa. "He should be back soon."

The tea arrived, the countess poured, and the conversation took wing.

It was hard to resist Lady Hartford, Clarissa thought, as she listened to Geoffrey telling her about his trip to the Continent last year. She sparkled with interest in what you were saying and her own remarks were both shrewd and funny. Geoffrey had sounded stiff when first he began to talk, but within five minutes he was rattling away in perfect comfort.

At exactly four o'clock, a nursemaid appeared in the doorway holding a baby in her arms. "Do you want him now, my lady, or shall I come back later?"

Alexandra leaped to her feet and crossed the room, her arms held out. "There's my baby! Did you have a good nap, darling?"

The little boy was passed from one pair of arms to the other, and Alexandra came back into the room bearing her son. She reseated herself next to Clarissa and said, "This is Alistair. Isn't he wonderful?"

The baby's soft silky curls were black, but he had his mother's gray eyes. Clarissa loved children and her heart melted. "He is beautiful," she said sincerely.

"Is he Alistair Wilton or Alistair MacDonald?" Geoffrey asked curiously.

The baby had grasped a loose curl of his mother's hair and was in the process of pulling it gleefully.

"No," Alexandra said firmly, as she detached his fingers. "You may not pull Mama's hair."

The baby's fingers entwined themself next around the pearls she wore at her throat, and she let him amuse himself with them as she replied to Geoffrey, "That was quite an issue with my husband, let me tell you. We finally decided that Alistair would be a Wilton and inherit all of Niall's English lands, while our second son will be called MacDonald and will have all the land in Scotland."

"Heavens," Clarissa said.

Alexandra turned to look at her, her chin elevated to avoid coming in contact with the baby's head. "It is very complicated," she explained. "Technically, my husband's name is Wilton, but he has been called MacDonald all his life, and that is what he considers himself. On the other hand, the earls of Hartford have been Wiltons since time out of mind, and it would be a great pity to let the name die out. So that is the solution we have come up with."

Another half hour passed as the baby crawled around the drawing room, pulling himself up on tables and getting his fingers on everything he could reach. His mother let him explore, only rescuing him once or twice when he fell down and began to cry.

"I say, Alex," Geoffrey said when the baby's exploration first began, "aren't you afraid he'll break something?"

"I put all of the breakable things out of his reach when he

first started to crawl," she said. "What's left is safe for him to touch." She glanced at her son and frowned. "But *not* for him to put in his mouth," and she jumped up and went to remove an exquisite silver snuffbox from between Alistair's teeth. He screamed, and she handed him something else and came back to her chair.

Clarissa glanced at the clock on the mantel, and said, "I am afraid we have overstayed our visit."

She had not yet called the countess by name. Geoffrey's cousin did not want to be called Lady Hartford, but Clarissa did not feel comfortable addressing her by her Christian name.

"You can't go until you have met Niall," Alexandra said.

Clarissa looked at her husband for help, and he responded, "We really must be going, Alex. My mother is expecting us back at Highgate."

Alexandra said, "I absolutely refuse to allow you to leave until Niall has returned."

Clarissa blinked. Was the charming countess always so determined to get her own way?

Geoffrey sighed and relaxed back into his chair. "Ten more minutes, then we really must go."

Five minutes later, the earl came into the drawing room. Clarissa looked cautiously at the tall, dark-haired man with the hard, arrogant-looking face who stood on the threshold for a moment, regarding his wife and her guests.

"Niall," Alexandra said. "Look who is here—Geoffrey and his new wife."

The earl's long legs covered the space between the door and the sofa with just a few strides. Clarissa put her hand into a very large very muscular grip and a pair of dark blue eyes looked directly into hers. "How do you do, Mrs. Wilton," he said.

"I am so happy to meet you, my lord," she returned.

Then the earl was going to shake hands with Geoffrey, who stood up to greet him.

"I have been hearing all about Geoff's trip to the Continent and his marriage to Clarissa," Alexandra said.

The earl nodded. The expression on his hard face never changed as he said to Geoffrey, "Are you back at Highgate for good now, Wilton?"

"Yes," Geoffrey replied. "There is quite a lot to do to get the land back into good heart, and I am anxious to get started."

The earl regarded him thoughtfully. Then he said, "Good. If there is anything I can do to help you out, let me know. We will be here for another month, then we shall be in Scotland until Parliament opens in January."

Geoffrey flushed. "Thank you."

Niall looked down. The baby was holding on to his leg, attempting to pull himself up.

"Well, well, well," he said. "Who do we have here?" And he bent to lift his son into his arms.

The baby laughed and patted his father's cheek.

Niall smiled, and said, "How many things have you managed to get into your mouth in the last half hour, laddie?"

The baby got a handful of his father's hair and pulled.

"*Dhé,*" Niall said, wincing. "He never gives up, does he?"

Alexandra laughed. "Perhaps we ought to wear wigs."

Niall's amused gaze met his wife's. "You probably have some old white ones stored away in the attic."

Clarissa couldn't believe what a difference the smile made to the earl's face.

"Would you like some tea, Niall?" Alexandra asked.

"Surely," he replied and looked around to see what he should do with the baby.

Clarissa said shyly, "Do you think he would come to me?"

"He will pull your hair," Niall warned.

"I don't mind," Clarissa said sincerely. "I love babies."

Both the earl and the countess regarded her with approval. Then the earl deposited his son in her lap and went to pull a chair up next to Geoffrey's.

"Alexandra told us that you are building a new bridge," Geoffrey said, and the two men proceded to discuss the bridge while Alexandra and Clarissa discussed the baby.

When finally they were in their carriage and on their way home to Highgate, Clarissa said to her husband, "I thought that Lady Hartford was very nice. She seemed to be very fond of you."

Geoffrey looked down into the soft brown eyes of the wife he truly cared for, and managed to smile. "She is like a sister to me," he said.

She smiled back and he picked up her hand and held it to his lips for a moment. Then he let it go and started to talk about something else.

Later that night, as they were getting ready for bed, Niall and Alexandra discussed Geoffrey's marriage.

"I liked her," Alexandra said. She was already in bed and was watching as Niall opened the bedroom window a few inches. Those inches were their compromise between Niall's love of fresh air and Alexandra's love of warmth.

Alexandra went on, "She seems a very sweet girl, and she likes children. I think she will be good for Geoff."

"She appeared to be a nice enough little thing," Niall agreed absently. He came over to the bedside and unknotted the tie on his robe.

Alexandra let out a long, relieved breath. "Thank God Geoff has finally gotten over his infatuation with me. Every time I've met Cousin Louisa during these last two years, I've known how Helen must have felt whenever she ran into Hecuba in the streets of Troy."

His preoccupied face blazed into laughter.

She frowned. "It's true, Niall. He stayed away for so long, and I know she blamed me. But he's home now, and he's married, and I can be happy again."

He dropped his robe over a chair. "I didn't realize that you've been unhappy these last few years."

"You know what I mean."

"I suppose I do." He got into bed beside her. "It's not a good feeling, knowing that you've made someone you care about unhappy."

"Exactly," she said, pleased that he understood.

Instead of turning out the light, he turned to look at her.

She said, "I think Alistair is getting another tooth. That is why he keeps putting things into his mouth."

"Mmm."

"Geoffrey wanted to know what Alistair's family name was, and I told him about our decision to name one son Wilton and the other MacDonald."

"Mmm."

She looked up into his narrowed eyes and knew immediately why he was not responding to her conversation. Desire, sweet as hot honey, rippled through her.

"Of course," she said, "in order for us to implement that plan, we need to produce another son."

A slow smile curled his lips. "That is precisely what I was thinking."

She lifted her brows. "Well, are you going to do anything about it?"

In reply, he growled, buried his face in her neck, and kissed the delicate skin over her collarbone. The touch of his mouth made the desire run sweeter and hotter, and she closed her eyes and gave herself up to familiar magic.

Afterward, as she lay drowsily in his arms, a memory of something that had happened earlier in the day floated into her mind. For some reason, she always felt chatty after sex, and she opened her mouth to tell Niall.

"Alistair did the funniest thing today," she began.

There was no reply.

"Niall?"

Still no reply.

Alexandra sighed. It was a rare occasion when she got to indulge her late-night, chatty tendencies. After sex, Niall usually went to sleep.

"We have nothing at all in common," she said now to her husband's recumbent body. "Nothing. How can I love you so much?"

"Alec," Niall groaned, "will you please stop talking and go to sleep?"

She smiled into the dark. "Oh, all right, but get your leg off of mine. It weighs a ton."

"You feel so comfortable," he mumbled.

She shook her leg and, grumbling, he removed his.

"Remind me to tell you in the morning the funny thing that Alistair did."

"All right."

"Good night, Niall."

"Good night, Alec."

And, finally, she settled down to sleep.

Fall in love with Joan Wolf

❧❧❧

"Romance writing at its best."
—Publishers Weekly

○ THE DECEPTION
(0-446-60-275-2, $5.99 USA) ($6.99 Can.)

○ THE GUARDIAN
(0-446-60-276-0, $6.50 USA) ($8.50 Can.)

○ THE ARRANGEMENT
(0-446-60-479-8, $6.50 USA) ($8.50 Can.)

○ THE GAMBLE
(0-446-60-534-4, $6.50 USA) ($8.50 Can.)

○ THE PRETENDERS
(0-446-60-535-2, $6.50 USA) ($8.50 Can.)

○ GOLDEN GIRL
(0-446-60-693-6, $6.50 USA) ($8.99 Can.)

AVAILABLE AT BOOKSTORES EVERYWHERE
FROM WARNER BOOKS

907-E